SUTTON'S
LAW

SUTTON'S
LAW

JANE M. ORIENT, M.D.

AND

LINDA J. WRIGHT

HACIENDA PUBLISHING
MACON, GEORGIA

This is a work of fiction. The characters (including names) and events described here are imaginary and fictitious. Any resemblance to actual persons, living or dead, is purely coincidental.

Hacienda Publishing
Macon, Georgia

1 3 5 7 9 10 8 6 4 2

Library of Congress Catalog Card Number: 97-072143
ISBN: 0-9641077-1-6

Printed and bound in the United States of America on acid-free paper.

MEDICINE IS A TRUST, NOT A HOLDING COMPANY

Chapter
1

"Is you the doctuh?" the patient wanted to know.

"No, suh. I'se the nuhse," Jim replied. He turned to Maggie with a wink. "This is Dr. Altman."

Maggie tried to look confident, though her pulse had quickened. As of today, July 1, she was the doctor. Not a medical student. Not a research assistant. Her fresh white coat had "Dr. Margaret Altman, Internal Medicine," embroidered above the pocket. This was the very first patient she would see since graduating from medical school. She was the intern assigned to the Major Medicine section of the emergency room, where patients were sent if the nurse at Triage thought they might have something serious. The intern's job was to evaluate the patients, arrive at a tentative diagnosis, provide lifesaving treatment if needed, and decide whether to admit the patient to the hospital. It was a heavy responsibility.

There had been some changes in the emergency room since Maggie had been a senior medical student two years ago. The sign over the entrance said "Texas University Regional Preventive Health Center" instead of "Woodlands Hospital." The area had been remodeled, so that now the twenty cubicles were arranged in a circle around a central nursing station and two "crash" rooms. The blackboard was still there, and listed the patient she was about to see: "Jefferson, SOB, Priority 1." "SOB" for "short of breath"; that terminology hadn't changed. Jim Thomas, the black nurse who usually worked nights, was a familiar face. But instead of recording the vital signs on a clipboard, he was punching them into the computer terminal that resided near the door of each cubicle.

"Mr. Jefferson was here just two nights ago," Jim told her. "Same problem, only worse this time. Will you be wanting some Lasix?"

"Let's try 40 mg for a start. And we'd better give him

about 5 mg of morphine too," Maggie said. The patient was sitting bolt upright, gasping for breath, and the legs that protruded from under the sheet were swollen to three times their normal size. Maggie could hear rattles in the lungs even without a stethoscope. She noted that Jim had already started some oxygen.

Heart failure, that much was apparent. From a heart attack? The EKG showed some suspicious changes. She did a quick examination of the patient, murmured some reassuring words, and decided that the admitting resident, Dr. Stemmons, had better know about this one. He obviously needed to be in the hospital. Especially if he had been here just two nights ago, and was not responding to treatment.

Brent Stemmons motioned for her to sit down beside him. He was absorbed in watching a colorful moving data display that just now was showing a graph of "EquaCare Resource Utilization." Another innovation. He made an entry on the computer terminal, then smiled at Maggie.

"Well, Maggie, you plunged into work so quickly I didn't even have a chance to say hello." He extended his hand, and shook hers warmly. "I hear you were working over in research last year, and I remember seeing you at Grand Rounds. Welcome to the Pit."

Maggie returned his appraising look. She remembered Brent Stemmons; he had been a senior student during her freshman year. Most of the students knew him; at least the women did. They were entranced by his dark good looks, the intense brown eyes, the aquiline nose, the tall, trim body. He was often chosen to present cases at conferences because of his impeccable style and manner. When other students were often bedraggled and irritable, Stemmons was always neatly groomed and relaxed. Just as he was now, despite the fact that nearly every cubicle in Major Medicine was filled. How did he do it, she wondered.

Maggie attempted to return Stemmons' smile. "Don't look so serious," he said. "The first day is always hard, but you're not alone here. Just bring all your questions to me."

"Thanks," Maggie said. "As a matter of fact, I have a problem for you. Mr. Jefferson, the man in Room 1, needs to come in." She was about to recite his history, but Stemmons held up his hand.

"I've got it all here," he assured her. "Two years ago, you would have had to plow through five volumes of old charts on this fellow. Then you would have had to recite the whole story to me. Now all the pertinent information is available on line. Age, social history, problem list, EquaCare eligibility rating. I already know more about this patient than you do. See?" He ran his fingers skillfully over the keyboard. Problem 1 is noncompliance. Problem 2, living arrangements. Also, congestive heart failure, hypertension, chronic obstructive lung disease, and diabetes. He was last admitted 3 weeks ago, discharged 13 days ago. Heart failure." Stemmons looked up from the display. "Probably from failure to take his medicine. Or maybe it was an overdose of peanuts and dill pickles." He sounded a bit cynical, Maggie thought.

"Jim said he was in two days ago," Maggie interposed.

"No," Stemmons said, "it would be in the computer."

"Well, here's his EKG." Maggie showed Stemmons the tracing. "He mentioned a little tightness in his chest. He may have had an MI, and maybe that's why he went into failure," she suggested.

"Hmm," Stemmons said, touching another function key. The old EKG appeared on the screen. "NSCSLPT. No significant change since last previous tracing. So, no evidence for an MI. How much Lasix did you give him?"

"Forty milligrams."

"Well, if he doesn't pee a lot, double the dose." Stemmons chose another function on the main menu, "EQUACARE CRITERIA FOR ADMISSION TO AN ACUTE CARE FACILITY." After scrolling through several screens, he shook his head. "As I thought. Not a keeper. He doesn't meet the duration of symptoms criterion. This is a chronic condition we're dealing with. We need to optimize his out-patient management."

"But, . . ." Maggie protested. She didn't care what the computer said. She was the doctor, wasn't she? This man needed to be in the hospital. But before she could finish her sentence, a stretcher came through the double doors, and Stemmons waved her aside.

"Double the dose," he told Maggie. "Then see about this OD. Feet first," he instructed the paramedics.

• • •

"Dr. Larkin, Dr. Jeannette Larkin, call 2824," the page operator droned.

"DRG 242 septic arthritis, severity 2," Stemmons said, recording it neatly in the admissions log, the first entry of the evening. "Dr. Larkin takes one hit. But it will be a shorter than average LOS."

"LOS?" Maggie asked.

"Length of stay," Stemmons explained. "Minimizing the LOS is the key to maximizing reimbursement ratios and cost-effectiveness. They didn't teach you about that in medical school, did they?"

Maggie shook her head.

"Well, you need to learn about it. Nobody can afford the luxury of being ignorant about the principles of efficient management these days. But that's one of the strengths of the program here at TURPH. Stick with me, and you'll soon be an expert." Stemmons patted his keyboard. "Computer systems like this one will revolutionize the practice of medicine."

They already had, Maggie thought. And not necessarily for the better. She was about to say so, but Dr. Larkin had come to find out about the new patient. Stemmons greeted her with a warmth that did not seem to be purely professional. Soon, the two were engrossed in a friendly conversation, and Stemmons seemed more interested in Jeannette's neckline than in a report on Mr. Jefferson's continued shortness of breath.

Men didn't look at her that way, Maggie thought, pushing back a recalcitrant strand of hair that had escaped from her neat braid. Of course, she wasn't a blonde like Jeannette, and even at her best, she wouldn't win any beauty contests. Although her best wasn't all that bad. In the plus column were a flawless complexion, and a tall, slim body. In the minus column were her ordinary features and lack of voluptuous curves. Make-up and more fashionable clothes would help. But then internship wasn't supposed to be a social occasion. Maggie picked up her clipboard and went back to work. The patient in Room 4, CP (chest pain), Priority 2, needed her attention. She'd catch Stemmons' attention later about Mr. Jefferson.

· · ·

"Well, now, here's a winner!" Stemmons said, showing Maggie a platinum American Express card, engraved with the name Milton Silber. "They sent him over from Surgery."

"Dr. Silber?" Maggie said doubtfully. The man on the stretcher certainly didn't look much like a Professor of Medicine. The Dr. Silber she had known four years ago had always been dressed in a dignified tie and a white coat, as he led an awestruck retinue of students and residents on attending rounds. This man was dressed only in a green hospital gown that barely covered his girth. His gray beard was unkempt and bushy; his eyebrows grew together across the bridge of his nose. There was a bulky pressure dressing on his head. "MVA"—motor vehicle accident—was entered as the chief complaint. The surgeon had sutured a scalp laceration, and referred him to medicine because of an irregular heart rhythm. The patient was obviously not happy to be there.

"I'm all right," he assured Jim. "Stupid enough to allow myself to be run over near Woodlands Hospital, of all places, but otherwise intact. Give me my clothes. I want to get the hell out of here."

"What happened?" Maggie asked.

Silber glared at her. "I was crossing the street with my mind on something else, when I heard some screeching brakes. I found myself in the middle of the road with a bruise on my thigh and blood pouring from a scalp wound. The ambulance insisted on bringing me here. Incompetent, arrogant bastards. I intend to sue their asses off!"

"Did you lose consciousness?" Maggie asked.

"Yeah. I got a concussion," Silber said, as he tried to climb over the siderails.

"Just a moment," Maggie said firmly. "We need to check

you, and you may need to stay in the hospital. For one thing, there seems to be a problem with your EKG."

"Trigeminy," Silber said. "I've had it all my life."

"Then we won't worry about that," Maggie said. She presumed she could trust his informtion on that point. "But Dr. Silber, I need to do a neurologic exam, at the very least. You did get quite a bump on your head."

Silber lay back down on the stretcher and looked at her more closely. "Well, I'll be damned. Maggie Altman." He extended his hand. "What is a nice girl like you doing in this Pit? I thought you were doing something sensible, like going into research."

"I did, for a while," Maggie said. "But then I decided that I wanted to be a real doctor."

"My condolences," he replied, shaking his head. "But very well. You may do a neurologic exam. As I recall, you know how to go about it, and I see that you still carry a reflex hammer in your pocket." He nodded approvingly at her bulging pockets.

Maggie did a careful examination. She remembered how meticulous Dr. Silber had been about the physical exam. Apparently, he judged her effort to be satisfactory, except for the test of coordination. He demonstrated a more sensitive test, and insisted that she perform it.

"Dr. Hendricks, Dr. Paul Hendricks, call 2824," the page operator said.

"As I told you, I am all right," Silber reiterated. "Now, if Jim will just get me my clothes, I'll be on my way."

"We have a bed for you, Dr. Silber," Stemmons interposed, having left his control station for a moment. "A private room."

Silber glowered at him. "Brent Stemmons, isn't it? Yes, I remember you. Well, you can just utilize your bed for somebody else. I don't need to be in the hospital. I am certainly not staying in Eisig's hospital. Oh no. My clothing, please."

"Dr. Silber," Stemmons said patiently, "I'm afraid I must insist. I cannot allow a patient with trigeminy and a recent concussion to be discharged. You need to be under observation."

"Bah!" Silber snorted.

"Dr. Hendricks is on his way down to examine you."

"Dr. Altman has already examined me." Silber lowered the siderail of the stretcher, and threw his legs over the edge. "Bring me my clothes," he said, louder this time.

"Dr. Silber, I hope you will reconsider," Stemmons replied, unruffled. "But if not, then I will need to ask you to sign out Against Medical Advice. You understand, I'm sure."

"Hmmf," Silber said.

"Good. I'll leave the form with the nurse at the desk. She'll give you your clothing as soon as you sign it." Stemmons smiled slightly, and turned his back on Silber's fury.

Silber waited until Stemmons had left the room, then jumped down from the stretcher, holding the hospital gown together in the back. "Blackmailer," he snarled. "I'm not signing his damned form! Dr. Altman, would you be so kind as to ask Mr. Thomas to bring me another gown?"

Maggie nodded. The patient was clearly determined to leave. And he was of sound mind, even if he possibly wasn't making the most prudent decision. Why should Brent Stemmons be making things difficult? Of course, Dr. Silber was behaving in a rather peculiar way himself. She shook her head in amazement as her former professor strode out the double doors of Major Medicine, barelegged, wearing the second gown—a white one with blue flowers—backward over the green one. Jim shrugged. "He insisted that I call him a taxi," he said.

"I hope he'll be all right," Maggie said.

Stemmons looked up from his console for a moment. "All right? He's certifiably nuts. Borderline personality. Can you believe that that man thought he should be Chief of Medicine!"

. . .

The rest of the night was a blur. Mr. Jefferson had gone. Stemmons had discharged him after his second dose of Lasix, before Maggie had had a chance to argue with him about it. A patient who had taken a heroin overdose was nodding off again, and required another dose of Narcan. He didn't meet the admissions criteria either, according to the omniscient computer. Stemmons had told Maggie to watch him until the heroin had worn off. She was also supervising three asthmatics, whose blood gases weren't bad enough to worry the computer, and two young women who had taken overdoses of pills in half-hearted suicide gestures. They were on stretchers out in the hall, retching from the Ipecac. Then there was an acutely intoxicated man, who would be on his way to the tank at the county jail as soon as she pronounced him fit.

Stemmons had withdrawn to the call room. "Call me if you need me," he said. "And don't write in the admission book. I need to check the EquaCare criteria on all admissions."

So this was what it was like to be the doctor. She was soloing on her very first flight. Fortunately, there hadn't been much time to worry about it.

"How are you doing, Doctor?" Jim asked, handing her a cup of coffee. She sipped it gratefully, although it was lukewarm and had a distinctly metallic taste. "When you get a chance, could you take a look at the man in Room 5. He has a fever of 103 and looks pretty sick."

Woody Brown, FUO (fever of unknown origin), Priority 2, never previously seen at TU, EquaCare eligibility not established, did indeed look sick. In fact, he was having a chill, an impressive bed-shaking rigor that Maggie had read about but never seen.

Jim had already set up equipment for drawing blood cultures, and as soon as the patient had stopped shaking Maggie put the tourniquet around his arm. Needle tracks. No veins.

"Oh, no, please don't stick me," Mr. Brown moaned.

"Have to. The only question is where," Maggie said firmly.

The patient sobbed a few times. "Other arm, Miss," he said. "I'll show you." He pointed to an unlikely looking spot, and directed Maggie to aim deep, in a certain direction. She followed the directions, and the blood flowed.

Mr. Brown's chest X ray showed the classic pattern for bacterial endocarditis—patchy infiltrates, the result of globs of bacteria being sprayed from the heart valve into the lungs. Staph, she guessed. No doubt about it. He needed admission, a central intravenous line, and high-test antibiotics. She would just have to wake up Stemmons. It was nearly 6:30 anyway.

Stemmons emerged before she could even knock. Amazingly, he looked quite refreshed. He was clean-shaven, and wearing a pressed shirt and a tasteful blue tie. "Good morning, Maggie," he said with a smile. "I trust everything has been nice and quiet."

"Not exactly." Quiet for him, maybe.

He took a look at the films on the viewbox while sipping some coffee. "Yes, I believe you're right about the X ray," he said. He seated himself back at his console, frowned at something on the moving display, and glanced at his watch. "But there's a suggestion of pleural fluid. We need a lateral decubitus film. Send the patient back to X ray."

"But why?" Maggie protested. "You probably wouldn't try to tap such a small amount of fluid. And we need to start the antibiotics as quickly as possible!"

"Yes," Stemmons said, a bit condescendingly. "And the way to get things started as quickly as possible is to send the man to X ray. Believe me, I know how to manage this system."

"We could hang some oxacillin first," Maggie said. "Or call the intern who will be taking care of him, and let him order the antibiotic he wants. And we're going to have to put in a central line—he doesn't have any visible veins. I'll have Jim set up the equipment."

"Relax, honey," Stemmons said, taking her wrist and pulling her toward a chair. "You just phone in the order to X ray. The rest will be taken care of. You don't have to do everything around here all by yourself."

Maggie sat down reluctantly. It seemed she had been doing things all by herself all night long. And who was Brent Stemmons to call her "honey"? She felt her temper building up steam.

Stemmons seemed to sense that. "Look, you've done a great job. But it's nearly 7:00, and you look just exhausted," he said in a concerned tone. "It was a long night. Why don't you go on home and get some rest? I already got some sleep. I can't leave for a while anyway, and I'd be happy to finish up this case for you."

Maggie had to admit that she was beginning to feel remote, and to lose her train of thought easily. Stemmons was the resident, after all, and had more experience with this system. Maybe the fatigue and stress were making her testy. She jotted down Mr. Brown's name and number on an index card, so she could follow up on him later. It probably was a Staph, but if other organisms could behave this way, she wanted to know.

"That's very kind of you," she said, although she felt a little doubtful.

Stemmons favored her with a disarming smile. "Things are much easier if we work together as a team."

. . .

Maggie blinked as she stepped outside. The sun was already bright, although the temperature hadn't yet reached 90 degrees.

"Today is Wednesday, July 2, and I am in Fort Bastion, Texas. Good. Still oriented times three. I have survived my first night as an intern." She could hardly believe it.

She found her car in the parking lot, where she seemed to have left it a year ago. Without remembering how she got there, she found herself on the doorstep of her apartment. She tossed the newspaper onto the table, headed straight for the bed, and fell asleep immediately.

Chapter
2

The phone's fourth ring finally penetrated Silber's fuzzy consciousness. He threw an arm out from under the covers and hunted around on his bedside table for the offending instrument, rapping his knuckles painfully on the clock radio and upsetting the dregs of a glass of bourbon.

"Damn it to hell!" he cursed, then putting the receiver to his ear, cleared his throat and demanded angrily "What?"

"Sorry to wake you," a pleasant voice said. "It's Ryan Fitzhugh. Something's happening here that I thought you should know about."

Silber cracked open an eye and looked at the blue figures on his digital clock. The numerals were just changing from 3:22 to 3:23. "At this time in the morning, it had better be World War III," he said, breaking into a fit of coughing.

"Milt, those cigars are going to kill you," Fitzhugh commented, as Silber gasped for breath.

"So what?" Silber wheezed. "Now tell me what you woke me up for."

"A piece of news just came across the wire from Paris."

Silber swung his legs out of bed and sat up. Switching on the light, he grabbed a pencil and paper. "Go on."

"Pontchartrain Frères, the big Paris-based medical supplier, has fallen 11 1/8 points in heavy trading."

Silber thought furiously. Pontchartrain was the European supplier for American Medical Instruments—a billion dollar company that supplied most of the major US hospitals with state-of-the-art instruments and diagnostic aids. Including a new computer-based diagnostic system which had been selling like hotcakes. He grunted. AMIX would, of course, not be trading yet—the US exchanges were not open—but one could deduce the direction AMIX's stock would take from the action of Pontchartrain. "Fallen on what news?" Silber demanded tersely.

Fitzhugh chuckled. "AMIX didn't renew its contract. And Pontchartrain derives over 80 percent of its revenues from AMIX." He paused. "And we know where AMIX derives most of its revenues."

Silber hooted. "EquaCare! So they're dropping AMIX as a supplier. Oho! Those idiots! Now they'll have to contract with another company. Or companies." He laughed unpleasantly. "They really should have stuck with AMIX. I wonder what's going on. Someone's idea of efficient management, I guess." He snorted.

"Just thought you'd like to know," Fitzhugh said blandly.

"So what's it going to cost me this time?" Silber wanted to know. "You Irish bastard, you never do these things for nothing."

"Milton!" Fitzhugh exclaimed, feigning shock. "Well, now that you mention it, you could short a couple of hundred shares of AMIX in that account you're managing for me."

"Hmmph!" Silber grunted. "Is that all?"

"How about lunch at your club on Tuesday? On you, of course."

"Oh, all right," Silber acquiesced, and hung up.

He staggered to the bathroom and washed his face, drank three glasses of cold water, and leaned against the basin, feeling a little ill. He touched the bandages that covered the sutures on his head, winced a little, and took a couple of aspirin. Then he padded out into the living room, and switched on the lights.

John Maynard Keynes regarded him balefully from his perch atop a pile of old *Wall Street Journals*. "Mrrf," he muttered in feline irritation.

"Go back to sleep, you useless old pelt," he told the cat. Keynes, however, had ideas of his own. He yawned hugely, gave his fur a few perfuntory licks, then sauntered to the front door where he stood eloquently lashing his tail.

"Go to the kitchen. Use your cat door, you peremptory beast!" Silber shouted at him. "I refuse to be the servant of a cat! Hmmf. Up and down at your every whim. Be independent.

Be a . . . cat, for God's sake!"

Keynes looked back reproachfully at Silber, then decided he had urgent business in the kitchen. The flapping of the cat door ended this latest battle of wills, and Silber sighed in exasperation. One day he'd sell that mangy beast to a suture-maker, he vowed, and be rid of it once and for all. But maybe not today.

Collapsing heavily in a chair at his desk, he looked at his watch. Almost 4:15. He dialed a number he knew by heart.

"Benjamin, Miller and Stein," a pleasant female voice said. "Richard Bell's desk."

"Let me talk to him," he said gruffly.

"Sure thing, Dr. Silber," the voice replied, seemingly oblivious to his rudeness.

"Morning, Milt," Richard Bell said.

"I want you to short 10,000 shares of AMIX for me at the opening," he told Bell, wasting no time on pleasantries. "It will soon be going down the tubes. Might as well make some money on their misery."

"Always were a bleeding heart, weren't you Milt?" Bell responded. "But AMIX? Silber, you old dog, do you have the inside track on this?"

"If you're asking me if this is insider information, the answer is no," he said testily. "So don't worry. You won't get your ass in a sling." He sighed, knowing he'd have to tell Bell more to satisfy him.

"News from Paris," he said. "Pontchartrain's dropping."

He heard the clicking of the Quotron machine's keys as Bell punched out the quote.

"You're right," Bell said. "Okay, I'm writing the order now. You know, Silber, one of these days I'm going to find out who your source is. I thought I was the only one who came to work at 4 a.m."

Silber grunted. "I'll call you later today. Let's try to get 10 points out of this. Got the order written?"

"Yup."

He hung up.

...

Silber measured three tablespoons of instant coffee into a mug, added hot water and a splash of bourbon, and took it into his living room. He sat at his desk for a few minutes, sipping coffee, and thinking about Fitzhugh. His meeting with the young currency trader had been decidedly odd. One evening before dinner at his club—the only luxury Silber permitted himself—his nightly perusal of the *Wall Street Journal* had been disturbed by a stranger.

"I'm Kramer's guest," a tall, redhaired young man had said, coming over to Silber where he sat under the lounge's one good reading lamp, astonishing the older man into unaccustomed silence. "But I've been stood up. It's too late to get a table at any of the decent restaurants, and I'm starving." He smiled and held out his hand. "I'm Ryan Fitzhugh, Foreign Exchange trader at Banque France."

Nonplussed, Silber shook his hand. "Milton Silber, financier and publisher of *The Silber Report*."

Fitzhugh raised his eyebrows in evident recognition of the name.

Silber snorted. "Come, come. I surely can't be that famous."

The young man shrugged. "I read you when I have time. Your advisory service is very influential. I've always had an interest in medicine." His eyes twinkled. "A profit-making interest, of course."

Silber grunted. "It's the best kind to have." He looked at Fitzhugh more closely. "I assume you want to have dinner with me, as Kramer seems to have stood you up."

Fitzhugh grinned.

Oh, what the hell, Silber had told himself. Besides, he might learn something. As it turned out, he had learned a great deal. Tonight was not the first time he and Fitzhugh had found ways to help each other—to their mutual profit, of course.

Silber tapped a pencil on the desktop, making quick mental calculations. AMIX had closed yesterday at 188 3/4. Shorting the stock at today's opening—in effect selling the stock at what he hoped would be its high, and purchasing it later in the day when it had fallen—should be good for 10 points, at least. A tidy profit of $100,000. Minus commissions. He grunted in satisfaction. Idly, he wondered which companies would get the contracts AMIX had lost. A rare smile flitted over his face. Oh, there was a way to find out—but Richard Bell would not approve of the method. So what? Bell didn't have to know. He weighed up the risk/reward, and tapped his pencil indecisively on the desk. Didn't he owe it to his clients? He was in the business of nosing out potential profit situations, after all. Would Eisig have had any influence over the choice of company? He snorted. Probably. The man was very persuasive. He sighed, torn by temptation. Of course he should wait until the news was announced. He knew that. Disgusted at his own indecision, he heaved himself up from his desk. There was work to be done. He drank the last of his coffee, scratched his hairy stomach, and got down to the business of making his clients rich.

• • •

". . . we believe the decline in AMIX should be good for between five and 10 points. Be sure to close your positions promptly, and don't be greedy. I'll update tonight, July 2, after midnight. Good luck with AMIX," Silber concluded, shutting off the tape recorder. Whistling a little, he took the tape into a back room, inserted it into another recorder—this one attached to a telephone—and closed the door. He looked at his watch. Just after 5:00. Clients usually began to call *The Silber Report* hotline about this time. Sure enough, he had hardly gotten back into the living room when the first call came. He heard the recorder click in after the phone's second ring, and smiled in satisfaction. Much better than the Internet, especially with the new caller ID feature.

He wondered how many of his clients would follow his advice and sell AMIX short. He shrugged. It took guts to sell short. The first time he had done it, it had scared him to death. But the boldness had paid off.

Just as boldness had paid off when he decided to leave

medicine and start a new career at the age of 48. Actually, it had been easy, although he would never admit it to anyone. Finance had always been his second love, and even while he was working at Woodlands, he had kept meticulous charts of the movement of publicly traded companies in the health care industry. He done quite well following his own advice. It had been a very profitable avocation, and once he had abandoned medicine, it had proved to be a very profitable livelihood. There were hundreds of investors out there, he discovered, many eager to pay $500 per year for his financial advice. And in a very short time, he had acquired a reputation for being one of the most reliable analysts of health care stocks. He had made himself, and his clients, very rich. Why then, did he feel so depressed?

Yawning, he threw open the living room curtains. It would be dawn soon. He was a doctor—had been anyway—surely he knew how to combat depression? More coffee. One of those Cuban cigars his Canadian client sent him periodically. And some Bach. The Concerto for Three Harpsichords and Orchestra in D Minor. Yes, the very thing. Then, perhaps a trip to see his old friend, pathologist Jacob Metzenbaum, in the bowels of Woodlands. He would pick up some onion bagels on the way and talk to Jake for awhile. Then, home to work on the latest issue of *The Silber Report*. He frowned a little, realizing that he hadn't decided upon a company to profile in the upcoming issue. As he hunted for the Bach tape, he wondered again about AMIX's replacement. He chuckled a little to himself. It would be so easy to find out. He could, for a fee, acquire an access number for the hospital's computer. Maybe he'd do it. Just to satisfy his own curiosity, of course. He chuckled again. The idea was almost irresistible.

Chapter 3

The ambulance turned in just ahead of Maggie and followed the sign pointing to "Ambulance Entrance." The sign was just above the one pointing to "Morgue."

It was only 6:30 a.m., so except for the lone ambulance, the emergency room looked pretty quiet. It was too early for Dr. Stemmons to be sitting behind the main computer terminal—the "bridge," as they called it now—but there he was. No more banker's hours for him, it would appear.

"Well, you're here early," Stemmons said, with an eyebrow raised. "Minor Medicine doesn't open until 8:00. Aren't you there today?"

"Yes," Maggie said. "But I want to check the admissions log. I'm doing a study of patients admitted for chronic lung disease."

"Can't give up the research, can you?" Stemmons said, shaking his head and taking a sip of coffee. He had brought his own stainless steel thermos. "Well, there's nothing in the book yesterday that fits that description. We're managing more of them in the Preventive Health Clinic these days. It's more cost-effective." He handed her the open log.

Maggie scanned it. No patients with chronic lung disease were on the list. She turned back to the previous day. "Well, while I'm here, I'd like to check on that man with the endocarditis." She fished some index cards out of her pocket. "Woody Brown was his name."

"Woody Brown?" Stemmons asked.

"Don't you remember? You were going to admit him after I left. But I don't see him on the list."

"Oh, of course," Stemmons said. "I was blanking on him. It was a most unpleasant affair. He signed out AMA."

"AMA!" Marjorie exclaimed. "But he'll die!"

"Very likely," Stemmons said, examining his nails. "I

17

explained that to him. I painted the most gruesome picture that I could about the complications. Damaged heart valve, fluid in the lungs, emboli in the brain. The whole bit. But he left, all the same."

"There ought to be something we could do in a case like that," Maggie protested.

"Well, there's not," Stemmons said. "Just like with Dr. Silber. He wasn't mentally incompetent. So he had the right to refuse treatment." He touched her hand. "Don't worry about it. You did all you could. This is just one of the frustrations of dealing with this patient population."

Maggie shook her head. Mr. Brown had a curable disease. It wasn't as though he had advanced cancer. And he hadn't seemed reluctant to come into the hospital when she had spoken to him about it. She should have stayed and seen to his admission herself. She suspected that Stemmons really hadn't tried very hard.

"Why don't you go have a cup of coffee now. I need to get my statistical summaries in order before the circus starts. By the way, you could help me out by keying in your provider number on each of the patients you see."

"My provider number?"

"Didn't you read the orientation manual?" Stemmons asked. "Your number has to go into the computer with every encounter. I put yours in for you the other day. It's part of the quality assurance program."

"I put my name on all the printouts."

"I know it, dear," Stemmons smiled. "And I realize that doctors are often insulted by having a provider number. But we really do need it. It facilitates many aspects of the system that you can't be aware of at this point."

"Are they going to start paging 'Provider Altman'?" Maggie asked.

"Now, now," Stemmons said. "Be a sweetheart, and key in the number. Even if you do think it is stupid."

"Dr. Stemmons, I'd appreciate it if you wouldn't call me things like 'sweetheart'," Maggie said.

"Sorry," Stemmons said. "I promise henceforth to call

you Maggie. If you promise to call me Brent."

"All right."

He smiled, but Maggie sensed that he was annoyed with her. Well, she was annoyed with him too. Such condescension was uncalled for, even if he was a mighty resident, and she a green intern.

The clerk at the desk wasn't happy to see her either. "We can't give out patient's telephone numbers," she informed Maggie haughtily.

"But I'm his doctor," Maggie insisted. "He had a head injury, and I need to check whether he is all right."

She really was worried about him. His behavior had been a little strange. And a subdural hematoma could also have delayed effects. Maybe Dr. Silber could recognize the signs. But maybe not. A doctor who treats himself has a fool for a patient, they say. And if he were alone, what could he do? Maybe he wouldn't be able to call for help. Or wouldn't want to. He certainly had a negative attitude about the hospital. Maggie wondered why. But her main concern was to find out how he was doing.

The clerk stared at her impassively.

"He refused to sign the AMA form," Maggie added. "Maybe I could ask him to do that."

Maggie had found the right words, and soon had the telephone number in her pocket.

• • •

The waiting area was the largest section of Minor Medicine: six rows of chairs with arms hooked together. There was a one-armed school desk where patients had their blood pressures taken by the nurse. A printer whirred almost continuously, spewing out hard copy with the pertinent social information and vital signs. The papers went into the "intake" box, to be picked up in turn by the doctors. By ten minutes after eight, there were already six papers in the box, and eight or ten people waiting to be "vitalized."

. . .

The patient, a young man wearing a green hospital gown, looked up in chagrin as Maggie opened the door. "Uh, can I see a man doctor?" he asked.

"Sure," Maggie said. "It'll be about an hour. Have you got a drip, or trouble with your nature?" She felt grateful for her student rotation in the clinic. One thing she had learned there was the proper Fort Bastion term for impotence.

"A drip." He looked relieved. The other possibility would obviously have been more serious.

"Oh, well, just put a drop of it on this slide, please, and a drop on the swab."

The patient complied, and also allowed Maggie to check for swollen nodes. Maggie headed for the microscope, grateful for a few minutes away from the eyes of the patients in the waiting room, who seemed to be watching her every move.

"Matches," she said, and added it to her list of things to bring. She had had to borrow a lighter from one of the nurses. The state of the laboratory was a disgrace. She pitched a number of soiled slides into the red trash bucket with the "biohazard" label. The path of that bucket would be carefully tracked with documentation in triplicate. Too bad the hospital couldn't keep track of the laboratory's need for chemicals. She would have to telephone the lab; the decolorizer for the Gram's stain was almost gone. Maybe it was supposed to be gone. It could be that mere physicians weren't supposed to look at slides, what with the Clinical Laboratory Improvement Act.

Sighing with frustration at how difficult a simple procedure could become, she got the stained slide of the discharge under the oil immersion lens. Pink bugs inside the white cells. Another case to report to the public health department.

"Rocephin, 125 mg," she ordered, on returning to the doctor's station.

"You mean Benemid, 1 gram, plus 4.8 million units of procaine penicillin?" the nurse inquired.

"That's not what I said," Maggie replied.

"That's what the formulary says," the nurse responded.

"You might be able to get the Rocephin, but it'll take hours, on a good day. Your patient will be out of here by then."

"But this is not 1980," Maggie said.

The nurse shrugged. Obviously, it wasn't.

"Okay, Benemid and procaine pen," Maggie agreed. It might work, and you had to pick your battles. "And draw a VDRL."

Maggie sighed. Clinical medicine was really glamorous. Her fourth case of sexually transmitted disease in one day. At least there was some variety. Crabs, and Trichomonas, and gonorrhea. The nurse had not looked happy when she had requested a set-up for a pelvic exam. She had had to fill out a special authorization form, certifying that the procedure was truly necessary. They seemed to ration the speculums and culture tubes. The nurse had informed her that she was supposed to refer these people to the VD clinic. But Maggie was afraid they might not go there, so she insisted on ordering the treatment herself.

This certainly wasn't exactly what she had visualized medicine to be like. But then two years in a quiet, well-organized immunology lab wasn't the best possible preparation for plunging back into clinical medicine, feet first. Maggie was confident that she would soon establish a routine, despite the seeming chaos of the situation.

• • •

"I'm turnin' into a dog! And I'm gonna die!" shrieked the patient. The man cowered in the corner, and howled when Maggie moved a little closer to him. His eyes were wide, and he was sweating profusely. He had gotten his injection of penicillin a few minutes ago. But there were no splotches on his skin, no swelling of the lips, and no audible wheezing, at least from a distance. It did not seem wise to move close enough to listen to his chest.

"You're not going to die," said a confident voice behind Maggie. "You'll just feel like it for about the next 15 minutes or so. Then you'll be all right."

The patient looked up suspiciously at Fred Jenkins, Maggie's fellow intern, who had heard the commotion from the next room. "But I'm turnin' into a dog, man!"

"No, we won't let that happen," Fred told him firmly. "If you'll just sit in the chair here, you'll be all right."

Looking doubtful, the man seated himself, never taking his eyes off Fred. He looked ready to leap at them if they made a suspicious move. Maggie tried not to move a muscle.

"Good," Fred told him confidently. "Already you're beginning to feel better. Pretty soon the fear will leave you completely."

"I'm turning into a dog," the man said, less insistently.

"You feel like you are, but you're not. It's the anesthetic in the shot that you received. It's making you feel very strange. But you'll be all right soon. It wears off real quick."

"Are you sure, man?"

. . .

"Thanks!" Maggie told Fred. "I've never seen anything quite like that before."

"Well, I just happened to see a case one summer when I was working with Dr. King, a GP back home. He used to let me help him in the office after I finished my chores on the ranch," Fred explained. "He uses the newer drugs now. The procaine in the penicillin really makes some folks go crazy. Then the doc thinks they're allergic to penicillin."

Maggie was impressed. Her new friend, a tall gangling young man with sandy hair and a sunburned face pitted with acne scars, certainly seemed to have a lot of common sense, not just book learning.

"Now you just yell if you need any help," he told her. "And by the way, did you know that we're neighbors? I saw you going up to your apartment just the other day."

So, there would be at least one person she knew in her apartment complex. Maybe this wouldn't be such a gruesome year after all.

• • •

The classroom was full; evidently, nothing was to keep
interns from Dr. Eisig's conference. Not even the pile of charts in
Minor Medicine. At precisely 12:05, Dr. Eisig entered. Maggie
took the last bite of her peanut butter sandwich, and studied him
curiously. This was the Philip Eisig whose innovative program at
TURPH was already attracting the attention of the *Northeastern
Journal of Medicine*.

Eisig seated himself on the desk at the front of the room
and blinked at his interns through his thick lenses. His appearance was not imposing. He was about 50 years old, of medium
height, with thinning gray hair, and watery blue eyes. A few years
ago, he had been just another professor of medicine, giving
rather boring lectures on metabolic imbalances. He had been
doing important research, she gathered. At least, it was
presented at a lot of national conferences. Now he had set aside
his lab coat in favor of a conservative gray business suit, as he
undertook his dual role as hospital administrator and
Chairperson of the Department of Medicine.

"Usually we have charts to go over at this meeting," Dr.
Eisig said. "But it's too early in the year. Dr. Blaine hasn't collected any for me yet." He nodded at Stephen Blaine, the chief
resident, who smiled tightly. Blaine was a stocky, dark-haired,
dour looking fellow, who seemed to have a habit of staring at
people until they obviously felt uncomfortable. Maggie had heard
that he would be doing a fellowship at the NIH next year, in
clinical pharmacology.

"Welcome to the Texas University Regional Preventive
Health Center," Eisig began. "You've all read the orientation
manual, which tells you about the mechanics of our program.
What I want to do is share with you something about our
philosophy." He pressed his fingertips together and rested his
chin on them.

"All of us have been distressed by the rapid changes that
have been occurring in medicine. Changes that threaten to
sweep away our concern for the underprivileged in our society.
Changes that threaten to place doctors and hospitals under the

control of the third party payers, with the major emphasis being on the bottom line."

He looked around the room, gazing over his wire rimmed glasses into several sets of eyes in turn. "Now we know that many of these changes were motivated by a very real concern about the rising cost of medical care. Society does not have unlimited resources. We can't change that. But we can see to it that the resources are allocated fairly, and efficiently, on the basis of medical necessity alone."

He paused. "It is our job as health care providers to determine how medicine will be practiced. And to see to it that everyone has equal access to high quality care, and that resources are not wasted on ineffective care. We mustn't leave the decisions to the clerks and the bureaucrats. But if we don't do our job, rest assured that they will be eager to do it for us."

That word again, Maggie thought. She wondered if Dr. Eisig meant that she, the health-care-provider intern, was supposed to make decisions, or whether the health-care-provider computer programmer had taken over that function.

"We must learn from the mistakes of the past," Eisig continued. "We know now that we need to concentrate on prevention, and wellness, rather than sickness. And that we need to consider the whole patient."

Good. But Maggie wondered about the ones who were already sick. Once they got to Major Medicine, it was a little late to talk about prevention, as far as those individuals were concerned.

Eisig was warming to his subject. "With EquaCare, we have had the opportunity to design a system properly, from the ground up. We will be applying the most sophisticated management techniques to plan and monitor our resource use. And to track all the important patient parameters, including the social ones." Maggie noticed that Blaine raised an eyebrow slightly. She suspected that he for one didn't much care about social factors.

"We are starting with the indigent population, the most neglected people in our society, the most difficult population. Once we have proven our system to work for this group, it will spread to revolutionize the entire health care delivery system."

The phrase made Maggie think of a van that delivered laundry, like the one her grandfather had driven. She needed to modernize her outlook, it seemed.

"It's just like doing cancer research on the patients with the most advanced disease," Eisig continued. "If a treatment works for the hopeless cases, its potential for curing early cancers is tremendous!" He looked off into space, perhaps visualizing a new disease-free age.

Blaine was paging through a binder filled with computer printouts. Clearly, Maggie would have to become more familiar with the computer. Meanwhile, she would continue to carry around her index cards. Even if they were on the verge of obsolescence.

"All of you will be participating in a historic event. A great experiment in health care delivery." Eisig paused to look around at his interns, with what Maggie supposed to be a fatherly expression. "We are counting on you," he said. "Your cooperation will be needed to make the system work. Of course, we expect some difficulties. The concept is new, the software is new, and most of us are unaccustomed to working with computers. But we will succeed. Texas University Regional Preventive Health Center will be the showcase for the nation. If you all do your part."

The room was quiet, except for some rustling of cellophane, and the sound of one of the interns biting into an apple.

"Please feel free to bring any problems to Dr. Blaine or to me. We are anxious to have your feedback. And we'll be giving you feedback too. We learn to be quality, cost-effective physicians by learning how our actions compare with the standard of care. I want to assure you, however, that you are not to look upon this feedback as a report card. Not at all. It's meant to be nonthreatening, simply an educational exercise. Now, are there any questions?" Eisig concluded.

Nobody raised a hand. Maggie wondered if she was the only one who had any questions. She thought of the former chief, Dr. Edgar Lowenstein, who had never been seen without his white coat. Before his sudden death, he had dazzled (and terrified) generations of students with his brilliant diagnoses.

Somehow, she couldn't imagine Dr. Lowenstein giving the presentation they had just heard. He would have spoken of the importance of getting autopsies, keeping flowsheets, and measuring the circulation time.

. . .

"Well, what do you think?" Maggie asked Fred on their way back to the ER. "So far, this place doesn't seem like the model of efficiency to me."

"No, ma'am, it sure doesn't," Fred agreed. "And I reckon the folks down here don't see it that way either." All the chairs were filled, and a number of patients were standing. Someone had put a "6" in the slot on the sign that said "Estimated Waiting Time: ___ hours." Maggie and Fred each grabbed a printout, and headed into an examining room.

. . .

The telephone rang eight times, as Maggie's apprehension grew. But eventually a gruff voice said, "Hello."

"Dr. Silber, please," Maggie said.

"Speaking."

"Dr. Silber, this is Maggie Altman. I was a little concerned about you, and wanted to see how you were doing."

"Hmmf," he said. "Nice of you to call. As a matter of fact, I was just calling the hospital."

"Oh," Maggie said, with concern. "Are you having a problem? Vomiting, drowsiness, weakness?"

"No, Dr. Altman, not a medical problem," Silber said sardonically. "If I had, I certainly wouldn't call Woodlands."

"Oh," Maggie said, uncertainly.

"I am having an administrative problem. The bastard in the business office refuses to allow my wallet and keys and clothing to be returned to me because I have not signed an AMA form. I told them what they could do with their form. They kept repeating that it was contrary to their policy for me not to sign their damnable form." Maggie could almost see the steam flowing over the wire.

"Oh, dear," she said, "is there anything I could do to help?"

"As a matter of fact, there is," Silber responded. "But you probably won't want to."

"Maybe I would," Maggie said, hesitantly.

"If you were to sign my discharge, Jim could get my belongings," he said. "But you would have to trust me not to sue you for malpractice, in case something bad ever happens to me that I could conceivably blame on you."

"I could probably get the chart from the clerk at the front desk," she said.

"You shouldn't," he admonished her. "They aren't legally entitled to keep my things, and I'm sure I'll eventually be able to recover them. But it's going to be a tremendous pain in the ass."

"I'll just sign the discharge," Maggie said. What a bureaucratic snafu. Of course, she would be taking a risk. She really ought to check the patient again first.

"Would you ask Jim just to put the things in a paper bag and send them to me by taxi? Offer the taxi driver $150, COD. Tell him to get Sam, if he can. In case he's forgotten the address, it's 4435 E. Hudson Drive."

Maggie jotted the number down, then exclaimed, "You know, you live just six blocks from me. I could just drop the things by on my way home."

"Totally unnecessary," he responded. "Just tell Jim to put them in the taxi."

Chapter
4

Maggie parked her car in the driveway of 4435 East Hudson Drive, and looked uncertainly out through the window. Was this really where Dr. Silber lived? The old, rambling white stucco house sat well back on its lot, and overgrown bushes and unpruned shrubs almost hid it from the street. The yard was a tangle of weeds. She shook her head. Gone to seed. Come to think of it, Dr. Silber himself had looked a little seedy when she had seen him in the ER. She wondered what he was doing now that he had left medicine. After Silber had stalked out of the hospital, Stemmons had told her the story—how Silber, in a fit of pique at being passed over for Chief of Medicine, had refused to cooperate with Eisig. He had become obstreperous and obstructive—positively unreliable. Finally, so Stemmons had said, Eisig had been forced to ask him to resign.

She gathered up Silber's belongings and slammed the car door. The man Stemmons had described to her did not sound like the Dr. Silber she had known. Apprehensively, she navigated the uneven flagstones of the front walk, stepping over a broken red clay tile that had presumably fallen from the roof, and knocked on the front door. A wild-looking figure pulled back one of the front room curtains and peered out at her. Then the door opened.

"You don't look like a cab driver," Dr. Silber said.

"Well, I wasn't sure a cab driver could be trusted with your things," Maggie told him, handing over the paper bag. "There are credit cards and cash in your wallet."

"Unnecessary for you to go to such trouble. But very kind. Come in, come in," he said expansively, looking ridiculous in a pair of khaki shorts and a rumpled pink shirt.

"Well," she replied, hesitating.

"It's all right," he assured her. "I'm quite tame, my performance at the hospital notwithstanding."

"Maybe for just a minute," she agreed, stepping inside. "Here are your things. I signed you out." he looked at the bandages on his head, which now sat somewhat askew, giving him a roguish appearance. "How are you feeling?"

He grinned, reminding Maggie of a grizzly bear, and she barely restrained a laugh. It's not at all funny, she told herself. The man can't help his appearance. Even though he did look like a bear—little suspicious eyes, mane of uncombed hair, wild beard, hairy arms and legs.

"How am I? Very well indeed," he replied. "Won't you come in and have a drink?" He peered closely at her. "You don't look like a drinker, though. Well, I think I have some sodas around somewhere."

"A drink please," she told him.

"Bourbon?"

"That would be fine."

He waved a hand. "Find someplace to sit."

She looked about curiously. Although there were armchairs and a comfortable looking sofa in the living room, every horizontal surface, save one battered old wing chair, was piled with paper. And that chair's seat was at least an inch deep in black cat hair. She shook her head in amazement. Stacks of old *Wall Street Journals*, back issues of *Barron's*, bulging file folders, piles of unfiled papers. The walls were lined with bookshelves, but half the books, it seemed, had been dragged off the shelves and now reposed in various states on the floor. Dr. Silber must practice the 80-20 rule, she thought in amusement. The theory stated, she recalled, that 20 percent of all books, papers and reference materials were used 80 percent of the time. Thus, those who wished to avoid unnecessary effort kept that 20 percent close at hand. A persuasive argument in favor of the cluttered desk. Or, as in this case, the cluttered room. And over everything lay a fine film of dust. She could feel a sneeze building up in her sinuses.

Silber disappeared into the kitchen, and she furtively studied the room he passed through. It must have been the dining room at one time. She could plainly see that a wall had been removed to join it to the living room. The combined space

29

overflowed with office furniture: a huge, battered oak desk and swivel chair. A long wooden table against the far wall. The table held a computer—distinctly out of place because of its shiny new appearance—attached to two printers and a telephone. Beside it stood a computer-like machine she didn't recognize. Quotron, it said. Six dented and scratched metal filing cabinets stood against the far wall, and on the floor were the inevitable piles of paper. But it was the wall itself that was most interesting. Three clock faces gave three different times—9:14, 11:14 and 2:14. Below that a large rectangular box, approximately 10' by 10', and was clearly a video display of some sort. The lower left hand corner of the box read "Trans-Jet LED" and the lower right corner, "NYSE". Very unusual indeed for the home of a professor of medicine. What in the world was Dr. Silber up to? She considered asking him but decided against it.

"Here we are," he said, returning from the kitchen. Seeing her still standing, he grunted, put the drinks down on his desk, and fetched a straight backed chair. "I don't have many guests," he apologized. He carried the chair into the living room and found a place for it between two stacks of paper. Maggie sat in it tentatively, and he handed her her drink, easing himself into the vacant armchair. "Cheers," he said, and they drank. "Thanks again for your help."

"No problem," she replied, wondering if she should ask him about his injury. That was why she had come, after all. But he seemed fine. Admit it, she told herself, you're a little intimidated by him.

"I thought you were safely tucked away doing research somewhere."

"Safely?"

He snorted. "Medicine can be harmful to your health, you know. But tell me what you were working on."

"Before Dr. Adamson left to go to Lilly, I was working on his monoclonal antibody project. It wasn't getting anywhere, so the grant wasn't renewed," Maggie explained.

"Typical," Silber growled. "Adamson spent too much time in the lab, and not enough time networking or interfacing, or whatever they call sleazy politics these days. Eisig will get rid of all the Adamsons before long. Too threatening to him."

Maggie was a little shocked. "It wasn't like that—Dr. Eisig tried to help him!"

"Like hell he did," Silber muttered unpleasantly. Such bitterness, Maggie, thought. The telephone rang in a back room, but Silber made no attempt to answer it. It stopped after two rings.

"But what about you?" Silber inquired. "Have you given up hope of pushing back the frontiers of science?"

Maggie laughed. "I was never that ambitious. But I did hope to continue with some clinical research during my internship."

"Oh?" Silber looked interested. "What would you investigate?"

"I'd like to follow patients with lung disease who are admitted over a three year period. See what kind of problems develop. And how their lung disease progresses."

"Too clinical," Silber commented cynically. "If you want to get it published, you ought to talk about how such patients 'consume health care resources.' And about how the resources could be allocated more fairly."

"But I want to be a doctor, not an economist!" Maggie protested.

"If you want to be successful in medicine, you'll have to be a politician," Silber said. "And are you sure you want to be a doctor?"

"Oh yes," Maggie assured him. "I always dreamed of having my own practice. Research was simply an attractive distraction." She laughed a little. "No night calls. I guess I was being selfish. In a way, I'm glad the grant wasn't renewed."

"You weren't being selfish, you were being smart," Silber grunted. "You would have been better off staying in research. Medicine is going straight to hell. You think you'll open up a practice of your own and make a decent living? Bah! Forget it. Fee-for-service medicine is almost extinct. Private medicine may go the way of the dodo. And who's killing it? Systems like EquaCare!"

"I disagree," she said heatedly. "I think I could succeed

in a practice of my own."

He glared at her. "You don't know enough yet to disagree. Wait awhile. Eisig and the Woodlands—pardon me, TURPH—will change your mind."

I don't want to fight with you, Dr. Silber, she thought. You may have reason to be bitter, but I don't. She swallowed the last of her bourbon, and felt a vague burning sensation in her upper abdomen. She probably shouldn't be drinking bourbon.

"You know," Silber said, as if embarrassed at his negative comments, "I have some books that might be useful to you in your research." He scratched his beard and looked thoughtfully at the bookcase. "In fact, I have several that deal with the analysis of data. Most important. You need to plan that from the start. You could drop in and use them if you like." He snorted. "It's for sure I won't be needing them again."

"That's very kind of you," she said, surprised. Then, she decided to ask the question. "What are you doing now?"

He laughed. "Getting rich." Seeing her surprise, he continued. "I've become an analyst of publicly traded health care companies. People pay me for my advice."

She was amazed. "But don't you miss medicine? You were such a good teacher."

A strange, stubborn look came over his face. "I don't miss it a bit," he assured her. "Not one bit. In fact, I seldom think about it." He bared his teeth in a smile.

"Woodlands, Eisig, medicine—that's all in the past. My new profession occupies all my time now."

• • •

On the short drive to her apartment, Maggie found herself unable to think about anything but Dr. Silber. He's so bitter, she thought. And so negative about medicine. And why should he bother to tell her such a blatant lie, assuring her that he never even thought about the hospital, let alone regretted leaving it? She knew it was a lie because there on his desk was this morning's copy of the *Fort Bastion Morning News*, an article about EquaCare circled in red. She hadn't removed a rubber band from a newspaper since starting her internship, but decided she wanted to read that particular article as soon as she got home.

EQUACARE SYSTEM HERALDED AS MAJOR ADVANCE

The state's innovative new health care delivery system gained national recognition in this week's issue of the prestigious *Northeastern Journal of Medicine*. The journal called EquaCare "a model for the nation in the concept of prepaid health care." The plan is designed to contain the rising cost of health care while assuring equal access to quality care for all.

Texas University Regional Preventive Health Center is the state's largest EquaCare provider. Formerly a chronic source of deficits in the county budget, it is now operating in the black.

Administrator Philip Eisig, MD, who also serves as Chairperson of the Department of Medicine, said that computer technology and innovative management techniques have been helpful.

"But it's the basic concept that's most important," Eisig said. "We have thrown off the burden of the profit motive in medicine. Our only concern is to optimize resource utilization. There is no incentive to overtreat, as there was under the antiquated fee-for-service arrangement. Resources are allocated in the fairest, most efficient, and most cost-effective way."

Although EquaCare was designed to care for the needs of the indigent, Eisig expects that TURPH Center will also have a waiting list of persons with all types of health insurance coverage.

"People will soon be aware of the advantages that our system has to offer," he explained.

TURPH Center has set up several satellite offices to accept applications for membership in this prepaid plan.

Maggie put the canned split pea soup in a saucepan, and stirred it thoughtfully. So, she and her fellow interns were subjects in an experiment—although, unlike most experimental subjects, they were expected to help make the system work. The article sounded a little too optimistic about the likely results, from what she could see so far. She wondered if EquaCare had been part of the reason for the apparent antagonism between Dr. Silber and Dr. Eisig. And what interest Silber still had in TURPH.

Well, it was too bad that Dr. Silber had withdrawn himself from medicine. But medical politics was not her field. What she needed to do tonight was read up on some subjects she had jotted down on an index card: subdural hematomas, penicillin-resistant gonorrhea, and heroin overdose. There was barely enough time to do that—it was nearly 10 p.m., and she had to be at work by 7 a.m. tomorrow.

The hard rolls were pretty stale, but they'd be edible if dunked in the soup. Maggie sliced some cheese and an apple, and decided to treat herself to some fig newtons. That should supply enough energy to complete a couple sections of *Harrison's Textbook of Medicine* before bedtime.

Chapter 5

He sat in the darkened apartment, curtains open, looking out at the nighttime city. Across the river, lights in the Twin Towers—the city's business and finance district—died one by one. His mouth twisted a little in disdain. Only the unimaginative worked from sun to sun. He finished the drink he had poured for himself, ice cubes tinkling against the expensive crystal of the glass. When the phone rang, he smiled. He had been expecting the call.

"Yes?" he inquired.

"Good evening," the caller said.

He smiled again. "Well?" he asked eagerly.

The caller sighed. "Well, what?"

"Oh, come on. Can't you unbend a little to congratulate me? It's been a very good month. You could be a little more appreciative."

The caller made a muffled sound of disapproval. "Please spare me your adolescent analysis. It's our mutual hard work that makes this endeavor profitable—not yours alone. An interdependence of utility factors, as it were. Everyone benefits from the work we are engaged in, although the narrow-minded would not agree with that point of view. Pioneers in our field are often suspect. That is, of course, why we must work behind the scenes. Together."

He stifled a laugh at this pedanticism. "Whatever," he told the caller blithely.

"You may look in the same place for . . . appreciation," the caller told him. "I think you will find it to be an agreeable amount."

"That's what I wanted to hear!" he replied.

"Until next time, then," the caller said formally, and hung up.

He stared at the receiver for a moment, shrugged, then

replaced it in its cradle. The man was a puzzle. He had never seen beneath that cool, controlled facade. Always in control. But no sense of humor. Ah well, one couldn't always choose one's business partners. His father often said that very thing. Yes, he'd just have to make the most of this opportunity. He grinned. His father would certainly be impressed if he knew how successful his son was becoming. And this was his business deal. His alone. No one had helped him this time. He considered briefly, as he did often, telling his mother, just to see the look of incredulous amazement on her face. Something accomplished without her help. He even savored the hurt it would cause her. And what about telling his father, who declared so often that he would never amount to anything? His grin became broader. Someday he would let them know how clever he was. But not yet.

Switching on a table lamp, he stretched a little. It had been a long day, but he felt restless rather than tired. He crossed the room to a tall, lacquered wooden cabinet, unlocked one of its drawers with a key he wore on a gold chain around his neck, and took out a small, ornate ceramic container. He unstoppered it, and poured a small quantity of a fine, white powder onto the glass top of the coffee table. Rolling a crisp $50 bill into a tight cylinder, he quickly inhaled the white powder.

He looked at his watch—only 8:00. He would go out, he decided, and stood up to go the bedroom and change his clothes. As he passed the sliding glass doors of his balcony, he paused in mid-stride, startled. There was an image in the glass, superimposed upon his view of the city, and for a moment he failed to recognize it. It seemed to be a giant, looming head and shoulders over the city's Twin Towers. The giant spread out his arms as if to gather to himself all of the city from the docks in the south to the oilfields and ranchlands in the north. The image pleased him. He walked to the window and pressed his hands against the glass. In fact, the image pleased him very much. He threw back his head and laughed aloud.

Chapter
6

"Medicine doctor to the Fire Department phone!" shrieked the intercom.

"Take that for me will you, Maggie?" said Stemmons, who was busy talking to Jeannette Larkin. They were seated very close together, Maggie observed.

"But I don't know the procedure," Maggie protested. It was the resident's responsibility to take calls from the paramedics.

"Don't worry about it. You'll do just fine. The fireman will help you," he said nonchalantly, without looking up.

Maggie felt a twinge in her stomach as she found her way back to the radio room. The fireman put away his paperback— one with a dead body on the front cover—and motioned for her to sit down. "Want some coffee?"

"Love some."

"It's 10 cents a cup, but this one's on me."

"Thanks. What's going on?"

"Black male of about 50 found down. Somebody at the scene started CPR. Paramedics just arrived. He had V fib on the monitor, so they already shocked him."

"We're sending you a tracing," said the radio.

"Doctor's here. Tell him your name, Doc."

"Margaret Altman."

"Looks like a straight line now, Dr. Altman. We're continuing CPR. Shall we try to tube him?"

"Guess you'd better. Does he have an IV?"

"Not yet, ma'am. That was our next question. Meanwhile, if we get the tube in, shall we squirt some epi down it?"

"Sounds good," she said.

"Don't look so nervous, Doc," said the fireman, named Smitherman, according to his badge. "Would you like to look at

37

our cheat sheet—I mean the protocol? See—straight line after defib—give epi, down the tube if necessary, and shock again."

"You seem to have it all worked out."

"We done it once or twice before, ma'am. And Dr. Wilkens, he wrote it all out, so, you know, the new residents would have something to go by."

"That was a good idea," Maggie said.

"Tube's in and I can hear breath sounds. Epi's in. Still nothing on the monitor. Shall we go for another 400 watt-seconds?"

"Sure," Maggie said.

For a few minutes, there was only static on the radio. "Nuthin'," said the fireman. Maggie hoped he was looking at a better quality tracing than she was. It could be ventricular fibrillation instead of straight line, as far as she could tell.

"You want an IV with D5W?" he asked

"How'd you know?"

"We're talkin' to the Medicine Doctor. The Surgery Doctor woulda said Ringer's lactate."

"Not for a cardiac arrest, I hope."

"We wouldn'ta called him for a cardiac arrest."

"How about two amps of bicarb?"

"You're gettin' ahead of us, Doc. Havin' a little trouble with the vein."

"Sorry." Maggie waited, sipping coffee and feeling helpless.

"OK the bicarb's in," the paramedic's voice said.

Maggie looked at the protocol and wondered whether to give a dose of calcium.

"We're not gettin' anywhere, Doc. Whaddya say to transporting him in?"

"Not much else to do."

"We're loading 'im up. ETA 10 minutes."

Maggie gulped the last of the coffee, and reported the ETA to Stemmons. Jeannette was just now pushing her patient's stretcher toward the elevator. Her skirt was tightly fitted, and ended well above her knees. For some reason, she looked a little smug.

"The third Code Blue today," Stemmons remarked, his eyes following Dr. Larkin's departure. "And it's only 10:00. Moore is up next."

The paramedic squad burst through the door, one pushing the litter, one administering closed chest massage, and one bagging the patient, all sweating profusely.

"Feet first," directed Stemmons, not moving from his chair. "Let me have a look at the tracing. Never had any rhythm, did he?"

"Dr. Moore, STAT, Dr. Louis Moore, STAT, 2824," the page operator called.

Maggie listened to the patient's lungs—the tube seemed to be well placed, and the firemen were generating a good pulse with their massage. The pupils were fixed and dilated. That could be a sign of brain death—but it could also be caused by the epinephrine. They had already tried every drug she could think of that might help. The situation looked hopeless.

Arriving breathlessly on the scene in wrinkled green scrubs, Lou Moore, the resident assigned to the "B" service, practically shoved Maggie aside, and yelled for a transthoracic pacemaker. He seemed to have taken charge of the code, and Maggie hovered around uncertainly, until Stemmons appeared in the doorway and signalled for her.

"Maggie, can you see the one in Room 8? The ambulance call said he had LOC and a 'personal hygiene problem.' He might be a keeper," Stemmons said. Maggie felt a little irritated, but she might as well go—Moore wasn't about to let her put in the pacing wire.

Attired in a surgical mask, gloves, and a brown and white striped seersucker bathrobe tied backward over his whites, Jim Thomas met her outside the room. Rolling his eyes, he offered her a gown and gloves, and opened the door for her. The stench was nearly overpowering.

The patient may have had LOC—loss of consciousness—before the ambulance arrived, but he was moaning loudly now. A whale of a man, he was wedged tightly between the siderails, with his feet sticking out from the end of the stretcher. There was filth caked beneath his horny, curved toenails. Maggie drew back the sheet, and involuntarily jumped back. An open wound on his thigh—a burn, she supposed—was crawling with maggots.

"I can't get a word out of him, Doc," Jim said. "He just moans. And he tried to hit me when I took his blood pressure, so be careful. His wife says she's been trying to get him to come in, but he refused. She waited for him to pass out, then called the ambulance. Evidently he's been lying on the sofa and drinking Thunderbird for days."

"Who brought him the Thunderbird?" Maggie wanted to know.

"Why his wife did, I guess," Jim said.

"He's been bleeding," Maggie said, looking at the black stool. The odor was pretty characteristic too. She suppressed an urge to vomit.

"I already drew a type and cross," Jim informed her, "although the CBC isn't back yet."

"Thanks," Maggie said, "you're a couple of steps ahead of me."

Maggie made a ginger attempt to do a physical examination. She thought there were rhonchi in the chest, but it was difficult to be sure because of the moaning and the moist cough. She knew it was important to examine the retina, but the patient closed his eyelids tightly, and coughed in her face. She replaced the ophthalmoscope in its wall mount and wiped the spittle from her glasses. She stepped back a few steps, and stared at the man. She had to admit to herself that at that moment she felt like hitting him with an IV pole. Instead, she punched a few findings into the terminal, which registered them with a blink, and fled out into the hall. It took several minutes to suppress the waves of nausea.

"I just wasn't able to do a good physical," she apologized to Stemmons.

"We got enough," he said. "DRG 174, GI hemorrhage, probably a winner." Maggie wondered what a "winner" might be in this context. "Severity 4, and complications present." Stemmons finished entering the data. "I already called the intern," he said.

"Dr. Fischbein, Dr. Charles Fischbein, call 2824," came over the intercom.

"He'll make a detour to the 5 East bathtub," Stemmons remarked, and turned his attention back to the moving display of patient parameters.

Maggie sighed. The blackboard listed five additional patients since she had been to the doctor's station. So far, only one had been claimed by another intern. "See to Room 7 next, would you please?" Stemmons asked.

"OK," Maggie said, stepping aside to allow a procession to pass from the crash room. Moore and two interns were taking a patient and a collection of equipment to the elevator. "Oh, I thought he would die," Maggie said. "Did he make it?"

"There was a rhythm on the monitor after they put in the transthoracic pacemaker. That means he's alive enough to count as an admission. Law IX," Stemmons informed her.

"Law IX?" Maggie asked.

"The only good admission is a dead admission," Stemmons said briefly. "This one's pretty good." He punched more keys on his terminal. He didn't seem to be in the mood for conversation; Maggie wondered if he was annoyed with her. Again. She thought better about making any comment.

· · ·

"What a troll!" Fischbein shouted. Since Maggie could hear him through the wall, presumably the patient heard him too. She hoped he didn't understand. "Is this a hospital, or a sanitary landfill?" Fischbein fumed.

"Really, Charlie," a calm voice said reproachfully. Stemmons' voice. "I must ask you to behave professionally in my emergency room. This is your patient. A human being. Now please take him upstairs."

"This dirtball looks like a veteran to me," Fischbein said.

"He's not," Stemmons assured him. "I always check."

"Are you sure?" Fischbein demanded.

"I'm sure," Stemmons said. "In any case, he is too sick to be transferred. You wouldn't want to be responsible for his death in the ambulance now, would you? The feds would call it dumping and sting you for 50 grand."

Fischbein's expletive was drowned out by a crash. He seemed to have run the stretcher into the door as he angrily shoved it out of the examining room.

Maggie winced, as the moans of Fischbein's patient turned into a guttural howl. The patient she was examining, an 83-year-old woman with the "dizzy weaks" and severe deafness didn't seem to notice.

. . .

"Code Blue, 5 East, Code Blue, 5 East, Code Blue, 5 East," the page operator shrieked.

Maggie helped herself to a swig of antacid from the nurse's station. Maybe she should try some Tagamet or something, if she could find the time to go to the drugstore.

"Code Blue, 5 East, Code Blue, 5 East, Code Blue, 5 East," the operator continued, after a brief pause.

"Do you think that was the patient we just admitted?" Maggie asked Stemmons. He seemed unperturbed by the repeated urgent message. How could he remain so unruffled, she wondered. "I hope I didn't miss anything important. I didn't do a very good exam," Maggie confessed. "And maybe we should've given him some uncrossmatched blood."

"Too risky. It's not on the protocol. Anyway, it was probably the bath that did it," Stemmons remarked. "Too bad. They'll never get him out of the water fast enough to shock him. See, I thought he was a winner."

Law IX, Maggie supposed. She recalled hearing that the hospital got paid by the diagnosis, regardless of how much it cost to take care of the patient. Well, this one hadn't cost very much. Were they to be congratulated for that? Stemmons evidently thought so.

. . .

Maggie checked the EquaCare number again, and

punched in the codes for the third time. But the computer blinked back, "NO ENTRY THIS ID AND DATE. ANOTHER QUERY (Y/N)?

Finally, she seated herself next to Stemmons, who was, as usual, watching the flow of parameters on the screen. "I don't understand it," she said.

"What don't you understand?" Stemmons looked up with a resigned expression.

"Mr. Jefferson is back again, with heart failure," Maggie reported. "I remember seeing him on my first night here. But there's nothing about it in the computer."

"You must have put in the wrong code," Stemmons said.

"I tried it three times."

Stemmons entered the patient's EquaCare ID number himself, but got the same response: the most recent recorded note was over two weeks ago, as the patient was being discharged from the hospital.

"Hmm," he said. "I've never known it to make a mistake." He tried the number again. "Well, you must have confused him with somebody else. We see a lot of bad heart failure."

"No, I'm sure this is the same man," Maggie insisted. "He was my first patient here. And we had the very same problem then. Jim remembered him, but there was no record of the visit in the computer."

"Oh, yes, now I remember. I wonder if there's something wrong with the software." Stemmons looked very concerned. "I'll have to tell Blaine about this tomorrow, before I go home. Don't worry. It'll be taken care of."

"I really wonder if we weren't better off with the old written records," Maggie said.

"No way," Stemmons responded. "This system has capabilities we wouldn't have dreamed of two years ago."

He took some papers from the clerk, and began glancing through them. He seemed to have forgotten about Maggie.

She waited until he had finished signing the papers. "Look, this time he really does need to come in. He had some prolonged chest pain last night. The EKG is unchanged, but he just doesn't look good."

Stemmons allowed his impatience to show, as he called up the data from the day's visit and the record of the old hospital admission. "Nothing objective has changed, compared with his last admission," he said. "And there's not an entry in the data base for female intuition."

Maggie felt her color begin to rise. She reached for the admissions log, but Stemmons stopped her with a look.

"I'll take care of the log book," he said coldly. "I already have a patient for Moore's team. Fischbein will be up next. Why don't you just call him and explain your reasons for admitting this patient."

Obviously, she had invaded Dr. Stemmons' turf. Men were so sensitive. Well, he would just have to be miffed. The patient needed to come into the hospital.

"Another dump!" Fischbein snarled at her. "Can't you do any better than this at outpatient management? And haven't you ever heard of preventive medicine?"

Maggie held the telephone several inches away from her ear, quietly replaced it in its cradle, and took a gulp of Maalox. There was no time to argue with Charlie, even if she had the taste for it. A disorderly, disheveled young man was being dragged in by two policeman. He smelled like model airplane glue.

"The fireman just made a fresh pot of coffee, Doc," Jim told her cheerfully, as he directed the policemen to one of the cubicles. "You better get some before it's all gone."

Chapter
7

"Hey, Doc, it's for you!" someone yelled over the raucous party music and shrieks of laughter. A hand rose above the partygoers' heads, brandishing the phone's receiver.

He took the cordless phone into the townhouse's bathroom, and locked the door behind him.

"It's Daniel, Doc," a familiar voice told him. "You're a hard man to find, you know."

"So you've found me, Daniel. Congratulations. What do you want?"

Daniel chuckled. "Got a surprise for you. Right here in the back of the ambulance."

"Oh?" he inquired, feeling his heart accelerate. "What kind of surprise?"

"The best kind. A dead one. Some old wino. Collapsed in an alley outside one of those fancy restaurants on Jackson Street. By the time we got there, he was dead. His EquaCare card was in his pocket; I took a look after I loaded him in. I figured you'd be interested."

"You're right, Daniel my friend. Give me 20 minutes to get there. I'll meet you at the usual place."

"All right. But listen, Doc—be sure to bring cash. And make it the whole $100 dollars this time, or I'll dump the stiff in the river."

He sighed. Daniel would do it, too. "The whole $100. I promise. Twenty minutes."

He came out of the bathroom to find that someone had put a red light in the ceiling fixture, and for a moment he saw everyone drenched in blood. He shuddered. A bad omen? Nonsense. He was just on edge tonight. He'd conclude his business at the hospital, and be back here as soon as he could manage it. Everything was going to be all right. Raúl would understand why he didn't have the full $5000 he owed him for the cocaine. Hell, he'd have to understand. Wouldn't he?

Threading his way through clots of clinging, dancing, chattering people, he headed for the front door. His friend Jay— the townhouse's owner—intercepted him there.

"Leaving so soon, old buddy?"

He frowned. "An emergency. Shouldn't take long."

Jay laughed. "A truly dedicated man. Well, I'll try to save some of your . . . refreshments for you. But I can't promise. Don't be long. You know Raúl's coming, don't you?"

He turned on his friend in irritation. "I can take care of Raúl."

"I sure hope so," Jay told him.

. . .

He drove east, toward the bridge, the Ferrari's top down, the night air cool on his skin. He was still angry, thinking of Jay's last remark. If there was anyone who could take care of Raúl, he was the man. So he still owed him $2000. So what? It was peanuts. Raúl knew he was good for it. And even if he couldn't get the cash, there might be another way to placate him. Raúl was in the pharmaceutical business, wasn't he? Yes, everything would be all right. He was a businessman. He knew how to turn adversity into opportunity.

A brief fireworks display lit up the eastern sky, and he smiled. Independence Day. He liked the sound of that word. If business went well, he too would be independent. He would never have to ask anyone for anything again. Not his father; certainly not his mother. He hummed a little, and tapped his fingers on the steering wheel, feeling ebullient. Tonight's business transaction should be worth at least $1500. Maybe $2000. Even after he had paid off Daniel. And Caroline. He picked up his car phone and dialed the hospital.

"Page Dr. Miltown to pathology," he told the page operator, and hung up.

Caroline. She, like Daniel, played an essential role in this business. However, unlike Daniel, she did not understand her proper place. Over the past few months she had become possessive and demanding. He frowned, wishing he had limited his involvement with her to business. But with Caroline, that was hard. She was so damned . . . willing. Yes, that was it. So maybe he had been a little too willing himself—so what? She offered and he took. Another simple arrangement. The emotional morass she now found herself in was hardly his fault. He hadn't promised her a thing. In fact, he reasoned, she should be grateful. He frowned again. He was going to have to do something about her. There was just too much money at stake here to take any chances with emotional females.

He pulled into the nearly empty parking lot, locked the Ferrari, and hurried to the Morgue entrance. Once inside, he looked around cautiously, but as he had suspected, there was no one around. Good. The last thing he needed was to be seen here. He waited just inside the door, listening for Daniel's ambulance.

Behind him, a door opened and closed, and he heard quick, light footsteps. Caroline.

"Well," she said sarcastically when she saw him waiting by the door. "Such dedication. Working on July 4th."

He sighed. She was going to be difficult. Well, he knew a way to deal with that. He pulled her to him and kissed her roughly. "We're both dedicated," he reminded her after a moment. "To ourselves."

Caroline laughed a little, and began to unbutton his shirt. He smiled. She was so predictable. Sometimes he thought that she wasn't in this for the money at all. He believed that if he told her he could no longer pay her, she would still do what he asked. The payoff? Him. A few minutes every now and then on the floor of the Morgue, or the chart room, or his office. He shrugged. Money, sex, what did it matter? They were both commodities, to be given in exchange for services rendered. It made little difference to him which one she preferred. That she demanded both only strengthened his hold over her. A knock at the door interrupted Caroline, and she made a little sound of exasperation.

"Later," he said, buttoning his shirt and walking to the door. With a sigh of relief, he saw it was Daniel. He helped him wheel the dead man into the Morgue.

"All right," Daniel said matter-of-factly, holding out his

hand. "My money."

He handed Daniel two $50 bills, and the ambulance driver examined them carefully, then put them into his wallet.

"That's more like it," Daniel said. His acquisitive glance moved to Caroline, and he grinned. "You folks have a nice time now, you hear?"

He waited until the ambulance pulled away, then locked the outer door. Curious, he looked closely at the dead man. Daniel had fastened the EquaCare card to the fellow's big toe. Johanssen, it read. He remembered him. A pathetic, frail old man who lived on the streets. As far as he knew, the man had no next of kin. Perfect.

"Let's have a nice time, just like the man suggested," Caroline said, grabbing him by his belt.

"Not just yet," he said. God, but the woman had a one-track mind. "We each have a job to do now," he reminded her.

She pouted.

"Go on upstairs and get things ready for him. I have to make sure he's entered in the computer." He laughed a little. "Mr. Johanssen won't be causing us any more trouble."

"Oh, all right," Caroline said reluctantly.

He looked at her appraisingly. She really was attractive, in a common sort of way. Blonde hair, blue eyes, a great body. Not a brain in her head, but then, who cared? Hmm. Maybe he did have time. "If you come to my office when you're finished, you can, ah . . . collect your pay," he said.

She grinned. "I'll hurry."

Chapter
8

Alarmed at his shortness of breath, Silber deposited himself on a park bench across the street from the hospital. Gasping like a netted trout, and you've only walked a mile or so, he thought in disgust. Mopping his brow with a large, checkered handkerchief, he considered shortening the length of his nightly constitutional. Might be a good idea in view of his recent injury. He touched his head carefully. Come to think of it, he hadn't felt quite himself since he had bounced his cranium off the asphalt in front of Woodlands. Hmmf. Perhaps a ten or twelve block walk would have to suffice. Face it, Silber, injured or not, you're getting old. Crotchety. Decrepit. Everything's running down. He grunted in irritation. Peering across the road at Woodlands, he checked the distance with a worried frown, and calculated that he was safe. The last thing he wanted was to be recognized, sitting here like a derelict on a park bench. Of course he wasn't just sitting here, gazing vapidly at Woodlands. Certainly not. He was simply resting from his rigorous walk. And the hospital happened to be in his line of sight. In a minute, he would catch his breath and move along.

As his pulse quieted, he noted with satisfaction that it would soon be dark. Good. The likelihood of being spotted by someone from Woodlands diminished by the minute. If it weren't for the occasional trip to see his old friend, pathologist Jacob Metzenbaum, he would never visit Woodlands at all. And no, he told himself irritably, he wouldn't call the hospital by that vile acronym, TURPH. It would always be Woodlands to him. When he bothered to think of the hospital at all. He frowned a little at his train of thought. Old fool, he chastised himself. Sitting here mooning over your past. He heaved himself upright and crossed the street, skirting the perimeter of the parking lot, heading for the doorway under the sign marked "Morgue".

He found the stairs and descended. The netherworld.

Fitting, he thought. A world turned grey and penumbrous in the scant illumination of a few night lights. Metzenbaum's world. Well, it was peaceful here with everyone gone. He knew his friend preferred it this way. No noise. No confusion. No questions and answers. No bumbling students or meddlesome colleagues. The place quiet, immaculate, scrubbed clean of the day's carnage. White tile and stainless steel. Silber passed the morgue and couldn't help glancing inside. A single bare bulb illuminated the place, casting huge, cavelike shadows across the walls. The only sound was the soft, high whir of refrigerator motors cooling cadavers in the lockers that lined the wall. Just down the hall, the door to Metzenbaum's office stood open slightly, spilling warm yellow light into the gloom. A shape moved inside the office and blocked the light momentarily. A bear in a cave. Silber smiled to himself.

"Are you there, you old butcher?" Silber asked, sticking his head into the office.

Metzenbaum sat morosely at his desk, black necktie in hand. His basset hound face looked more mournful than usual, and to Silber's amazement, his friend seemed to have lost weight since he had last seen him. Why, the man must weigh no more than 150 pounds, Silber thought. On Metzenbaum's 6' frame, that was too little. And his clothes! His friend always had been a very conservative dresser—neutral colors, nothing flashy. But now he looked like a funeral director. Or a penguin. His shirt was stark white, his vest black, and the suitcoat that hung on the coatrack behind him matched the vest. Most disconcerting.

Metzenbaum looked up at Silber and sighed. "It's Ellen," he said, making a global gesture that seemed to include his tie, his suit and perhaps his life.

Silber eased himself into the chair across the desk from Metzenbaum. Something was amiss here. He prepared to listen. "Ellen?" he asked.

Metzenbaum leaned over the desk and whispered to Silber, "She's gone gaga. Bonkers. Loopy."

Silber forced himself not to laugh. "Oh?"

"I'm supposed to be meeting her and the kids," Metzenbaum told Silber. "At some bloody French restaurant." He scowled, and ran a hand through his springy grey hair. "I'm just on my way out." He looked at his watch. "I've been on my way out for an hour." A thought seemed to cross his mind. "Want a drink? Maybe a little fortification is just what I need."

Silber felt a little stab of envy at Jake's mention of joining Ellen and his children for dinner, but quickly suppressed it. "Let's have that drink," he said encouragingly.

Metzenbaum fished in his bottom drawer, brought out a bottle of bourbon and two glasses, and poured them each a healthy belt. "They're at La Petite Colombe drinking champagne and eating snails." He shivered. "Snails, for God's sake. Milt, I spend all weekend trying to poison the slimy little buggers in my garden. They're pests, right? No one in his right mind would want to eat them." He made a strangled sound. "I can't do it." He poured himself some more bourbon. "Last month it was Greek food. Squid rings, and something wrapped in grape leaves. The month before it was Japanese food. Baby octopus. Whole." He shuddered. "I gagged twice on the tentacles. It was touch and go for a few minutes." He looked at Silber mournfully. "I haven't had a decent meal in ages. Even the dog's dinner is starting to look good to me. Milt, I don't think I can take any more. And next month it's going to be haggis. Do you know what that is?" he asked in horror.

Silber nodded, feeling a little queasy himself. "As a matter of fact, yes. It's a dish made of the heart and liver of a sheep or calf, minced with suet and oatmeal, and boiled in the animal's stomach. I'm told it's quite tasty," he offered encouragingly. "Thousands of Scots thrive on it." He felt amused at his friend's squeamishness. Didn't pathologists name diseases after food—bread and butter pericarditis, for example? And didn't they state that some exudations resembled currant jelly or anchovy paste? The bottled organs on shelves along the wall didn't seem to bother Metzenbaum, and at autopsies he sliced the livers with great enthusiasm. Curious.

Metzenbaum hastily poured himself another drink. "I'm being driven insane," he whispered. "Between my wife and that damned nun . . . "

"Which nun?" Silber prompted.

Metzenbaum waved a hand. "Sister Mary Patrice. Damned meddler. Thanks to her, I haven't done an autopsy in three months. Three months! How will the students learn anything?"

"I don't understand." Silber shook his head. "What's she doing? Stealing corpses?"

Metzenbaum looked up quickly, and Silber hooted with laughter. "Jake, you old body-snatcher! Are you still running that scam?"

Metzenbaum looked offended. "Scheme. Not scam. And, yes, I'm still doing it. The money for unclaimed bodies might as well go into Pathology's budget as some mortician's pocket." He looked through his bushy eyebrows at Silber. "I had hoped you'd forgotten all about that."

Silber snorted. "Not a chance. That little gem is going in my memoirs." He saw Metzenbaum's look of alarm, and decided to let his friend off the hook. "Just a joke, Jake. Of course I'd never tell anyone. Besides, who'd believe it? But tell me, what's Sister Mary doing to you?"

Metzenbaum's nostrils flared. "Discouraging next-of-kin from permitting autopsies. She's very persuasive. Could talk the birds out of the trees. Irish, I think."

"Mmm," Silber agreed. "Reminds me of another Irish charmer."

"Of course, I've complained to Eisig," Metzenbaum said, "but he's about as useless as . . . well, you know," he broke off in embarrassment, evidently remembering Silber's antipathy for the man. "Sorry. Didn't mean to rub salt in the wound," he apologized.

Silber sighed. "Don't expect any help from Eisig. He's not interested in medicine. He's interested in cost containment." He spat out the last two words as if they were oaths. "The bottom line. Woodlands—or TURPH, as he calls it—is a model of the EquaCare system at work. Nothing is going to disturb Eisig's balance sheet. I guess your autopsies just cost too much. And return nothing. So, he's supportive of Sister Mary Patrice and her mission." He snorted. "A simple matter of economics."

Metzenbaum belched. "Maybe you did the right thing,

Milt."

"Oh?" Silber raised an eyebrow.

"Look at you. You're doing all right."

"Yes," Silber had to agree, "I am."

"A bloody tycoon," Metzenbaum exulted. He poured each of them another drink.

"Mmm," Silber equivocated. "You, too, could be financially better off, you know, Jake," Silber told him, taking up an old refrain. "Let me put together a portfolio for you."

Metzenbaum heaved an immense sigh. "Then I'd stay awake nights worrying about it. I don't know, Milt. Maybe sometime. If I live through Ellen's adventures in continental cuisine." He looked over Silber's shoulder out into the morgue. "What I really want is to work. At what I was trained to do." He sighed again. "Do you know I've been offered another job?"

Silber was amazed. He couldn't imagine Pathology without Metzenbaum. "You have? What? Where?"

"Forensic pathologist. Chief Medical Examiner for Fort Bastion."

"You, a civil servant?"

Metzenbaum belched. "Milt, you should see the set-up they have over there. Every piece of equipment you could imagine." He groaned. "It's pretty tempting."

Silber shook his head. "I can imagine it is. You know as well as I do that things are just likely to get worse here. For anyone who cares about medicine, that is." Silber could feel his blood pressure rising. "However, if you're interested in making money," he said cynically, "that's quite another matter. Everyone wants to 'contain costs' and they're willing to pay a bundle to anyone who claims to be able to do it. With so much money concentrated in systems like EquaCare, opportunities are boundless. There's a whole new game afoot in the health care industry. Fortunes to be made. And I intend to make some of them. And to bail out before the liabilities come due." He was suddenly aware of Metzenbaum looking at him oddly, and he retreated to safer ground. "Winners and losers," he explained. "Companies which adapt, and those which don't. And picking the winners is my business," he said. "But, if you don't want me to help you . . . " he trailed off. Metzenbaum, eyes closed, humming a little, was unsuccessfully attempting to knot his tie. Good. His friend had probably not paid close attention to Silber's fulminating about "fortunes to be made" from systems like EquaCare. Silber sighed and got up to help him. "Snails, eh?" He stood behind Metzenbaum and knotted his tie, and helped his friend into his suit jacket. Then he called a cab.

With only a little urging, Metzenbaum, still humming, walked to the door of the morgue. Silber opened the door, poked his head out, and closed it quickly. Coming down the sidewalk to the ER was someone he definitely didn't want to see—Maggie Altman. Damn! She had already looked his way. Well, perhaps she hadn't recognized him. He groaned. A car, presumably the cab he had ordered, pulled up and honked its horn. Grinding his teeth in frustration, he risked another look outside. All clear. She had disappeared into the ER entrance. He steadied Metzenbaum, making certain he could stand upright, then urged him out the door and over to the cab. It was, of course, by design, and not by accident, that the body of Jacob Metzenbaum served to shield Silber from potential onlookers. No, it wouldn't do to be seen here.

"La Petite Colombe!" Metzenbaum told the cab driver happily, collapsing in an alcohol-sodden lump in the back seat.

Silber rolled down the window, wondering guiltily how he was going to explain his friend's state to Ellen. She would be sure to blame him. Wives. Hmmf. Silber wondered why Metzenbaum put up with all this restaurant nonsense. He looked gloomily out across the river as Metzenbaum, made mellow by alcohol, hummed contentedly. Silber envied him.

Chapter 9

Maggie looked again at the door leading to the morgue. She was sure she had just seen Dr. Silber. But apparently he had gone back inside, just as she had started to wave to him. Strange. Especially at 7:30 p.m. She had thought Dr. Silber made every effort to avoid TU. Well, perhaps she had been mistaken. She took a deep breath and walked through the double doors, wondering what the night had in store for her.

"Sure thing, Chief," Stemmons was saying to Blaine, as Maggie entered. "I can have those stats compiled for you every week."

The chief resident was leaving the bridge with a sheaf of computer printouts. He gave Maggie a curt nod of recognition. Stephen Blaine never had a smile for the interns, Maggie had noticed, although he certainly knew all of them, from his erratic but frequent visits to the Pit. She wondered what he did with all that computer output.

"For some reason, the chief has developed an interest in ODs," Stemmons informed Maggie. "And as it happens, we've got a special on them tonight." There were already six listed on the blackboard. "How about taking on the one in seven?"

"Sure," Maggie said.

• • •

Maggie had never seen anything like it. A young girl, only 14 years old, looked at Maggie appealingly. She appeared to be very frightened. She kept sticking her tongue out, and couldn't seem to get her chin away from her right shoulder. Maggie had no idea what to do. She would have to ask for help.

"Show her the pictures," Stemmons suggested, handing Maggie a booklet containing photographs of pills. "I'll bet it's that blue one. Haldol. Very popular these days. Why, I can't imagine.

But some of these kids will try anything."

"Really?" Maggie asked. "It's certainly a strange reaction."

"Just give her a shot of Benadryl," he advised. "It'll make you an instant heroine."

"Thanks," Maggie said.

The medication worked just as dramatically as Stemmons had promised. Her opinion of him went up one notch. She had something to learn before she could sit on the bridge and dispense knowledge like that.

. . .

"Ewald tube for this one," Stemmons directed. The firemen wheeled a semiconscious boy, who appeared to be in his late teens, into the crash room. He had a bizarre spike haircut, and a safety pin in one ear. His purple, sequined vest was stained with vomit. The boy tried briefly to focus his eyes on Maggie, then passed out again. He smelled unmistakeably of alcohol.

"Found down next to his Fiat in the Oz parking lot," the fireman reported to Maggie.

"Oz?" she asked.

"Yeah, Oz. Famous Fort Bastion nightspot. Or should I say notorious? You don't get around much, do you, Doc?" the fireman said with a grin.

The medics moved the patient onto the crash room stretcher, and wheeled their own litter away. The beeper on the fireman's belt was already summoning them to another emergency.

Maggie pried the patient's mouth open with a tongue blade, and made sure that she could elicit a gag response. The patient flailed at her with both hands. Probably wouldn't have to put a tube in the trachea, she judged. But the Ewald tube was fatter than her thumb. How was she going to get it down his throat?

"Restraints, Doc?" Jim asked.

"Please," Maggie said.

After Jim had applied the leather wrist restraints, Stemmons materialized and gave a smooth demonstration of how to pass the tube. With a large syringe, Maggie sucked out a quart of liquid. Alcohol. She lavaged the stomach with several quarts of water. "I wonder if this is what they mean by the 'stomach pump?' " she asked Jim.

"I reckon so, ma'am. And I think you just saved this young man's life," Jim said, grimacing as he poured the stomach contents into a container for the lab. "He must have drunk enough to kill himself before he passed out."

The patient did not appear to be grateful. He made a tremendous effort to cough up the tube, and struggled to free his hands. Stemmons appeared again and removed the tube. "We're sorry for the discomfort, Mr. Bancroft. But it was necessary. We have a more comfortable room ready for you now."

Dr. Larkin appeared, and Stemmons himself helped her wheel the stretcher toward the new elevator—the one that led to the private floor, Maggie noted. The patient's name had not appeared on the blackboard. Bancroft? The mayor of Fort Bastion? But the loudspeaker was demanding a medicine doctor, and since Stemmons was away from the bridge, that meant Dr. Altman.

• • •

It was 5:00 a.m. before she had a minute to sit down. Stemmons had disappeared, presumably to the call room to catch a nap. Fred came to join her in the small nurse's lounge, and she offered him a piece of banana bread. "The benefits of advertising," Fred observed.

"Advertising?" Maggie asked.

"Yes, don't you notice the billboards when you drive? Or listen to the country western station? 'EquaCare patients' choice: TU first.' Well, they're all trying us out."

"So that's why," Maggie said. "I never remember being this busy when I was a student. I thought I was doing some selective forgetting."

"I couldn't say. I was in Louisiana then. But why don't you rest your feet a minute, and let me take care of that FUO that just came in. And by the way, have you tried the tacos at

57

Ojeda's?" Fred swallowed the last bite of banana bread, and grabbed his stethoscope.

"No," Maggie said.

"How about 7:00? I'll treat."

"Sure," Maggie agreed.

"Dr. Miltown, Dr. Miltown, call 2262," the page operator said. Maggie blinked. She hadn't met a Dr. Miltown yet. And wasn't that the brand name of a tranquilizer? She shrugged. Another CP had been brought in, and the EKG machine was being rolled out of his room. She pulled herself to her feet, and splashed some cold water on her face.

· · ·

"This place may look like a dive," Fred assured her, "but they make the best tacos in Fort Bastion."

Maggie looked around a little doubtfully. The dim lights served a purpose, she thought. The table was covered with a red and white checkered oilcloth, and the legs were all a different length. Or perhaps the floor wasn't level.

Fred handed her several small napkins from the aluminum napkin dispenser, and passed the plastic dish of tortilla chips. "Careful with the sauce," he advised. "Especially until they bring the beer."

His warning was a little late, and it was fortunate that the pitcher of beer arrived soon.

Fred dunked another chip into the sauce, and munched on it thoughtfully. "Ojeda's tacos," he said, in a tone of mock seriousness, "are one of the best things in Fort Bastion."

Maggie thought she noticed a twinkle in his eyes, and she laughed a little. "Well," she said, "You'll have to show me. But I may not be a very good judge, since I haven't been anywhere in Fort Bastion except to the hospital and the grocery store."

"Well, I didn't mean to include the hospital in my culinary comparisons," he said. "It just wouldn't be fair. I mean, have you tried the Egg à la King yet?"

"Well, no," Maggie said.

"It's not like the steak sandwiches they used to have at

midnight, when I was a student in Louisiana."

"Probably not. But I just don't feel like eating anything when the Ipecac brigade is in the Pit," Maggie said. "And there certainly were a lot of them last night. Really depressing. I bet none of those kids would take that junk if they knew what we were going to do to them. It's really horrible to have them sitting out in public like that, throwing up."

"It's pretty awful," Fred agreed. "But we have to get the stuff out of them somehow. That's the safest way. And you have to admit, we didn't invite them to come see us."

"That's for sure," Maggie said, glumly.

"But enough of TU," Fred told her. "This is dinnertime. Here come the tacos. Enjoy!"

Someone had turned on a recording of mariachis, making conversation difficult. Maggie signalled that the tacos were as good as advertised, and reached for another handful of napkins. Fred kept refilling her beer glass.

"Oh no, I shouldn't," she protested. Her stomach agreed.

"It's all right," he said. "You can afford to relax a little. Otherwise TU will get you down."

"It's pretty depressing all right. I'm beginning to wonder whether I made the right decision to do an internship here. Even if it is the best place west of the Mississippi."

"Already?" he asked. "The average time it takes to wonder about that is two months, or so I hear."

"Maybe things will get better," Maggie said, "But I have this feeling that all my circuits are overloaded. Like last night. I was just sure that the T-wave inversions on a patient's EKG were new. But when I went to show them to Dr. Stemmons, and he called up the old EKG, the two tracings looked identical."

"It's a good thing they invented writing. And computers." Fred took her hand reassuringly and held it for a moment. "It's easy to make a mistake like that, when there's so much going on."

"But it's so embarrassing," Maggie said. "Especially when I had already told Charlie Fischbein about the patient. He was hanging around there to see what was happening. He was not happy about that admission. Called the patient a scuzzball or something. And accused me of shirking my responsibility for out-patient management by dumping the patient on him. I said to him that Dr. Stemmons would just have to decide. And he decided all right. You should have seen the smug look on Charlie's face."

"I can imagine," Fred said, sympathetically. "Charlie's not a very happy person. In fact he's pretty weird. I hear that he roams the building even when he's not on call. You can't let the things he says get to you. You just have to do your job."

"That's what I try to do," Maggie said. "But sometimes it seems that that isn't the most important thing. It seems that, as far as the hospital is concerned, the computer output is all that counts."

"Well, it gives the managers something to do," Fred shrugged. "So it helps to fight unemployment. You don't need to worry about it. You just need to have dinner and a good night's sleep. Would you like a sopapilla? They're pretty good too."

"OK," Maggie agreed. She probably was obsessing about things too much. Fred just wanted to be a country doc, he had told her. She should try to keep things in perspective, as he did. Just learn as much as possible, concentrate on the tasks at hand, and not trouble herself about the workings of the Health Care System. Didn't TU have a team of managers to take care of the administrative details?

Fred was right. What she needed now was sleep. And a large dose of Maalox.

Chapter 10

He had scarcely gotten into the apartment when the phone rang. Collapsing heavily into a leather armchair, he grabbed the receiver and held it to his ear.

"Yes?" he demanded irritably.

"Hmm," a familiar voice said. "You sound out of sorts."

"Oh," he replied, affecting nonchalance. "It's you." Damn! He had hoped to avoid this conversation. But he might as well get it over with. "Isn't it a little too early in the month for you to be calling?"

"Normally I would call later, yes. But there seems to be a problem."

His heart sank. So the caller had noticed it, too. Well, it could hardly be covered up. "A problem?"

"Yes," the voice continued. "I've been reviewing the data in the computer so far this month."

"And?" he said irritably. Why didn't the man just come to the point?

"And it seems you haven't been doing your job."

"What?" he shouted. "I've been doing the same job I always do! A damned good one."

"You may think so," the voice replied, "but the statistics contradict you."

He felt ill, and his mind flipped to the bottom line. If what the voice said were indeed true, he could expect a smaller paycheck at the end of the month. He recalled with a little thrill of fear the amount of money he owed to Raúl.

"Are you there?" the voice inquired.

"Yes, yes. I'm thinking." And he was. Furiously. First he'd check the computer records for himself. But he had no doubt that what the voice was telling him was the truth. If he were honest with himself, he would admit that he had seen something like this coming.

61

"I hope your cerebration includes a method of rectifying the problem," the voice continued.

"Oh yes," he assured his caller. "I have no intentions of allowing the situation to get any worse."

The caller sighed heavily. "I certainly hope so. In fact, I'm counting on it."

His palms had begun to sweat. "I won't let you down," he assured him.

• • •

In the kitchen, he poured himself a large snifter of brandy, then paced about the apartment in the dark, drinking it. The "problem" of course, was that damned woman. The Dragon Lady, he called her. He hadn't wanted to believe that she was interfering with his work, but he knew now that it was true. Well, it simply couldn't go on. Why couldn't she have gone to another hospital, he wondered petulantly. She could have been making someone else's life miserable. Why him? And why now? Just when things had been going along beautifully.

He sank down into his favorite armchair, and finished the brandy. All right. Something had to be done. But what? Various ideas presented themselves, but he discarded them. Something subtle? It might miss the mark. Something direct? An unambiguous message? What could it say without giving too much away? He'd give it some more thought a little later. One way or another, though, the obstacle was going to have to be circumvented. He stroked his chin thoughtfully. Or removed.

Chapter 11

As Maggie waited for Brent's arrival, she found, to her surprise, that she was nervous. Really, she chided herself. You're just going to dinner with him. Relax. Still, the fact that he had asked her for a date seemed hard to believe. She had thought that he found her plain, and perhaps even irritating. But he had told her that he appreciated her work, and wanted to get to know her better! And to show her a little of the real Fort Bastion.

"You look beautiful tonight!" Brent exclaimed, when she opened the door. "You should wear your hair down more often."

Maggie blushed a little. Men never told her she was beautiful. She knew that she looked tired, that her eyelids were a little puffy, and that her straight brown hair was plain. But she had put on some make-up, and one of her few dressy outfits: a blue silk blouse and skirt. Very feminine. She knew that she looked as good as she could, and it was gratifying to receive a compliment, even if it was a bit exaggerated.

"I have reservations at the Downtown Club," he said. "If that's all right with you. They have excellent seafood. I thought you might like that."

"Oh, that sounds nice," Maggie said. "How did you know I love fish?"

Brent held the car door open for her. An old fashioned custom that she thought men had abandoned. She found she liked it. She noticed that Brent had a sporty red car, with plush bucket seats, and carpet on the inside of the doors. She had heard that his father was a wealthy man—from oilwells, or something.

Brent maneuvered the car expertly onto the Expressway, and turned on a tape player. Vivaldi, she thought. "Look at the magnificent sunset," he said. "It makes Fort Bastion look like a paradise."

The tall glass buildings reflected the colors of the clouds

in ever changing patterns, giving the heart of the city an other-worldly appearance. It was hard to imagine that the effluent of this ethereal city discharged into the emergency room of Texas University. Maggie resolved that she should try to set her sights on something more elevating than the TU parking lot at dawn or dusk.

Brent was apparently well known at the Downtown Club. The maitre d'hôtel greeted him warmly, and escorted them to a table with a view of the oldest, most beautiful part of the city. They looked down at the river and its bordering woodlands, and Brent pointed out a few of the more famous old mansions.

"This is my favorite view," he said. "Although if you'd rather see downtown, we could sit on the other side next time." Next time? What was happening here? Brent smiled at her over his crystal goblet of Perrier. She looked away in confusion.

"This is beautiful," Maggie said, when she had regained her composure. The surroundings were so elegant, in fact, that she felt a little out of place. The cutlery was of heavy sterling silver, the napkins of finest linen, the carpet a rich Oriental. She was not used to such opulence.

"I wanted to bring you to a fine place," Brent said, touching her hand gently, and gazing into her eyes. "It suits you."

Maggie looked away, not sure what to make of Brent's apparent change of character. Brent took the cue, and changed to a less personal approach. He described the various delicacies on the menu, and made several recommendations. The cuisine was sure to be outstanding, Maggie thought, but the names of many of the dishes were unfamiliar.

Dinner arrived, and she had never seen anything quite like it. The first course was a chilled potato soup, served in china that rested on ice in a silver bowl. The salad contained several interesting vegetables that she hadn't tried before: hearts of palm, Brent said, and artichoke hearts. He told her that the dressing contained caviar. The salmon was quite good, she thought. Brent advised her not to have too much of the crisp French bread, to save room for dessert.

"I'll bet you're a chocolate lover," he said.

"How can you tell?"

"Oh, I can tell," he said mysteriously. "Let's rest up for it." Brent filled her glass again with the wine: a French wine, he told her, a Chablis. She felt it was a little too sour, not as good as the California variety she was used to, but decided to keep her opinion to herself.

"The Academy of St. Martin's in the Fields will be here a week from next Friday," he said. "I have a pair of tickets. Would you like to hear them?"

So he really had meant what he said about "next time"! "Let me see," she said. "I'm on call Saturday. My first day on the wards. So Friday should be all right." You can do better than that, she scolded herself. "I'd love to go," she told him, truthfully.

"I'll look forward to it," he replied. "You know I used to be a violinist myself, but I no longer have enough time to practice. Medicine is such a demanding mistress."

When the waiter brought chocolate mousse and coffee, Brent smiled at her obvious enjoyment. Careful, Maggie told herself. You could get used to this. She looked thoughtfully at Brent's handsome face. It didn't seem to belong to the Brent she had known several years ago. That Brent certainly wouldn't have asked that Maggie for a date. Well, maybe he had changed.

• • •

After a short drive to point out some of the night time sights of Fort Bastion, Brent escorted her to the door of her apartment. He placed his hands gently around her waist. She had been thinking about this moment, and wondering what Brent would do. And about how she would respond.

"I can't tell you how much I enjoyed this evening," he said. "You are so different from other women. I can talk to you. But I don't want you to think that it's just your fine mind that attracts me, either!" He looked into her eyes as if asking permission, then gently kissed her on the mouth. She couldn't have been more surprised if he had shaken her hand. This was Brent Stemmons, playboy?

"Good night, Maggie," he whispered.

"Good night, Brent," she managed to say.

"See you soon."

He was gone. Maggie let herself into her apartment and locked the door. She stumbled into the bedroom without turning on the light; she didn't want to wake up from her dream. A handsome man, treating her to a dinner like that, was a rare occasion.

"Silly romantic," she muttered to herself. "Are you going to try to get ready for bed in the dark?" Resolutely, she turned on the harsh bathroom light. Yes, there was her white coat, soaking in a bucket of Clorox solution. With a sigh, she felt she had returned to reality. Where she worked with another Brent Stemmons. Which one of them was for real?

Chapter 12

Because he was preoccupied, he didn't see them coming. One of them stepped out from the darkness between two cars in the hospital parking lot, and the other came at him from behind. The one behind him clamped a forearm across his throat, and the one in front of him flicked open a thin-bladed knife, grabbed his right ear, and held the knife to his earlobe. He tried to say something, but found his mouth was too dry to allow him to speak. He was, he admitted to himself, terrified.

"Raúl says hello," the man with the knife told him. White teeth flashed in a thin, Hispanic face as the man smiled. "He hopes you haven't forgotten that you owe him money. He's gonna pay you a little visit at the end of the month. You're one lucky hombre, y'know?" He felt the knife slice his flesh, making his eyes water with the pain, and a thin stream of blood ran down his neck. His knees began to shake. Oh God, what was going to happen to him? Would they cut off his earlobe? And this was lucky? "Usually, Raúl don't give no credit. But in your case, he said he'd make an exception. He knows you're good for it. Right, Doc?"

"Right," he managed to whisper.

"Of course, there'll be interest on the loan. But you can handle that." The knife cut into his flesh a little more, and he moaned. Were they really going to cut off his earlobe? Or even the whole ear? He found that he couldn't breathe properly.

"What's the matter, Doc? Can't stand a little blood?" The man with the knife chuckled, enjoying his joke. "You're lucky Raúl is so considerate. He told me not to cut your nose. I like to cut noses," the man told him, grinning. "They bleed a lot. But then, you'd know that, wouldn't you?"

He forced himself to nod. Maybe he was lucky. If this thug had cut his nose, he would have had ended up in TURPH's ER. But earlobes were different. Not much to cut. He could probably take care of the damage at home. If he just didn't get cut any more.

"You can handle the interest, can't you," the man inquired. "For you, Raúl says it's only 100 percent. But you gotta have it on time for sure. Otherwise, I'm gonna have to pay you another visit." He gave the injured ear a vicious tug. "Maybe take the whole ear then."

Hating himself for playing the victim's role so neatly, he answered desperately, "I'll have the money. All of it. Tell Raúl." How he would take care of it he had no idea, but he would have said anything to make the man put his knife away. Please, he begged silently, just stop. As if in answer to his plea, the man with the knife stepped back, wiped it elaborately on his tie, then flicked it closed, putting it in his pocket.

"Smart man," he told him. "Gonna pay his debts. I'll tell Raúl you got the message. Right, Doc?"

He nodded.

"I can't hear you." The arm around his throat tightened. "Yes! I got the message."

The arm released him. The two men melted into the darkness at the edge of the parking lot. He fought an urge to vomit, and pressed a clean handkerchief to his earlobe. It hurt like hell, and would probably require the services of a plastic surgeon. The last thing he needed was embarrassing questions about what had happened. This would happen now, just when he had started to put his plan into action. What lousy timing! Shaking, he was barely able to climb into his car and drive away.

Chapter 13

"No!" the patient screamed, and looked at her wildly. For a moment, Maggie took her bearings. It was 1:00 A.M. She was on Ward 6 West. She was alive. The impression that this was a chamber in the underworld was just her imagination. The patient was in the bed. The two objects on the windowsill that ended in high-heeled shoes were her artificial legs. The ravages of diabetes.

The patient was drenched with sweat, and her heart rate was very rapid. Maggie tried to find a vein so that she could draw a blood sample and give some 50 percent dextrose. But the woman was enormously fat, and the tourniquet kept slipping off because of the sweat. Besides, she was struggling, and was surprisingly strong.

Maggie decided that a fingerstick would have to do. The blood sugar reading, as far as she could tell in the dim light afforded by the bedside lamp, was about 30. Dangerously low. It was surprising that the patient was not unconscious. Well, if she couldn't get in an IV, she would have to give some glucagon, a hormone that would raise the blood sugar.

The pharmacy didn't have any glucagon.

Maggie tried again to start an intravenous, but without success. The nurse suggested squirting the glucose solution into the patient's mouth, slowly and cautiously. Doubtfully, Maggie tried it. She didn't have any other ideas. It must have been effective, because eventually the patient seemed to come around, complaining of a massive headache.

Maggie reviewed the chart. The blood sugars were not filed among the lab reports, and the ward's laboratory terminal was not functioning. She called the lab. A surly technician advised her to look for the results on the chart. Finally, the tech agreed to look in the lab's computer and call back. She didn't. By the time Maggie got around to calling the lab again, the first technician had "stepped out," and the one who answered didn't know how to query the computer, or said she didn't. Astonishing, in a place that seemed totally dependent upon the electronic record.

"Dr. Miltown, Dr. Miltown, call 2262," the page operator called. Fortunately, not the ER, and not one of the admitting interns, Maggie noted.

She sighed with frustration. She didn't see any other way of getting the old lab reports. For now, she just cancelled the patient's insulin, and ordered a fasting blood sugar and frequent observations for the rest of the night.

"Dr. Jenkins, Dr. Fred Jenkins, call 2824," said the operator. The ER extension. Dr. Jenkins wouldn't see the call room tonight, Maggie thought. And she probably wouldn't either. She was up for the next patient now.

Maggie went to the sink in the doctor's station to splash some water on her face, and made a sound of disgust. She had just cleaned up the room about half an hour ago. She simply couldn't concentrate when surrounded by scraps of paper, coffee cups, crushed up tablets for serum acetone tests, half filled urine specimen cups, and even an occasional used needle. She thought she had left the place tidy, but there, on the edge of the sink, was a styrofoam cup containing a half inch of dirty gray coffee and a cigarette butt. "Charlie Fischbein?" she asked out loud. Fischbein was a chain smoker, and she had seen him using styrofoam cups as an ashtray. What a slob, she thought to herself, pouring out the repulsive liquid and discarding the soggy butt. But that diabetic was his patient; Fischbein wasn't on call tonight. So what would he be doing here? Certainly, he wasn't taking care of the patient. Apparently, he didn't pay much attention to her glucose during the daytime either. Well, there was no time to worry about it. The page operator was calling Dr. Margaret Altman again. At least the sixth time in one hour. This time to the dreaded ER extension, 2824.

• • •

"How long have you been sick?" Maggie asked. She

70

couldn't remember whether she had already asked him that. At 2:30 a.m., her mind was dull.

Mr. Jones, an emaciated 66-year-old man with no established address, seemed to think it was about two weeks.

"Why did you wait so long to come in?" she wanted to know.

"Well, ma'am, I did come in about a week ago, and the doctor gave me some black and yellow capsules. I took a couple of them, but they made me sick. So I didn't take any more. Tonight I got worse."

Maggie finished her examination, and had Mr. Jones cough up some rust colored sputum. He spat most of it into a jar; some dripped down the side. He had pneumonia in both lower lobes; a half hour search in the X-ray department had finally turned up the films. The slides of the sputum had to dry, before she could do a Gram stain and a stain for tuberculosis.

The computer terminal blinked. TOMMY JONES, 66-YEAR-OLD MALE, EQUACARE NUMBER 8993251, DRG 89, SEVERITY 3, ADMISSION CRITERIA L1, P5. RESOURCES EXPENDED TO DATE IN THIS HOSPITAL STAY $963, TOTAL ALLOWED $3935. No previous record was available. That was strange. Maggie was sure he had said he had been here one week ago, not somewhere else. Maybe he didn't remember correctly. But this was not the first time that the patient's memory differed from the computers. And it always seemed to happen with patients like this.

The computer queried her for the medical data base. It was the intern's job to complete the initial data base for all patients not already in the computer; for subsequent admissions, the job would be easier. Most of the blanks on this patient could not be filled in. Maggie sighed with discouragement. The patient just didn't know what medicines he had taken in the past, or what operation he had had to account for his midline scar. She asked Medical Records to send up any old charts from pre-computer days. When she had finished the history and physical as well as she could, she noted that the computer added to the problem list: "Incomplete Data Base."

Finally, the IV was started, and the first dose of an

antibiotic was running in. Maggie decided that an hour's nap would be better than no sleep at all.

Fred was already asleep in the call room. In the dim light of early dawn, Maggie noticed idly that he hadn't even taken off his scuffed boots. An intern from the "B" service snored in the other lower bunk. Maggie took off her heavy pockets, climbed into the upper bunk, and rested her head on the slippery, plastic-coated pillow.

• • •

The telephone seemed to ring for a long time before someone answered it. Maggie felt that she had to climb out of a deep pit, as Fred handed her up the telephone receiver. Her pulse pounded in her ears from the surge of adrenalin.

"Dr. Altman, this is Sueann on 6 West. I need to clarify an order on one of your patients. Does SPEP stand for 'serum protein electrophoresis'?"

"Yes."

"Thank you. And have a good morning," Sueann said cheerfully.

Maggie was tempted to throw the telephone through the window. Having just fallen asleep, she was now wide awake. Her back ached, and she had a burning sensation in her upper abdomen. Well, it was 6:30. Maybe there would be time to wash her face and change her stockings before the student nurses descended on their locker room, making intolerable noise. Maggie certainly couldn't change in the coeducational call room. She got up as quietly as possible, and headed for the stairway.

She nearly ran into Stephen Blaine, who grumbled "Good morning," but looked at her as if to say "What are you doing here?" As usual, he was carrying a stack of computer output.

Well, she had to admit that she didn't want to see anybody at this hour either. She wondered whether Blaine had spent the night at the hospital, or whether he just came in this early. The chief resident shouldn't have to do either. Blaine evidently took his job very seriously.

Chapter 14

"When did you have time to do this?" Silber inquired from under the table. Supine, a well-chewed power cord in one hand and a screwdriver in the other, he waited for an answer.

"Mrrnnh," Keynes answered from his bed in Silber's "out" basket, clearly bored.

"You perambulating rug, you sleep 23 hours out of 24," Silber accused him. He cursed as the screwdriver slipped, slicing his finger. "I fail to see when you had either the time or the energy to wreak havoc on my electronic minion."

"Nrrff," Keynes replied.

"All right," Silber declared, sitting up and brandishing the destroyed power cord. "I've replaced it. But this is the last time." He thrust his face into Keynes'. "Hear?"

The cat opened one yellow eye, sighed malodorously into Silber's face, and resumed his nap.

"I don't believe what I put up with from you," Silber told him. "Such insolence." He stood up, dusted off the parts of his anatomy that he could reach, and wandered into the kitchen to pour himself a glass of bourbon. As he powered up the computer, he noted that Keynes had disappeared. Just as well. A reassuring "beep" and the whir of the disk indicated to Silber that his surgical efforts had been successful. He was almost ready to relax, when sounds of chewing emanated from under the table. "No!" he roared. "You damned Luddite!"

Keynes shot out from under the table as if jet propelled, the flapping of his cat door attesting to a successful escape from Silber's wrath.

"The day of your delivery to the suture maker may be at hand, you flea-infested technophobe!" Silber shouted after him. "Why do I keep you around?" His voice, echoing through the empty rooms of this lonely house, told him why.

• • •

"No, not Persis Instruments," Silber muttered to himself. "Too little working capital. Nor ISCO, nor SurgiMed, nor Interhealth. Hmmf." He ran his fingers through his mane of hair, thinking. Finally, he had to admit he was stumped. Having just reviewed the current balance sheets of all the companies he considered to be candidates for the EquaCare contract, he couldn't find one that he would select to replace AMIX. What had the EquaCare decision makers been thinking about when they decided not to renew AMIX's contract? Of course, it was none of his business, but he was curious nevertheless. In fact, the question had become an annoying, irritating itch in his mind. One that demanded to be scratched. Sighing, he sat back and shut off the computer. Perhaps he should give in to the temptation. Buy his way into the Woodlands' computer and ferret out the information. Hmmf. Failing success at that, access the Equacare computer's database. But it would be theft. Did he really want the information that badly? And what would he do with it once he had it? He could hardly publish it in *The Silber Report*. He snorted. Purloined information was probably even worse than insider information. So he would have to keep it to himself. Was it worth all the effort involved just to satisfy his curiosity? Hmmf. Well, he would just take the first step. He picked up the phone and dialled a number he knew by heart.

"Forex desk. Fitzhugh," a voice on the other end of the phone answered. Silber smiled.

"Silber here," he told him. "Fitzhugh, I need a favor."

"Name it."

Silber took a deep breath. "I need the current codes for the Woodlands and the EquaCare financial records data base."

Fitzhugh whistled. "All right. I think I can get them for you." He laughed a little. "Milt, you old hacker, I thought you were pretty adept at that sort of thing."

"Out of practice," Silber informed him tersely.

"Then I guess Banque France's computer is safe from you?"

"Quite," Silber answered. "Besides, its balance sheet is

74

pitiful. Too many loans to oil drillers."

"Aha!" Fitzhugh exclaimed. "So you have cracked it!"

"Not at all," Silber told him. "It's a matter of elementary deduction. You only have to have lunch at the Petroleum Club and keep your ears open."

"Ah, Milt, you were wasted on medicine," Fitzhugh said. "But let's get back to the reason for your call. The access codes. I'm afraid they'll cost you."

"How much?"

"I'm not sure yet. At least $2000 though."

"Good God, I don't want to buy the computers, I just want the data base access codes!" Silber groused.

"Come off it, Milt," Fitzhugh chided him. "My contacts will be risking a lot to get those codes. I have to make it worth their while."

"Hmmf," Silber replied. "And what's your cut?"

"My cut? Why, Milt, I'm surprised at you. You know I don't take a commission for doing a friend a favor."

"But you wouldn't refuse a favor done in return."

"Certainly not."

"Oh all right, you Irish chiseler," Silber capitulated with mock irritation. "Saturday night at the Club? On me, of course."

"Sounds good to me," Fitzhugh replied. "It'll take a couple of days to get the information. Why don't I just bring it with me on Saturday?"

ORIENT & WRIGHT

Chapter 15

"It's very kind of you to offer to drive me home," Maggie told Brent as they walked through the TU parking lot to his car. "But it's really not necessary. I can manage on my own."

"You should have let me know your car is in the shop," he said admonishingly. "If I hadn't overheard you talking to Fred about it, I might never have known. I certainly wouldn't have wanted you to take the bus," he told her, putting one hand on her elbow and urging her gently toward his car. Maggie felt a moment's irritation. What she really wanted was solitude. After nearly 36 hours on the wards, she had no desire to see or talk to anyone. Not even Brent. Or perhaps especially not Brent. She wanted a shower and her bed. Don't be so ungracious, she chastised herself. It would be nice to have a ride, without having to wait for Fred to finish up with a patient. And it was nice of Brent to offer. Maybe he really was concerned about her welfare. Despite his recent brusqueness with her in the ER. She was sure he wasn't really seeking out the most difficult cases for her—it just seemed that way at times. Probably paranoia due to lack of sleep. She always did seem to be the last intern to make it to the call room. She looked at Brent just in time to catch his worried frown as he hurried around to the passenger door and unlocked it. He held it open for her and she capitulated, tucking herself into the bucket seat. "And the cab companies in Fort Bastion are unreliable. Especially on Sundays." He closed the door firmly, as if to end the discussion.

Maggie sighed, and allowed herself to sink into the plush upholstery of the seat. "What kind of a car is this?" she asked him curiously. "I have cars on the brain. Mine seems about to give up the ghost." That was probably the wrong thing to say, she thought. There was no way in the world that she could ever afford a car like this. And people who had such cars probably wanted everyone to recognize them. Otherwise, how could they

76

be a status symbol? Well, it was too bad. To her, a car was just a mode of transportation. If it reliably got one from point A to point B, it was good.

Brent didn't seem to be offended. He just laughed. "This is a Lamborghini," he said. "A very impractical vehicle. But it was a gift from my mother. She likes to give me sports cars," he said, "so I drive them to please her." He looked over quickly at Maggie. "I don't really like this one, although I'd never let her know. It's so . . . garish. And ostentatious." He sighed. "I'd really prefer something more discreet. And practical. A Volvo, say. Gray. Or maybe a BMW. In a nice off-white. What do you drive?"

"An elderly Duster. It's given years of noble service, but I'm afraid its time has come."

"You know," he said, changing the subject, "I have an ulterior motive for wanting to drive you home."

"Oh?" she replied, curious. "What?"

"I wonder if you'd mind dropping by my house."

"Your house?" She was confused. "I thought you lived in an apartment."

"No. I mean yes, I do. I meant, of course, my parents' house."

"What, drop by now?" Maggie was appalled. Her hair felt oily and stringy, she knew she needed a shower, and she had a run in her stocking. Worse still, she had two spots on the front of her skirt where patients had respectively bled and vomited on her. She looked and felt like a scullery maid.

"Well," Brent said, "I have to drop by to see Mother, and as I've been telling her so much about you, I thought this might be a good time." He smiled and put a hand on her knee. She instinctively moved away. This really was a little odd. After two dates, why would a man be taking her to meet his mother? Especially Brent Stemmons. That really wasn't his style. What was going on?

"Aren't you tired?" Maggie asked him. "You've been up almost as long as I have."

"Oh, maybe a little. But Mother asked me to stop by, and, this is the first chance I've had. She sounded very insistent. Besides," he said, "I'd like you to meet her."

77

Maggie didn't know what to say. She looked at him quickly to see if he were putting her on. But apparently he wasn't. He simply looked at her and smiled. She shook her head in amazement. "I'd love to meet your mother," she told him.

"Great!" he exclaimed. "I just know you'll like each other. You have so many similar interests! Did you know she collects antique musical instruments? The music room in our house is climate controlled so the instruments are kept at the proper temperature and humidity. She has a wonderful 18th century harpsichord that you'll just love. Of course, that's where she keeps the Stradivarius, too."

Maggie's brain was reeling. A Stradivarius? Wasn't that the world's most expensive violin? Brent's family must be fabulously wealthy. That shouldn't be too surprising. So what was Brent up to, bringing home a bedraggled intern who had been up all night? Did he intend to overwhelm her? Well, she had no intention of being overly impressed. She could manage. Anyone who could manage the cows on a Kansas farm, or the patients at TU, was not going to be intimidated by one aging socialite, she told herself.

Exhausted, she put her head back and closed her eyes. She couldn't believe that Brent didn't feel as tired as she did. Where did he get his energy? Something tugged at her memory, and she recalled her last date with Brent. The concert at Symphony Hall. The Academy of St. Martin's in the Fields. Baroque music. Handel, Vivaldi, Bach, Purcell. Her favorites. How uncanny that Brent seemed to know her tastes. In restaurants, in music. Still, the concert had been largely wasted on her—she had been so tired she had nearly fallen asleep during the Handel. A quick peek over at Brent had confirmed that he, too, was nodding off, and for that reason she had felt a little better. Then, at the intermission, Brent had yawned, stretched, and excused himself. He had barely made it back when the lights went down. And he had seemed so . . . different. Revived. Alert. Full of energy. Restless, almost. It was with great difficulty that she had been able to convince him that she could not possibly go for dessert and liqueurs after the concert. That what she had desperately needed was to go home to bed. As she did now.

She yawned.

They turned off the Expressway onto Riverside Drive, and Maggie had to restrain herself from exclaiming aloud. All the houses were set well back on immaculately landscaped grounds, and some of them seemed to occupy several acres. Every so often between the oaks that lined the riverbank, she could see private docks, and here and there, a yacht.

"Here we are," Brent said, pulling into a driveway and pausing before a pair of immense iron gates set in a stone wall. He pressed a button on the car's dashboard and the gates swung open. Maggie looked around curiously. The driveway seemed to go on for miles, but at last they pulled up in front of a huge two-story stone house. "It's certainly big, isn't it?" Brent said off-handedly. "It was featured in *Architectural Digest* in 1981. Mother was very pleased." He lowered his voice. "Father and I think it's a little, well, showy." He shrugged. "But Mother likes it." He got out and opened the car door for her. Maggie took a deep breath and preceded him up the steps and into the house.

"Why don't you make yourself comfortable in here," Brent said, taking her elbow and ushering her into a bright cheerful room filled with plants and white wicker furniture. "Oh," he said thoughtfully, "there's a powder room just there off the hall if you want to freshen up. I'll send Carmelita to see what you'd like to drink. Now, if you'll excuse me, I'll go find Mother, get my business over with and we'll join you for a cold drink." He smiled dazzlingly, and left her.

As soon as he was out of sight, she made a dash for the "powder room." Looking at herself in the mirror, she shook her head. What could be done in a few minutes to disguise her evident fatigue and disheveled state? She sighed. Not much. She washed her face, dried it, then decided against putting on any makeup. Still too pale, though. A little lipstick would have to do. But she did unbraid her hair, and brushed it vigorously, deciding that it looked better loose. There was nothing else to be done. She looked at herself critically, squared her shoulders and walked out.

A plump Hispanic woman was waiting for her in the room she had just left. "Mrs. Stemmons says you should make yourself comfortable. She will join you soon. What may I bring you to drink?"

"Um, some iced tea, please," she said.

Tentatively, Maggie seated herself on the edge of a white wicker chair, and surveyed the opulent surroundings. It was hard to believe that such a magnificent room was on the same planet as the wards of TU.

When Carmelita reappeared with her iced tea, Maggie took it and held it uncertainly. Should she drink it? Wait for her hostess? Her smattering of etiquette did not include situations such as this. An urge to laugh hysterically came over her, and she only suppressed it with great difficulty. To think that she was pondering seriously over a decision such as this one, after such a night! To hell with it, she thought, and compromised. She drank half the tea.

Brent appeared in the doorway looking flushed. A stately, blonde haired woman, casually dressed in a pair of white linen slacks and a green short-sleeved silk blouse accompanied him. Maggie looked at her reflectively. The woman had the sort of aristocratic, offhand beauty that never seemed to require any assistance. And although she was plainly well past 40, she appeared to be in wonderful physical condition. In fact, she seemed to glow. Maggie blinked several times, quickly, and stood up.

"Mother, this is Margaret Altman. Maggie, this is my mother, Alyce," Brent said, looking pleased with himself.

Mrs. Stemmons absorbed Maggie's appearance in one quick glance, then stepped forward and pressed her hand warmly. She gave her a quick, sympathetic smile that immediately endeared her to Maggie. "I'm so happy to meet you," she said in evident sincerity. "Brent has told me so much about you."

"I'm very pleased to meet you, too, Mrs. Stemmons—"

"—please, call me Alyce. And do sit down." Carmelita appeared in the doorway, and Alyce ordered two iced coffees.

"Alyce," Maggie said, resuming her seat gratefully. She gestured self-consciously at her clothes. "I must apologize for the way I look, but I'm afraid that I've been on the wards for nearly 36 hours."

"You poor thing!" Alyce exclaimed, looking reproachfully at Brent. "The very minute we finish our drinks you must take this young woman home." She gave her son a long, inscrutable look, and Maggie quickly averted her eyes. That there was some undercurrent of tension here was obvious. She wondered what it was. Brent had been so eager to come. Alyce, however, seemed positively cool towards him. Almost as if she would rather he hadn't come. But that must be wrong. Brent had told her that his mother had sent for him. Strange. Well, it was none of her business.

Carmelita brought the iced coffees, and Maggie was relieved to note that Brent drained his in two swallows. She had never been any good at small talk, and she had to admit that Alyce Stemmons and this lavish riverfront estate actually were a little overwhelming. This was a world she had only seen in movies, or on television. An unfamiliar world. What on earth did someone like Maggie Altman say to someone like Alyce Stemmons? The woman could have no possible interest in EquaCare. Or TU. Or probably even medicine. Maggie realized that those topics comprised her whole world, at least for the present. You really ought to do better, she reproached herself. Broaden your horizons. Brent stood up abruptly.

"I suppose I'd better get you home, Maggie," Brent said.

Alyce stood up gracefully, smoothing down the front of her slacks. Maggie was again aware of Alyce's understated elegance. "Do come again," Alyce said earnestly. "You will bring her, won't you?" she asked Brent.

Brent smiled. "Of course, Mother."

"Good!" Alyce said emphatically. She turned her impossibly blue eyes on Maggie. "We're having a cocktail party next Saturday. It will be outdoors, in the evening. If you two young people could possibly make it, I'd be delighted."

Maggie looked at Brent for a cue. And saw a curious thing. For just a moment, she could have sworn there was a look of stubborn anger on his face. She blinked, and it was gone. Had it ever been there? She was so tired, she wasn't sure. Now, she saw only his smile. Must be the fatigue, she thought. But what do I say to Alyce? Brent solved the problem for her.

"I'm afraid next Saturday is out of the question for me. I'll be at TU for 24 hours straight. I'm covering for someone."

"Well, another time then," Alyce said, walking with them to the door.

. . .

After Brent dropped her off, Maggie headed straight for the bed. She kicked off her shoes, pulled off her blouse and skirt, and threw them in the direction of the laundry basket. Shower and food later, she thought, crawling under the bedspread in her underwear. She yawned. What an unbelievable morning! Later, she'd have to give it some thought. And Brent, too. What was happening to her? She shook her head ruefully. She felt as though she were playing a part written for someone else. Things like this just didn't happen to her. A cocktail party at a Riverside Drive mansion? That might be an interesting experience, even if she did feel a little out of place. It was novel to be invited, even if she couldn't go. And tired as she was today, she would have enjoyed seeing Mrs. Stemmons' harpsichord. And the Stradivarius. Brent must have forgotten. He undoubtedly had a lot on his mind. Who was he covering for at TU on Saturday, she wondered. And where did he get the energy to take on an extra shift? He certainly seemed to work in the ER more often than any of the other residents. But further thought was impossible, as she fell asleep.

Chapter 16

"Dr. Miltown, Dr. Miltown," the page operator called again, the second time in ten minutes. He closed the door to his office and sat in the dark, waiting. Where in hell was she? He hadn't intended to see her tonight, but as he had to come to the hospital to check the computer records, he had decided he might as well speak to her.

Someone knocked tentatively at his door.

"Come in," he said irritably.

Silhouetted by the faint light from Pathology, she slipped quickly into the office. He recognized her cap, and her figure. God, but she was a real knockout! He felt his resolve slipping away. She giggled a little in the darkness and came to sit on his lap. He groaned.

"I locked the door," she told him, pulling his hair a little. Her hands explored his face, and when she touched his ear, she gasped. "What happened to you?"

His interest shrivelled and died, replaced by a sudden, graphic memory of the men in the parking lot. He stood up, standing her unceremoniously on her feet and backing off a little. "Nothing happened to me," he lied to her.

"All right, don't tell me," she pouted. "Keep your secrets. Just come over here and undress me."

He ground his teeth. "No."

"No?" She sounded incredulous. "What's wrong? Have you taken a vow of celibacy?" She put her arms around him. "Or are we short of time?" She began to unbuckle his belt, giggling. "That's all right. I don't have to get undressed. We'll manage."

Pulse racing, he pushed her away from him. "Please," he said. "We have to talk." He switched on his desk lamp and buckled his belt.

"Talk? About what?"

He glowered at her. "The way you're doing your job.

Daniel tells me he telephoned you last night. He had a body for me. Why didn't you call me? You know how important something like that is."

She pouted. "I asked someone where you were. Out on a date, they told me. With that—"

"—it doesn't matter who I was with!" he interrupted, shouting. "You're supposed to call me! God damn it, I could get 20 other people to help me. To do what you're supposed to do. To do what I'm paying you to do!" Breathing heavily, he looked at her in disgust. "So you decided—you dared to decide—that because I was out with another woman, you'd punish me. Right?"

She looked at him triumphantly. "Right. You don't pay enough attention to me as it is. How come you never ask me out anywhere? Not good enough for you, is that it? So I decided to send you a message."

A message? He couldn't believe his ears. Raúl was one thing, but this . . . damned woman was something else. He was sick and tired of getting messages. "Message received," he said through his teeth. He was so angry he was shaking. "Now, here's one for you. That little stunt of yours cost me $2000. So, you know what I'm going to do? I'm going to pass the cost on to you."

"You wouldn't dare!" she told him.

"Oh? Why not?"

"I'm not working for you for nothing, you egotistical bastard! I'll go straight to the hospital administrator with your dirty little scheme. I'm sure Dr. Eisig would be interested. And the press, too. It would be the end of your career."

"You dumb bitch," he told her contemptuously. "You're so stupid, you can't see any farther than your petty revenge. Do you really think this 'scheme' stops with me?"

She stared at him, open-mouthed. "What do you mean?"

"What do you mean?" he mocked. "Well, let me spell it out for you. I pay you, right? And Daniel."

She nodded.

"Do you think I do it out of the goodness of my heart?"

She swallowed, shaking her head.

"Of course I don't," he continued. "Someone pays me." He shook his head. "This 'scheme' is bigger than your insufficient brain could possible imagine. There's a fortune at stake." He stepped towards her menacingly and took a handful of her hair. Only a massive effort of will prevented him from striking her. "Do you really think I'd let you spoil it?"

"No," she answered weakly.

"All right, then," he said, stroking her hair. "Now that you understand the situation better, I'm sure you'll be more conscientious. Right?"

"Oh yes. I will be."

He smiled. "Better get back to work."

She fled.

Frowning, he fingered the healing cut on his ear—a pretty good job. No one but Caroline had noticed it. He should feel elated. Things were going better with that damned woman. And he had gotten the money for Raúl. All of it. Why then, did he feel so depressed? Everything was under control. Well, wasn't it?

Chapter 17

Dr. Eisig removed the top chart from the pile that Stephen Blaine had collected for the weekly noon chart conference. The interns, seated at school desks in the conference room, all looked apprehensive. The chief smiled at them genially.

Eisig opened to the front sheet in the chart. "Velma Harris, 43 year old black woman with diabetes complicated by peripheral vascular disease and renal insufficiency. Bilateral AK amputations. Admitted for criterion 4A-1, blood sugar above 300, by Dr. Marchak." Eisig looked quizzically around the room. Dr. Marchak was not present. Maggie felt a twinge in her stomach; this was a patient she had cared for one night. She had done the best that could have been done under the circumstances. It couldn't be her care that was in question.

"He's at the VA now," Blaine said, consulting his schedule.

"No documentation of an adequate attempt to control this patient in the Preventive Health Center," Eisig commented, thumbing through the record. "This is a hospital stay that might have been prevented." Eisig read on for a moment. "A perfect example of how utilization review and quality assurance go hand in hand. A most instructive case. First, a preventable admission. Then, an iatrogenic complication." His eyes turned to Maggie. "There's a note by Dr. Altman. Tell us about the case."

Maggie swallowed a bite of apple with some difficulty. Her throat felt dry. She summarized the situation as well as she could remember it.

Eisig listened noncommittally, then stared at her reflectively for a moment. "The blood sugar, Doctor," he said quietly. "Wouldn't it be a good idea to document the blood sugar in a patient you say is suffering a hypoglycemic reaction?"

"It was between 20 and 40," Maggie said. "Something

like that."

"Something like that?" Eisig asked. "I cannot locate any laboratory report."

"Oh," Maggie explained, "I couldn't get the blood from any of her veins. I had to stick her finger."

"You couldn't get the blood," Eisig said reproachfully. "So you instituted treatment based on a guess. 'Somewhere between 20 and 40'."

"I did a Chemstrip, sir," Maggie said.

"Oh?" Eisig said, raising an eyebrow. "But that isn't documented on the chart."

"Isn't it in my note?" Maggie asked in dismay.

Eisig handed her the chart. The report was not in the computer printout of her note. But she felt sure that she had entered it.

"I guess I just forgot to punch it in," Maggie said.

"If it isn't in the chart," Eisig said evenly, "it isn't done. Documentation is everything. This chart is a legal record." He looked at her note again. "Also, Dr. Altman, your treatment was not standard, and you did not document your reasons for employing such an unusual method." He looked at her sternly over his glasses. "Fortunately, the patient survived."

Maggie felt someone staring at her and turned, just as Fischbein looked away. He certainly looked smug, she thought. What did he think he could have done differently? What was unusual about giving glucose by the only means available when the patient needed it? Didn't it make any difference that she had saved the patient's life?

Eisig tossed the chart aside and reached for the next. After scribbling some notes, Blaine studied Maggie closely. She felt her blood pressure rising. This was certainly not a fair review. But an acerbic reply wouldn't help. She tried thinking about swimming to music: Paderewski's Minuet in G. She missed hearing about the next few patients, but some of Eisig's words filtered through.

"The real problem with medicine is the behavior of physicians in the traditional physician-patient relationship," he was saying. "This tradition neglected the responsibility that we have to society as a whole, to conserve resources and to allocate them fairly and efficiently. Physicians need to develop new skills in order to fulfill their social responsibilities: better management and legal and political skills. Our program here is uniquely designed to prepare the doctors of the future, who must be prepared to sit in board rooms, not examining rooms. That is why we will be emphasizing compliance with the criteria for UR and the standard of care." Eisig smiled and dismissed them. He looked pretty satisfied, Maggie thought. As the interns left, Blaine handed each of them a computer printout.

"Our UR/QAC reports," Fred commented, coming up behind her.

"UR/QAC?" Maggie asked.

"Utilization Review/Quality Assurance Committee," Fred explained, folding his up and stuffing it in his pocket. "Sounds like a Babylonian god, doesn't it?" He pulled something else out of his pocket and handed it to Maggie. A Snickers candy bar.

"A nonstandard treatment," he said with a wink. "Take one p.o. stat for your blood sugar."

"Dr. Altman, Dr. Margaret Altman, call 2824," said the page operator.

Another admission. It was just too much, Maggie thought. She muttered a thank you to Fred, and headed for the stairwell to keep him from seeing the tears of anger and frustration. She had to dry her eyes before reaching the ground floor.

• • •

She could feel the heightened tension the moment she entered the double doors of the emergency room. But the source wasn't immediately apparent.

Medicine A was moderately busy. Brent was just leaving his station at the bridge, apparently to supervise the activity in one of the crash rooms.

"Hello, Maggie," Brent said, favoring her with one of his charming smiles. "If you'll just sit down for a minute, I'll be right back to tell you about your case."

Maggie sat down in the chair next to the main terminal, and saw her name listed on the admission book, next to the patient, Frank Post, 65-year-old white man, DRG 96, bronchitis and asthma. One for her research series. She paged through the book, and found several others over the past few days who might be suitable for her project.

"You're going to need bigger pockets," Brent said, pulling at the corner of her left hand jacket pocket, "if you keep stuffing all those index cards in there."

"I guess I'll have to sew it," Maggie replied. The top inch of the pocket had pulled away. She hoped she had a safety pin for an emergency repair job.

Brent tapped her gently on the forehead. "Treatment isn't enough," he chided her. "I was thinking of prevention. Stop making so much extra work for yourself."

"My research isn't exactly work," Maggie responded. "I enjoy it."

Brent shook his head. "You need some other enjoyment too. I can tell. You're looking a little tired. And discouraged."

Maggie sighed. He was certainly right about that.

"I have just the prescription for you. Doctor's orders."
"Oh?" Maggie asked.

"Much better than one of Mom's stuffy cocktail parties. How about dinner at Pierre's a week from Saturday?"

Maggie calculated a minute. "Yes, I'll be on call Thursday. So Saturday I'll even be awake."

"Great. I'll look forward to it," Brent gazed into her eyes for a moment. "But business before pleasure. Here's the story on Mr. Post. A lunger. But pretty straightforward."

• • •

"Can you believe it?" Maggie heard the conversation from the nurses' lounge as she wheeled the stretcher toward the double doors. "At 7:00 in the morning. She was just getting off the night shift. Raped and stabbed. I'm going to check with the OR. She should be out of surgery by now."

"I'm going to start bringing my gun to work," another

said. "especially if security won't escort us to our cars."

Maggie shuddered. No wonder everybody down here seemed to be a little more on edge than usual. They liked to think of themselves as immune to the violence that brought people into the ER. But apparently nobody was safe. Not even in the parking lot, near the police and ambulance entrance to the hospital. She wondered who the victim was.

• • •

"No, he doesn't have any risk factors," Maggie said, exasperated. "He hasn't been in bed, or in a cast. But I still think he had a pulmonary embolus, and I want him to have a lung scan."

"Well, you're the doctor," the clerk on the other end of the line said. "But I can tell you that this patient doesn't have any of the standard indications for a lung scan. You'll need to get an authorization form signed by the chief resident. Call me back if you do."

• • •

Maggie found Stephen Blaine in his office on the tenth floor. It was at a corner of the building, and had a splendid view of the city. The spacious office had a computer station and a moving display similar to the one presided over by the Pit Boss. A printer was clattering away industriously. More UR/QAC reports, she suspected. The walls were lined with floor to ceiling shelves, filled with neatly labeled computer printouts, and loose-leaf volumes labeled "Standard of Care Criteria." The chief's white coat was hanging on a hook, and he had loosened his tie. He was intently working at the terminal; Maggie sensed that she was an unwelcome interruption.

"It's your decision," Blaine said, signing the form with an air of boredom. "You're the gatekeeper, and you're responsible. I can't tell you for sure what UR/QAC will say, but you may get an error statement for this." Blaine fixed her with his expressionless dark eyes.

"But what if the patient had an embolus, and I miss it?" Maggie wanted to know.

Blaine shrugged. "Then you are responsible for the consequences. It goes with the gatekeeper role."

"So what else can I do?" Maggie demanded.

Blaine sighed impatiently. "Look, I didn't invent this system. I'm just trying to make it work. I'm not going to tell you what to do; but I keep track of the retrospective reviews. Those who have good profiles will do well. Those who don't . . . well, it's time physicians had some meaningful peer review. Some real quality control, as they say."

Maggie thought his voice had a trace of hostility. Blaine clearly didn't want to discuss the issue further. He was already looking at his terminal again. She took her form, and headed for the stairs; although Nuclear Medicine was on the second floor, it was faster to walk than to wait for the elevator.

• • •

"A stroke," Fred informed Maggie, returning from the telephone. "It can wait until after dinner." He moved a piece of hard biscuit around in the gravy. "We're going to need some Church's fried chicken to get us through the night, I suspect. With jalapeno. The other team's already gotten a hit too, so you're already up again."

Maggie stared disconsolately at the beef stew. Giving up research had definitely been a mistake. She would have to try to get some results out of her clinical project; it might improve her chances of getting back into a lab somewhere.

"But we'll have to send two or three of the guys for it."

"What?" Maggie asked. She hadn't been paying attention to Fred's cheerful banter.

"For the chicken. Church's is in a bad neighborhood. Even worse than our parking lot." Fred became serious. "I heard that they had to give Lisa four units of blood. You'll let me know when you're ready to leave tomorrow, won't you? I'll walk you to your car."

"Thanks," Maggie said. "I just got it back from the

garage. It has a new battery, so I hope it won't leave me stranded."

"I always carry jumper cables. And you shouldn't be going to the parking lot alone, anyway."

"Well, sometimes there isn't any choice. I'll be all right."

"Promise you'll let me walk you to the car."

"Okay," she said, amused at his gallantry. She had always been able to take care of herself in the past. But Fred seemed so worried that she capitulated.

"And how about some Texas barbecue and country western music? I have tickets for a week from Saturday."

"Sure," Maggie said. Then she remembered. "Oh, no. I'm sorry. I can't go that night."

Fred's face fell in disappointment. "Well, give me a rain check then."

"Dr. Jenkins, Dr. Fred Jenkins, call 2824."

"The fans won't leave me alone." Fred gulped down the last bite of stew, and pushed his chair away from the table. "Say, how did that lung scan come out?"

"Positive," Maggie said.

"See, kiddo," Fred told her, pressing her hand quickly. "You were right." He jumped up and headed for the telephone.

Maggie watched him depart. She sighed a little. She didn't like to disappoint Fred. He was nice, although a little lacking in polish. For example, he didn't seem to notice the ink blot on his pocket that had been there for at least a week. Brent, on the other hand, had savoir faire. It wasn't really important, she knew, but it was rather nice.

She pushed these extraneous thoughts aside. She had to try to organize her work for the night, in so far as that was possible. First stop was the lab, to check whether she was giving Mr. Post enough heparin to dissolve the clots in his lungs.

Chapter 18

Silber waited for Fitzhugh in the Club's lounge, an open copy of *Barron's* on his lap to discourage casual conversation. He squirmed a little in his chair—his trousers were a trifle too tight. How old was this suit, he wondered? At least a dozen years. He'd have to take it to the tailor. Have it let out. Or buy a new one. Or lose some weight. He sighed. Over the past five years, since he had left the Woodlands, he had become positively degenerate. He ate when he wanted, slept when he was tired, saw whom he pleased, wore whatever was at hand. And it worried him. You're going to seed, he told himself. Fitzhugh came through the door, and Silber was surprised at how pleased he was to see the young man.

"You're early," Silber told him gruffly. "I haven't finished reading my paper."

Fitzhugh, his beige summerweight wool suit a little rumpled, his tie loose, raised an eyebrow. "Well, I'll just have to catch up on my reading, too," he said, pulling out of his pocket a folded copy of *The Silber Report*. A white-coated waiter materialized, and Fitzhugh ordered a vodka and tonic.

Silber harrumphed in pleasure and rattled the pages of his paper, peering furtively at Fitzhugh now and then. But the young man seemed absorbed in his reading. Finally Silber could bear it no longer.

"What do you find so interesting there?" Silber asked him. "I thought you limited yourself to *The Interbank Bulletin, The Federal Reserve Bulletin* and the *London Daily Market Report*."

"Among other things," Fitzhugh told him. He sighed heavily. "I'm usually up to my ears in correspondence from the Bundesbank, The Bank of France, Suisse National, Mobilaire, Banco Hispana. Not to mention the "hot" postings—the daily rate sheets—every morning." He sighed again. "It's getting to me,

Milt. I'm too old for this job. They told me I'd last five years, and I've been with Banque France for seven." He shook his head. "Now I have to go in every Saturday and catch up. The young hotshots are miles ahead of me." He massaged his temples. "I've got a headache and an overbought position in spot pounds, value Wednesday."

"Hmmf," Silber said. This was the second person in two weeks to tell him he was unhappy in his work. The virus of dissatisfaction. He hardly knew what to say to Fitzhugh. The young man's job was a tough one, Silber knew. At the office at 4 a.m. to synchronize his arrival at work with the 9:30 a.m. opening of the market in London. And he was at his desk at 8 p.m. for the next day's opening of Tokyo-Singapore. Similarly, Fitzhugh's colleagues on the west coast in San Francisco would be keeping late hours so they could trade with New York-London on one side and Tokyo-Singapore on the other. The money never slept, Silber knew, nor could those who followed it for a livelihood. Quite naturally, therefore, most of the traders were young—under 30—and tough and resilient enough to endure the stress and long hours. Most, too, were unmarried, and all made a great deal of money. "Well," he told Fitzhugh roughly, "quit, then."

Fitzhugh looked up and smiled ruefully. "I might just do that. Kate urges me to quit every other day."

"Kate?" Silber inquired."

"My father's widow," Fitzhugh explained.

"You mean your mother, surely."

"Well, not really. My stepmother. But Father married Katherine—Kate—very late in life, after Mother died. The two of them lived abroad, in Ireland, until just recently. So I never really knew her. When Father fell ill, they came back here to Fort Bastion, bought a bankrupt dude ranch, and hired staff to take care of Father." He shrugged. "I moved into one of the guest cottages. To help out. Then, when Father died, I just stayed on. Kate asked me to. There were a lot of legal details to sort out regarding Father's estate. Then, I got the job at Banque France, and haven't had the time to think of moving."

Silber snorted. "So Kate wants you to move out? About

time, I'd say."

"Oh no. Not at all. She wants me to quit Banque France and go into partnership with her." He looked embarrassed. "Father left us equal halves in the ranch. She wants to refurbish the place. Raise horses. That's what her family did in Ireland—bred horses. The O'Mara steeplechasers are famous." He sighed. "About the only thing I know about horses is not to bet on them. I don't see myself as a horseman. I can't even ride. They make me nervous." He looked up at Silber. "I'm probably boring you. But, as you can see, I do think from time to time about quitting the bank. Not for the horse business, though. Something else in finance. But who'd want a washed-up Forex trader?" He folded his copy of *The Silber Report* and put it back in his pocket.

Silber tossed his *Barron's* onto the table in front of him, and they went in to dinner.

. . .

"So," Silber said as he mopped up the last drop of juice from an enormous, rare slab of roast beef, "did you get me what I want?"

Fitzhugh handed him a piece of paper. On it were written two strings of letters and numbers. "Good 'til the end of the month," Fitzhugh told him.

Silber folded it and put it carefully away in his wallet. "How much?" he sighed.

"Not as bad as I thought," Fitzhugh grinned. "Only $1500."

Silber moaned aloud, and reached into the inside pocket of his jacket. He withdrew a brown legal-sized envelope, extracted five $100 bills which he pocketed, and passed the envelope to Fitzhugh. "This exchange should take place in a dark alley," he said. "It makes one feel quite larcenous."

"Milt," Fitzhugh said soberly, "I don't know what you want the codes for, and I don't want to know. Just be careful. Don't leave any indication that you've been in the computer."

"What do you mean? How could anyone possibly tell?"

Fitzhugh sighed. "Milt, the new security systems automatically record incursions into the computers' data bases. They record the data accessed, and the code number that allowed the access. Unless you know how to bypass that feature of the security system. That information is written at the bottom of the piece of paper I gave you. Be sure to follow the instructions carefully. We don't want the code numbers traced back to their source. My informant would probably lose his job."

Silber nodded. He'd do his best to be careful. He motioned the waiter over. "Coffee and brandy?" he asked Fitzhugh. The young man nodded, and the waiter cleared the table. A spasm of generosity seized him. "Oh," Silber called to the waiter, "make that brandy Remy Martin, would you?"

"Why, Milt," Fitzhugh teased him, "you've never treated me to Remy Martin before. What's the occasion?"

Silber glowered at him. "No occasion, you Irish peasant. I'm simply helping you prepare for your retirement from Banque France. As you've wisely decided not to waste yourself on horses, you're going to have to learn how to live like civilized people do."

"Oho," Fitzhugh said, eyes sparkling with mischief. "Grooming me for the company of cultured men and women. To whom, I suppose, I shouldn't confess my propensity for Egg McMuffins or chocolate milkshakes?"

"Exactly," Silber told him, shuddering. "You Forex traders are a bunch of barbarians. No class at all. But I think we might salvage you. Just." He shook his head. "Horses," he said in disbelief.

Chapter 19

"Smile now," Brent said. "You've been preoccupied all evening. Aren't you enjoying your dinner?"

"It's excellent," Maggie assured him, frowning as she took another bite of the filet mignon. She certainly couldn't complain about the food at Pierre's. Attentive waiters had plied them with sumptuous trays of hors d'ouevres, followed by an artistically arranged salad. The steak was tender and juicy; Maggie thought she had never tasted anything better. She didn't want to think about how expensive it must be. Her copy of the menu had not had any prices listed; Brent himself had suggested the filet mignon.

"Then why are you frowning?" Brent persisted.

Maggie set down her fork and looked at him thoughtfully. "I guess I was frowning, wasn't I? I'm sorry to be such poor company. I'm having a hard time putting last night out of my mind. Or Thursday night it was, when I was on call."

Brent nodded sympathetically. "I understand. I wasn't on that night. Did you have a lot of admissions?"

"Only three," Maggie said, stirring the stuffed potato. "And I had some time while I was waiting for the lab. So I tried to work on my research. It is just so frustrating."

"You're trying to do too much," Brent admonished her. "You need to relax when you can, instead of running around and making extra work for yourself all the time."

"I suppose you're right," Maggie sighed. "But it really shouldn't be that hard. The place just isn't very efficient."

Brent raised an eyebrow. "Really, now, you certainly must have high standards. Didn't you read about our efficiency award?"

"The rubber bands are still on all my newspapers from the past three weeks. But you must be joking."

"Not at all," Brent assured her. "TU has been named the

97

most efficient hospital in the EquaCare system. We're going to receive a much bigger contract next year. And more than that, we had the lowest mortality and morbidity of any hospital in our class. Dr. Eisig is really proud of us."

"Where did you hear that?" Maggie wanted to know.

"At morning report," Brent said. "I guess the word will filter down to the interns eventually."

"Well, I sure wouldn't have guessed it," Maggie said, wrinkling her brow. "And I bet we don't get any awards for medical records. You know I even lost my temper last night. I yelled at the clerk."

"Maggie Altman, losing her temper!" Brent exclaimed. "I don't believe it! You must have been very tired. Eat more of your steak—that will help your stamina."

Maggie felt the color rising to her cheeks. "Well, I bet even you would have been angry. The clerk gave me the runaround for two hours. Finally, I went down myself to look for the charts. They weren't in the file. I decided to check to see if they were in the pile being returned from the clinic. They weren't there either. But it so happened that the dumbwaiter had stopped a little above the countertop. Just on an impulse, I shone my flashlight into the shaft—and saw a whole pile of charts at the bottom! The janitor helped me fish them out. And three of the five that I wanted were in that pile!"

"That's strange," Brent said. "Maybe they all went to clinic on the same day."

"They didn't."

Brent looked concerned. "I've heard about this happening before," he said. "Some of the clerks didn't want to do their filing, so they just pitched the charts down the shaft. I'll have to talk to the chief about it. Fortunately, with the computer, it makes less of a problem for the people taking care of the patients."

"I'm not so sure." Maggie set her fork down. It was a shame that her dinner was getting cold, but her appetite just wasn't as good as usual. And she felt the familiar burning in her stomach. Odd that the steak hadn't relieved it.

"Oh, come on," Brent said. "How many times have you

rummaged through an old chart when you could get the same information with a few keystrokes on the terminal?" He looked at her thoughtfully. "Why did you want those old charts anyway?"

"For my research. I wanted to get the blood gases from old admissions that hadn't been put in the computer. And while I was looking for them, I noticed something else."

"Oh?" Brent asked. Maggie noticed that he, too, had stopped eating. She looked away from the remains of his sweetbreads.

"The blood gases that were in the computer—that I had written down on my index cards—were not the same as the ones on the original lab slips!"

Brent refilled her wine glass, although she had only drunk a few sips. He frowned. "Are you sure you didn't make a mistake?"

"Quite sure. I checked everything again. It wasn't just one or two that didn't match. And they weren't the sort of mistake that you tend to make when you're typing."

When Brent finally exhaled deeply, Maggie realized that he had been holding his breath. "You know, it's really easy to make mistakes when you haven't been getting enough sleep," he suggested.

She didn't answer, but Brent must have sensed that he had hurt her feelings. He touched her hand gently. "But I'm sure you checked it out carefully."

"I did," Maggie said, a trifle acerbically. "You know, I really wonder if it isn't a mistake to rely on that computer so heavily."

The waiter interrupted to ask if everything was satisfactory. Brent motioned him away. He swallowed a few sips of water, and studied the glass carefully for a few minutes. Then he regarded Maggie with a very serious expression.

"I think you're right," he finally said. "There seem to be too many bugs in the system. I have talked to Blaine about the problems you mentioned before, and he promised to investigate. He did say that we could rule out the possibility of unauthorized access to the system. The security coding is state-of-the-art."

He paused, and weighed his next words very carefully. "I hesitate to say this out loud, even to you." He lowered his tone. "When this system was installed, there was a lot of controversy in the medical center. Some of the old guard—who shall remain nameless—were bitterly opposed to it. They were set in their ways, and wanted to turn back the clock. They constantly complained about the system, and hindered its full implementation for a year. Now I don't mean to suggest that they deliberately sabotaged the software. But they certainly were obstructionist in every way. Fortunately, we don't have to deal with them any longer."

Maggie took a sip of wine. "So you think it's a software problem? Or sloppiness on the part of people entering the data?"

"Could be either, or both," Brent said. "We don't seem to have problems all that frequently. At least, you're the only person who has noticed anything so far. That makes it harder to track down. But Blaine will get to the bottom of it. I want you to tell me if you have any more problems and to keep a record of exactly what they are. Can I count on you?"

"Sure," Maggie said. "I can even give you a list of the ones I've had to date." She was grateful that Brent was taking her seriously. She had told her ward resident, Stuart Collins, about the old charts under the dumbwaiter. But he had been three admissions behind, and had been annoyed with her for bothering him. He seemed to think that such occurrences were normal.

"Just leave your list with me the next chance you get," Brent said. "I'll take it from there." He squeezed her hand, and looked into her eyes. "I'm glad that you didn't have anything more serious than that weighing on your mind. I really do appreciate your being so conscientious—but you could let it spoil your enjoyment of life." He reached over and stroked her cheek.

"Thanks for listening," Maggie said sincerely.

"Now, let's ask Henri to warm up our plates a little. Then I want to have a few dances with you in the lounge. Slow dances," he added with a wink. "The pianist is very good."

Maggie smiled. She vowed to think of nothing else this evening except the raspberries and cream that Brent had ordered for dessert, and the soft music.

Chapter 20

"Outside. And for once in your misbegotten life, no arguments," Silber said. "Look, I'm even holding the door open for you. That's one you win."

Keynes approached the open back door, paused, sniffed it thoroughly, then lay down on the threshold, half his body inside the kitchen, and half on the porch outside. He looked back over his shoulder at Silber and smiled.

"Oh, get on with it," Silber told him. "I can't spend all evening being doorman. Go be catlike. Climb a tree. Investigate a garbage can. Visit an alley. Catch something." Silber immediately regretted the suggestion.

He recalled one morning 11 months ago when Keynes (then a scruffy, unnamed black cat who had taken to hanging around Silber's back porch) had come bearing gifts—the uneaten hands and feet of a field mouse which the cat had deposited on the kitchen counter next to the coffee maker. They had been clearly meant for Silber's breakfast. Finding the pinkish, oddly human appendages before he had consumed his morning coffee had almost ended his budding realtionship with Keynes. He had barely suppressed a gag, reminding himself that these were feline gifts. The cat, who obviously planned to move in, was showing Silber what a good provider he was. Feeling strangely touched, Silber had hastily scooped the revolting appendages into the garbage, shielding the ungrateful deed from Keynes' eyes. Then, because the cat had continued to sit at his feet, looking up at him expectantly, he had made himself pat the beast on the head, and murmur "Good boy." Unfortunately, that had clinched it. Gifts given and received. A contract sealed.

Silber sighed, remembering. Those had been only the first in a string of offerings which had included, in the 11 months of their cohabitation, a particularly fetching pair of pink lace underwear; a tin of kippered herring from the local delicatessen;

a woman's leather glove, size 7, left hand; a hotel key for room 228 of the Fort Bastion Hilton; a toupee; a turtle (live, which Keynes had clearly meant to adopt, and which now resided in a roasting pan in the laundry room); a nauseating succession of dead birds, voles and lizards; and only last week, the *piece de resistance*—the head of a freshly killed road runner, placed in the exact center of the kitchen floor. Keynes' tastes were, apparently, quite catholic, and Silber contemplated each feline offering with appalled awe.

But as he now glared down at the unabashedly grinning animal sprawled over the threshold, he wondered if Keynes hadn't been playing one long, convoluted cat joke on him. But what? He shook his head. Inscrutable beast. "So beat it, already," he said, prodding Keynes with his bare foot. Keynes smacked Silber sharply on the ankle with claws sheathed, as if to discourage such unseemly advances, then decided he had business outside. He stood slowly, stretched, and crossed the threshold with studied nonchalance. "Hmmf. Cat burglar." Silber grunted indulgently.

He took the bourbon bottle with him to his desk, poured a healthy belt, and powered up his computer. The piece of paper with the result of Fitzhugh's latest investigations on it, he placed within arm's reach. Then, feeling a quickening surge of adrenalin, he proceeded to break and enter the EquaCare and the Woodlands computers.

• • •

"I don't believe it," Silber muttered to himself. He sat back in his ancient swivel chair and contemplated the cobwebs on the ceiling. An hour's work had given him the information he needed and more. Much more. It was all rather unsettling.

As he had suspected, EquaCare's choice was beyond his comprehension. In the first place, he could not imagine why EquaCare would want to drop AMIX. AMIX was a well established company with a good balance sheet and an excellent growth record. It distributed low-cost, high-quality medical instruments from its parent company Pontchartrain Frères, in, as far as Silber knew, a very timely and economical manner. Why suddenly discontinue doing business with a tried and true supplier in order to take a chance on a very new, very small company which had just begun to trade publicly? Chapman Health Enterprises, Inc., symbol CHEP. A NASDAQ stock. Really! It didn't make sense. Was this another example of EquaCare's cost-cutting measures, its obsession with the bottom line? If so, this was very short-sighted indeed. Chapman might have convinced the decision makers at EquaCare that they could deliver the goods more cheaply than AMIX, but Silber was skeptical. No one could do a better job than AMIX. And he should know, he thought immodestly. After all, in the course of investigating companies to be profiled in *The Silber Report*, he had traipsed through more plants, factories and warehouses, shaken more hands, and interviewed more managers than he wanted to remember. He had seen every operation personally. He had met management. He had pored over balance sheets, annual reports, financial statements. He knew these companies. And he was very doubtful about Chapman. Cost cutting, indeed!

He frowned and poured another glass of bourbon, dismissing EquaCare from his mind. It was what he had found in the Woodlands computer that was worrying him. He had accessed the Woodlands' database in order to determine the amount Chapman was receiving—nothing more. His only desire had been curiosity. And, as he had suspected, he had discovered a quarterly payment to Chapman in an amount considerably smaller than the previous year's payment to AMIX. True, Chapman was saving Woodlands money. This quarter, anyway. He snorted. You usually get what you pay for, he thought. In the long run, Chapman would be unable to continue delivering low-cost goods and services. Well, Woodlands would learn. To its detriment.

Then, having found what he wanted—having scratched his mental itch—he was just about to exit the database and shut off the computer. But some demon of curiosity had made him scroll down through the list of current payees. He had almost choked on his bourbon. There, among companies large and small on Woodlands' payroll, one had fairly leaped off the screen at him. One that shouldn't have been there.

"What the hell?" he demanded. He gaped at the data, blinked furiously, then looked again. But it hadn't disappeared. His pulse quickened as the full import of his discovery hit him. He forced himself to be calm. Just settle down and think this through, he told himself. His thoughts raced in three directions at once, and he reined them in with difficulty. One step at a time, he told himself. This must be approached analytically.

He knew what had drawn his attention to the entry. But someone else might not have noticed. What would make it stand out, anyhow? Its position in the alphabet? The name of the company itself? Probably not. The astronomical amount it received quarterly from Woodlands? Possibly. The nature of its business? Less likely.

It was simply another of Woodlands' payees, he told himself. Who would get excited about that? Who would even care? Well, the Auditor General might. But presumably it had escaped his notice. So far. Hmmf. What he needed to do now was clear: try to ascertain how far a clever person could follow this trail. A paper chase. See where it led. He tapped his fingers thoughtfully on the keyboard, noting that his pulse had begun to quiet. And then? What if this hypothetical clever person were successful? What then? Silber clenched his jaw. That problem could be taken care of later. If and when. Right now, he needed to select his clever person. And persuade him to do what he wanted done. Under close supervision, of course. He smiled and picked up the phone. He knew just the person for the job.

• • •

"Forex desk, Fitzhugh here."

"I thought you'd be there," Silber said accusingly. "You apparently live at that bank. Are you planning to quit for the night, or are you going to hang yourself up in the coat closet like a vampire bat?"

"Oh," Fitzhugh answered, "I guess I'll knock off around midnight. The Paris market will be closed tomorrow. Hurricane Constance knocked out their equipment. Thank God. I'll be able to grab a few hours' sleep before Singapore opens."

"Hmmf," Silber said. "Can you drop by? I have an interesting proposition for you."

"Can't you propose over the phone?" Fitzhugh said, yawning.

"No," Silber answered testily. "I can't. Are you holding out for another evening at the club, you Celtic chiseler?"

"The thought never entered my mind," Fitzhugh said, innocently. "But we could discuss it, though. Just after midnight, when I drop by. Oh, and Milt, send out for something to eat, will you? I'd like roast beef sandwiches on rye. Lots of mustard. See you soon."

. . .

"Damn!" Silber said to Fitzhugh, as the knocking sounded again at the front door. He walked reluctantly to the window and looked out. Maggie Altman? At this hour of the night? He groaned. She had no doubt seen his windows blazing with light and decided to drop by. Well, he had invited her to come over and consult his library. His own fault for being so generous. "Oh, all right, I'm coming," he called in the direction of the door.

"I don't want to explain what you're doing here," he told Fitzhugh. "Grab the printouts and look them over in the back room, will you? I'll take care of this young woman as fast as possible."

Fitzhugh took the papers in question, his glass of bourbon, and his sandwich, and hurried off in the direction of the little room at the back of the house. When Silber judged that Fitzhugh had had enough time to get out of sight, he opened the front door.

"I was just driving home and saw your lights," Maggie said apologetically. "If your offer's still open, I'd like to look at one of your books. But if you'd rather I came at a better time . . . "

"You're here now, aren't you?" Silber said, forcing a smile. "No point in wasting a trip. Come in and do what you need to do."

Chapter 21

Maggie already wished she hadn't come. But it was too late to change her mind. Silber had closed the door behind her and was raking his beard thoughtfully.

"The books you'd be interested in are in that bookcase over there. The one closest to the desk. Unless they're on the floor. Hmm. Better go paw through them yourself." He looked about uneasily, then seemed to remember his manners. "A drink," he muttered to himself, then peered at her. "Would you like one?"

Taken aback by his abruptness, she was slow to reply. Silber evidently took her silence for consent, grunted and disappeared into the kitchen. She shrugged.

"Just take the books to the desk," Silber called from the kitchen. There's a free chair there. I'm afraid the best seat in the house is taken."

Maggie navigated the tortuous path through the cairns of papers, and was just passing Silber's favorite armchair—presumably the "best seat in the house"—when she felt her leg touched, then held. Incredulous, she looked down. An enormous black cat now had both arms around her right leg, just below the knee. The creature looked up at her in a very self-satisfied manner, and butted its head against her knee. Now what, she wondered? Tentatively, she held out a hand. The cat sniffed it, seemed to find it agreeable, and released her. As she edged past, it patted her bottom gently with a paw the size of a teacup. "Nice kitty," she said doubtfully.

She found the books she wanted, and took them, as Silber had told her, to the desk. There was scarcely any room to work amid the clutter of papers. As she laid the book on the desk, a single piece of paper fell to the floor. She reached to retrieve it and her eyes were drawn to something written on the paper "Texas University Regional Preventive Health Center—

C56 42833019 FD88". She frowned. What could it mean? The other line of letters and figures fairly jumped off the page at her "EquaCare—WRT01 5549 767VZT0100". Her heart began to beat a little faster. The first string looked to her very similar to her own password for the TU computer. With the exception that hers was shorter. Why would Dr. Silber have such a password? Hadn't he terminated his affiliation with TU? And what about the other one? Was it an EquaCare password? And what did the last line on the paper mean: "After ID prompt, type RECORD DECLINED, wait for ackowledgement, then enter codes." Her thoughts in disarray, she found herself pulling out an index card. She began copying the numbers.

"Finding what you want?" a voice called from behind her.

Guiltily, she stuffed the index cards back in her pocket. "Yes, thanks," she said, trying to keep her voice from betraying her. "But I wonder if I could take this book home. There's a rather long article I need to read."

Silber appeared behind her, bearing drinks. She looked at him cautiously. Why, he seems positively relieved, she thought. He wants to get rid of me! "Of course, of course," he told her.

She tucked the book under her arm and was just preparing to navigate the living room debris when a tremendous crash came from the back of the house. Silber's cat sat straight up in his chair and with a frightful yowl, sprang over the piles of papers and disappeared in the direction of the noise. She thought she heard a muffled voice yell something, and then there was silence. Thoroughly alarmed, she looked at Silber.

"That damned turtle!" he shouted, hustling her to the front door.

"Dr. Silber!" she said in alarm. The man obviouly wasn't well. "A turtle? More likely a burglar. Shouldn't we check? Or call the police?"

"Totally unnecessary," Silber told her.

A door opened in the back of the house, and Maggie's blood ran cold. She looked in the direction of the sound, and plainly saw a dark figure tiptoe carefully through the kitchen. It was a tall man, and he seemed to be carrying a large roasting pan. He was limping. Dr. Silber's cat followed him.

"Look!" she exclaimed. "There! A man! In the kitchen!"

"Aaargh!" Silber yelled. "Damned clodhopper!" He opened the door and all but pushed Maggie out onto the porch. "Goodnight," he told her abruptly. Peering closely at her, he scowled. "There's really nothing wrong. Don't be alarmed. Simply another guest. A clumsy one. Let me know how you make out with the book. Must go now." He slammed the door.

• • •

Maggie's tires spat gravel as she floored the accelerator. Heedless of traffic, she rocketed her car out onto Hudson Drive. She was angry at having been shooed out the door like . . . like Silber's cat! And, she had to admit, she was just a little frightened. What was going on there? Leaving Silber behind was the only thought in her head. She shifted into Drive and put her foot to the floor. The Duster squealed in protest, but responded nimbly, and she risked a fleeting glance at Silber's front window. To her relief, she did not see him there, watching. Evidently Silber and his mysterious guest were preoccupied with other things. The curtains were now drawn, and the porch light had been turned off. The house sat in darkness.

She realized she was driving too fast, and turned off the street at the first blaze of bright lights she saw. A MacDonald's. Locking the car, she hurried the few yards to the front door. Three teenaged couples sat at one table, laughing over fries and cokes, a truck driver sat drinking coffee in the corner, and four uniformed employees from the all night supermarket across the street were nursing soft drinks and coffee, evidently relaxing on their break. It all looked perfectly normal, she thought, relaxing a little. She ordered a chocolate milkshake (for the gnawing pain in her stomach) and took a table that faced Hudson Drive. Closing her eyes, she tried to put some order into the stream of chaotic thoughts and impressions that tumbled through her mind.

• • •

By the time she had finished half the milkshake, Maggie had sorted out her thoughts sufficiently to realize that Dr. Silber was not simply the reclusive financial analyst he claimed to be. He was not someone who had turned his back on medicine forever. And certainly not someone who had forgotten his past at TU. The computer access codes on his desk disproved those claims. So what was he? She took another sip of milkshake as a spasm of pain stabbed her.

What a fool she had been. If things had gone differently at Dr. Silber's—if she hadn't found that slip of paper, and if that person hadn't been in the back room—she might have confided in Dr. Silber. Over the past few weeks she had become more and more convinced that there was outside interference with the computer, as opposed to just a glitch in the software. She might have told Dr. Silber her suspicions that someone was tampering with TU's computer. Tried to use him as a sounding board for the half-formed theory she had. What a mistake that would have been! She shuddered. And felt immediately guilty for the suspicions she had been focusing on Blaine and Fischbein. Blaine, with his stacks of computers printouts and dour manner. Fischbein, who so often seemed to be unaccountably close by when an error occurred. And both of them seemed to prowl the hospital corridors at odd hours. But what could either of them gain from sabotaging the TU computer? She felt more than a little foolish for having suspected them on the basis of such weak circumstantial evidence. Well, now she had another suspect.

She finished her milkshake and looked out into the parking lot. Everything appeared ordinary, and she sighed in relief. But what about a motive? She frowned. What would Dr. Silber's motive be? Revenge? A desire to make the hospital—and therefore Dr. Eisig, its new administrator—look bad? Or could it be something more sinister? She shuddered, recalling Dr. Silber's strange behavior. The man was probably capable of anything. Now what, she asked herself, frowning. If she wanted anyone to listen to her, she would have to have proof. She'd better start writing everything down. And making copies of corroborating information. And should she tell someone? But who? Maybe Brent. After all, he had agreed with her assertions that there were problems with the computer. Yes, perhaps Brent was the person to discuss this with. He was both knowledgeable and interested. And he was turning out to be a gentleman, despite her first impressions of him. But first she needed some proof. She threw her milkshake container in the trash, and walked thoughtfully to her car.

Chapter *22*

"Raúl?" he said in surprise to the slim, impeccably dressed young Hispanic who stood at his door.

The man smiled, showing even white teeth.

"Please come in," he said in confusion. This was certainly not what he had expected. Not after his encounter with Raúl's enforcers in the hospital parking lot. Why, this expensively dressed, urbane young man could be anyone—a young lawyer, a stockbroker. Even a doctor. "Have a seat."

Raúl placed a thin leather attache case on the coffee table and took a seat on the couch, fastidiously straightening the crease in his trousers as he did so.

"What would you like to drink?" he asked him. "I have most everything."

"I'm sure you do," Raúl replied in a cultured, unaccented voice. "But I don't drink. I would, however, enjoy some Perrier if you have it. With fresh lime."

"Oh. Yes, sure," he replied, surprised. Raúl, a teetotaller? Maybe the rumors he had heard about drug dealers were true after all—they didn't take recreational drugs. Never their own products, and seldom anything else. As he poured the Perrier, he wondered nervously why Raúl was here. He could have sent his thugs for the money. He handed Raúl his drink and sat warily in an armchair opposite him, waiting.

Raúl took a few sips of his drink, and wiped his moustache delicately. "To business, then," he said. "I'm sure you're wondering why I myself have come to pay you a visit. After all, I could have sent Benny and Carlos." He smiled. "How is your ear, doctor?"

He swallowed nervously. "It's okay. Wasn't that a little extreme, though?"

Raúl lifted one eyebrow. "You think so?" He appeared to consider the matter. "Perhaps it was. But in my business, Doctor, it is often necessary to emphasize to the borrower the serious-ness of his indebtedness." He smiled again. "Were I in another business, I might have my lawyer write you a letter, or a collection agency pay you a call. But I cannot do either of those things. Benny and Carlos are my collection agency. I have never known anyone to ignore a message from them." He shrugged. "Extreme? Yes. But effective. You were, after all, in my debt." He took another few sips of Perrier.

"I have the money," he assured Raúl. "All of it. Interest, too." He handed over an envelope.

Raúl smiled again. "Good." He placed his attache case on his knees, snapped it open, and put the envelope inside. "Now for the second item of business."

His mind raced furiously. What else could Raúl possibly want with him?

"As you know, Doctor, I am a businessman. I operate according to the laws of supply and demand. What my . . . customers require, I provide. At a profit, of course. That is the nature of business." He spread his hands. "But things change. Oh, not the demand—that is a constant factor. It is the supply, or rather the nature of the supply that is changing."

He thought he understood. "And so you're going to be charging more. No problem, I—"

Raúl held up a hand. "—not more. Less."

"Less? I don't understand."

Raúl reached into his attache case and brought out a small glass vial. He placed it carefully on the coffee table.

"What is it?" he asked, picking it up and looking closely. Inside were five crystalline lumps, each off-white in color, and about the size of his little fingernail.

"Cocaine."

He shook his head. "No way."

"I assure you it is, doctor. This is called 'rock' or 'crack'. It's freebase cocaine."

He blinked. "But what about the other stuff? The powder."

Raúl shook his head. "This is better. It will cost you less, because it costs me less. I no longer have to go through the elaborate and time consuming procedure I did to 'cut' the coke I received from Colombia. Shall I tell you about it?" He smiled. "You're a professional, as I am. In a not unallied profession. I think you'll be interested."

He nodded. It was true—he was fascinated.

"The cocaine I receive from my Colombian source is approximately 40 percent pure. Each ounce weighs 28.3 grams. From each ounce 25 grams of cocaine is weighed out and mixed with 25 grams of lactose, thereby producing 50 grams of 20 percent cocaine. There is, of course, 3.3 grams of 40 percent cocaine left over from each ounce. This is used to pay my chemists." Raúl laughed, seeing the expression on the doctor's face. "You're surprised? Surely you didn't think I did this myself? Oh no—I hire chemistry students from the university to do the 'cutting'. All the procedure requires is minimal dexterity, a digitized pan balance, a five pound jar of lactose, a large mortar and pestle, and a box of paper squares. And not too larcenous a soul." He paused. "That, unfortunately, is one of the problems. Quality control. So few people are trustworthy." He sighed. "Never mind. Fortunately, the industry is moving in a different direction. To freebase." He gestured to the glass vial. "This is virtually pure. It has never been adulterated. Of course, anyone who wished to could prepare crack from the adulterated cocaine sold on the streets. In fact, many people do it now. But I predict they won't do it for long."

He frowned. "Oh? Why not?"

Raúl laughed. "First of all, it's dangerous. Why assume an unnecessary risk? Second—economics! Why spend your time doing something that someone else will do for you." He shook the vial. "This has never been adulterated. And it's so much more . . . accessible. Such civilized little pieces. Requiring so much less in the way of capital investment."

He took the vial from Raúl. "How much would these five civilized little pieces cost me?" he asked curiously.

"About $25," Raúl told him.

"Yeah—that's more accessible if you're an individual of, ah, limited means. Fortunately, I don't have to worry about that. But I see your point."

"And consider another thing," Raúl said. "This is close to 90 percent pure." His eyes glittered. "The high that you'll get from this is so intense that you'll never go back to that inferior white powder."

He swallowed nervously.

"This is not available everywhere yet," Raúl told him. "But I wanted my good customers to be able to try it. You're a man of discernment, Doctor. I know it won't be wasted on you."

Pure? That would mean it was potentially more addicting. His respect for Raúl as a businessman climbed a notch. And he himself didn't need to worry about getting addicted. He only used the stuff recreationally. And sometimes to energize himself. He handed the vial back to Raúl. "You've sold me. When can I have some?"

Raúl pushed the vial back toward him. "Right now. That's a free sample. After all, you're one of my best customers." He placed a small glass pipe on the table beside the vial. "This you can buy anywhere, but I want you to have the best." He smiled. "I take care of my people. I don't want any of my good customers trying to make crack themselves, and I don't want them ingesting it improperly."

He nodded.

"Good," Raúl said, standing up and brushing an imaginary piece of lint off his trousers. "Oh, one last thing, Doctor. I'm in the market for an associate. Someone with good connections in the professional world. Someone discreet. Someone presentable. The nature of my business is changing, as I explained. I have plans for expansion, and I will require a suitable . . . partner. Do you know of anyone who might be interested?" Raúl's mouth smiled, but his shrewd, dark eyes did not.

He swallowed nervously. Why not? "I might," he equivocated. "But the ah, financial details would have to be extensively discussed. The individual I have in mind would place top dollar on his services."

"I would certainly hope so," Raúl told him. "Only top-flight people are of interest to me. Perhaps you might mention the prospect to your associate and let me know."

He nodded, walking with Raúl to the door. "I will."

"Good." Raúl paused and looked back at the coffee table. "Enjoy yourself, Doctor. But be a little cautious at first." He held out his hand. "It's been a pleasure. And do speak to your associate soon. Although men must sleep, money never does. Don't you agree?"

Chapter 23

"I'm in the middle of attending rounds just now," Maggie said, holding the telephone with her shoulder while scribbling on the clipboard in her lap. "Can't I talk to you about this later?" The Utilization Review/Quality Assurance Committee really thought that they were the most important people in the hospital, Maggie grumbled to herself.

"Well, I suppose so." Miss Brophy's assertive voice sounded dissatisfied. "But we're working under a deadline. You should come to my office as soon as possible."

Maggie added the errand to her growing list. Along with two infiltrated IVs, three X ray results to check, two blood cultures to draw, and Mr. Pearson, whose nurse said he couldn't urinate. She shifted her posture a little on the hard desktop and sighed. The medical student droned on with a Weed Problem-Oriented presentation on one of Fred's patients. Their attending, Malcolm Long, was a stickler for the Problem-Oriented Medical Record, the POMR, and they would probably spend 15 minutes making sure that the active and inactive problem lists were properly set up and the diagnoses ranked in the proper order. Fred winked at her and slipped out the door for a moment.

"Dr. Altman, STAT, Dr. Margaret Altman, STAT, call the Operator" came over the intercom. Maggie suppressed a laugh, as the Operator told her that Dr. Jenkins needed her on 6 West.

"Thanks," she mouthed to Fred, exiting the room as he entered. She could probably get a couple of things done without arousing Dr. Long's ire. Later, she could return the favor for Fred.

Mr. Pearson had a bladder as large as a basketball, and a history of urethral stricture. They had tried to pass a catheter, the nurse told her, and failed. There was one last resort before calling the urologist, Maggie thought. The two of them helped Mr. Pearson stand up, draping his arms over their shoulders. He was certainly heavy. Maggie held the urinal for him, and he

116

obligingly filled it up.

"My first, and probably last, therapeutic triumph of the day," Maggie sighed, as she and Nurse Marilyn helped the patient back into the bed. Now for priority 2: a visit to the UR/QAC office.

• • •

"This isn't Burger King: you can't have it your way," announced the sign on the wall in the UR/QAC office, adjacent to Medical Records. This morning, it didn't strike Maggie as funny. Especially after she had to look at it for ten minutes, while Miss Sylvia Brophy, UR/QAC Chairperson, finished a telephone call.

"Oh, yes, Dr. Altman," Miss Brophy said, with a smile that Maggie felt was forced. "Let me just pull the file on Frank Post." Another wait ensued, while Miss Brophy slipped her high heeled shoes back on and headed for the long section of shelves labeled "DRG Problems." Maggie studied her. She was obviously dressed for success in a royal blue suit of stylish cut. Her dark hair, streaked with gray, was elaborately arranged, and her coarse features were carefully made up. Every detail of her appearance was meticulously cared for, including her perfect long enameled fingernails.

"Here we are," Miss Brophy said, seating herself behind a large desk, which held the obligatory computer terminal, telephone, and little else. Miss Brophy also called up Frank Post's updated EquaCare profile on the screen. "This patient has exceeded the LOS for his DRG by 17 days now."

"But he got pneumonia," Maggie protested. "Just as I was ready to send him home. He is much too sick to go home now."

"Pneumonia is not listed as one of the expected complications of pulmonary embolus," Miss Brophy said, scanning through a file on that diagnosis. "So it doesn't extend the LOS."

"I can't help that," Maggie said. "He has chronic lung disease, and he's susceptible to pneumonia, and he got it."

"A hospital-acquired infection," Miss Brophy said sternly, pursing her lips. "It will affect our M & M profile too."

117

Maggie shrugged helplessly. What was she supposed to do?

"As I said, this patient needs to be discharged," Miss Brophy continued. "He's already an outlier. Pneumonia, you realize, often does not require the intensity of care that we provide in this acute-care facility. You have not documented that this case meets the intensity of care criteria. He is not even getting an IV."

"But his blood gases. . ." Maggie began.

"Chronic," Miss Brophy interrupted.

"But I can't send him home yet," Maggie protested. "He's just not ready. His wife can't possibly manage him."

"We're not asking you to discharge a patient who has a medical necessity to be in the hospital," Miss Brophy insisted. "But the convenience of his family does not justify the consumption of resources in an acute-care facility."

"But you can't send him home," Maggie insisted, realizing that the pitch of her voice was rising.

"That's right, we can't," Miss Brophy responded her with a tight smile. "You're the doctor. You write the orders. We're only here to advise you. You make the final decision. Please don't hesitate to call on us if we can be of any help."

Maggie found herself escorted to the door. She hurried back to rounds, pausing only to take a dose of Maalox at the nursing station. What on earth did that woman want her to do? Give Mr. Post IV aminophylline, when it always made him vomit? Just so he could meet some "intensity of service" criterion? Well, it didn't matter what Miss Brophy wanted, as long as she, Maggie Altman, was the doctor. Maggie found herself hoping that somebody else would apply for that job.

• • •

Noon chart conference had a new feature, Maggie noticed: an overhead projector. Blaine was fussing with it as she arrived. She tried to see what was on the screen, but Blaine quickly switched off the light as the interns began to file in with their brown bags. Gathering up the transparencies, Blaine took his seat in the front. He sat with his hands in his pockets, looking over the interns and residents. When Maggie met his eyes, Blaine hastily looked away. I just don't trust him, she told herself. He's so cold and mechanical, like the computers he seems to love so much. Could he be an accomplice of Dr. Silber's? The notion wasn't too far-fetched. Someone who was trying to destroy EquaCare would probably need inside help.

Dr. Eisig entered promptly at 12:05, with a smile more genial than usual. "Good afternoon," he said. "You have probably noticed that the stack of charts is very short today. We're going to try something a little different." He smiled again, looking very pleased with himself.

"In the past, peer review has always been a retrospective sort of thing: criticizing mistakes after the patient has gone home. By then it's already too late," he explained. Some of the interns tittered. "Well, here at TU we are about to introduce a much more meaningful process: an ongoing peer review, which looks at patient care concurrently, so that we can anticipate and correct any potential problems." Eisig paused for dramatic effect.

"The data gathering capability of our computer expedites the process tremendously, and has allowed us to establish standards of care much more precisely." He nodded to Blaine, who was standing beside the overhead projector.

The first transparency was a bar graph. "Allowed DRG reimbursement" was in black; "utilization of resources" in red. Along the left margin were provider numbers, which represented individual interns. There was one intern whose red line was twice as long as the black one; most of the others had red lines that were shorter than the black ones. Maggie noticed that Drs. Fischbein and Larkin were looking pretty self-satisfied. She guessed that they were among the cost-effective doctors.

"On the whole," Blaine said, "We're really doing quite well. Most of the housestaff are rapidly learning how to work more efficiently, and how to remain within the economic constraints faced by society, without sacrificing quality." He put up a second transparency. "In fact, there is even a positive correlation between cost-effectiveness and quality. You can see that the very same individual who has accumulated the highest nonreimbursed costs, also has the same number of deviations from the accepted standard of care."

That was her provider number, Maggie noted. Not surprising. Her last individual DRG profile had shown a big excess in consumption. But "deviations from the accepted standards of care"! What did they mean by that? She just felt numb. She wondered whether Blaine was going to reveal the name of Provider Number PGY1-14 to everyone, but he didn't. He studiously avoided looking at her.

Provider Number PGY1-18 was probably Fred, she speculated. His "debit" was not nearly as large as hers, though. He had a high number of "deviations" too. Maggie shook her head. Fred was a good doc.

Blaine had a third transparency, that listed principles that should help them improve their performance.

"1. Clear documentation of how the patient meets the criteria for continued hospital stay.

"2. Careful selection of the DRG most appropriate to the patient's condition.

"3. Adherence to the standard of care.

"4. Prevention of complications.

"5. Early discharge planning."

Fine, Maggie thought. That really helps me a lot. And what if the patients are sicker than they're supposed to be? Was it just her imagination that she somehow was assigned the sickest patients? Even her phlegmatic resident, Stuart Collins, was beginning to remark—jokingly?—on his rotten luck: he had both Maggie and Fred as interns, and the resident on the other service got a lot more sleep.

"Now, don't misunderstand," Dr. Eisig explained. "We're not trying to alter the diagnosis. Or to omit any needed tests. The main thing is to emphasize documentation. When you order a procedure, document the need for it. When a patient needs to stay longer than usual, document the reasons, so that EquaCare won't deny the stay. Work with the Utilization Review/Quality Assurance Committee. They're here to help you."

Maggie raised her hand. "Yes, Dr. Altman," Eisig said.

"What if there is a difference of opinion between the

doctor and the Utilization Review Committee?"

"Well, of course, the doctor makes the final judgment," Eisig assured her. "The UR/QAC department only establishes guidelines."

"I should add something to that," Blaine interposed. "All of you need to understand the importance of cooperation with UR/QAC. They're part of the team. Because if you think you don't like them," he looked directly at Maggie, "you should ask yourself what the alternative is. If doctors don't control the cost of medical care, then somebody else will."

Dr. Eisig blinked his watery eyes behind his glasses, and smiled again. "I hope that answers your question, Dr. Altman."

Fischbein spat out a grape seed. Maggie thought she heard him say "Buff the chart." Over the crackling of his waxed paper, she couldn't be sure. Is that how he got such a good rating? She wondered.

Chapter 24

"But I am taking care of it!" he told the caller in exasperation. "The problem will gradually fade away. I'm not a magician, you know. I can't make it disappear in a puff of smoke. And furthermore—"

"—Listen my young friend," the caller interrupted. "We've had the last three weeks' profits totally wiped out. Now it looks as though this week's profit picture will be dismal as well. Perhaps you are willing to tolerate another down month, but I'm not. I've never been fond of red ink." He paused for a moment. "You know, I've begun to wonder lately if you're the right man for this job. You seem to be considerably less . . . effective than you were."

"Oh, come on!" he exclaimed. "I'm as effective as I ever was. It's not my fault that this particular problem appeared. And it is in your department now, isn't it? For God's sake, you could express a little gratitude. At least you don't have to get your hands dirty. So give me a break. I said I'd take care of it and I will. I have something in the works. A plan. Trust me."

"Oh? Tell me about this . . . plan."

Trying to sound optimistic, he went on. "Well, it's got to be discreet. This is a person we're talking about, not a figure on a balance sheet. She can't just be erased. She's got to be persuaded to lay off. But in such a way that she thinks it's her own idea. And in such a way that no attention is called to us. Or our . . . business. But I need just a little more time. You have my word that the problem will resolve itself. Damn it, you know I'm interested in the bottom line just as much as you are. But you're going to have to let me do the job my way."

There was silence for so long that he thought the caller had hung up. But no, there were sounds of breathing on the line. "All right," the caller told him. "I'll agree to give you until the end of the month to resolve the problem your way. At that time, I'll review the situation, and if there has been no improvement, something more drastic will have to be done. Do you understand?"

He swallowed. "Yes."

"And although I agree to give you the necessary time to resolve the problem, I don't see why our—pardon me, my— profit margin has to suffer."

"I don't understand," he said.

"No, I'm sure you don't. Listen, then. Manipulation of the case mix from your end is not the only method of assuring profits. If we can't trust the staff to make cost-effective decisions, more direct intervention may be necessary. Aggressive intervention."

"You don't mean . . . " he trailed off, shocked.

"That's exactly what I mean, my squeamish young friend," the caller replied matter-of-factly. "It is perfectly in accordance with our social responsibilities. It merely assists nature in accomplishing the inevitable. Besides, such action would hardly arouse suspicion. People die in hospitals every day. Especially those with the appropriate severity-of-illness parameters. And Woodlands, thanks to your little problem, has recently acquired far too many unprofitable cases. And too few profitable ones."

He closed his eyes. How had things gotten so out of control? This was a nightmare. "I couldn't do anything like that," he told the caller weakly.

"I didn't suppose you could," the caller replied. "If it's necessary, I'll take care of it myself."

• • •

After the caller hung up, he sat in a state of shock, unmoving, for many minutes. So it had come to this. He held out his hands and looked at them. They were shaking. Angrily he clenched and unclenched his fists. It was all her fault. That damned woman! He found himself hating her. Easy, he told himself, easy. She's just a woman. An obstacle. You've got until the end of the month to see if she can be brought around. You needn't think about something more drastic just yet. But another month with no money! He groaned. He'd have to see if Raúl would give him credit again. Probably. He'd done it once. But what about paying back the money—and the interest. He scowled. The end of the month would tell the tale. Either the woman would be brought under control, or she would have to be erased. Like an error in an equation. He closed his eyes, not wanting to think about it. Something nagged at him, and he tried anxiously to pin it down. What was it? He was having more and more trouble concentrating these days. Sleeping, too. Oh yes— Raúl's offer of partnership. He hadn't had time to give it much thought, but now, suddenly, it began to look very attractive. Perhaps he should hedge his bets. Have one foot in a totally different business. Yes, that seemed like good economic sense. Maybe he'd better talk to Raúl about it soon. He chuckled. Wouldn't his director be surprised if he found out! Yes, that's what he'd do. In fact, he'd call Raúl right now and set up an appointment. As he reached for the phone, he felt a surge of optimism. No, things weren't out of control. The problem at the hospital, the need for direct intervention from the top—those were just minor setbacks. He needed to think in a more businesslike way about things. It was the bottom line that mattered, after all, wasn't it? His bottom line. He smiled, and began to dial Raúl's answering service.

Chapter *25*

"Amazing," Silber told Fitzhugh. He swung his legs out of bed and took a firmer grip on the telephone receiver. "Absolutely amazing."

"Well," Fitzhugh said, sounding excited, "it's pretty odd, anyway."

In the background Silber could hear the sounds of Banque France's Forex department. He assumed Fitzhugh must be busy, and was grateful to him for taking time to call.

"What did you tell your young associate in the legal department?" Silber wanted to know.

"Nothing," Fitzhugh replied. "Stevens is our law clerk. A very enterprising young fellow. And very close-mouthed. He never asks why he's asked to do things. He just does them." Fitzhugh laughed. "And here he's asked to do some pretty crazy things. But he's very thorough. If he says that Ararat Management Consultants may be nothing but a shell, then I believe him."

"Hmmf," Silber said, his pulse racing with excitement. "Tell me exactly what he found."

Fitzhugh rustled some papers. "Let me see—I have his report right here. I'll get a copy to you. Look at this! 'Ararat Management Consultants Inc., a close corporation, was incorporated August 15, 1993, in Wilmington, Delaware.' That's common enough practice," Fitzhugh told Silber. "If you're a big corporation. It's done for tax reasons. Nothing at all shady about it. But small companies usually don't do things that way. They usually incorporate in the state in which they do business. So right off the bat, Ararat looks a little odd. Stevens goes on to note that 'The registered office of the corporation is stated in the certificate of incorporation to be 1100 Wharf Street. This address is, in fact, not the address of Ararat, but the address of an agent'."

"An agent?"

"Right. A company set up for the sole purpose of providing out-of-state corporations with a Delaware address. It's perfectly legal. A convenience, really."

"Hmmf," Silber replied. "What else was he able to discover?"

"Let's see," Fitzhugh said, reading from Stevens' report. "'Financial data for the corporation was unavailable, as were names of the corporation's officers.' Hmmm. That's highly irregular. Minutes of meetings and names of the officers should be public information. They're required to be on file in Newcastle County. Stevens does note, however, that Ararat is described in its incorporating statement as a 'close corporation of various medical management consultancy firms', and the name and address of the managing stockholder of Ararat is then listed as yet another company. That's what made Stevens suspicious."

Silber could hardly contain himself. "Another company? Which other company?"

Fitzhugh riffled pages noisily. "Can't find it. Damn. Well, it will be here somewhere in the report."

"I need to take a look at that report right away."

"All right. I'll call the courier service and have it driven over to you. Of course, I'll put the charge on your tab."

"Yes, yes," Silber said in irritation. "Listen. I want young Stevens to go on."

"Go on?"

"I need to know more about Ararat. And the company that's given as its managing stockholder, which is probably another shell. I don't want him to stop until he turns up a name. A person, blast it! And I need to know the financial data. How much is Ararat worth? The other company, too. There must be a way to find this information!"

"Milt, there's always a way to find things out," Fitzhugh told him. "Information is a just another commodity. But it would cost you more money. File clerks are notoriously underpaid, and Stevens will have to offer someone enough money to persuade her—and it probably will be a her—to go and hunt up this information. Assuming it's been filed, that is."

Silber groaned. "Oh all right. How soon can I have it?"

Fitzhugh sighed. "Milt, Stevens does have other chores."

"When?"

"Well . . . the beginning of next week if he can do it over the phone. The following week if I have to send him there."

"Where?"

"Delaware. Where else?"

Chapter 26

"I just have this feeling that he's not going to make it home," Mrs. Post confided to Maggie. "Not ever."

"It's been pretty discouraging," Maggie admitted. "First the blood clots, then the pneumonia. He's been here over a month now. But he's a lot better, and I think he'll be able to go home in the next few days."

"Do you really think so?" Mrs. Post asked, her eyes becoming moist.

"Yes, I do," Maggie assured her, taking her hand.

"I just hope something else doesn't happen." Mrs. Post shook her head sadly. "But thank you, Doctor."

Mrs. Post made her way to the elevator, slowly, with the aid of a cane. Maggie felt a little surge of anger. This case had been a constant battle, and not just against disease. Miss Brophy had called her in again today to discuss the "excessive use of resources." In fact, Miss Brophy had said that the hospital would lose its favored status, and face much tighter scrutiny by the government, if this patient was not sent home within three days. Some sort of statistical criterion would be met. Maggie didn't understand what that was, but she got the idea that all the doctors would have much more paperwork, and that she, Maggie Altman, would be held personally responsible for it. Fortunately, Mr. Post was finally on the road to recovery.

Maggie returned to the doctor's station to query the computer about the day's lab results on her patients. That at least was a convenience. She didn't have to go to every ward to look at the charts, or telephone the lab. She just had to get the patient's number from her index cards.

The pack of cards was becoming too fat for the clip. Maggie decided to sort them into several piles: currently in hospital, discharged, and research. The last card just had some code numbers on it. Maggie stared at it, apprehension flooding over her. The numbers she had scribbled down at Dr. Silber's house.

You've been repressing things, she accused herself. You haven't wanted to think about it. You're afraid of what you might find. Being too busy is no excuse. Maggie felt her heart pounding. She listened carefully, but did not hear anyone approaching the doctor's station. It was nearly 9 p.m.; everyone who was not on call would be gone by now. She took a deep breath, and punched the numbers into the terminal.

"ILLEGAL FORMAT," the terminal replied. Maggie tried again. Same response. She wasn't sure whether she wanted to curse, or sigh with relief.

"Good evening, Dr. Altman," Stephen Blaine said. Maggie started. Blaine was picking a chart out of the rack. He could probably see the terminal, though. She punched a few more keys to clear the screen.

"Oh, good evening, Dr. Blaine," Maggie managed to say, gathering up her cards in what she hoped was a leisurely fashion. "You're working late."

"Not really," he replied somewhat curtly.

"Dr. Miltown, Dr. Everett Miltown, call 2262," said the page operator. Maggie was briefly tempted to ask Blaine who Dr. Miltown was. She thought that he glanced at the telephone when he heard the page.

"Well, I've got to see a patient," Maggie lied, feeling a need to make an excuse for leaving the doctor's station. The truth was that Blaine just made her uncomfortable. He was reviewing one of Charlie's charts, she noted. He just grunted, without looking up.

Maggie headed down the hall, just to be going some-where, anywhere. She found herself at the door to the stairwell. Blaine's office was at the top of those stairs, four flights up. He might have left the door unlocked, she thought, then shivered at her boldness. Well, here was opportunity staring her in the face. Would she be too cowardly to take advantage of it? It probably wouldn't present itself again. She raced up the stairs, trying to outrun her fears.

No one was in the hall on the tenth floor, and the door

to the chief resident's office was ajar. Maggie quickly darted inside. The computer was already powered up. She noticed that her hands were shaking, as she retrieved the card from her pocket. Her fingers were so clumsy that it took three attempts to type in the numbers correctly. A disk drive whirred, and the date and time appeared on the screen.

After a brief delay, a menu appeared. Maggie chose the first entry, and the screen filled rapidly with what appeared to be financial information about the hospital. Companies on the hospital's payroll. The laundry, janitorial service, and so on.

At the bottom of the screen, a query flashed: "CONTINUE? Y/N." Maggie pressed the "Y," and more of the same type of information appeared. There was even a consulting firm. Ararat Management Consultants. Well, TU certainly could use some advice on efficient management. Despite what the newspaper articles claimed. But it certainly was expensive. The payment to Ararat was a couple of columns wider than any of the others.

Why was Dr. Silber interested in this information, Maggie wondered. And, what was more important, why did he have the password? Access to this data base was restricted.

Obviously, he had a grudge against Dr. Eisig and the hospital. Would he be bitter enough to try to sabotage the EquaCare system? Or did he have some sort of financial interest in it?

She pressed the "Y" several times. Each time, she heard a whirring sound, and noticed that the red light on one of the disk drives was briefly illuminated. She wondered whether it was recording something. Her anxiety mounted, and began to override her curiosity.

She glanced at her watch. How long was Blaine planning to stay on the wards? Probably not long, she thought, otherwise he wouldn't have left his door unlocked. How was she going to turn this program off, she wondered, and felt her stomach constrict. She remembered the trouble she had once had in figuring out how to log off a computer after she had logged on. She could always turn off the power, but that might wipe something important out of the memory, and Blaine might be very upset.

She tried answering "N" to the next query. To her relief, an "ABORT" option appeared. The whirring sound occurred again, and the screen gave her the message "EXITED 2120, ACTIVE 12 MINUTES, 18 SECONDS." How could she get that message off the screen? The "delete" key didn't work. She would have to think of something fast. She had the overwhelming sense that Blaine was on the way back to his office. In desperation, she hit the "reset" function. The screen blanked. Whatever else it did, she would never know. She bolted from the office and into the stairwell. On the second flight, she passed Blaine, who looked at her strangely, but said nothing.

"Dr. Altman, Dr. Margaret Altman, call 2824." Well, there would be no time for speculation now. Maggie felt the familiar rush of anxiety that accompanied each new admission. She had hoped that feeling was just a phenomenon of early internship and that she would someday find a hospital admission to be just a routine chore. But so far, it hadn't happened.

• • •

Maggie sipped her third cup of coffee of the morning, and tried to concentrate on the student case presentation. About her last patient, admitted at 3 a.m. The page operator interrupted her thoughts again.

"Dr. Altman, Dr. Margaret Altman, call 7654."

An unfamiliar extension. Maggie picked up the telephone to dial, but couldn't remember the number. She was also having trouble remembering where her various patients were. And she would occasionally stop in the middle of the hall, unsure of what her destination was. Symptoms of sleep deprivation. She tried to be an objective observer of the phenomenon. That seemed to make it a little less distressing. She dialed the operator, who repeated the extension for her.

It was Blaine. "Dr. Altman, would you please stop by my office just after attending rounds?"

Maggie felt her heart skipping beats. "Certainly, Dr. Blaine," she said. So she had been found out. She was too numb to care. She almost hoped that he would send her away from TU

131

immediately.

Blaine was eating his lunch when she arrived, but he pushed it aside, and offered Maggie a cup of coffee.

Blaine looked at her thoughtfully, and—could it be?—apologetically. "As you know, Dr. Altman," he began, "We're doing concurrent peer review these days, trying to identify problems early. The computer constantly monitors patient care, and compares it with predetermined criteria for quality."

Maggie paled at the mention of the computer. When would Blaine get around to mentioning her unauthorized access last night? Or did he want to keep her in suspense?

"Your cases keep falling out, whether we are looking at deviations from the standard of care, or excessive costs. As we are finding out, cost-effectiveness and quality of care usually go hand in hand."

"Quality of care?" Maggie asked, feeling her face flush. And, she imagined, a squirt of acid from the glands in her stomach.

"I have reviewed several cases," Blaine said. "Frank Post, for example." His expression seemed inscrutable to Maggie. "And it is hard to find a specific criticism of your management. Except for a certain lack of documentation."

Maggie felt indignant. "It seems I am documenting all the time," she protested. "I think that sometimes the computer just eats my notes."

Blaine made an impatient gesture. "You know, sometimes we think we do things that we haven't done. It's easy to blame it on the computer. But this system has been thoroughly tested, and I just haven't had any other complaints about it."

Maggie wanted to say something, but checked herself. She wondered if Brent had spoken to the chief resident, as he had promised.

Blaine continued, "As I said, on individual cases, your performance looks all right. But the pattern is consistent. Longer than average stays, many complications, and documentation problems. And at night, many complications involving other doctor's patients."

Maggie clenched her fists. Yes, she frequently did have to

take care of patients who "crashed and burned" at night. Was that her fault? Or their doctors' fault for failing to notice the 6 p.m. fever of 104?

Blaine paused. "Again, I am just going by the pattern. But I think it is only fair to let you know about our concern."

"What should I do?" Maggie said quietly.

"Well, for starters," Blaine said, pulling his chair up to the terminal, "you could try calling up the quality of care criteria for each of your patients' diagnoses, and making sure that you have documented adherence to the criteria." He demonstrated with Mr. Post's diagnosis.

Maggie wanted to protest that the criteria didn't exactly apply to Mr. Post. But her opinion wasn't worth much, it would appear. She was only the doctor. Blaine wrote down the sequence of commands for her, reminding her—somewhat condescendingly—that they were also to be found in the intern's manual.

"I'm really hoping that you will improve," Blaine told her. "We want all our interns to succeed."

"Thanks," Maggie mumbled, as he opened the door for her.

• • •

"Dr. Altman, Dr. Margaret Altman, call 2824." Oh no, Maggie groaned. Why at 4 p.m., when I'm just about to go off call?

"Hello, Maggie," Brent Stemmons' voice said cheerfully. "I haven't seen you for ages."

"Several days, anyway," Maggie said.

"Seems like ages. And it's been only business for the past couple of weeks. Well, I do have a patient for you—a bounceback—Mr. Turpin, a lunger that you discharged 7 days ago. He's back in with wheezing. I'm afraid he needs to come in again."

Maggie sighed. Another blot on her record. Up for automatic review because of readmission within 14 days. A premature discharge.

"I know it's not very exciting," Brent apologized. "But it

does give me a chance to see you. And how about a quick cup of coffee while they're doing his paperwork? Meet you in the cafeteria."

"OK," Maggie said. She was more than a little glad that she would get to see Brent. It would be nice to think about something besides work for a few minutes.

• • •

Brent paid for the coffee, and carried it to the table for her.

"I'm worried about you," he said, looking at her in concern. The sight of a friendly face was too much for her, and her tears started to flow. Damn, she said angrily to herself, not here!

He moved his chair a little closer to her, and took her hand. "Maggie, what's the matter?"

"I had to go to see the chief resident today," Maggie told him, trying to blink away the tears. "It seems that I'm not doing very well."

Brent looked perplexed. "That's ridiculous," he said. "Everybody can tell what a good doctor you are. What is he talking about?"

"The statistics," Maggie said. "You know, the UR/QAC profile."

"Oh, that," Brent said.

"Maybe I'm just getting paranoid from lack of sleep," Maggie said, "but it almost seems that Blaine has it in for me."

"Hmm," Brent said thoughtfully, "why do you think that is?"

"Well," Maggie said, "I'm becoming more and more convinced that something is going on here. I don't know what it is yet. But I intend to find out."

"Oh," Brent said, looking at her intently. "What has happened?"

"Dr. Miltown, Dr. Everett Miltown, call 2262," interrupted the page operator.

Maggie considered whether now was the time to tell him

about what she discovered at Dr. Silber's house. But she had to see Mr. Turpin, and Brent probably was preoccupied with his responsibilities as Pit Boss.

"It's a little complicated," she said. "I'm not sure we have time now."

"Well, I do have to get back to the Pit," Brent replied. "And you have that patient to see also. Why don't I call you sometime soon?"

"All right," Maggie said.

"Maybe this weekend," Brent added.

Maggie smiled. Well, there was at least something to look forward to.

Brent excused himself to go to the men's room, and Maggie found a bed for Mr. Turpin. Fortunately, he wasn't all that sick. It wouldn't take long to get him settled for the night.

$$\bullet \ \bullet \ \bullet$$

"Yes, he is wheezing a little more today," Maggie told Mrs. Post. "But I still think he'll be able to go home by the end of the week." Mrs. Post seemed to be reassured.

Maggie signed out to Charlie Fischbein, then stopped by the call room to pick up her survival bag. It was 7 p.m. More than 36 hours since she had entered the building. And no sleep at all, if one didn't count the naps on the elevator. On the way out, she heard herself being paged again. It was a long way to the nearest telephone, and she was so tired she could barely focus her eyes. Besides, she had already signed out. To hell with it, she said, and headed straight home to bed.

Chapter 27

It was only 6 a.m. Most interns would not arrive for at least an hour. Anticipating a little peace and quiet in the doctor's station, Maggie hoped to get caught up on some paperwork.

The elevator doors opened onto the sixth floor, and Sister Mary Patrice stepped aside as Maggie got off. "Good morning, Doctor," she said, with an otherworldly smile.

"Good morning, Sister," Maggie replied, as the doors closed on the little woman wearing the old fashioned white veil. Maggie had a sinking feeling. The chaplain would not be making rounds at this hour unless something bad had happened.

As she passed the conference room, Maggie learned the reason for Sister's visit. Mrs. Post was inside, sobbing.

"What happened?" Maggie asked, sitting down beside her. She knew the answer to her own question, but didn't want to believe it.

"He . . . died," she said. "Last night he was fine, except that his mouth was drooping a bit . . . And he told me he thought he was having a small stroke because his left side felt weak." Guiltily, Maggie remembered the page she hadn't answered last night. Could that have been about Mr. Post? She tried to tell herself that it wouldn't have made any difference.

Mrs. Post blew her nose, and continued. "They called me an hour ago. By the time I got here, he was gone . . . The doctor said he hemorrhaged." She buried her face in a tissue. "I don't understand . . . He was almost well."

Maggie sat with the old woman in silence for a while. What could she say? "I'd like to speak with Dr. Fischbein, and find out exactly what happened. Would you like me to come back and talk to you?"

Mrs. Post nodded, and continued to sob.

Maggie intercepted the chart in the doctor's station, just as it was about to be sent to the morgue. The nurse's note said that the patient had developed a mild left-sided paralysis. Another complication, just as he was ready to be discharged! He would have had to stay longer—UR/QAC wouldn't have been pleased about that. But simple strokes weren't very often fatal. Had he had a hemorrhage? Maggie was sure that the pro-thrombin time had been under excellent control. She checked the lab notes again. Of course, he might still have bled. But at least her dose of anticoagulants had been correct. She turned to the doctor's progress notes. Charlie Fischbein had written tersely: "Left sided weakness. CT scan showed extensive sub-dural hematoma. Prognosis poor. Patient found pulseless at 0500. Pupils were fixed and dilated, and patient felt cool. He was pronounced dead at 0503. Family refused autopsy."

Maggie stared unseeing at the chart for a time. Well, it made perfect sense. He needed the blood thinners for the blood clot in his lung. But they had apparently caused him to bleed into his head. Even with normal blood pressure, and careful control of the dose. Tragic, but an unavoidable risk of treatment.

Still, there was something that didn't seem right. Maggie reread the nurse's note and recalled what Mrs. Post had told her. The patient had complained of difficulty using his left hand. That meant he must have been alert. Whereas patients with subdurals usually became confused before they developed other signs. He could have deteriorated rapidly. But why hadn't Charlie gotten a neurosurgical consult?

Reluctantly, Maggie returned to speak with Mrs. Post.

"Apparently, he did hemorrhage," she said.

"He was on that blood thinner," Mrs. Post said.

"Yes," Maggie said. "But his blood wasn't too thin. We checked it just yesterday."

"I don't blame anybody," Mrs. Post said sadly. "You did all you could."

"Well," Maggie said. "I think that we did. But I feel I don't completely understand why this happened. I really would like to be sure of the diagnosis." She could see that Mrs. Post looked more distressed, anticipating the next question. "Sometimes, you know, it helps the next patient."

"I just don't want to put him through any more

137

suffering," Mrs. Post said.

"He won't suffer any more now," Maggie said quietly.

"But I don't want him cut up," Mrs. Post sobbed, looking in her purse for another tissue. "I want him to have a decent Christian burial." She looked quite panic-stricken. What did she think they wanted to do?

"Of course," Maggie said. "But I wonder if you would allow us to do an autopsy first. The pathologist and I would just take a look inside. It really doesn't delay the arrangements for long. And that way we could be sure we understand why he died. We might learn something that will help us treat someone else."

Mrs. Post looked doubtful. "You would be there?"

"Of course," Maggie said.

She shook her head. "I just want him to be left in peace. And to have a decent burial."

"And he will," Maggie said. Mrs. Post probably didn't understand about autopsies. Maggie wondered how she could tactfully find out what the woman was worried about.

"The Sister said he didn't need to have an autopsy," Mrs. Post volunteered, "and that they could go ahead and make arrangements for a funeral unless I wanted to sign that form."

Surely Sister Mary Patrice understood the importance of autopsies, Maggie thought. The chaplains had always reassured the patients' families about the procedure. But this chaplain certainly wasn't explaining things very clearly. Apparently, she had given Mrs. Post the idea that her husband couldn't be properly buried afterward!

"That's right," Maggie said, "he doesn't have to have an autopsy. But it doesn't affect the funeral arrangements at all. Really. People can come to visit him, and they won't even be able to tell."

"Oh," Mrs. Post said. "Well, if it won't hurt him, and if you think it might help somebody else, of course I'd like for him to have one."

"I really think it's important," Maggie assured her. "And I'll be glad to call you to let you know what we find, if you like."

"I'd appreciate that," Mrs. Post said. She signed the form.

"Let me call someone to help you make the arrangements," Maggie suggested.

"Thank you," Mrs. Post said. She seemed to have recovered her composure a little. "And just one more thing, Doctor. Mr. Post wanted to donate his eyes. He was a Lion, and they have a special program for that. I called the Lions' Eye Bank, and they said to put some ice in a glove and place it on his eyes, until they could get here. The autopsy won't interfere with that, will it?"

"No, of course not," Maggie said. "And I'm glad you thought of that."

"Mr. Post told me that the doctors usually forget," Mrs. Post said. "He made me promise to take care of it." Maggie nodded sadly. It seemed unfair that nice people like Mr. Post were usually the ones to die too young.

There didn't seem to be anything else Maggie could do for Mrs. Post. Now she had to call pathology about the autopsy consent, and dictate the death summary. Guiltily, she remembered the page once again. What if the patient had been examined sooner? Charlie apparently hadn't gotten the scan done until early morning. It hadn't even been ordered "stat"; it was surprising that X ray hadn't postponed it until the next day, or the day after. During the night, Mr. Post might have drifted, unobserved, into coma, as the blood put pressure on his brain. Surgery might have saved him. If only she had been there!

• • •

"Say, Maggie," Charlie Fischbein dropped a cigarette butt into the remains of his coffee, "one of yours expired last night. Bled into his head."

"Yes, I know," Maggie replied. "There'll be an autopsy."

"Nah," Charlie contradicted her. "The wife refused. Don't need one anyway. I got the CT scan. Sutton's Law."

"Sutton's Law?" Maggie asked.

"The money was in the head," Charlie said. He returned her blank expression with a look of disdain. "Don't you know about Willie Sutton, who robbed banks because that's where the money is?"

"Oh," she said. So that's why Stuart Collins frequently advised them to "go where the money is" when deciding which lab tests to order first. She had assumed that "money" or "paydirt" meant a brilliant diagnosis. Although she was beginning to suspect that it just meant money these days. They were trying to save money by looking for the most likely diagnosis first. It sounded callous, but economics was a fact of life. She supposed Charlie was right—the diagnosis was on the CT scan. Well, there would be an autopsy anyway in this case. Even if it did cost the hospital money. She wanted to ask Charlie more about the clinical findings, but he was already halfway down the hall.

• • •

"Code Purple. Code Purple," the page operator announced. Maggie asked Fred to make apologies for her at rounds, and headed for the basement. There were no signs pointing the way to the morgue, and she made a few wrong turns before she found it. The door was locked. A placard hanging from a hook invited her to press the buzzer.

"Who is there?" a deep voice wanted to know.

"Dr. Altman."

"Just a moment." Maggie waited several minutes, then a white smocked diener opened the door and led her to the autopsy table. Yes, that was Mr. Post on the table. No, his body. The yellow flesh had a translucent, waxy appearance. The body cavities were already opened with a Y-shaped incision, and a stream of water washed the fluids through a hole in the stainless steel table to a drain in the floor. Dr. Metzenbaum, gloved and wearing a brown plastic apron over his white coat, was weighing the liver in a scale like the ones in the produce department at the grocery story.

"Good morning, Dr. Altman," he said. A sepulchral voice, she thought. "This was your patient, I presume."

Maggie nodded.

"Welcome to the altar of truth." Metzenbaum dictated a

description of the liver into a tape recorder, and proceeded to remove the spleen. "Perhaps you could present the clinical history."

As Maggie reviewed the events of the past month, Metzenbaum continued with his work, occasionally nodding, or interrupting to dictate a comment to his recorder.

She finished the story as Metzenbaum started to examine the lungs. "Some emphysema," he said. With an enormous knife, he sliced the left lung on a cutting board. "See the blebs." Maggie moved a little closer to look. She had found herself backing up because of the odor. "But no sign of pneumonia at present. Or of clots, for that matter."

"He seemed to be over his pneumonia," Maggie said.

"Hmmm," Metzenbaum continued. "An unexpected death. We'd better take a close look at the heart." He opened the coronary arteries, and sliced the heart muscle. "Look at those coronaries. Quite clean for a man his age. Well, he could have had spasm. How long does it take to see a myocardial infarction at autopsy?"

Maggie thought for a moment. "About 24 hours, I think."

"Close," Metzenbaum said. "Up until about 12 hours, you may see nothing more than perhaps a slight pallor. It takes an electron microscope to see the structural changes. So he could have had a heart attack, which we would miss." Maggie nodded. "So far, we haven't found the cause of death."

"Well, I guess we weren't expecting to find it in his chest," Maggie said.

Metzenbaum fixed her with his penetrating gaze. "At the autopsy, we look for the unexpected," he growled.

"Yes, Dr. Metzenbaum," Maggie agreed.

The internal organs had all been examined. The diener would sew up the incision later. Now, he was pulling the scalp down over the patient's face, exposing the skull. Maggie steeled herself for the sound of the bone saw, which would open the top of the cranium.

"What skull deformity does this patient have?" Metzenbaum asked.

"Cranial synostosis," Maggie said, "from premature

closure of the coronal sutures."

"Very good," Metzenbaum said. "You did a complete physical examination. What were the clinical findings on the day before death?"

"The nurse's notes reported that the patient complained of a left-sided weakness. And his wife said his mouth was drooping," Maggie responded.

"Any headache?"

"I don't know," Maggie admitted.

"Vomiting?"

"They didn't mention any."

"Physical exam?" Metzenbaum continued.

"Well," Maggie said with embarrassment, "I didn't see one on the chart. And I wasn't there last night."

"Hmmf," Metzenbaum snorted in disapproval. "Level of consciousness? Signs of herniation? Blood pressure?"

"I guess they weren't recorded," Maggie said, feeling disgraced. "Or else I just missed them when I reviewed the chart. The only thing I saw was the result of the CT scan."

"They just sent this patient down to X ray?" Metzenbaum fumed. "Without even checking the neuro signs?"

"It looks that way."

"And the CT scan report?"

"Subdural hematoma," Maggie said.

The diener lifted off the top of the skull, and stepped aside. Maggie couldn't believe what she saw.

"Damn shadow docs," Metzenbaum said, contemptuously. "Those radiologists think they know everything. Look at this brain, Doctor," he commanded Maggie. "Do you see a hemorrhage? Or any displacement of the midline?"

"No," Maggie had to admit.

"Neither do I. Well, we'll cut it in a week. After it's been fixed. I suspect we'll find a stroke." Metzenbaum looked at her intently. "The cause of death is unknown, Doctor," he said. "And I suggest that the clinical record is not adequate."

Maggie had to agree with him. It was humiliating. Mr. Post had been her patient, even though she hadn't been on call that night.

"The microscopics take time," Metzenbaum informed her. "The final report will be out in about six weeks. I'll see that you get a copy of it."

The diener had removed the brain to place it in a jar of fixative. Then he would replace the skull, and suture the scalp back over it. Maggie looked away. She was beginning to feel sick. She wanted nothing more than to escape from this gruesome place.

. . .

Maggie decided to take the stairs. Maybe a brisk walk would make her feel a little better. And she should stop by the X ray Department. She needed to have a look at those films.

As she opened the door to the stairwell, someone jumped back out of the way. Stephen Blaine. Maggie wondered what his errand could be in the basement. She had just passed by a nurse from one of the medical floors too—she thought she recognized the elaborate coiffure topped by a pert white cap. Could Blaine be chasing nurses? Unlikely. He didn't seem human enough.

"Was that your Code Purple?" Blaine asked brusquely.

"Yes."

"I heard about the death at morning report. Iatrogenic complication, no doubt." Blaine sounded as though he thought it was her fault. "Do you know how much a Code Purple costs the hospital?" he asked.

"No," Maggie replied.

"At least $2500," he informed her. "Unreimbursed. Now I've heard the propaganda about the importance of autopsies. But with our modern imaging techniques, they're really outdated. Better we should utilize our limited resources to take care of patients. And to make the diagnosis while the patients are alive," he concluded pointedly.

"But . . . " Maggie started to tell him about the results of the autopsy.

"Instead of being wasteful," he interrupted. Maggie thought better of arguing with him. In any case, he had already slammed the door behind him.

. . .

"Look at the log yourself," the girl at the desk told her, pushing it in Maggie's direction. Clearly, she was annoyed at being interrupted in the middle of a personal telephone conversation.

"I don't see his name either," Maggie persisted. "But I know that the films were done this morning. Otherwise, how could we have gotten a report on the results?"

"Oh, all right," the girl said, pushing back her flamboyant blonde curls. Debbie, according to her name tag. "I'll look in the file." Maggie followed her back into the file room. She checked the box of unread films first, then went to the alphabetical file. She pulled out an envelope and handed it to Maggie. She actually looked surprised to have found them, Maggie thought.

"Thank you," Maggie said, and took the films to the nearest viewbox. There it was. The diagnosis was obvious, even to someone inexperienced in interpreting CT scans. A large density between the skull and the left cerebral hemisphere pushed the midline structures to one side. The structures were compressed and distorted. She stared at the film for a while. Methodically, she checked the name and the date: Frank L. Post, September 19.

She shook her head. It just didn't make sense. This should have shown up at the autopsy. She would take these films to Dr. Metzenbaum.

"Where are you going with those films?" Debbie demanded, toddling after her in high heeled sandals.

"To show the pathologist," Maggie replied.

"Films are not allowed to leave the department," Debbie informed her peremptorily.

Maggie wondered where they all went, in that case. About half the time, they couldn't be located. Well, these films were going downstairs. No file clerk was going to stop her.

Chapter 28

Hands clasped behind his back, Silber stared moodily out the living room window. It was barely dawn. Mid September already, he thought. Fall aways depresses him. It had been September when he left Woodlands, and September when Marsha had left him. He sighed heavily. That was in the past, though—surely he had no reason to feel depressed this September. After all, he had just completed the latest issue of *The Silber Report*. His weekly market advisory tape had only an hour ago been placed on his answering machine, and already the phone was ringing steadily in the back room. The *Fort Bastion Morning News* had sent a pretty young thing out to interview him for a series they were running on finance and investment. And last month he had acquired half a dozen new subscribers to his service. He sighed again. I'll go out, he decided. Take that floppy disk over to the typesetter instead of downloading it onto their machine. Check with my mail service. Maybe even get a haircut. He snorted, recalling that he had promised to let the lady journalist come back and take some photos to use with her article. Then perhaps he'd stop in at Goldblum's for some of their onion bagels and Mrs. Goldblum's wonderful coffee. He began to feel more optimistic. Maybe he'd continue on downtown and drop in on Jake. He chuckled a little, recalling the night of the snails. Yes, that's what he'd do. He stretched, and scratched at his beard which was beginning to look positively rabbinic. Maybe a trim would be in order, too. Why not? If he didn't soon attend to himself, he'd look as mangy as Keynes. Cheer up, old man, he told himself. There's no point in worrying about Stevens' expedition to Delaware. He'll find what he'll find, and you'll deal with it when you know what it is. Sighing, he headed for the bathroom.

. . .

"Food!" Metzenbaum said in amazement, as Silber

145

spread the feast out on his desk. "Goldblum's onion bagels. Cream cheese. And coffee!" He groaned. "Milt, you may have saved my life. I sneaked out of the house this morning before Ellen was up. She had planned to feed me some middle eastern glop for breakfast—curdled goat's milk with amaranth. I couldn't face it. But I was so overcome with guilt that I couldn't bring myself to stop anywhere for breakfast. I don't know what's come over her, Milt."

Silber spread cream cheese on a sliced bagel and offered it to Metzenbaum. His friend accepted it reverently, chewing and swallowing with eyes closed as if in some private communion.

"Whatever's come over her," he told Metzenbaum, "it's likely to be the end of you. Look at you for God's sake—you look like a wraith! Amaranth. Really, Jake."

Metzenbaum lowered his eyes in embarrassment. "I know. Maybe I shouldn't indulge her. But this thing with gastronomy began just after Lisa went away to college. The empty nest, I guess." He shrugged. "It gives her something to do. She'll snap out of it sooner or later." He took another bite of bagel. "Sooner, I hope."

"Hmmf," Silber said, disapproving. "Have you made up your mind about your job offer yet?"

Metzenbaum frowned. "No. Not yet."

"You'd be crazy to pass it up," Silber told him. "What's keeping you here?"

"Beats me," Metzenbaum told him. "Maybe someone has to fight the good fight. You know," he grinned, "I did an autopsy yesterday. First one in weeks. That young intern Maggie Altman snatched the body right out of Sister Mary Patrice's clutches."

Silber burst out laughing. "That would've been something to see! Maggie Altman versus the Forces of Good. What did they do? Arm wrestle for it? The good sister is as tenacious as a Gila monster, so I've heard."

"I don't know how she did it," Metzenbaum chuckled. "But I don't think they went head to head. I would have liked to see that damned nun's face when she realized she'd been thwarted, though."

Silber wiped his eyes. The thought of Maggie Altman wrestling Sister Mary Patrice for a dead body sent him into snorts of laughter again. Finally he calmed himself and grabbed the last bagel before it disappeared into Metzenbaum's maw. His friend lit up a cigar, offered one to Silber, and they both sat in companionable silence, puffing and musing.

"Given any more thought to your financial future, Jake? You said you would."

"Nope," Metzenbaum replied.

"Time's a wasting, my friend. When all this," he gestured to the hospital above them, "comes figuratively crashing down, what will you do?"

Metzenbaum shrugged. "I like to think that I'll have enough brains not to be here. I have to tell the city yes or no by the end of the month. I'm still thinking about it." He held up his hand to stem Silber's tide of comments. "I know the ship is going down—I just haven't decided which way to jump. I don't have the head for business you have."

"Hmmf," Silber replied. Well, if his friend stubbornly refused to look the future in the eye, what business was it of his? One could only do so much.

Chapter 29

Maggie frowned as she descended the stairs to Pathology. She didn't know whether Dr. Metzenbaum would care or not. He apparently didn't think much of the new imaging technology. But pathologists were supposed to look at the premortem record, to correlate the autopsy findings, weren't they? And this one would be pretty hard to correlate. The blood, as far as she could tell, was not buried deep in the brain; it was right under the table of the skull. On the left.

Maggie paused in the middle of the flight of stairs. Mr. Post's symptoms had been on the left. So the blood should have been on the right. Well, maybe she had put the films up backward. She would have to recheck the markers.

The door to the morgue was unlocked, now that the Code Purple was over, and Maggie quietly stepped inside. She didn't know exactly where Dr. Metzenbaum's private office was; perhaps behind the closed door just beyond the autopsy room. She was about to knock, when the sound of raucous laughter came from within, ending in a paroxysm of coughing.

Maggie could detect the odor of cigar smoke. And the voice was familiar. Dr. Silber?

"What good would it do, Milt?" Metzenbaum asked. "It might make you feel better, but it wouldn't change anything in the long run. Eisig will take the credit if this scheme succeeds. But it's sure to be someone else's fault if it comes crashing down."

Maggie wondered just what Dr. Silber had suggested. Clearly, this conversation was not meant to be overheard. Maggie had a momentary desire to slip away, but she was determined to find out what was going on. Was Silber really trying to destroy Dr. Eisig's reputation? Silber was so embittered that she had never heard him speak of the mild-mannered, dedicated Dr. Eisig without hostility. And as to the demise of EquaCare, was Silber trying to engineer it?

She wouldn't learn the answer today. The conversation was interrupted by the sound of metal scraping against metal and a stream of expletives from across the hall. Alarmed, Maggie fled into the autopsy room. The odor of death still hung on the air, but Mr. Post's body had been removed, and the stainless steel table had been cleaned and polished. She pressed herself against the wall nearest Metzenbaum's office.

Footsteps, two men probably, crossed the hall, and fists pounded on Metzenbaum's door.

"Business is good today, Doc," a loud voice said. "We brought ya another stiff. If you'll just sign the ticket, we'll put 'im in the cooler."

Maggie could hear a pen scratching on a clipboard. "Number 12?" a different voice asked.

"That should be fine," Metzenbaum responded. His office door closed again, and feet clumped across the hall. From the sounds, Maggie visualized a corpse being shoved into one of the lockers that lined the wall of the morgue. Then elevator doors opened and closed. The service elevator around the corner from the ER had a set of back doors, she had noticed. Maggie shivered a little. Evidently it was designed to deliver the bodies directly to the morgue.

"Jake, you old body snatcher," Dr. Silber said, laughing again. "And you don't want to get your hands dirty in the stock market!"

"Have to pay the bills somehow," Metzenbaum responded.

Maggie felt shocked. Just what was Metzenbaum willing to do, in order to make money? She shook her head in disbelief. She wouldn't have been inclined to suspect the pathologist. But his very immunity from questioning made him a prime suspect. He was isolated from public view, down here in his basement. Nobody even liked to think about what went on in his domain. And in medicine, the pathologist was the one with the final word. Who would ever question a path report? The pathologist, like the police detective, was always on the side of the law. But something wasn't right at TU, and it seemed that something pretty strange was going on in Pathology too. And hadn't she seen Dr. Silber lurking around the morgue before? Dr. Silber, who claimed to have no interest in TU at all. Dr. Silber, who clearly wanted the TU experiment to fail, and Dr. Eisig to be ruined. True, she herself was not particularly fond of Dr. Eisig, and she didn't like the EquaCare system either. But that would not be an excuse for sabotaging it. And so many things were going wrong that one had to wonder about sabotage.

Well, Maggie could hardly walk into Dr. Metzenbaum's office with her packet of X rays now. And what if they found her, leaning against the wall of the autopsy room? She really didn't want to try to explain. Forcing herself not to run, she had just passed the service elevator when she heard him behind her.

"Dr. Altman?" The voice was Silber's. Pretending not to hear, she didn't turn around, but hurried down the hall to the stairwell. To her relief, no one followed.

Chapter 30

It was 2300 hours. Bedtime for most people. Maggie sighed. She'd just had another page to the ER.

The youth who was sharing the elevator with her—Ned, according to his nametag—grinned. She often saw him around. An FLK—"funny-looking kid"—with a high forehead and a long narrow skull. Maggie couldn't remember what syndrome that was. He was from the Sheltered Workshop, she supposed. Placing such workers at TU was one of Dr. Eisig's pet projects.

"Hello, Doc," the youth said.

"Hello," Maggie replied. "You always work nights, don't you?"

"Yup."

"Did you work last night?" Maggie asked.

"Sure. I come every night. Except Sunday," he told her proudly.

On an impulse, she decided to ask about Mr. Post. "Do you remember taking a Mr. Post for a CT scan yesterday morning early?"

Ned looked at her blankly. Of course, how would he know the patient's name? "From 6 East," she added. "About 4:00."

"Yup. I go to 6 East," Ned nodded vigorously.

Maggie smiled at him. What did she hope to learn from the orderly, she wondered. One couldn't expect him to do a physical exam. This one might not even notice whether or not the patient was alive.

"You have a good night now, Doc." Ned maneuvered his empty stretcher out of the elevator onto the fourth floor. It had a large sign on it that said "4W." Probably to remind him of where he was going, she speculated.

• • •

"Dr. Blaine, Dr. Stephen Blaine, outside call," the page operator said, as Maggie wearily headed for the doctor's station. And there was Dr. Blaine, sitting at the terminal she had planned to use to record the history and physical—or data base, as they now called it—on her most recent patient. It was midnight. Maggie wondered when the chief resident ever slept. Blaine reached for the telephone, but appeared to stop in mid motion when he saw Maggie. Evidently, he decided to use a different phone.

"Excuse me," he said, brushing past her.

Well, she thought irritably, she would have to find a free terminal, because Blaine was in the middle of something. She couldn't help noticing what it was. A book of diagnostic codes was open on the desk, and a simple list of commands was on the screen. SEARCH PROBLEM LIST. A cue to enter the diagnosis code. A menu that included "all inpatients." And LIST ID,LOC. Hmmm, Maggie thought. This might be easier than looking at the ER log for cases for her study. Why hadn't she thought of using the computer before? She jotted down the commands.

"Dr. Miltown, Dr. Everett Miltown, call 2262," the page operator droned. Not the ER, Maggie noted gratefully. Dr. Miltown, whoever he was, wasn't getting an admission, so she wasn't up for another one yet.

• • •

Sunrise over the TU parking lot, viewed through the grimy window of the tenth floor laboratory, was not a particularly inspiring sight, Maggie thought. She put aside the slides of Gram-stained sputum from her early morning admission, and stretched a little. Her eyes were stinging, and her back ached. But the gray morning light had evidently informed her biological clock that it was daytime. She really wasn't sleepy enough to nap for half an hour.

And nobody would be waiting to use the computer terminal in the doctor's station. Maggie decided to try out the procedure she had seen Blaine using last night—maybe the access number of a mere intern wouldn't work, but it would be worth a try.

• • •

Patient Matthew Portman had been admitted this very morning, the computer said, but he was not in his neatly made-up bed. A green washbasin holding a box of tissues, a urinal, and a towel remained sealed in plastic wrappings on the bedside table. If Maggie wanted to ask him any questions, she'd have to try to come back later. And there were some interesting features in his history. She hardly hoped to find the answers in the chart, but it wouldn't hurt to look.

"Can I help you, Doctor?" asked someone who was looking over her shoulder. Caroline, her nametag said. Was she the nurse who had been with Dr. Blaine in the basement yesterday? Not very many nurses wore caps these days, and Caroline's was certainly distinctive. Maggie pushed the unprofessional suspicion aside.

"I was looking for Mr. Portman," Maggie explained. "He isn't in his bed."

"He's in X ray," Caroline informed her, "but who are you?"

"I'm Maggie Altman. I don't believe we've met."

Caroline ignored her extended hand, and Maggie felt herself shrinking a little under the woman's hostile stare.

"You're not Mr. Portman's doctor," Caroline announced.

"No," Maggie said. "I'm doing a research project. A chart review of . . ."

"You have no right to read this," Caroline interrupted her, scooping up the chart and replacing it on the rack. "The medical record is confidential, Doctor, in case you have forgotten."

Maggie stared at her, dumbfounded. Well, there was no point in arguing with this woman, Maggie decided. Even though it seemed that anyone in the hospital with a computer access number could read any record any time. Maggie wondered what Caroline's problem was and resolved not to get angry. She would just go for breakfast and coffee. Food usually quieted the unpleasant sensation in her stomach.

• • •

Someone had intended to create a cheerful atmosphere with a random assortment of brightly colored chairs. But in Maggie's opinion they only accentuated the shabbiness of the TU cafeteria, with its peeling wallpaper and chipped, dirty gray floor tile. She took her tray to a small table by the window, which offered a scenic view of the expressway. Traffic was already heavy. Thankfully, the shifts hadn't changed yet, so the cafeteria was still relatively quiet.

"Mornin', Doc." Ned greeted her cheerfully, placing his tray on the table next to hers. He favored her with a wide smile.

"Good morning, Ned." Maggie returned the smile. "Busy night?"

"No, ma'am. Nuthin' to do all night long." Ned shook his head back and forth emphatically.

"Nobody needed an X ray?"

"Nope. Not on my route."

"You got some rest then."

"Boring, boring, boring." Ned continued shaking his head.

"Ned, stretcher to 6 West please," a metallic voice squawked, and Maggie started. Ned jumped up, patting the beeper on his belt with a look of satisfaction.

"Gotta go Doc," he said. He set off with a purposeful stride. Evidently, he took his work very seriously.

Maggie stirred her Malt-o-meal thoughtfully. Her brain was dull and unfocused after a sleepless night. But something didn't make sense. She was sure it wasn't just her imagination. Ned hadn't taken anyone to X ray all night, he said. Yet 6 West was clearly on his route. Might he simply have forgotten? Or had Caroline been confused when she had told her that Mr. Portman was in X ray? Maggie had not checked the bathroom, she had to admit. Or the lounge. The patient might have gone for a smoke. And there was something else. The patient's name had been in

154

the computer, but not on the ER log. She had checked the book on her last trip to the Pit. And no interns had been paged to the ER after her last admission. She would surely have noticed that. Maggie swore at her own dullness. She hadn't even noticed which doctor's name had been on the spine of the chart.

"Dr. Altman, Dr. Margaret Altman, call 2379," the page operator said. That would be 10 East. What now, Maggie wondered.

• • •

She would have to wait for the next elevator, Maggie thought impatiently, as she saw the doors close on Ned's back. For a moment, his narrow skull was framed by the doors.

Maggie caught her breath, and felt her heart contract. The idea that had struck her was terrifying.

Until now, she had had only a vague hunch that something was wrong with Mr. Post's CT scan, besides the absence of the hematoma at autopsy. Now, she could have absolutely no doubt about it. Mr. Post had had an abnormal skull too, except that his was flattened from front to back, instead of from side to side as Ned's was. But the films had shown a normal cranium! The labels for right and left could have been accidentally reversed, but there was no way to change the shape of the skull.

Those films could not have belonged to Mr. Post.

Could his films have been mixed up with those of another patient? Was a patient sitting on the ward somewhere with a huge, unrecognized subdural? Or had he already died of it? A year ago such gross incompetence would have seemed unthinkable. Now Maggie was ready to believe it could happen.

The alternate explanation was even more incredible. Who would have switched the films deliberately? Had Charlie done so, to hide his mismanagement of the case? Not likely. She doubted that he would be so clever. But suppose someone had had a stronger motive. Concealment of a homicide, for example. But who would want to kill Mr. Post? As far as she knew, he lived in quiet retirement with his wife. He was too disabled to get around much. He had such a pleasant personality that it was difficult to imagine anyone being angry with him. And he was on EquaCare because of being medically needy. Unlikely that anyone was in a hurry to receive an inheritance.

With a start, Maggie realized that she had been so engrossed in thought that she had missed the elevator.

Chapter 31

"What now?" he demanded irritably. "We talked just a few days ago. Surely you can't have expected a miracle so soon?" He was tired, anxious and depressed. And didn't give a damn if the caller was put off by his manner. Who did he think he was, anyhow? Oh, sure, he was the "boss" of this operation, but who was down here in the trenches, on the front line, making sure everything ran smoothly? Oh no, not him. Well, maybe it was time to remind him who really did the work around here.

"No, I don't," the caller replied. "But it seems there's been another development."

He groaned. What now? "Well, can't you handle it? I've got enough to do."

The caller laughed. "My young friend, this is something you said you'd take care of."

"I don't understand. Get to the point."

"It's Dr. Altman."

"So?" He hesitated, stalling for time. "I'm doing my best. It's not my fault that she turned out to be such a pain in the ass!"

"She's a troublesome type, I agree. When you've had a little more experience, you'll know how to spot them. She really has no business being here. Her DRG profile is way out of line. She's unable to take direction, and she's costing the hospital a small fortune. In itself, that is not an unmanageable problem. We can compensate in other ways. That's why, up until now, I've been willing to let you handle matters in your own way."

"But now there's something else?"

The caller sighed. "I'm afraid so. Someone has been making unauthorized incursions into several of the computer's data bases. I was unable to pin down the ID until last night when someone queried the patient record data base for all inpatients. The ID belonged to Dr. Altman. It seems she's looking for something."

"Looking for what? She can't possibly know anything about us."

"Probably not. But she's intelligent and persistent. And if she keeps snooping around in the data base, she's bound to put two and two together, whether she suspects something or not."

"Well, I'm doing what I can. But I can't keep her from using the computer. Unless you have some ideas."

"Oh yes. I have several ideas. But let's try this one first—it's less drastic than the others. I think she should be discouraged from her current career choice. Didn't she come from research? Well, redirect her career path. Encourage her to go back there. And be persuasive. It would be much better for everyone if she decided to leave Woodlands. Pardon me, TU."

He sighed, feeling a now-familiar depression settle over him. In his own way, that's what he'd been trying to do. "All right."

"But remember—you have until the end of the month to call Dr. Altman off. I don't know how you think you're going to effect a change in her, but if she stays here, her attitude and her performance will have to be much different. Frankly, I don't think you can do it."

"Well, give me a chance! You're wrong. She can be brought around."

The caller made a skeptical noise. "We'll see. And if your scheme doesn't work, there are always other solutions. Ones I'm prepared to undertake. This is serious business, my young friend. I have no intentions of letting one idealistic young woman ruin everything."

. . .

He massaged his aching temples and tried hard not to give way to the panic that threatened to engulf him. This mess really was all Maggie Altman's fault. Things had been going so well before she came. Damned interfering woman! And now there was this business with the computer. What in hell could she have been looking for? Well, his efforts had better start to pay off. And soon. Otherwise, he'd have to let the boss dispose of the problem. That cold-blooded bastard would do it too. No question about it. Just like he'd disposed of Mr. Post.

Chapter 32

Silber wiped his sweaty palms on the sides of his trousers and tried to control his breathing. You're likely to have a heart attack, you old fool, he chided himself. Calm down.

"There's Stevens," Ryan Fitzhugh said, peering through the bar's window. "Let's go in, Milt."

Silber bared his teeth in what he hoped would pass for a smile and followed Fitzhugh into the noisy, crowded interior. As the door swung shut behind him, he groaned. The interior reverberated to the raucous squawks and thumps of punk rock. Although a few of the patrons seemed normal—secretaries, office boys and mail clerks from the Twin Towers across the street—most of the clientele gave the impression of having just beamed down from another, more benighted planet. One young woman with orange hair arranged in a bizarre crest resembling that of a hoopoe, winked suggestively at Silber. He blushed.

"Why on earth did we have to meet Stevens here?" he complained to Fitzhugh, who stepped aside to allow the hoopoe-haired girl to pass.

Fitzhugh shrugged. "It was Alan's choice. Ask him." He made his way to a table near the back where a young man with dark, curly hair and sunglasses, dressed in coveralls bearing the logo of the telephone company, sat over a cup of coffee. "Hi, Alan," he said, pulling out a chair. "Nice place you picked."

The young man took off his sunglasses and grinned at Fitzhugh. "We sleuths have to be careful not to blow our cover. Mingling with the natives is a must." He held his hand out to Silber. "I hear you're my employer. I'm Alan Stevens, Banque France's law clerk."

"Good God," Silber said, shuddering. "What kind of an education is Fitzhugh giving you?"

Fitzhugh chuckled. "Don't worry about Stevens' being corrupted. Before he went to law school and joined Banque

France, he was engaged in some pretty shady activities. He even taught me a thing or two. But he's turned over a new leaf, haven't you, Alan?" he said, elbowing his young associate.

Stevens smiled. "Definitely. I may not make as much money on your side of the law, Fitz, but, as you keep telling me, I'll sleep better at night." He looked at his watch. "Almost 6:00. The place should be deserted by now. But let me bring you both up to date on what I found out in Wilmington."

Silber stared. "You're back already? I thought you weren't going until next week. If at all."

"Surprise, Milt," Fitzhugh told him. "After our conversation last Friday, I asked Stevens to try his luck over the phone. No dice." He shrugged. "So I packed him off to Wilmington on the first flight. He just got back this morning. So, what did you find out, Alan?"

Stevens frowned. "There are five corporations. Four are shells. Each lists another corporation as incorporating stockholder, and gives that Market Street address in Wilmington—the agent's address. Except the last one. Harvey Consulting Corporation." He bent forward eagerly. "I knew I'd hit the jackpot when I found it. It gives the office tower across the street as the address of the incorporating stockholder. The stockholder's name is conveniently blurred." He passed a brown envelope across the table to Silber. "The information is all there. I made photocopies of everything. Then, when I got back here, I borrowed these coveralls and tools from a friend of mine and spent the day repairing phones on the 18th floor. During the four hours I spent in the hall, I didn't see one person enter or leave Suite 1805—the offices of Harvey Consulting Corporation. The phone rang a few times, and someone answered, or I thought they did, so I went downstairs and made a call myself." He shrugged. "All I got was an answering machine. 'Leave your name and number at the tone'—the usual thing. And that's all I can tell you." He yawned. "If you don't mind, I'd like to go home to bed. Didn't get a wink of sleep last night. Sleuthing is really tough work. I had to take the Wilmington agency's file clerk out to drinks, then to dinner, then to the disco, then—"

"—aargh!" Silber interjected. "Enough! Don't go on. I'd

prefer not to know in detail how you squandered my money."

"All right, then," Stevens said, standing up. "I'm off. See you in the morning, Fitz."

Silber watched Stevens until he left the bar. A most enterprising young man. Really! Fitzhugh did have some unusual acquaintances. Useful, though. He clutched the brown envelope. So Stevens had managed to run the corporation to the ground. But not without a certain amount of trouble. And not everyone could have extracted the information from the Wilmington agency's file clerk. He smiled a little. As he had thought when he had come across Ararat's name in the Woodlands financial data base—the parent company was very well hidden. A cursory search would never have turned up the Fort Bastion address—of that he was confident.

"So, what now?" Fitzhugh inquired.

"What? Oh, well, nothing I suppose."

Fitzhugh's eyebrows shot up. "Nothing? You must be joking, Milt. Don't you want to see what lurks behind Harvey's door? I haven't a clue about what you're up to, but I'm so curious that I know I can't go home without knowing more. Why don't we just pay Harvey a little visit?"

"Well, I don't think that's a very good idea." His mind raced. How was he going to call Fitzhugh off the scent? Without arousing his suspicions. Damn it to hell! He was just too curious. And too intelligent to be put off with some half-baked explanation.

Fitzhugh leaned over the table. "Let's go and see."

Silber couldn't think of anything to say to dissuade him.

• • •

"I really think you're making a mistake," Silber said in a hoarse whisper as the elevator deposited them on the 18th floor. "A big mistake."

Fitzhugh chuckled. "Relax, Milt. There's no one around. Who in his right mind works overtime?"

Unfortunate, Silber thought, looking around. Fitzhugh seemed to be right. The other offices on the floor appeared empty. Well, all wasn't lost yet. Perhaps someone would emerge from one of the offices, and Fitzhugh would lose his nerve. He knew he had lost his long ago. Damn! Where was the janitor? Or the night watchman? Would they really have to go through with this?

"Come on, Milt. Harvey is this way."

He padded disconsolately along after Fitzhugh, who seemed to regard the whole thing as a lark. Hmmf. Breaking and entering was a crime, wasn't it? He could just see the headlines in the *Fort Bastion Morning News*: "Prominent Financier Revealed to be Cat Burglar" or "The Secret Life of Milton Silber—Second Story Man." With his luck the news story would run in the same issue as the article lauding his financial acumen. He wondered idly if they would use the same pictures. Blast the luck! They had arrived—1805. All right, Silber—time to do something. Fitzhugh had to be called off—enough was enough. He took a deep breath.

"I've changed my mind," he told Fitzhugh. "I really don't want to know what's behind the door."

Fitzhugh spun around. "You're joking!"

"No. I'm quite serious. This has gone far enough. It's too risky. We have both our reputations to consider."

Fitzhugh grinned and rattled the knob of 1805. "The oversights of business always amaze me. They've probably got thousands of dollars of office equipment in there, and they're guarding it with a crummy $20 lock. This one would open with a sharp look." He took out his wallet and extracted a credit card. "Or a strip of rigid celluloid." Silber cringed. Fitzhugh knocked, and waited a few moments. "No one at home," he said. "Shall we try my key?"

"Wait!" Silber whispered. "What about an alarm systems? How can you possibly know there isn't one?"

Fitzhugh raised his eyebrows in surprise. "Stevens would have told us. He spent enought time mucking about with the phones—he would have found out."

Silber was suddenly unable to breathe. "Ohhhh . . . " he moaned, wishing he were dead.

Fitzhugh knelt in front of the door. "Move a little, will

you, Milt. Stand between me and the elevator. There, that's it."

Silber briefly considered dragging Fitzhugh bodily away from the door, but quickly abandoned the idea. The heaviest thing he had hefted in years was Keynes. Well, what else could he do? Clutch his heart? Swoon? No, that was out of the question. Too undignified. What, then? Quick, think! Silber put his hand to his head and groaned. He tried to swallow, but found his mouth suddenly dry. Abruptly, the elevator whirred into life, and he moaned in terror. Light-headed with relief, he watched it go on past to the 22nd floor. He felt his knees tremble, and experienced a sudden urge to visit the men's room. Fortunately, the feeling passed.

"Got it!" Fitzhugh exclaimed in satisfaction. He stood up and put away his credit card. "Be my guest."

Well, there seemed to be nothing for it but to continue this little performance to its end. For Fitzhugh's benefit, if nothing else. Taking a deep breath, he pushed the door open with his left hand, reaching with his right for the switch on the wall. He fumbled for a moment, then succeeded in turning on the lights.

"Well, I'll be damned!" Fitzhugh exclaimed. "This is crazy!"

Silber had to agree. Illuminated by the harsh fluorescent overhead light, the Fort Bastion office of Harvey Consulting Corporation yielded up its secrets. This company, the ultimate recipient of 1.3 million dollars paid to Ararat from the Texas University Regional Preventive Health Center, occupied, as one might expect, an address in the financial district's prestigious Twin Towers. A very spacious and expensive corner office. With a view of the river. But it was, save for a telephone and an answering machine on the floor near the windows, absolutely empty.

Chapter 33

After the next summons to the chief resident's office, Maggie could hardly sit still during rounds. He must have just discovered her use of his computer. Why else would he want to talk to her again so soon? Possibly the rude remark she had made the last time Miss Brophy had called about her "outliers," patients who had overstayed their welcome. She had invited Miss Brophy to write and sign the discharge order. "That's your job, Doctor," had been the indignant reply.

Maggie appeared at precisely the appointed time, and Blaine arrived 30 seconds later.

"Hello, Maggie," he said, as he tossed a pile of printouts onto the bookshelf. "Sorry to keep you waiting. I didn't think you'd get here so soon."

He pushed aside a stained coffee cup and some empty boxes from Church's Fried Chicken, and pulled a folder from a desk drawer. Her profile, evidently.

"You already know that your DRG profile has been a cause for concern," he told her. "We've been plotting those all along for each of our interns. But we have just introduced a new program, one that flags individuals for special attention when a certain parameter is exceeded." He looked at her thoughtfully, and perhaps not unsympathetically. "It's called an early detection system."

Like for cancer, Maggie thought, a little bitterly.

"The protocol seems a little arbitrary to me," Blaine said, avoiding her eyes, "but it requires me to talk to you. Even though we spoke just recently."

Maggie stared into space. Apparently, they were trying to get rid of her. At the moment, she almost didn't care. But that was just fatigue, she knew. Well, she wouldn't make it easy for them.

Blaine thumbed through the folder. Maggie said nothing,

and Blaine finally broke the uncomfortable silence. "Now, I don't want you to take this personally, Maggie. Sometimes we find ourselves in a situation where we don't fit in. One of my responsibilities as chief resident is to try to identify such situations. And to offer constructive help."

Oh, really, Maggie thought. How did he plan to help?

"I know you've been interested in research," Blaine said, "and Dr. Adamson gave you a fine recommendation. He was even sorry, he said, that you had decided on clinical medicine."

Sometimes she was too, Maggie thought. And the moguls in charge of EquaCare seemed to be even more sorry. So what could she do? She didn't give the patients their diseases. Nor was she the one who commissioned the billboards, inviting them all to sign up for EquaCare.

"I do have some contacts at the NIH," Blaine offered. "Would you like me to make some inquiries for you?"

"That would be nice of you," Maggie responded dully. "In case I decide to apply there at some point. A couple of years from now."

"I'll do it," Blaine promised. There seemed to be a forced sincerity in his voice. "In the meantime, I would suggest that you pay more attention to the computer. After all, a lot of work and expertise went into the development of those programs."

Expertise at what, Maggie wondered. The bottom line? But she held her tongue. She felt that she had been dismissed. And the page operator was calling her again.

• • •

"I was afraid for a minute that you'd gone home early," Fischbein said, blowing smoke in her direction, "and left me with another one of your disasters."

"What happened?"

"Six twelve B fell out of bed," Fischbein informed her.

"I checked your patient." Fred had just come into the doctor's station. "I hope you don't mind, but I was close by. I think she's fractured a hip."

"Halleluja, as they say in Fort Bastion," Fischbein interposed. "An iatrogenic complication—but a turf to the orthopods. A score for Dr. Black Cloud." He laughed unpleasantly.

Maggie felt her anger rising. So they called her "Dr. Black Cloud," did they?

"Do be sure you take care of it before you go, won't you?" Charlie continued. "Instead of dumping on me?"

"I sure will," Maggie said, reaching for the telephone to order an X ray. She hated trusting any of her patients to Charlie. Especially after what had happened to Mr. Post. Charlie might as well have killed him, she thought bitterly. Could he have? No, she thrust the thought aside. Charlie was obnoxious and careless, but he wasn't a murderer. She took a swallow of Maalox from the bottle she carried in her skirt pocket. It was getting to be automatic; she didn't even bother with a paper cup.

"Scotch?" Charlie sneered. "Or rum?"

Maggie closed her eyes and counted to ten. When she opened them again, Charlie had disappeared.

"What a case of hoof-and-mouth disease," Fred remarked. "Want some tea?"

"Thanks," Maggie said. "X ray might not get around to that film for an hour."

"Have you ever thought of going back into research?" he asked, bringing her a styrofoam cup of tepid tea from the ward's small kitchen.

Fred too? She had thought he was her friend. Maggie bit back an angry reply. "The idea had occurred to me," she acknowledged.

"I've thought of cattle ranching, myself," Fred confessed. "But, unlike managed medical care, it isn't profitable these days."

"Profitable?" Maggie asked, staring into the teacup.

"That was supposed to be a joke," Fred told her.

Maggie managed a feeble smile.

"But, seriously, now that you're back, I've got to go see to my albatross upstairs. The one that proves the basketball theory of life."

"What's that?"

"Each bounce is a little lower than the one before." Fred

illustrated with his hands. "But he's a fine fellow. He used to ride broncos in the rodeo. He has lots of interesting stories to tell."

Maggie suspected that Fred had his problems with UR/QAC too. How did he manage to be so cheerful, she wondered.

• • •

It was 7 p.m. by the time Maggie could get the patient transferred to orthopedics. All the cafeteria had had to offer was spinach souffle, Polish sausage, or liver with onions. When she looked at the steam table, she had imagined that she saw Mr. Post's liver being sliced on Metzenbaum's cutting board. So she had skipped supper. She would just get her survival bag from the call room, so she could take her stockings home to wash.

"Oh!" someone shrieked, as Maggie unlocked the door. She felt a resistance; evidently the someone was trying to keep the door closed.

"Sorry," Maggie muttered. "I guess I should have knocked. I didn't think anyone would be there. I just wanted to get my things."

Jeannette Larkin opened the door, and finished zipping her skirt. "It's okay," she said. "You just startled me. You have to get a little rest when you can."

Maggie thought her fellow intern might be blushing a bit. "Yes, I take naps too. I just wasn't thinking. I hope I didn't wake you up."

"Oh, no," Jeannette said. "I have to go answer my page."

"Well, have a good night," Maggie said. She gathered up her bag and quickly headed for the stairs, hoping to escape before the page operator called her again. She nearly collided with Brent Stemmons, who was emerging from the men's room.

"Maggie!" he exclaimed, straightening his tie. "I was just thinking about how long it's been since I've seen you. Outside of business, I mean. And then you suddenly appear. Amazing!"

"Yes, it has been a while," Maggie said. "Time flies when the week has only four or five days in it." Brent hadn't called her for several weeks—except to receive patients in the ER. She hadn't thought much about it; after all, she had never expected him to be socially interested in her in the first place.

"I really have been awfully busy," Brent said. "That's no excuse, I realize." He looked into her eyes and smiled.

"No need to apologize," Maggie said.

"Yes there is," Brent replied. "Even though I've been the loser."

Yes, he certainly has a charming smile, Maggie thought. He used it every time he admitted a really awful case to her service. Well, it wasn't his fault that her life was so difficult. He could just as easily be unpleasant while doing his job. On occasion, he even told her that he missed having her help in the Pit.

"How about dinner this Saturday?" Brent asked. "I know a place that you'll really like."

Maggie hesitated for just a moment. Really! What's the matter, she asked herself. Was getting to bed early to become the major preoccupation of her life? Did she have any other offers? "Sure, I'll look forward to it," she heard herself saying.

She wondered whether anyone ever told him no.

As she closed the door to the stairwell, it occurred to her that Brent's appearance on the sixth floor was itself a little curious. And running into him just after Jeannette was an interesting coincidence. Well, she was seeing coincidences everywhere these days.

Chapter 34

"Dining here is always an event," Brent said. The waiter brought a bottle of wine, opened it deftly, and waited at a discreet distance while Brent tasted the wine. He nodded, and the waiter filled both their glasses. "To us," Brent toasted, smiling at Maggie.

She raised her glass and drank dutifully, but found she couldn't muster a bit of enthusiasm. Not for the restaurant—the Trou Norman—or, strangely enough, for Brent. What's the matter with you, she chastised herself. A handsome man has asked you out to dinner at a very chic and expensive restaurant. He's gazing soulfully into your eyes, and all you can think about is how you'd rather be at home. What would you do there, anyway, but brood about TU? She tried to manufacture a smile for Brent's benefit, but found instead that she felt like crying.

"What is it?" Brent asked her, full of concern.

"Oh, nothing," she said, unwilling to go into the events of the past few days. Maybe Blaine was right—maybe clinical medicine wasn't for her. She thought he was mistaken, and that the system was at fault, but it was sometimes hard to maintain her self-confidence. Surely Brent didn't want to hear about her self doubts. After all, this was his time off, too. She took a sip of wine and shook her head.

"It's TURPH, isn't it?" Brent said, frowning. "It's getting to you. I can tell."

Her eyes filled with angry tears, and she brushed them away with the back of her hand. Damn. She was not going to start crying here in the middle of the restaurant. "Yes, it's TU," she managed.

Brent nodded and reached across the table for her hand. He held it tightly. "Do you want to tell me about it? I'd be happy to listen."

"Really?" she asked, doubtful.

He smiled encouragingly, and squeezed her hand a little.

"Really."

So it all came pouring out. Once she got started, she found it impossible to stop, and before she knew it, she had told him everything, culminating with her last two humiliations—Charlie Fischbein's taunting her with her nickname "Doctor Black Cloud", and Blaine's suggesting that she leave TU and go back into research. Soon.

Brent raised an eyebrow. "Back to research? In mid-year? He said that?"

She nodded, indignant.

"Hmm," Brent said. He looked at her thoughtfully. "But do you want to go back to research?"

She withdrew her hand from his with an apologetic pat. "I just don't know," she said, gesturing. "Evidently Blaine thinks I belong there. I don't think he's vindictive. Why should he have it in for me? And he's certainly not stupid. He's seen lots of interns come and go. So maybe he's right. Maybe I'm just not suited for clinical medicine. At least not for medicine at TU." She began shredding her dinner roll, relieved to note that she no longer felt like crying. Now she felt like kicking something. Or someone.

"But you thought you were," Brent said.

"I still do, Brent. In spite of everything. Or maybe even more so because of everything. There really are some problems with the way the system treats the patients. Like input into an equation leading to the bottom line."

Brent looked at her strangely. "And so you fight the system. Instead of trying to make it work."

"How can a mere intern 'make it work'? Anyway, it does work. The question is, who does it work for?"

"You're on a soapbox, Maggie," Brent said. He held up a hand to ward off her angry rejoinder. "You have to learn to be a team player. It's part of being a good doctor these days. I'm not saying that everybody always agrees with the system. I'm just saying that's the way it is. That's how medicine is, and how it has to be in this day and age. You have to work within the system. We can't turn back the clock to the 'good old days,' which of course weren't all that good. And if you're going to stay at

TURPH, you'll have to accept it. If you can't accept it, then everyone says you're a good scientist. You'd probably be much happier doing what you do best."

The waiter appeared with their first course, and Brent poured more wine for them. "How do you like it?"

"What? Sorry, I wasn't paying attention."

"The pâté," Brent said reproachfully. "It's made here on the premises. The truffles are flown in from Provence. A house specialty."

"It's delicious," she told him, taking a sample. The food really was delicious. She resolved to try to enjoy herself. Why not? The problems at TU would remain every day, but the opportunity to have a meal like this was rare.

"Just relax and enjoy the meal," he suggested. "We can't let TURPH spoil our digestion."

"You're right."

"You're in for a surprise," Brent said, smiling mischievously.

"Oh? What?"

"Did you notice that the name of the restaurant—Le Trou Norman—means, literally The Norman Hole?"

Maggie laughed. "No, I didn't. Not a very auspicious name, though, is it?"

"Aha—but it doesn't refer to the establishment. It refers to an old Norman custom of pausing after the salad course and drinking a glass of calvados—apple brandy—to make room for more food. Making 'the Norman hole.' Ah! Here comes the calvados."

The waiter deposited two glasses of amber liquid in front of them, took their plates and smiled as he left them.

"*Eh maintenant, ma jolie demoiselle, faisons-nous le trou norman?*" Brent asked, holding up his glass and smiling.

She raised hers, drank and gasped as the apple brandy burned all the way down. It brought tears to her eyes, and she quickly swallowed some water. "Wonderful," she lied as soon as she caught her breath. "What's next?"

"Veal poached in apples and cream," Brent said. "Then, a dessert if you like, or fruit and cheese. And, of course, cafe au lait."

"Of course," she said, forcing herself to smile back at him. He really was handsome. And he had such savoir faire. And he took her to the most interesting places. But the discussion about TU was not going to be dissolved in apple brandy or buried in a Norman hole. Not for long. If Brent really wanted to be friends, he would need to hear her out. What were friends for if you couldn't confide in them, or have a serious discussion with them? She found herself growing impatient with the small talk that accompanied the meal, and was glad when the china was cleared away.

She could hardly wait to tell Brent that she had been able to make her decision. Just talking over dinner had made things clearer for her. She was not, after all, going to run back to the refuge of some lab. No, she was not a quitter. She had never failed at anything she had put her mind to, and she wasn't going to fail at clinical medicine. She was going to stick it out at TU.

. . .

"Well," Brent said, yawning as the waiter returned his credit card, "I'm beginning to feel just a little tired."

"Maybe you should go home and get some rest then," Maggie suggested. She felt a little disappointed, but then she was usually the one who was exhausted.

He sighed. "I'll be all right. I do think we need to talk a little more. I might be helpful to you. You know—I could listen while you talk out the pros and cons of going back to research. I know it's a big decision."

She took a deep breath. "I've made that decision, Brent."

He stared at her. "You have? When?"

"While we were eating." She shrugged. "I don't want to do it. If I go back to research at all, it will be because I chose to do it, not because I flunked out of clinical medicine. No, I'm determined to continue." She paused for a moment.

He finished the last half glass of his wine in a single gulp. "How can you make a decision about your career just like that?" he snapped his fingers. "Are you sure that your desire to stay at

173

TURPH isn't motivated more by mulishness than by good sense?" He reached for her hand. "You're killing yourself at TURPH, and for what? A bunch of people who don't appreciate you. A system that you don't like, and that isn't going to change." He shook his head sadly. "You're wasting yourself there, Maggie."

Embarrassed, Maggie stared at him. "I wouldn't say that," she told him.

Brent looked steadily at her for a few minutes, then squeezed her hand. "I would. But excuse me for just a moment. I need to wash my hands. Then we need to think about this together."

As Brent hurried away, Maggie felt her anger rising. To leave TU or to stay was her decision. One she thought she'd made. Why did Brent want to try to change her mind? She shook her head. He was beginning to sound just like Blaine. She shook her head. No, he wasn't. Brent seemed to care about her, whereas to Blaine she was just another intern. She was being too hard on Brent, when he probably had only her best interests at heart. He was more of a realist than she. But she really wanted his support, not his advice. And she also wanted to talk to him about what she suspected was going on at TU, not just about her career plans. A thought struck her, and she sat upright in her chair. Maybe Brent did know, or at least suspect, something! Perhaps that was why he wanted her to reconsider her decision—he cared about her and was trying to protect her! Trying to keep her out of harm's way. Perhaps he really was old fashioned in that sense, for all his modern ideas about medicine. But how could she persuade him that she didn't want to be protected? That it would be better to get to the bottom of the mystery. Better for her, better for TU, better for everyone. She looked at her watch. He had certainly been gone a long time.

Deep in thought, Maggie didn't notice that he was back until he sat down opposite her. She looked over at him and frowned. He seemed . . . different. A little too intense. He drummed his fingers restlessly on the table and stared at her for a moment.

"Maggie, I'm worried about you," he told her. Then he leaned over the table. "We need to go someplace where we can talk. Privately." He stroked the back of her hand gently with one finger. "You could invite me up to your place for a nightcap."

Uncertain of how to respond, she looked back at him. Yes, she did want to talk to him. Even if her decision was made. Perhaps she shouldn't seem so definite about it. If she let Brent believe she was undecided, maybe he would try to persuade her. Give her reasons to leave. Perhaps give her some clues. Was it possible that he knew what was going on at TU? Brent smiled at her, then raised her hand to his lips and kissed her palm. Maggie blushed to the roots of her hair.

"Come on, Dr. Altman," he said quietly. "Invite me up to your apartment. This is hardly the place to continue our . . . discussion."

Maggie found it difficult to breathe, let alone to answer. So, he had finally gotten around to propositioning her. Idly, she wondered what it would be like to go to bed with Brent. The prospect might even be tempting. Out of the question, of course. But she did want to talk. Oh well, it will be all right, she told herself. Brent was a gentleman, wasn't he? He wouldn't insist on anything she didn't want. She was sure of that. She returned his smile. "All right," she told him. "Let's go to my place. For a nightcap. And a talk."

• • •

"You have quite a CD collection," Brent said appreciatively. "Do you mind if I play something?"

"Go ahead," Maggie called from the kitchen. She poured herself a large glass of cold milk and drank it quickly, then filled two glasses with wine and brought them into the living room. Brent had taken off his suit jacket and was standing with his back to her, bending over the turntable. She looked quickly around the room, hoping everything was in order. It could use a cleaning, but at least it was tidy. She sighed. Functional was the best adjective to describe her home. One wall of the living room was nothing but bookcases—holding her books and compact disks, as well as a fold-down desktop. Along the other wall was a comfortable rust sofa with a large coffee table in front of it. Her one concession to interior decorating was the Navajo carpet on the floor. She had bought it shortly after she had arrived. Its rusts and blacks pleased her. What did Brent think of such humble accommodations, she wondered. She thought guiltily of the pile of unread newspapers in the corner, and hoped he wouldn't notice.

The curtains were already drawn across the living room windows. The strains of Julian Bream playing Rodrigo's "Concierto de Aranjuez" filled the room. She smiled. That was one of her favorite pieces. She carried the glasses to the coffee table and sat down. Brent joined her. She decided to get right to the point.

"Brent, don't you think there's something odd going on at the hospital?" Seeing the smile on his face, she bristled. "Don't you dare laugh! I'm not imagining things."

"Maggie, I know there are weird things going on at TURPH," he told her.

"You do?"

"Sure. Glitches in the computer program, lost charts, even lost patients. I know all that. Don't you think I've lived through the same frustrations you're experiencing?" He set his wine glass down and put his hands on her shoulders. "It may seem like a vast conspiracy, but it's simply a ponderous and rigid system displaying its inefficiencies. That's all. Nothing more sinister than that. You'll be much happier once you're away from that place."

He bent to kiss her cheek. Maggie shivered a little. He was making it impossible for her to keep her mind on what she wanted to tell him. She took a deep breath and drew away from him a little in order to concentrate. "Brent, you're wrong," she said emphatically.

He sighed. "I don't think so. I've been at TU longer than you. Don't you think I'd know it if there were something going on? Maggie, you worry too much, you know. That's because you think too much." He stroked her hair. "You should concentrate on feeling once in awhile." He drew her firmly toward him.

She smiled a little ruefully. "Well, maybe once in awhile," she told him. When he kissed her, she was surprised at her own response.

"You know, if you were to leave TURPH, we could see a lot more of each other," he whispered. "I'd like that. Wouldn't you?"

Was he teasing her? He must be. And he must seriously think she was still undecided about leaving. Perhaps it was time to make things clear. "Brent," she said, disentangling herself from him with some difficulty, "I'm going to stay at TU."

He seemed not to be paying attention. "You'll probably go off to some research lab somewhere else, but we could have a really good time before you left Fort Bastion. The kind of time we could never have with our present schedules." He smiled at the amazed look on her face. "Oh, you won't admit it, but I know you'd like to leave TURPH. Put all the hassles behind you. Who would blame you?" he asked sympathetically. "So do it, Maggie. Do what you want to for once, not what you feel you should do."

What was he talking about? "I want to stay," she told him firmly, "and I want to find out what's going on there! I was hoping you'd help me."

He blinked rapidly a few times. "Me? But I've just told you there's nothing going on. It's your imagination. You're overworked." He put his arms around her. "Overworked, overwrought and underloved. I can remedy that. Starting now."

Maggie felt trapped. He wasn't interested in discussing the subject at all. Apparently, he was only interested in one thing. She should have known better. He leaned forward and nibbled her ear. "Let me show you some more enjoyable things than growing old at TURPH."

Maggie sighed. Whatever romantic inclinations she had felt earlier were now completely gone. Brent was positively exasperating. Worse than Blaine, in fact. Underneath his off-color banter, it was clear that he really did want her to leave TU. But why? Was it pure male ego? Maybe they'd butted heads about patient care once too often. She stood up and crossed her arms, feeling absolutely ridiculous and more than a little angry. Who did he think he was, anyway? Underloved, really! What arrogance. Did he really believe that she would consider having more time for romantic liaisons with him to be a good reason to leave TU? No one could be that egomaniacal.

"Brent, I'm really very tired. Why don't we finish our wine, and say good-night?"

To her amazement, he reached over and pulled her down on the sofa beside him. "Come on, Maggie," he said soothingly, putting his hands on her shoulders and using his weight to push her down. "I'm not ready to say good-night. And neither are you. You don't want me to leave, and you know it." He laughed. "We both know what you really want, don't we? You really didn't want to talk about your career decisions. You'd already made up your mind. So what did you invite me here for? Admit it, Maggie—your fantasies about TU were another pretext. No, you wanted me here for another reason. I know that women like me—it's nothing to be ashamed of. So why don't we stop playing games?"

She looked up into his eyes and was appalled. There wasn't a trace of warmth or affection in them. The handsome, aristocratic face seemed to belong to someone else. This was not the Brent she knew. Or was it? A chill passed over her. This was more like the Brent she had known in medical school—his reputation for never taking "no" for an answer had been well known. But he had seemed so different recently. She cursed her own naivete. Brent may have seemed different, but underneath he was obviously the same arrogant, insensitive bastard he had always been. He had simply taken pains to disguise it. How could she have been so stupid? But what had he wanted with her, anyhow? She was hardly his type. No doubt he had found it amusing to play the gentleman with her, just waiting for a moment to . . . to what? And to think that earlier in the evening, she had found him attractive. What kind of a game was he playing? She struggled to sit up. Fortunately she had come to her senses in time.

"Look, Brent," she said reasonably. "I really do want you to go. We're both tired. And you don't want to do something you'll regret."

"Go? Why? I'm not going anywhere until I get what I came for. And as for doing something I'll regret, well, that's a laugh isn't it?"

She began to struggle in earnest, and he laughed. "Oh,

come off it, Maggie," he said roughly. "You know you want it as much as I do. Stop playing the affronted virgin. You damned women are all the same," he sneered.

"Let me up!" she told him fiercely, genuinely frightened now. "I said no and I mean no."

He laughed. "Are you kidding? Every man alive knows what a woman's 'no' means. Ultimately, it always means yes. There's really no such thing as rape, if only you women would admit it. Now, come on, Maggie. Relax. You might even enjoy it." He struggled to get a knee between her legs. "Damn it! Are you going to make me rough you up a little? I will if I have to!"

Maggie felt a great rage well up in her. He was not going to rape her! But what to do? There was no point in yelling—several of her neighbors had their stereos turned up as loud as hers. So she was on her own. She looked around for a weapon. There! On the coffee table was the oversized ceramic candy dish that Fred had given her as a housewarming present. It was just within reach. She picked it up in her right hand and brought it down on the back of Brent's head with all her strength. The leverage was bad, so the blow didn't do any actual damage, but it was enough to startle Brent. He let out a yelp of surprise and pain and let go of her, rising to his knees to feel the back of his head. She got one leg free, put her foot in the middle of his chest and pushed. As he toppled backward, off balance, she struggled off the couch and staggered upright, putting the coffee table between them. He put his hand on the back of his head and looked at her in amazement.

"Hey, you didn't have to do that."

She threw his jacket at him and, crossing the living room quickly, opened the apartment door. "Get out," she told him, shaking with rage.

"Maggie, I—"

"—don't say a word, you bastard! If you're not out of here in five seconds I'm going to scream for help."

Clutching his jacket, he walked dispiritedly to the door. In the hall outside the apartment he turned to say something to her. She slammed the door in his face, surprised at the satisfaction it gave her.

179

She walked aimlessly around the apartment for a few minutes, feeling indignant and hurt. A spasm of pain pierced her stomach and she ran to the kitchen and poured another glass of milk. The whole thing was incomprehensible, she thought angrily as she banged shut the refrigerator door. Brent Stemmons was a psychopath! No, she amended that. He was a sociopath.

In the bedroom she took off her clothes and hung them carefully in the closet. She took her shower, put on her pajamas, brushed her teeth—all the routine things that she did every night before bed. They must have had a calming effect, because when she sat down on the edge of the bed to wind her alarm clock, her pulse had returned to normal. And she even felt a little sleepy.

So her misgivings about Brent had proven to be well-founded. Obviously she should listen to her intuition more often. How many other women had Brent treated this way, she wondered. And did he really believe all those awful cliches about rape, and what women wanted? Lots of men did, but Brent? And should she warn Jeannette Larkin? She laughed a little bitterly, imagining herself telling Jeannette the sordid little story. What, after all, had happened? Nothing. Brent Stemmons had tried to rape her—she knew that. And he knew it, too. But she had no proof. And if she said anything about it, he would deny it. She yawned, shook her head and turned out the light. Fortunately, no real harm had been done. Except to her ego. Well, that would probably survive. It was proving to be tougher than she had ever imagined.

Chapter 35

Fitzhugh's ranch—the Flying V—was, so Ryan had said, just outside the city limits of Fort Bastion. Silber pulled off the road into the shade of a clump of cottonwoods and studied the map. Just about here, he should turn toward the river, onto Tanque Verde Road. He looked around for a turnoff. Yes, that seemed promising up ahead.

This had been a surprisingly pleasant drive, he thought as he drove slowly along Tanque Verde. Most salubrious. Perhaps he should get out into the country more often. It might improve his outlook on life. He looked uncertainly at the large area of fenced-off property. No, not Fitzhugh's. This particular ranch proclaimed itself to be Zimara's Arabians. Silber snorted. These people who lived here along the river were horse mad. Why, already he had passed something called Palomino Estates, which actually had a hitching post outside the entrance; the Rancho Paso Doble, a riding school; and various small unnamed expanses of equine inhabited property. Hmmf. What people saw in the enormous dumb brutes was beyond him.

Ah—here it was. A weathered wooden sign identified this particular acreage as the Flying V. And the gang of horses that hurried over to the fence to stare and whinny at him as he drove down the lane confirmed that he was in the right place. They kept up their infernal noise all the way down the lane, intimidating him thoroughly. One particularly nasty-looking speckled beast, fixing him with what Silber fancied to be a bold and malevolent stare, stamped his forefoot meaningfully on the ground. Equine thug, Silber muttered to himself, grateful for the corral fence that separated his Buick from the brute. Coping with the idiosyncrasies of a feline fool was one thing; dealing with the foibles of these deranged monsters was quite beyond his imagination. Fitzhugh was definitely right to prefer the perils of the Forex desk.

He parked his car between a dusty Jeep and a grey BMW and emerged cautiously, looking about for any maddened horses that might have escaped the corral. He had no desire to become involved in a staring match with one of them outside the safety of his car. However, the way seemed to be clear. He gave his trousers a perfunctory hitch and was just about to make a dash for what he guessed was the main house when a familiar voice hailed him.

"Milt! You made it!"

"Barely," Silber told Fitzhugh. "There's a particularly evil-looking horse over there who has designs upon my person, but I managed to fend him off."

"I feel the same way," Fitzhugh whispered. "But for God's sake, don't tell Kate! Come on, we'll go inside and have a beer. Then you can tell me what brought you all the way out here."

"A beer would be nice," Silber said, following Fitzhugh into the house. "Two beers would be nicer." He sank gratefully into an easy chair as Ryan disappeared into the kitchen. "What do you do out here," Silber called to him, "besides traipsing about in that ridiculous looking cowboy outfit?"

Fitzhugh reappeared with four bottles of beer and a couple of glasses, and looked down ruefully at his jeans and boots. "Do you think this is a silly outfit? I never thought of it that way before."

Silber grunted. "Are you a farmer or a financier?"

"Well, I'm certainly no farmer," Fitzhugh said. "But I'm open to other suggestions. As you know, I've had it up to here with Banque France." He shrugged. "But where do I go when I leave? All I know is money. I can't see myself in the unemployment line at my age. And the idea of loafing around the Flying V in my cowboy outfit isn't a very appealing one." He shook his head. "Still, raising horses sometimes seems the easy way out."

Silber barked out a laugh. "Yes, I can see how much affection you have for them. You'd be about as good as I would at it. Hmmf. The only useful thing I ever learned about horses was not to walk too closely behind them."

"Well, then," a pleasant voice called from the kitchen

doorway, "that shows how little you learned."

A small, slim woman with salt and pepper hair, dressed in riding breeches and boots, and a plaid cotton shirt, leaned against the doorframe and glared at him. Silber sprang to his feet.

"Er . . . Kate! Hello!" Fitzhugh exclaimed, struggling to his feet. "Milt, this is Kate Fitzhugh. My stepmother. Kate, this is Milton Silber, financial—"

"—wizard," Kate interjected with raised eyebrow, speaking to Ryan. "A paper charts and numbers prodigy." She turned next to Silber, looked him up and down, glowered, and left.

Silber found himself staring after her open-mouthed, and with an effort sat down to pour the rest of his beer. "Hmmf," he said to Fitzhugh, trying to make light of the whole thing.

"Oh, don't mind her," Fitzhugh told him. "If you don't have four legs and a tail and eat oats, you don't count with Kate."

"Hmmf," Silber said again, trying to communicate to Fitzhugh that he didn't care a whit what Kate thought of him. He swallowed his beer and stared moodily into the empty glass. Damn—she was the most attractive woman he'd seen in a dozen years. And he'd managed to get off on the wrong foot. What an ass you are, Milton Silber, he told himself.

"Well, are you going to tell me?" Fitzhugh asked him.

"What? Sorry. I was thinking about . . . something else."

"What you were so mysteriously alluding to on the phone. The reason for your visit." Fitzhugh handed Silber another beer. "You know I'd be happy to see you under any circumstances, Milt, but this sounded like business."

"Hmm. Yes, it is." Silber took a deep breath. "Fitzhugh, aren't you wondering why I wanted to find out who was behind Ararat? Why I went to such lengths? Spent so much money?" He looked at the young man carefully.

Fitzhugh shrugged. "Yeah, I suppose so. But I concluded that you were on the trail of some terrific prospect for your advisory letter. Companies in the health care industry are hot these days."

"And now? What do you conclude now? You know as well as I do that neither Ararat nor the other companies—

including Harvey, where the money is—is publicly traded. They're close corporations."

Fitzhugh stared thoughtfully at his boots. "Now I conclude that you've figured some other way to make a profit from the information besides using it to help you select stock. You didn't invest all that time and money for nothing. You've got some plan to make it all pay off."

"Hmm," Silber said. "You're sharper than I thought. What plan might that be?"

Fitzhugh frowned. "Beats me. But I have faith in you. You've got something up your sleeve."

Silber nodded slowly. This was going to be easier than he had feared. On the drive out to the Flying V he had reviewed in his mind the variety of elaborate reasons he had invented for his interest in Ararat, and ultimately Harvey—reasons he was prepared to give to Fitzhugh. All false, of course. But Fitzhugh had come up with a reason of his own—profit. Silber chuckled. Trust a fellow financier. And Fitzhugh seemed to think nothing of the decidedly odd lengths to which Silber had gone to obtain the information. Perfect!

"You know, Milt," Fitzhugh continued, "when Alan Stevens and I were younger we were not exactly law-abiding characters. Oh, we never did anything very reprehensible, but we sure bent a lot of rules and regulations." He smiled at Silber. "Nowadays, both of us have found it less nerve-wracking to make our profits inside the law. So, I'm not about to be judgmental about whatever you have planned for the Harvey information." He shrugged. "It's certainly not my business. But if you need my help," he looked directly at Silber, "I hope you know that you can ask."

Silber harrumphed and took another swallow of his beer. Perfect! He congratulated himself again. On having deceived Fitzhugh, and on the young man's unbelievable loyalty. Well, if he were going to be so gullible, and so evidently uninterested in Harvey, there was something else he could do. "Well," Silber said diffidently, "there is one last minor piece of information you might get for me. It's certainly not essential to my plans," he winked conspiratorially at Fitzhugh, "but it could be useful."

"Sure, Milt. What is it?"

"The name of the principal stockholder of Harvey. The number of shares of stock outstanding, and the stockholders. Plus the size, and location, of Harvey's bank account."

Fitzhugh grinned. "It just hit me—I know exactly what you have in mind, you old fox."

Silber thought his heart would stop. "You do?" he said weakly.

"Sure. This Harvey is obviously a hot prospect. You wouldn't be interested in it otherwise. I'll bet you're going to try to buy it! Take it over. Put old Harvey out of business. That's it, isn't it?" Fitzhugh laughed again. "C'mon, Milt. Tell me I'm right!"

Silber forced himself to smile. "Well, let's just say you're not very far wrong."

Chapter 36

Maggie shivered as she climbed out of the pool, after doing the 50 laps that she assigned to herself whenever there was time. It was well into October. She wouldn't be able to swim much longer. Although Fort Bastion did not boast an impressive display of autumn colors, the change in seasons was apparent. These days, it was dark when she left the apartment, and dark when she returned.

However, today she'd been able to leave the hospital by noon, and a whole Sunday afternoon stretched out before her. It would be good to have a few hours to herself—to sort out her thoughts, as well as the laundry. She scooped the warm linens out of the dryer, and tossed in her uniforms.

How much longer would she be wearing them, she wondered. Of course, no one had actually said she might not be allowed to complete the year. That would leave a hole in the call schedule, after all. Her fellow interns would have to take extra admissions—the Margaret Altman Memorial Service. The chief resident might want to avoid that situation.

But did she really want to finish the year? Even though she had told Brent otherwise, she sometimes had ambivalent feelings. This week, two of her patients had been transferred to another service. She had found their beds occupied by strangers, and their charts missing from the rack. The head nurse had informed her that they had been reassigned at the behest of UR/QAC. They had been discharged soon after. Much too soon, in Maggie's opinion. She had started to read at least one section of the newspaper: the public notices. One of the patients had died.

If only she could talk to someone. Her resident, Stuart Collins, went strictly by the computer recommendations, when he was available. "Call me if you need me, but remember, it's a sign of weakness," he had told her. As soon as his pro forma notes were done, it was difficult to find him. He was either running a marathon, or in the shower. The attending physician was preoccupied with fulfilling the charting requirements to document his visits, or with lecturing about the Problem Oriented Medical Record or mixed collagen vascular disease, his specialty. Fred refused to worry about the system. He just took care of his patients and ignored the computer's idiosyncrasies. He had remarked that fewer sick patients were being admitted to his service; he suspected that they were being shunted to the interns who had a better cost profile. But Maggie was still taking the very worst patients, often at 3:00 am, after they had languished in the ER for hours. Especially when Brent Stemmons was the Pit Boss. It almost seemed that Brent held certain patients there until it was Maggie's turn.

Brent Stemmons. She tried not to think about him. She could not avoid seeing him when he was on duty in the ER. That was almost every time that she was on call. It was certainly unusual for a resident to be in the Pit for this long. Most could hardly wait to move onto another rotation, according to Fred. Brent had told her he was planning to specialize in emergency medicine; he must be spending all of his elective time in the Pit. So Maggie just had to endure working with him. He was so cool, distant, and professionally correct. As if they had never met socially. As if that night in her apartment several weeks ago had never happened. He spoke to her in as few words as possible and had even taken to calling her "Dr. Altman."

How could he be so cool? He seemed to be completely free of remorse. Or so egotistical that he couldn't admit to having done anything wrong. Did he really think that "no" meant "yes"? What a male chauvinist! In any event, there seemed to be plenty of women willing to give him what he wanted. Maggie felt that one recent performance with Jeannette Larkin had been staged just for her benefit.

So maybe she had handled it wrong. And had she led him on just a little? Well, that couldn't have excused him. She had never expected him to behave the way that he did.

Some strange transformation had come over him that night. Maggie wondered what might have happened. Could the stress of being the Pit Boss be taking a toll, despite his outward coolness? Not that it mattered what his problem was. He shouldn't have reacted as he did.

More important was the question of what had come over her. Why had she been taken in by his apparent friendliness and concern? Certainly it had been nice to do something on an evening off besides folding the laundry. And it had been pleasant to be treated like an attractive woman instead of just one of the guys. Still, she shouldn't have abandoned her common sense. She really had known from the beginning that it wouldn't work out. Still, she was feeling depressed about it. And angry with herself for feeling that way.

She resolved—again—not to think about Brent. It was too painful, too humiliating.

No, she would concentrate on the problems at TU. First, there was the computer. She was sure that that was part of a scheme. She could have imagined one or two strange discrepancies, but certainly not all of them. Or her memory might have failed her on some occasions. It did so often enough, especially when she was tired. But she wasn't depending entirely on memory. She had her index cards too.

Maggie didn't understand that much about computers. But now that she thought about it, it didn't seem likely that a software problem would introduce the kind of errors that were occurring. She wasn't seeing screens filled with hearts and spades and other strange symbols, nor did the system crash. The electrocardiograms and laboratory values that turned up looked very reasonable. It might be that there was a problem with filing the dates. Or that the people who entered the data were just incompetent.

Maggie regretted that she hadn't asked Brent in more detail about what sort of errors to expect from various causes. He appeared to be knowledgeable about computers. But she had been too interested in enjoying herself. She had been a soft-brained romantic female, instead of a cool-headed, analytic scientist.

The timer beeped. The white skirts and coats were done. She made a quick trip to the laundry room, noticing that several people were sunning themselves beside the pool. She didn't recognize any of them. It occurred to her that she didn't even know the people who lived on either side of her; only Fred, around the corner, and the manager, a cigarillo-smoking, no-nonsense woman who accepted her rent check every month. She was certainly isolated. She pushed away the feeling of loneliness which was about to overwhelm her, and added distilled water to the steam iron. She needed to formulate some theories.

Hypothesis 1, Maggie thought. There is just a problem with the software. It's a new system, so it's bound to have bugs. Also, it is obvious that not everyone at TU is of the highest competence.

Hypothesis 2. Someone is deliberately sabotaging the system. This seems more likely, in view of the type of errors. The questions are: who, and why. Maggie decided to suppress her suspicions about individuals for the moment. They were based primarily on intuition, in any case. First, concentrate on the question of motive.

If EquaCare failed, who would benefit? Lots of people would certainly be hurt. The hospital might go bankrupt, the medical school and residency programs would see their reputations ruined. And where would the patients go for care? It was hard to imagine that anyone would benefit. And would anyone be so evil as to damage the system out of spite?

Wait a minute, Maggie thought. What if somebody, instead of sabotaging the system, was attempting to profit from it? The system was supposed to benefit from improved efficiency, after all. They had even hired a consulting firm, she recalled from her incursion into the financial data base. She had been shocked to discover how much Ararat Management Consultants was being paid for its advice—$1.3 million in one quarter alone. They were presumably earning the money, since TU was supposed to be making a profit, despite its apparent inefficiency from Maggie's standpoint. Mightn't all that money create a temptation to skim some of it off?

But would it be a strong enough motive to commit murder? Maggie shivered. She had temporarily allowed her personal problems to distract her attention from Mr. Post's death.

But she would find an explanation for it eventually, she vowed.

And what about a suspect? Whoever might be involved, he would have to have expertise with computers. And access to both the TU and the EquaCare computers. And probably an inside accomplice to manipulate the system. Someone with authority. Someone who would not be directly responsible for the consequences of bad decisions. And someone who didn't care about the patients. Obviously, the hospital would make money by keeping unprofitable patients out, and admitting profitable ones. And by discharging patients as soon as possible. Of course, that strategy was exactly what they were all supposed to be doing, for sound economic reasons and for the benefit of all! But it would take a thoroughly unscrupulous person to "manage the case mix" for his own personal benefit.

Maggie considered Stephen Blaine, making his midnight rounds, keeping his profiles and records, carrying around piles of computer output. Disapproving of autopsies. And trying to pressure noncooperative people—like herself—out of the system. She had never seen Blaine display any sympathy for a patient. And he sat before a computer display, monitoring events all over the hospital. He could go anywhere in the hospital, look at any chart, without being questioned. As far as Maggie knew, he had no outside interests. He seemed to spend every waking hour at TU, and probably spent the whole night there on occasion. All in all, he was a strange individual.

It was hard to imagine any of the other residents having the time or the ability to do the job. And hadn't the problem with the computer been called to Blaine's attention? He certainly hadn't done anything about it. But what could he gain personally from altering the performance of the system? The residents all got the same paycheck every month.

Once again her thoughts turned to Dr. Silber's role. Previously, Maggie had always admired her former professor, and had also found him very likeable. He had made her the generous offer of the use of his books. But his actions were distinctly unusual, to say the least. She reviewed the unexplained facts: the mysterious telephone calls; the visitor hiding in his house; the furtive visits to TU, while claiming to have no interest in the place; his hatred of Dr. Eisig; his unabashed interest in money; and above all, his access to the EquaCare computer. What possible interest could the financial data in the computer have for him? Unless he was skimming off profits.

It was all speculative, of course. Maggie had to admit that she didn't really have any hard evidence that deliberate manipulation of the system was occurring. And she wondered whether her evaluation could be entirely objective. Fatigue and uncertainty about her future were taking their toll. Also, she forced herself to consider the possibility that she might be looking for excuses for her own inadequacy. Could Dr. Blaine be right about her clinical performance? Many of her patients hadn't gotten well; she had missed some diagnoses; and she had prescribed treatments that caused complications.

But on the whole, Maggie felt that her own performance was satisfactory. She could see that she was doing as well as the other interns. Sick people got complications and sometimes died, regardless of who their doctor was. She was not going to allow Stephen Blaine to intimidate her.

Still, what could she do without evidence? Or even with evidence? She supposed she would have to report it to someone. But to whom? She could hardly go to the State Attorney General, without going through the proper channels at the hospital, whatever they were. Should she speak with Dr. Eisig? Yes, that was probably the thing to do. But what if he didn't believe her, and thought that she was just incapable of coping with the stress of internship? A recommendation to seek counseling would not look good on her record.

The most sensible thing to do would be to stop asking questions, since she wouldn't know what to do with the answers. But she thought of Mr. Post, and knew that she would have to continue her investigation.

But where to start? The only thing she could think of to do was to visit Dr. Silber. The idea filled her with apprehension, which she resolutely suppressed. She had indeed felt frightened during her last visit. Probably just guilt at having copied the computer codes, she told herself. Silber couldn't have known that she had even seen them. In fact, he had no way of knowing that she suspected anything. She had a pretext for visiting, after all. He himself had invited her. She would simply have to screw up her courage, and plunge into the investigation. She didn't know exactly what she would say. But she put away her ironing board, grabbed a notebook, and headed for the car, before her instinct for caution could take over.

. . .

"Well I'll be damned," Silber said, peering through the peephole in his front door. "It's Dr. Altman." He opened the door, and Maggie thought she caught a whiff of alcohol. Silber looked a little less disheveled than usual—he seemed to have had his hair cut and his beard trimmed—although his unironed shirt was missing a button. His house seemed to be less dusty, though just as cluttered as before.

"I hope I didn't pick a bad time to come by," Maggie began. "I really should have telephoned."

"No problem," Silber assured her. He fetched a chair for her from the other room. "Just tell me how I may be of help. Would you like a letter of recommendation for a research position? Advice on your stock portfolio? My recipe for shish kabob? How about a beer?"

"Yes, I would like a beer, thanks."

"You're looking very pale and tired," Silber said from the kitchen.

"Well, I am tired," Maggie acknowledged. "But it's more than that, I think."

Silber handed her a beer, and sat down opposite her. "Discouraged, too?" he asked.

Maggie sighed. "Yes. And sometimes I wonder whether it's all worthwhile. And where medicine is going."

"Straight to hell," Silber said. "Any difficult questions?"

"Is it that simple?" Maggie asked. "Isn't there a reason for it? Can't something be done about it?"

"What do you think?" Silber asked. She took a sip from her beer, then set it down on the table beside her chair. Her stomach was hurting, and she hoped Silber wouldn't notice if she didn't drink any more.

Maggie thought for a moment. Maybe she could draw him out a bit. "Well, hasn't medicine become too commercialized? Too concerned about profit?"

Silber laughed unpleasantly. "Right. Blame everything on the profit motive. Anything that's profitable is bound to be evil."

Maggie was a little shocked. "But is it right to make a profit from illness?"

"Who profits from illness, pray tell?" Silber inquired.

"Lots of people," Maggie said. "Doctors, hospitals, corporations that sell supplies, drug companies, . . ."

"Wrong," Silber interrupted.

Maggie stared at him.

"Illness is never profitable," Silber explained. "Treating illness can be profitable, and it's a good thing." He paused, watching her expression. "Otherwise nobody would do it."

"I hope they would," Maggie protested. "Or we could hardly call our society civilized."

"Nobody professional, I mean," Silber amended. "There would be grandmothers, and a few monks and nuns. Professionals get paid. By definition."

"I thought professionals were people who were trained."

"You were mistaken," Silber said tersely. Dr. Silber always had been sure of himself, Maggie reflected.

"But as you have probably realized by now," he continued, "treating illness is not very profitable. And it's a hell of a bother. Wellness is a much more lucrative racket. If you want to make some money, I'd suggest you purchase shares of Vitality Enterprises; Creative Power, Unlimited; and NutriSoul. Just be sure to enter stop loss orders. Better still, try not treating illness, after collecting the insurance premiums in advance. You have to be more careful with outfits that do that—be sure to bail out before the liabilities catch up with them."

"I'll remember that," Maggie replied. "And what do you think about Ararat Management Consultants?" The words escaped before she could censor them.

Silber's jaw dropped, and he was speechless for several

minutes. "Why do you ask?"

"I . . . overheard some people talking about it," Maggie ventured.

"Oh," Silber said. "Who?"

"Um . . . I don't know who they were."

"Where?"

"In the cafeteria at TU," she said. Maggie had no knack for inventing stories. What could she say if he continued his interrogation?

"What did they say?" Silber said, leaning back in his chair. He seemed to have recovered his composure. He did not take his eyes off her for a moment, did not even blink.

"Um . . . they were expecting to make a good profit."

"Were they going to buy Ararat's stock?" Silber wanted to know.

Maggie tried to swallow, but her mouth was too dry. "Yes, I think they were."

"Oh, were they? Are you sure?"

"Well, no, I'm not sure. I thought they were talking about that."

Silber trimmed a cigar. "The stock is not publicly traded," he said quietly.

Maggie felt trapped. She should have known better than to lie to this man. Or to bring up this subject.

"I sincerely doubt that anyone would have spoken of this particular company in the Woodlands cafeteria," Silber said. "You must know of it from some other source."

Maggie didn't know what to say. Should she blurt out the truth?

"Please try to remember how you learned about Ararat," Silber urged, leaning toward her. Involuntarily, she leaned away. "It's really very important that you tell me. More important than you can possibly suspect."

Maggie said nothing. She wondered whether he would try to stop her if she ran for the front door.

Silber changed his tack. He sat back and looked at her reflectively. "Why did you come here today, Maggie?"

For a moment, she considered telling him the whole

story. He really did look concerned about her. But of course, he knew about bedside manner, and had emphasized psychiatric issues in his discussions about interviewing patients. He could get them to tell him anything. She should be very cautious.

"You were hoping that I could help you in some way, weren't you? Well, maybe I can. Won't you please give me a chance?"

The telephone rang in a back room. Twice. Then was silent. Maggie wondered whether Silber had another guest today too. One that he didn't want her to know about. She thought of the shadowy profile she had seen in the back room on her last visit, and a feeling of panic flooded over her. What was she doing here? Her legs evidently propelled her to the car of their own accord, for she found herself speeding down Hudson Drive. She remembered hearing Silber call after her from the front door, "Maggie! Damn it, listen to me!"

Chapter
37

"I'm sorry," the caller told him. "There isn't any room for discussion. It's past the deadline. I gave you that long to clear up your problem. To do something about Dr. Altman. To get her out of the way."

"I just need a little more time," he said wearily. Why couldn't the man understand?

"No, my young friend. No more time. Now we do things my way. To be accurate, you do things my way. Right?"

He was too depressed and anxious to object. And why should he care, anyhow? Maggie Altman was the biggest pain in the butt he had ever encountered. A thoroughly unlikeable woman. And she was standing between him and future profits. Obviously, she had to be removed. God knows, he had tried his best to dissuade her from staying at TURPH. He had hoped for a while that she had been seriously considering going back into research. But his efforts had been unsuccessful. Well, maybe the boss was right. Maybe doing things his way would be better. "All right," he told the older man. "What do you want done?"

"Oh, I'll leave that up to you. Use your imagination. The only thing I insist on is that it be something drastic and definite."

He laughed bitterly. "Like Mr. Post?"

"Certainly not. At least not right now. No, we simply want the inquisitive Dr. Altman to leave Woodlands. We want her to walk away of her own accord. Having seen the error of her ways in wanting a career in clinical medicine, that is. Do I make myself clear?"

"I'm not sure. You want her dissuaded, but . . . "

The caller sighed. "Hurt her, but not too badly. Frighten her a great deal. There. Is that plain enough?"

He shuddered. "Yes. It is."

"Good. Get on with it, then. I presume you are capable of making the arrangements?"

"Yes."

"Fine. Call me when it's done. I'll want to express my condolences."

· · ·

He threw the glass pipe across the room and sat with his head in his hands. It didn't work anymore. Nothing made him feel better. His days were one long swamp of misery. And his nights were horrible. The coke made him so jittery he couldn't sleep without consuming what seemed to him like gallons of alcohol. And the next morning he could hardly get out of bed, his head ached so much. He clutched his hair. It was all the fault of that damned woman. Well, it seemed as though she would finally get what was coming to her. It served her right.

He thought about the man's icy tone and shivered. There wasn't a drop of blood in his veins. How long would it be before the cold-hearted bastard decided that he could do without his junior partner? He shook his head. To hell with it. He wasn't going to put himself at the mercy of a man like that. He was capable of anything. If he could cold-bloodedly discuss the "persuasion" of Maggie Altman, he could discuss the "termination" of his no-longer-useful junior partner, couldn't he? And what was he supposed to do for money this month? No, it was time to look out for number one. Before he could talk himself out of it, he dialled Raúl's number.

"Hello, Raúl. It's me," he told the answering machine. "I've thought over the financial details you mentioned. The arrangement sounds fine to me. I can probably move as much of the stuff as you want moved. Just tell me when I start work. Oh, and one more thing—I want to engage the services of Benny and Carlos. I have a little job for them to do—a job that has to be done right away. Call me later on tonight, all right? I'll be waiting to hear from you. Thanks."

Chapter 38

The envelope from Jacob Metzenbaum, Department of Pathology, had to be the autopsy report. Maggie tore it open, and hurriedly skimmed over the six single-spaced pages. Final diagnosis: small ischemic infarct, right cerebral hemisphere. A number of expected or insignificant findings: chronic obstructive lung disease, diverticulosis of the colon, small residual patch of pneumonia. The cause of death was undetermined.

Sudden death due to an irregular heart rhythm? It could not be proved one way or the other. Maggie stuffed the report into her pocket.

All day long, Mr. Post had been on her mind. Every time she reached for something in her pocket, her hand felt the report, reminding her of the autopsy. Finally, she decided to review the chart again in detail. Perhaps there was some clue as to what had really happened. Something she had previously overlooked. Maybe he had died a natural death, for all her suspicions. In that case, she had to admit, it was possible that there might have been some way she could have averted the disaster. Had she missed a laboratory finding? An irregular pulse? An atypical angina attack? It wouldn't help Mr. Post, of course. But she had to know.

The chart was no longer available on line since the patient had died two weeks ago. Medical records didn't have it either. The clerk didn't have time to try to trace it.

Maggie found it herself. On the shelf marked "death reviews" in Sylvia Brophy's office. Miss Brophy smirked a little and informed her that the chart was awaiting committee action. Maggie could look at it, Miss Brophy supposed, as long as she didn't remove it from the office.

She began to read. Yes, she had been checking the electrolytes. Normal potassium and bicarbonate even the day before he died. Daily tests for coagulation factors were duly recorded, and showed good control. No irregular pulse on her daily physical examinations. And no complaints from the patient about chest pain, once he had been started on treatment for his blood clot. Charlie's note. Very terse, it just named the complaint, the telephone report on the CT scan, and the fact that the patient had been found dead in bed. It was not entirely clear whether Charlie had actually seen Mr. Post before he had pronounced the patient dead. He might have just ordered a CT scan—by telephone—based on the nurse's account of the complaint. Maggie flipped to the section where radiology reports were filed. She could not find the official report of the scan. Could it have been misfiled? She looked at every page of the chart. Twice. The report was simply not there.

And there was something else odd—an electrocardiogram that showed changes typical for coronary artery spasm. And some dangerous looking extra beats. Maggie looked at it in disbelief. Her note had said the cardiogram showed changes consistent with chronic obstructive lung disease. Nothing more. She could not have made such a gross error! Yes, there was the admission cardiogram, just as she had described it.

Maggie looked more closely at the unfamiliar tracing. It had been taken at 11:00 p.m., the night before Mr. Post died. She didn't remember ordering it. But she had been the intern on call that night. She stared at the tracing, and her palms began to sweat. How could she have missed seeing this before? And who had ordered it?

When the committee reviewed the chart, there would be no doubt about their conclusions. Dr. Altman had ignored a seriously abnormal EKG.

The autopsy findings were compatible with the clinical picture, as revealed by the chart. Sudden cardiac death. Possibly preventable. If the intern hadn't been so appallingly negligent!

Was she losing her mind? She could not have forgotten a late night call about Mr. Post having chest pain.

Maggie knew that if she were called before a committee to explain her treatment, no one would be likely to believe her. Documentation—the medical record—was everything these days. A sense of unreality came over her. Could this be a nightmare? Complete with the drone of the page operator calling Dr. Miltown, disapproving looks from Sylvia Brophy, and the frequent jangling of the UR/QAC telephone?

. . .

"Are you able to read?" said a voice dripping with sarcasm. Maggie was on her knees in the file room, searching one of the lower shelves. The clerk in charge, Debbie, was standing at the end of the aisle, arms akimbo like an indignant schoolmarm.

"Oh, you weren't at the desk," Maggie explained. "And I thought I'd just save you the trouble. But maybe you can help me. Mr. Post's CT scan. I can't seem to find it. Although I remember we found it here before."

"That's why we have the sign," Debbie informed her. "Authorized Personnel Only. To keep the films from being misfiled."

"Sorry," Maggie said. "I was just trying to be helpful." Well, that wasn't entirely true. "I have the patient's EquaCare number here."

"I'm extremely busy at the moment," Debbie said. "But I'll look for the films when I have time. I just hope somebody didn't remove them from the department." She looked at Maggie accusingly. Obviously, she remembered Maggie absconding with the films once before.

"I brought them back," Maggie reminded her. "Within 15 minutes."

Debbie was not to be mollified. She watched Maggie start down the hall, then emphatically closed and locked the door to the files.

. . .

"Charlie, did you examine Mr. Post before you sent him for a CT scan?" Maggie asked.

"Mr. Who?"

"The patient of mine who died when you were on call about six weeks ago."

"Oh, yeah, the gomer with the bleed. Hell, no. I was up to my ass in alligators."

"You just phoned in an order for the CT scan?"

"Look, I do the best I can with the trolls you dump on me," Charlie said defensively.

"Do you remember," Maggie persisted, "who called you with the report?"

"You've got to be kidding."

· · ·

The only thing good about this day, Maggie thought, was that she was going to be able to leave at 5 p.m. She could never remember feeling so depressed. It was tempting just to give up. But beneath the depression was a smoldering anger. Why had Mr. Post died? It hadn't been mere misfortune. And it probably wasn't just incompetence. Because somebody was trying to cover it up. And then make use of the incident to ruin Maggie Altman's clinical career. And incidentally Charlie's as well. She was quite positive that she had not overlooked that EKG. It just hadn't been there before.

Maggie shuddered. That Mr. Post had met an untimely end was becoming more and more likely, almost undeniable. How could anyone do such a thing? A shadowy figure lurking in the X ray department, engaged in the gruesome task of "managing the case mix"? Impossible? Once she would have thought so. Now, she just didn't know.

There were certainly a lot of questions to be answered. But in her present state of mind, she was not capable of critical analysis. She needed a bath, and a good night's sleep. A week of normal sleep would be better, but that was as unlikely as receiving a letter of commendation from the chief resident.

Maggie walked quickly out of the building. If she stayed a minute longer, she risked hearing another page. As usual, she left through the ER entrance, which was closest to the parking lot. She tried not to look at the people standing in line at triage or loitering outside the building.

She didn't look back when she heard footsteps behind

her. What an active imagination you have today, she told herself sternly. It's 5 p.m., broad daylight, and there are a lot of people around. Don't be paranoid.

When she reached into her pocket for her car keys, a voice behind her said, "Good afternoon, Doctor. Don't turn around."

She froze.

"Just be very quiet and unlock the doors. You and my friend and me are going for a little drive."

So there were two of them. Well, what would happen if she turned around? She supposed that they were armed. Would they kill her right here in the parking lot, near the ambulance entrance? A police car might happen by. Then again, it might not. But wouldn't she be better off here than on an abandoned road?

She made a decision. As she tried to reconstruct it afterward, she apparently grabbed the Kelly clamp from her right hand jacket pocket, and with one smooth motion turned around and closed the serrated clamp on the nasal septum of the man on the right, locking it tightly. The other she kicked in the kneecap with her left foot. She jumped into the car, locked the door, and started the engine. Howling, the men scrambled to get out of the way as she backed up and roared out of the parking lot.

. . .

For some minutes, she sat in the middle of the living room floor, shaking. She couldn't remember exactly what had happened. But her Kelly clamp was missing, and her thumb hurt from squeezing with all her strength. She knew that she could have been killed, if her assailants had been serious and skilled with a knife. Or if she hadn't caught them off guard. She might easily have become a missing person on the police blotter.

Should she call the police? She lifted the receiver but replaced it. Why bother? She'd have to talk to the detectives. That would probably take hours. And they might even accuse her of assault. Or sue her if the thugs had suffered an injury. It might be her civic duty to report the crime. But she doubted that it would save anyone from a similar fate. She knew she couldn't give any kind of description, although she might recognize them if she saw them again. The men had been Hispanic in appearance, and of medium build, but so were millions of others. And one would have a bruised nose. That gave her a sense of satisfaction, followed by a twinge of guilt.

She didn't want to call her parents. They would just be frightened. But she had never felt so alone.

There was a tapping on the front door, and she jumped up with a start. She had retreated halfway across the room before she got control of herself.

The knocking came again, then a familiar voice. "It's me, Fred. I didn't think you'd be home, but I thought it wouldn't hurt to check," he said cheerfully. "How about some supper?" He stared at her as she opened the door. "Maggie!" he said, with alarm. "What's the matter?"

. . .

The waiter brought a large pitcher of beer. Fred filled her glass. "To better days," he said.

Maggie smiled feebly. She was determined not to start crying again. Certainly not here at Frank's Barbecue Pit.

"You've been looking pale, kiddo," Fred told her. "You need some red meat. And Frank makes the best barbecue beef in the world." He ordered two ranch size portions. "You have to keep your strength up if you're going to be taking on muggers single-handed. I hope you broke that thug's kneecap. I'd like to break his neck myself. Damn hoodlums are taking over the world."

Maggie shuddered. The feel of the kick was pretty sickening. She couldn't help visualizing the cartilages in the knee. It didn't seem like Fred to be so matter-of-fact about violence. But then she obviously didn't understand men very well. She sipped her beer in silence, staring at the sawdust on the floor.

"We really need to do something about that parking lot," Fred told her. "An escort service, perhaps."

"I don't know," Maggie said dully. "How would it help when people arrive in the morning? It's usually dark then too."

"At least when you arrive it is," Fred told her. "You certainly get an early start on the rest of us. Put us to shame."

"Who, Provider Number PGY1-14, with the worst profile in the hospital?" Maggie asked bitterly.

"Oh, that," Fred shrugged. "You know as well as I do that that's pure garbage."

"It sure is important to someone though," Maggie said. "And they plan to screen out the bad doctors that way."

"They did say something about that, didn't they?" Fred remarked. "But I can't believe that Blaine is that foolish. He knows that the computer printouts don't tell the whole story."

The waiter in a stained butcher's apron brought the food. Large plates of thinly sliced beef drenched with sauce; corn on the cob; crocks of baked beans; and a large loaf of hot French bread. Maggie made an effort to eat. But her stomach was in rebellion. She asked for a glass of buttermilk.

Fred looked at her with concern.

"I'm really worried about you," he said. "And not just because of the shock you had today."

"I'm all right," Maggie said. "I think. It's just that things really haven't been going well at all. Dr. Blaine told me that I ought to consider a research job."

Fred broke off a chunk of bread and mopped up some barbecue sauce. "Maybe he's right," he said. "Medicine is going to hell. It doesn't deserve you."

The opinions seemed to be unanimous, Maggie observed. She toyed with the beef. Fred continued to devour his food with relish.

"You know, I sometimes wonder," Fred paused to take another mouthful, "if there isn't something fishy going on. Other times, I think that some of us are just like that guy in Li'l Abner— the one who went around with the storm cloud over his head."

So that's where the "Dr. Black Cloud" epithet had come from, Maggie thought. She had to admit, it suited her well enough. Her thoughts were wandering, and Fred had to repeat the question.

"Have you ever wondered if somebody isn't manipulating the system? Doing all those things they tell us we're not supposed to do? Like fudging the DRGs, for example?"

"Yes," Maggie said slowly. "I've been giving it a lot of thought lately." So Fred was finally beginning to become suspicious. She wondered why he had changed his mind; he had always brushed off her questions before. She considered how much she should tell Fred. She wanted to talk to someone about her hypotheses, and especially about Mr. Post. But she really didn't feel well. Maybe some other time.

"I'll bet you're as good at detective work as you are at other things," Fred continued. "Have you come up with a theory?"

"Not really," Maggie fibbed.

"Come on, you at least have some suspects, haven't you?"

"Well, Blaine seems the most likely one," Maggie said finally. "Who else is in the position to stage manage things?" She took a sip of her milk. It couldn't hurt to mention the other part of her theory to Fred. "But it occurs to me that he needs an accomplice. A senior partner. Somebody with even more influence. Somebody who has the combination to the bank vault, so to speak." Fred was leaning across the table, as she lowered her voice. "After all, we need to find a motive. Money's always a good one. And there could be a lot of money involved in fudging DRGs, for example, couldn't there?" Maggie asked. "EquaCare is rolling in money. Maybe someone's helping himself to some of it." Why, according to the financial data she had seen, TU was paying over a million dollars to a consultant. "And maybe there's another motive too. Spite for example. What if somebody wanted to destroy TU?"

"It's a thought." Fred looked very serious. "But who could it be?"

"I shouldn't say," Maggie shook her head. "It's pure speculation."

"You can tell me," Fred said. "I'd never breathe a word of it, I promise."

Maggie debated for a moment. Of course, there wasn't

205

anyone she trusted more than Fred. But at one time, she had trusted Brent. And what a mistake she'd made there! One instinct told her she should tell Fred all her suspicions. Another held her back.

"Well, don't tell me if you think you shouldn't," Fred patted her hand. "Maybe I'd just better get you home." He signalled for the waiter and paid the bill. "You aren't looking well at all."

Maggie allowed him to help her with her jacket, and was grateful for his arm around her as they walked to his pickup. She was actually beginning to feel a little nauseated and light-headed.

Fred was thoughtful and quiet on the way home, and frequently looked over at her. Finally, Maggie decided she could not forego the opportunity to ask someone about her theory. "Fred, do you think that Dr. Silber could be behind some scheme at TU? You remember—the strange old man who left the ER AMA on our first night."

Fred had to brake abruptly to avoid running a red light. Strange, Maggie thought. She hadn't noticed before that he was an inattentive driver, but he had been looking at her instead of the road just as the light changed. He continued watch Maggie curiously. "Whatever gave you an idea like that?" he asked. "He may look odd, but I hear he's a financial genius. Rich too."

"Well, I suppose it's far out," Maggie acknowledged. Fred certainly had appeared to be startled.

"It sure is," Fred agreed. She decided to say no more. She was in no mood for arguing about anything.

He escorted her to her apartment door, but didn't turn to leave. "I'm worried about your being alone tonight," he said. "I'd be happy to sleep on your living room floor, if you like."

Maggie shook her head emphatically. No, not that mistake again.

"It's not that I think that you were singled out for an attack," he explained. "But after an experience like that, I thought you might feel nervous about being alone. And I have a gun. A Colt .45."

"No!" Maggie exclaimed. "Not in my apartment! A bullet could go right through the wall and injure a neighbor."

"Only if you missed," Fred pointed out. "I wouldn't miss."

Maggie shivered. What a gruesome thought. She supposed that Fred was just trying to be kind, and protective. But she hoped that he would just go away without her having to insist.

"Good night, Maggie," he said gently. "Lock your door. And you have my phone number if you change your mind."

"Thanks, Fred. Good night."

She checked the lock on the door three times. Once after brushing her teeth and washing her face, once after setting the alarm, and once after removing her uniform. She hadn't even changed before going to dinner. Then she lay down in her underwear to rest for a minute, and fell into a restless sleep.

Chapter *39*

Maggie stopped retching and stared incredulously into the toilet bowl. It was filled with what appeared to be shiny black coffee grounds. She tried to tell herself that it was the barbecue beef. But she knew better.

She stood up to wash her face, and immediately sank back down to the floor. She was sweating, she observed. She counted her pulse. One hundred twenty. Maybe she could just drink more Maalox, and hope that the bleeding would stop. It usually does, eventually, she knew. In any case, her blood pressure was so low that she was afraid to try to drive to the emergency room. She might pass out and cause an accident. No, it would be better just to lie on the floor and rest. She didn't even want to walk to the kitchen for a glass of water, although she felt very thirsty.

She probably fell asleep again for a few minutes, but was roused by another wave of nausea. This time there was bright red blood mixed with the coffee grounds. "Fool!" she said aloud. She who has herself for a doctor has a fool for a patient. She fumbled for the telephone directory. She hated to disturb Fred. But the only other choice was 911 for the ambulance.

"Hello," Fred's voice was muffled. He listened to her description of the problem. "What?" he said. "I'll be right over. Can you get to the door?"

Maggie stood up slowly and managed to walk to the door. As soon as she had unlocked it, she had to sit down with her head between her knees.

"My God!" Fred exclaimed, bursting in. "You're pale as a ghost." Hurriedly, he felt her pulse.

"I'm not decent," Maggie observed.

"Do you want me to get a robe or something?" Fred asked.

"In the closet," Maggie said numbly. He wrapped her in

her old blue bathrobe, and helped her into a coat. "We're going straight to the ER," he said. "Do you think you can make it to my truck, or shall I call an ambulance?"

"I can walk," Maggie said, though not feeling very sure of it. She had to stop and sit down several times. Finally, Fred picked her up and carried her the rest of the way. She just hoped she wouldn't have to throw up in the truck.

"Why didn't you tell me you were sick?" he wanted to know.

"I guess I wasn't sure myself," Maggie said.

"Doctors make the worst patients, as they say. Here, bend your knees and put your head down on the seat."

Maggie was vaguely aware of being helped onto a stretcher at the triage desk, and of receiving the horizontal view of Medicine A. Unceremoniously, Fred pushed the stretcher into one of the crash rooms, without consulting the resident presiding at the bridge: Brent Stemmons.

She felt a tight band around her arm, and saw Jim Thomas looking down at her. "Evenin', Dr. Altman," he said cheerfully. "Haven't seen you for a while. I'm just going to take some blood from your arm."

He was an expert, Maggie noted. Then she must have passed out.

"Swallow for me, Doc," Jim instructed, as he gently inserted the well-lubricated end of a Salem sump tube into one nostril. Obediently, she swallowed. She had an IV now too. It was dripping very fast. "Just relax, Doc," Jim said soothingly. "We're gonna take real good care of you."

Chapter
40

He could hardly contain his excitement. Things had finally started to go right! Unable even to sit down, he paced back and forth in the deserted office, savoring a moment alone. Smiling a little, he looked at the phone. In a minute, he would make the call.

Late last night Raúl had returned his phone call. Yes, he would be happy to have him as an associate, Raúl had said. Consider it done. Now, in a few days, as soon as Raúl's "mules" from Colombia arrived with the cocaine, he would begin selling it at the hospital. Well, of course, he himself wouldn't actually handle the stuff—Raúl had warned him about that—but he knew just the person for the job. Caroline. And Raúl had put him in touch with Benny and Carlos who had, apparently, thrown such a scare into Maggie Altman that she had ended up in TURPH! And in pretty serious shape, too. He found he was able to think about her without a trace of compassion. After all, she was nothing but an obstacle to be removed.

Yes, removal seemed like the best bet. Although he had made it perfectly clear that he had no intention of doing the job himself. Let his senior partner figure that one out. What more could he be expected to do? Thanks to his having hired Benny and Carlos, Maggie was now at TURPH—ill and helpless. And people died in the hospital all the time, didn't they? God knows, they wouldn't be there if they weren't sick. So maybe with just a little bit of help she could have an unfortunate accident. Untraceable, of course. He'd let his senior partner devise something. After all, he was the expert, wasn't he?

He picked up the phone and began to dial.

Chapter 41

"What?" Silber shouted into the phone. He sat bolt upright in bed, shocked into wakefulness. His digital clock read 2:23.

"Yeah, she was brought in just a little while ago," Jim Thomas told him. "Seems to be in pretty bad shape. I thought you'd want to know."

"Hmmf," Silber said hauling his bulk out of bed. He stood indecisively in the dark, scratching his beard.

"Mrrarr," Keynes complained gruffly from under the covers. "Nrrff," he added for good measure.

"Oh, go back to sleep you useless foot-warmer," Silber told him.

"Beg pardon?" Jim asked in surprise.

"No, no, not you," Silber said testily. "Who's Dr. Altman been assigned to? And where is she?"

"Dr. Fischbein. And she's on 6 West now."

Silber frowned. "Fischbein . . . don't know him. And Dr. Altman's in bad shape, you say? Hmm. Well, maybe I'd better come over. In case I have to take care of things myself. You can't trust anyone to do a job properly these days. Not if you want it done right. Hmmf. Thanks, Jim. I'll see you soon."

Chapter 42

A blue curtain was pulled around the stretcher. Also, the place was too quiet to be the ER. "Sign here," a nurse was instructing her. "Consent for endoscopy" the form said. Maggie signed. She observed that she was almost too weak to hold the pen.

"Give her 10 mg of Valium IV," a voice outside the curtains instructed. Although the words were clear enough, the sounds seemed to come from miles away. A young physician, dressed in scrubs and looking very sleepy, poked his head inside. "I'll be using the Olympus." Maggie remembered seeing the collection of long black snakes hanging from the walls in the endoscopy suite. She hoped that she wouldn't gag too much. But she felt very calm. Very distant. She even imagined her body to be floating on a cloud.

She drifted in and out of awareness. "Duodenal ulcer," she heard the voice remark. "Actively bleeding. More suction please."

Maggie gagged a little as the endoscope was withdrawn. "She's an intern, isn't she? Somebody better notify the chief. He's gonna have to do something about the schedule."

"No," Maggie started to say. "I'll be there in the morning." Then she fell asleep again.

She felt the stretcher lurching around the corner. Clumsily, the orderly held the double doors open and simultaneously pulled the stretcher between them. 6 West, Maggie noted. Well, it didn't matter, did it?

"What the hell!" a female voice exclaimed. "We can't handle a bleeder here!" Maggie thought she recognized the voice and the face. Caroline, as she recalled.

There was a clatter, as someone in a short white coat set a stainless steel basin down on the bedside table. A medical student. Maggie flinched a little as he squirted some of the ice water from his syringe onto her face. She opened her eyes briefly and saw that the nasogastric tube had been reinserted. It was full of bright red blood.

But it couldn't belong to her. She wasn't having pain now, and she felt very calm and peaceful. She was quite sure she'd be able to work by morning.

"I said put her in Trendelenburg. That means with her head down," an impatient voice told the medical student. "And run see if the first unit of blood is ready yet."

The student scuttled off, and Dr. Fischbein leaned over her to do his examination. He seemed to be annoyed with her. She didn't blame him. He'd inherit some of her work tomorrow, unless she got better very quickly. But she certainly didn't feel any better. She was perceptibly weaker.

"Caroline!" Charlie yelled.

"Yes, Doctor?" Caroline answered. She hadn't hurried, Maggie noted.

"See if the lab has that hematocrit yet. And find out how much Valium they gave her," Fischbein directed. "She's just not very with it."

Maggie was vaguely aware of someone else in the room, near the head of her bed. It was Dr. Eisig! How dedicated of him, to check on her himself. It must be an ungodly hour by now. He smiled at her and patted her hand. "Everything's going to be all right," he told her, reassuringly. "You're in good hands."

"Thank you, Dr. Eisig," she said gratefully. Hearing the tension in Charlie's voice, she had started to worry a little. But the confident, white-coated figure of the chief of medicine set her mind at ease, and she went back to sleep.

• • •

"BP 80/60, pulse 140," somebody was saying, a nurse's aide apparently. "Do you want me to get a pressure bag for the blood?"

"Yeah, why don't you. And maybe we ought to call Dr. Fischbein." Maggie opened her eyes briefly. The medical student—she couldn't remember his name—was still doing his

213

ice water lavage, and a unit of blood was hanging. The drainage from the nasogastric tube looked almost as dark as the blood flowing through the intravenous line. Surely the bleeding should have stopped by now, Maggie thought.

"Since you want to be the doctor, I'd transfer her to your service if I could," Fischbein's voice was just outside the door. "But given your rating, inter-service transfers aren't allowed. Too bad. But do me the favor of getting off my case."

"I'm not trying to interfere," Fred said, reasonably. "I just wanted to sit with her for a while."

"Caroline will tell you when visiting hours are," Charlie said rudely.

Maggie couldn't hear his response. Charlie blustered into the room, and the student seemed to be showing him the results of the lavage. "Do you think we ought to call a surgery consult?" he asked timidly.

"Nah," Charlie said bluntly. "They don't do surgery for duodenal ulcer anymore. Not since Tagamet has been around. Just keep up the lavage. She did get some Tagamet already, didn't she?"

"They got in a dose before the last unit of blood," the student replied.

"Fine," Charlie said, departing abruptly.

Maggie felt a hand on hers, and saw Fred looking down at her with great concern. "I'm all right," she said. "Please go home and get some sleep. You'll need it tomorrow. I didn't even want to call you."

"Dr. Jenkins," Caroline said icily. She had apparently followed Fred into the room. "Do I need to remind you what hospital policy is? We can't allow you to impede patient care."

"Don't worry about me, Fred," Maggie whispered. "Please. Don't get yourself in trouble." She sensed that her usually cool-headed friend was about to blow his stack at Caroline. And it was not necessary. Surely the bleeding would stop soon. Everything was being done. Even Dr. Eisig had been in to see her.

Reluctantly, Fred left the room. Maggie sighed. You sometimes didn't find out who your friends were until too late. Brent, she had noticed, had not found it necessary to check on

214

her.

The student read her armband again and checked the name against the one on the label for the next unit of blood—he seemed quite conscientious, Maggie noted. She had lost count of the number of transfusions by now. She was so tired. She closed her eyes again, and gratefully accepted the embrace of sleep.

Chapter 43

Silber entered through the side door, staying away from the bright lights of the ER entrance, and headed for the back stairwell. Thank goodness, he hadn't passed anyone in the hall. He was acting like a thief, sneaking into the hospital this way. He ought to just stride stride right up to the main elevator and push the button. Instead of puffing up six flights of stairs. He was winded after only two, and had to stop to rest. But he didn't want to have to give any explanations. With his luck, an officious nurse would ask him to leave because visiting hours were over. He had no time to argue with her.

Silber emerged on 6 West, in a small room at the end of the corridor that served as a combination storeroom and makeshift conference room, where he had once met his team for morning bedside rounds—a custom made archaic by the advent of EquaCare and other modernist innovations. He was ready to retreat back into the stairwell, if any nurses were taking a smoke break. But the room was deserted. Fortunately, the door that led to the corridor had a window. He flattened himself against the wall and watched the hallway for several minutes. Room 615 was about six doors down; a lot of doorways to pass. He was about to take a deep breath and plunge into the hall when a young man in a white coat emerged from 615. Silber jumped back out of sight again. But now was the time. The student, or whoever he was, might be coming back soon.

His heart skipping every other beat, he tried to walk down the hall at a normal pace. But he couldn't help moving a little too fast as he entered the room. He stumbled on the bedside table, and it ran into the bed, splashing ice water onto the sheets and the patient. Maggie opened her eyes, and looked up at him. As soon as she recognized him, her eyes opened wider in what he supposed to be fear.

"Pardon me, Dr. Altman," he said. "I was hoping not to

call attention to my presence quite so abruptly. Jim Thomas called me from the ER. He was worried about you." Silber evaluated the situation quickly: the nasogastric tube, the ice water, the blood transfusions. He turned on the light and pulled down her lower eyelid. "About 7," he muttered. And her pulse was 130. She was shocky, or else very frightened. Well, who wouldn't be, after an entrance like the one he had just made. Her hemorrhage must be frightening too. Probably a duodenal ulcer.

He knew that his intrusion was quite irregular. It certainly wasn't acceptable to barge in on another doctor's patient and start to do a history and physical. And to take over the therapy. But at the new Woodlands, the usual rules hardly applied. He looked at the untidiness around the bed and snorted in disgust. Lab values scrawled on a scrap of paper towel (yes, the hemoglobin was 7.4); a puddle of water on the floor; two used needles; and a partly filled tube of blood. The kind they used for a type and cross. It was right on the edge of the table, where it could easily be brushed onto the floor. Silber picked it up and stuffed it into his pocket.

It was too late to retreat when he heard someone approaching. The medical student. Silber stuck out his hand. "Milton Silber, internal medicine." No defense like a good offense. He certainly wasn't going to be intimidated by a student.

The student shook his hand. "Jack Wilson," he said. He returned to his duties as if Silber's presence were part of the normal routine. "They haven't got the next type and cross done yet. There's some sort of problem with it." He pulled back the plunger on the syringe, and bright red blood returned from the nasogastric tube.

"How many units has she had?" Silber asked.

"Four, sir," the student replied.

"What did the endoscopy show?"

"Duodenal ulcer, actively bleeding."

"Surgery consult?"

"Uh, no, sir. I asked Dr. Fischbein about that, and he felt that wasn't appropriate for a duodenal ulcer."

Not appropriate! Silber was furious. The patient was in shock, they couldn't stop the bleeding or crossmatch the blood, and there was nobody with her but a medical student, who was mindlessly squirting ice water into the stomach! It looked as though they were trying to kill her. Silber broke out in a cold sweat. Maybe they were.

Silber thought for a moment. He could hardly sling the patient over his shoulder and take her to another hospital. But he had to do something. First, the blood. There must be a public telephone nearby, probably near the elevator.

The number rang and rang; finally, someone answered.

"Ellen?" Silber asked. There was a noise he took to be an affirmative.

"Milt Silber. Have to speak to Jake."

There was a moment's pause and some coughing. "My God," Metzenbaum said, "You're calling a pathologist in the middle of the night? For an emergency autopsy, perhaps? Has there been an outbreak of plague? A—"

"—Jake, do you trust the people who are doing the blood banking?" Silber interrupted. This was no time for levity.

"I trained most of them myself," Metzenbaum assured him. "But wait a minute. Oh, my God! I don't know who's on tonight. It could be Rathbone. Or Rathman, whatever his name is. I've been trying to get rid of that bastard for years, but the equal opportunity committee insisted I put him back on regular rotation."

"Jake, Maggie Altman is at Woodlands with a bleeding ulcer. They're having trouble with a crossmatch, I hear."

"Dammit!" Metzenbaum said. "Sorry, Milt. I stubbed my toe! Look, I'm putting on some clothes. I'll be right over."

The telephone clicked, and Silber replaced the receiver. He still had the tube of blood in his hand. He had meant to look for a wastebasket. But there was something very strange. He tilted the tube a couple of times. Then held it up to the light. The blood was liquid. Without any sign of a clot forming. Silber's heart began to race, and he felt a tightness in his throat. Did she suffer from a severe, heretofore unrecognized, hereditary coagulation defect? Unlikely. Had she developed disseminated intravascular coagulation? Possible. A circulating anticoagulant? The differential would include pregnancy, liver disease, collagen vascular disease . . . or a drug effect. Silber headed for the main elevator, heedless of whether anyone saw him.

• • •

"You need to sign in at the triage desk, sir," the Major Medicine A clerk informed him primly.

"I need to speak to Jim Thomas," Silber wheezed. "Now. Immediately. Get him for me, please."

The clerk turned to the resident for help. Oh no, Silber thought. That swine Stemmons was on. What lousy luck. But what the hell. It would take more than that arrogant son of a bitch to stop him now.

"Good evening, Dr. Silber," Stemmons said frostily. "Can I help you?"

"Yeah. Page Jim Thomas for me. STAT. He'll know what it's about."

"I'm sure you understand, Dr. Silber, the importance of proper procedure. We can't interrupt patient care to deliver personal messages."

Condescending fool, Silber fumed silently, his blood pressure rising. He tapped one finger on the desk in irritation. He was tempted to slug the cocky bastard. Deck him right here in the ER.

"Shall I call Security, Doctor?" the clerk inquired of Stemmons.

"Feel free," Silber muttered to her, stepping behind the desk. If he was going to be treated like a disruptive visitor off the streets, he might as well act like one. The clerk looked horrified, but stood aside. Stemmons' eyes smoldered with rage, but he stood there indecisively. Coward, Silber thought. Silber picked up the the telephone, and punched the intercom button. "Mr. Thomas, to the desk, please."

Jim appeared almost immediately. He obviously recognized the voice. He walked toward the nurse's lounge, Silber following. "Get me some protamine, Jim." Silber showed him the tube of unclotted blood. The man's eyes widened.

"I'll have to get it from pharmacy," Jim said. "We don't

keep any down here. Wait for me by the surgery elevator."

The two men walked back to the Pit, where the clerk was picking up the telephone.

"I'm leaving," Silber informed them.

"I got rid of him, Doctor," Jim said to Stemmons, as Silber exited through the double doors.

. . .

Silber noticed that his knees were suddenly weak, now that the immediate crisis was over. He wouldn't be surprised if the clerk called Security after all, to search the hall for suspicious characters. And it wouldn't take long for the guard to arrive. An officer with a sidearm was continuously on duty near the ER.

But he had to get the protamine. Should he just stand near the elevator and try to look nonchalant?

A better idea soon presented itself. The surgery waiting room was across from the elevator; he could just sit with the patients. Patients were said to have been lost in surgery for days. Probably, no one would notice him. At least he wasn't over-dressed for the role—in his hurry, he had thrown on the shirt with the torn pocket, an old pair of slacks, and worn, unshined loafers.

Despite the late hour, business appeared to be brisk. Several patients were seated in school desks, soaking a wounded part in a basin of water and Betadine scrub. Parked on stretchers were patients with more severe injuries, some with splints. One such patient shrieked an obscenity from time to time, and one snored raucously. The place stank of alcohol and blood. Nobody looked at him as Silber cautiously lowered himself into a chair.

They all did watch, fascinated, as a team in scrubs pushed a stretcher onto the elevator, which led directly to the operating rooms above. Silber did a double take. The patient's chest was open, and one of the residents had his hand buried inside, doing cardiac massage. Or perhaps plugging the hole from a stab wound. Woodlands had the reputation for saving more "elevator cases" than any other hospital in the state. That ability might become a thing of the past, but the surgery department was, so far, faring a little better than the medicine department under EquaCare. At least they didn't have Eisig.

Silber was beginning to think Jim had abandoned him, but soon the nurse appeared, carrying a paper bag. It contained a vial and a syringe. And a set of scrubs. Jim really thought of everything. Silber followed him out into the hall. "Sorry it took so long," Jim said when there was no one in range of his voice. "I was afraid I was going to have to steal it from pharmacy. They didn't believe my story at first."

"Thanks, Jim," Silber said. He headed in the direction of the back stairs, but Jim steered him toward the elevator in the lobby, where several people were standing around.

"I think they alerted Security," Jim warned him. "Better to stay in plain sight."

• • •

Silber's hands fumbled as he drew up a dose of protamine. What a scandal if he were caught just at this moment, he thought. He could see the headlines now: "Former TU Professor of Medicine Found Shooting Up in Restroom." He nearly dropped the syringe when the door opened. But from the sounds, it was just someone on an errand of necessity. Silber cursed under his breath. He supposed the individual must now be combing his hair, and taking a long time about it. Finally, the door opened and closed again. Hastily, Silber changed into the scrub suit, dropped his own clothing onto the floor, and emerged from the cramped stall, the loaded syringe in his pocket.

He would just have to walk into the room and slip the injection into the IV. What could be difficult about that? He had done such things hundreds of times. He concentrated on breathing at a normal rate. Honestly, he told himself, one would think that he were the one who had tried to poison the patient.

Luck was with him. The student was leaving the room, just as Silber arrived on the floor. He slipped inside, found the IV tubing and inserted the needle. Pinching off the line, he pushed down on the plunger. Maggie opened her eyes, and for a moment, he thought she was going to scream.

She didn't, but a voice behind him demanded to know: "Just what the hell do you think you're doing?"

How could he have been apprehensive, Silber wondered. This was going to be easy. It was even going to be satisfying, in a perverse sort of way. He turned and stared her down, noting her nametag. Caroline, it read.

"Protamine, Nurse," he said. "How much heparin did you give her?"

"I don't know what you're talking about," she said contemptuously.

"The dose of heparin is important for calculating the correct dose of antidote," Silber explained.

"I know," Caroline said.

"So, how much did you give her?"

"Who the hell are you?" she asked.

"That doesn't matter," Silber responded. "But the dose of heparin does."

"I'm going to call Security," she announced.

"No, call the police," Silber advised her. "I want to report an attempted murder." Caroline looked shocked. "But first bring me a stool specimen cup, some test tubes, and a syringe for drawing blood."

• • •

When Dr. Eisig arrived ten minutes later, he found Silber tilting a test tube of blood, then sticking it back into one of three holes in the lid of a stool specimen cup. Eisig's expression was inscrutable.

"Good evening, Dr. Eisig," Silber said. "I am impressed to see you here so late attending to your patients. Or so early. Shall we go to the nursing station? I have a telephone call to make."

Silber led the way, and the two men seated themselves. Silber consulted his watch, and tilted the test tube again. Then he dialed the number for pathology. "Give me Metzenbaum, please."

Silber leaned back in the chair and studied Eisig's face

while he waited for the pathologist. What a mask. Perhaps his eyes were watering a bit more than usual. But otherwise he was as cool as could be.

"Milt, I was just about to page you overhead!" Metzenbaum said excitedly. "The blood doesn't clot. That was the trouble with the crossmatch. Rathbone, the idiot, didn't have enough sense to call the intern. It still hasn't clotted. The girl is anticoagulated out to infinity! There's only one possibility that I can think of, given the other test results."

"I've reached the same conclusion," Silber said, looking straight at Eisig. "And I just gave her a shot of protamine. In fact," he tilted a test tube again, and found the blood to be solid, "The Lee White clotting time is now 14 minutes. Obsolete test, I know. But it doesn't have to go to the lab where some idiot can screw it up. I guessed pretty well on the dose."

Eisig was staring at the test tube. "I was right!" he said, with a hint of triumph in his voice. "I just felt uncomfortable about this case. That's why I came in," he explained. "Besides the fact that the patient is one of my own interns."

Silber snorted. What an outrageous lie! But how would he ever prove differently? The dedicated Dr. Eisig. Personally supervising his house staff. And the patient wasn't even a Senator. She was a mere intern. The story was enough to bring tears to a person's eyes.

"Heparin," Silber pointed out, "is not a standard treatment for bleeding, as I recall."

Eisig ignored the sarcasm. "We have to find out who is responsible for this error. This is intolerable. We must be sure that such a thing can never happen again." He reached for the chart, and began to peruse it.

Fine, tell that to your board of directors, Silber thought angrily. If I had my way, you'd be explaining it to a jury. But that would never happen. He might have to be content with making sure that Dr. Altman got out of the hospital. Alive.

Silber left Eisig poring over the chart, and returned to sit with the patient. When the next unit of packed red cells was running, and he had assured himself that the bleeding had slowed, he placed a chair for himself just inside the patient's door. They wouldn't dare throw him out now, he thought.

"Dr. Silber," Maggie said weakly, "I want to apologize for being rude the other night."

"No, I should apologize," he said, "for being dimwitted." He squeezed her hand. "With your permission, I'm going to sit by the door here. Bad things can happen in hospitals."

"Did they give me heparin by mistake?" she asked.

"Apparently so," Silber replied. Why tell her the truth? She had enough to worry about for the moment.

"You know, I think they killed one of my patients," she said. So, she already suspected.

"We have a lot of things to talk about," Silber said, "when you're better. Including Ararat Management Consultants."

Maggie nodded. She wasn't afraid of him any more, Silber thought. He sat down near the door. Even if he dozed off, he would surely be awakened if anyone entered the room. He could hear some angry voices in the nursing station. The intern, apparently, was trying to blame the nurse and the medical student for the debacle. Silber was willing to bet that the intern would be fired for incompetence. He snorted. But that same intern wasn't too incompetent to be entrusted with the care of the patient for the rest of the night! Hmff! Well, he, Jake Metzenbaum, and the medical student would make sure that Maggie Altman did all right. And as soon as she was stable, he would arrange for her to leave this place, against medical advice if necessary. He knew just where to take her.

Chapter
44

Someone was tapping softly on the door of her bedroom. Maggie came awake with a start. Where was she? For a moment, she had been dreaming that she was back home in her parents' house in Kansas, with her mother knocking on the bedroom door to wake her for school. But that, of course, was wrong. Or was it? She opened her eyes. Was she still dreaming? The flannel nightgown she was wearing belonged to someone else, and this certainly wasn't her bed. Or her room. She realized that she hadn't the faintest idea where she was.

"Maggie?" a familiar voice called. "Are you awake?"

Dr. Silber! The events of the past two days came back with a rush: the attack in the parking lot; the midnight ride to TU's emergency room; the blood that wouldn't clot; Dr. Silber's miraculous appearance in her hospital room; a half-heard argument between Dr. Silber and Caroline (or maybe that, too, had been a dream); and finally, the next morning, a ride in Dr. Silber's car somewhere out into the country. She wondered how much of what she remembered was real, and how much imagined. Well, she would soon find out.

"Yes, I'm awake," she called.

Dr. Silber backed into the room, carrying a dinner tray. She found she was ravenously hungry. She wanted a thick, juicy steak. But it seemed she was getting chicken soup. He set the tray down on her night table and stood awkwardly beside the bed. He looked even more disheveled than usual, she noted. And he was wearing blue hospital scrubs. Could she be at Dr. Silber's house? And why?

"Where am I?" she asked him, looking about apprehensively. She had the impression that this man had saved her from something terrible. Something at TU. Yet only two days earlier he had been at the top of her list of suspects. Which perception was correct, she wondered. Had he somehow managed to deceive

225

and kidnap her? What was going on? "I think I'd like to make a phone call," she said.

He gestured to the bedside table. "Help yourself."

She picked up the phone, listened for the dial tone, then put it down again. She didn't really want to make a call; she wanted, rather, to be sure she could if she chose.

"Is anyone else here?" she asked.

"Oh. Yes. That is, Kate's here," he said, seeming to understand her line of questioning. "I'll call her if you like."

Maggie remembered now. Kate must be the woman who had put her to bed this morning. She also thought she remembered having her finger stuck several times. Presumably Dr. Silber's work. She felt oddly touched—Kate and Dr. Silber were certainly taking care of her.

Silber crossed to the window, and looked over his shoulder at Maggie. "There's Kate. I mean Mrs. Fitzhugh. She's in the paddock. This is the Flying V Ranch. Owned by her and her son. If you stretch up a bit, you can see Kate. Do you want me to call her?"

Maggie lifted herself up and peered out the window. It was late afternoon, she noted in surprise. She must have slept the day away. Sure enough, there was a small, wiry-looking woman in a fenced-off area watching a Hispanic man who had a horse tied to the end of a long rope. The woman laughed at something the man said, then walked over and gave the horse an apple and kissed its nose. She could see the river in the background. Maggie sighed. It looked all right. She shook her head no.

"You're safe," he told her earnestly. "You weren't, you know, but you are now." Seeing her skepticism, he gestured to the phone. "Please. Call your friend Dr. Jenkins for confirmation."

She looked at him steadily. She didn't want to bother Fred. And if Silber were urging her to call her friend, whatever he told her could probably be believed. "I don't remember everything that happened," she said. "But I do remember something about heparin. And about your being in my hospital room. And Dr. Eisig. You went outside to talk with him. Why?"

Silber glared at her, and she saw anger in his eyes. But she soon realized the anger was not directed at her. "Dr. Eisig was trying to kill you," he said.

• • •

"I don't really understand all of it," Maggie told Silber, finishing the last of her soup. "But there is something pretty strange going on at TU. And I have made a perfect nuisance of myself there. But enough of a nuisance to make Dr. Eisig want to kill me? It doesn't make sense." It certainly seemed incredible. But it was clear someone had been giving her heparin. There was proof—the tube of unclotted blood that Dr. Silber had found in her room. She shook her head. It could have been a mistake. Mistakes were made all the time in hospitals. And who could have administered the injection? A number of people had been in the room: the medical student (Jack Wilson, she thought his name was); Charlie Fischbein (who had been taking care of Mr. Post!); Caroline; Fred (no—it couldn't have been Fred!). She closed her eyes to help her remember—Dr. Eisig had been in the room twice. Once before Dr. Silber arrived. He could have done it then. It was certainly possible. But why? On one level she was gratified to learn that she hadn't been crazy after all—that there was someone masterminding a sinister scheme at TU. But on another level she was shocked and sorry to learn that it might be Dr. Eisig. Even if she never had liked the man. The thought made her profoundly depressed.

"Oh, it makes sense all right," Silber told her. "And I should have been able to put the pieces together earlier. I could have saved you from Eisig's tender mercies. When you asked me that damned fool question about Ararat Management Consultants, I knew you were in trouble," Silber told her. "No one could have known about Ararat unless they'd had access to TU's financial database. And the access code, as well as the security disarm code, had cost me a lot of money. So, I figured that you had stumbled across the access code, used it to get the information, but had probably been identified as an unauthorized user." He shrugged. "It was just a matter of time before Eisig found out. Although I myself didn't know that the mastermind behind this little scheme was our friend Dr. Eisig. Oh, I suspected it, but I wasn't certain until Ryan Fitzhugh brought me proof—the name of the principal stockholder of Harvey Consulting Corporation. Ararat was only a shell, you see. And, of course, I needed to know the size of the stockholder's bank account." He snorted. "Philip Eisig."

Maggie frowned. "So he was skimming profits. Arranging to be paid for consulting work he never did. And counting on the fact that TU's consistently profitable status would mean that its finances wouldn't be subjected to a thorough scrutiny."

"And even if they were," Silber pointed out, "who would inquire into the corporate status of Ararat? Even if they did, the paper trail would lead them to an address in the Twin Towers. All very plausible. No, our friend hid himself well."

Maggie was silent for a moment. "I suspected you," she told Silber bluntly. "I had you figured for the mastermind."

Silber hooted. "Me? I don't know whether I should be flattered or insulted. Whatever made you suspect me?"

So she told him: the fragments of conversation she had overheard between Silber and Metzenbaum; Silber's unabashed pursuit of profits; the phone that rang in the back room and was never answered; the dark figure she had seen skulking through his kitchen; and, of course, the computer access numbers she had found on his desk.

"Hmmf," Silber said. "My hotline. And yes, Fitzhugh did trip over the roasting pan the night you were at my place. And Metzenbaum's little scheme to increase Pathology's budget is a bit irregular. So I guess it could have added up to something incriminating." Silber smiled. "If you had a suspicious mind, that is."

Maggie blushed. "I'm sorry." She thought for a moment. "You know, Eisig must also be behind all the things that have been going wrong at the hospital. The unprofitable cases being turned away, and the profitable ones being admitted." A chill ran up her backbone. "Maybe even Mr. Post's death." The idea was absolutely appalling. Could Eisig have killed him for the few thousand dollars that his hospital stay was costing? Or to protect himself from close scrutiny by the feds? Miss Brophy had mentioned that the hospital was about to lose its "waiver" if Mr.

Post wasn't discharged. And she couldn't have discharged him without evaluating his stroke.

"Mr. Post may have to remain unavenged," Silber told her. "I'm sure there will be no proof that he was murdered."

"I can't believe Dr. Eisig would have done that!" Maggie exclaimed.

"Why not? He was ready to kill you! Who knows how many others there have been?"

Maggie shuddered. "But what can we do about it? Can't he be stopped somehow?"

"How?" Silber laughed bitterly. "He seems to have covered his tracks too well. We haven't a shred of evidence."

"The tube of blood! The heparin!"

"So sorry, Dr. Altman. Simply an error on the part of the intern. Poor Dr. Fischbein has probably been fired by now—Eisig looked appropriately concerned when I pointed out the error to him."

"But I can't believe there's nothing we can do!"

"Well," Silber pointed out reasonably, "we managed to save your life. Maybe that's good enough."

"Do you think it is?" Maggie asked him.

"No," he admitted, scratching his beard. "But I don't have any bright ideas at the moment. In fact, I have hardly any ideas at all." He yawned. "I was up all night, and I'm not a youngster like you. I need to check your hematocrit one more time, then I'll have to go home. Keynes needs his dinner." Silber stuck her finger with a lancet and collected a little blood in a capillary tube. He placed the tubes in a centrifuge and set the time for five minutes. "Metzenbaum borrowed a little equipment from the Woodlands for us. Your hematocrit has been running about 30. I wasn't sure which was riskier—having you here where no one could find you, but without hospital facilities, or putting you in a different hospital."

"It's nicer here," Maggie told him. "Much more restful. And I can check my own hematocrit."

"Kate will be here if you get into trouble," Silber said. "I'm at the end of the phone. Now here's your Tagamet."

Maggie obediently swallowed the pill, and Silber took the

blood from the centrifuge. "It's 31. We're all right for the moment. So, I'll be off." He took the tray from her nightstand.

"Dr. Silber," Maggie called after him, "do you think Dr. Eisig suspects that you know about him—about his being behind Ararat?"

Silber shook his head. "I can't think of any way he could have learned that."

"Good," she said, immensely relieved. "And of course still doesn't know that we suspect him of masterminding the 'profitable' running of TU. And of Mr. Post's death."

"And the attempt on your life," Silber reminded her.

"Yes. That too." She looked thoughtful. "So maybe we have an advantage after all."

"Oh?"

"Knowledge. For whatever that's worth."

"It's a valuable commodity," Silber said, backing through the door. "It's always worth something."

. . .

Showered and dressed, her hair shampooed and blown dry, Maggie tentatively tried on the sweater and skirt Kate had offered her. Fortunately, Kate seemed to be about her size. The sweater was a very attractive shade of green, and the wraparound skirt, a matching plaid. She looked at herself in the mirror. A little pale. Well, that was to be expected. She certainly felt better. In fact, she was ravenous. What she intended now was a late night raid on the kitchen. Kate had told her that she would be working on the ranch's books in her office if she needed anything. Well, she supposed she could make a sandwich on her own.

She found her way to the kitchen without much difficulty—the house was enormous, but laid out in a logical fashion. She just followed the long hall directly off her bedroom. The kitchen was a little intimidating. In fact, it looked as big as her whole apartment. Obviously a lot of cooking was done in here. Cooking for a great many people. A large double doored refrigerator was built into the wall at one end of the kitchen, and she opened it tentatively. Hmm. On a plate, covered with plastic, was half a roasted chicken. Her mouth began to water. Yes, that was just what she wanted. She put it down on the island in the middle of the kitchen, and considered which cupboard to open first in search of cutlery and dishes.

"How about some biscuits and gravy?" a cheerful voice asked.

Startled, she turned around. There, at a table she had hadn't noticed at the other end of the kitchen sat a red haired man reading a newspaper and eating. "Oh!" she exclaimed.

"You must be Maggie," he said, getting up. He was very tall, she noted. And had flaming red hair.

"Yes, I'm Maggie Altman. Who are you?"

He extended his hand. "Ryan Fitzhugh. Kate's stepson. We own the Flying V together."

She shook his hand awkwardly. Now what? She really wasn't up to a lot of small talk. Even though this man was clearly her host.

"How about those biscuits?" he asked.

"I'd love them," she confessed. "Gravy too, if you're still offering."

"Consuela is the best cook in the world," he told her. "She made extra for dinner, thinking you might want some later. Go ahead, sit down. You deserve to be waited on after the rough time you've had."

She sat down, feeling grateful, but also a little foolish. Ryan wasted no time. He heated the biscuits and gravy, produced another place mat and cutlery, and had her dinner in front of her in only a few moments. Then he picked up his paper—an issue of *Barron's*—and prepared to leave. "Sorry I have to run," he said. "But my work day is just beginning."

"Oh? Are you in the same business as Dr. Silber?"

He smiled. He had quite a nice smile, she thought. Not at all self-assured, and certainly not charming. But nice nonetheless. And he didn't seem at all the clumsy type. She wondered how he had managed to trip over the roasting pan in Silber's back room.

"Well, we're both in finance. So I guess you could say it's related. I'm a foreign exchange trader at Banque France."

She was impressed. "Sounds stressful."

"It is," he told her earnestly. "And I've been doing it for too long. I'm really too old for it," he admitted. "It's a young person's game." He looked thoughtfully off into the distance. "I daydream about quitting. But then I ask myself what else I'd do. Finance is all I know." He looked at his watch. "Got to run. Perhaps I'll see you later. Just yell for Kate if you need anything. Nice to have met you, Maggie."

As soon as he was gone, Maggie attacked her chicken and biscuits. It seemed to her that nothing had ever tasted so good.

Chapter 45

On the drive home from the Flying V, Silber was unable to appreciate the beauty of the sunset. He was, by turns, depressed, frustrated, and seething with rage, although he had done his best to conceal these emotions from Maggie. Damn it to hell! There had to be a way to get at Eisig. He ground his teeth and cursed the driver in front of him.

What did you really expect when you began this hunt, he asked himself. He had had no good reason to suspect Eisig of any criminal wrongdoing—he simply hated the man. No, it had all begun with the phone call from Fitzhugh, alerting him to profits to be made from AMIX's decline. That had led him into an unauthorized incursion into the EquaCare and Woodlands computers, where he had found the name of the company selected to replace AMIX. It was then he had come across Ararat Management Consultants, and the totally ridiculous sum it had received—$1.3 million. He snorted. All that money for management advice? In three months? Ridiculous. That was when his suspicions had been aroused. Because proper management of Woodlands was Eisig's job. The man would never have acknowledged that his administration was so poor that the services of a consulting firm were necessary. Never. He was too arrogant. Silber had vowed to himself then and there that he would pursue the matter, fully expecting that at the end of the road he would find Eisig, hiding like a snail under a rock. However, his thoughts had gone no farther than that. Now what, he asked himself.

He sighed, and turned onto Hudson Drive, approaching his house. Eisig had turned out to be guilty of much more than Silber ever dreamed. Murder, it seemed, and attempted murder. And now Maggie was involved. He slammed the car door and stomped across the yard. If the knowledge of Eisig's theft were his alone, or if the man were guilty only of theft . . . well, he might drop the matter. He waddled disconsolately into the house.

Keynes regarded him with a reproachful yellow stare.

"I know, I know," Silber said guiltily. "I've neglected you. Mea culpa. Would a plate of sardines mollify you? No? How about herrings in cream? Smoked salmon? Tinned shrimp?"

Keynes yawned. Then turned his back on Silber, feigning indifference.

"Go ahead. Be like that," Silber told him, shoving a can of shrimp under the electric can opener. He changed Keynes' water and placed the shrimp in a china saucer, depositing both dishes on the cat's place mat in the corner. Keynes favored him with a look of ennui. "Of course, you're not hungry," Silber told him. "I understand. I'll leave this here anyway, shall I? In case you think you might want a snack later." Keynes made a great show of washing his hind leg. Silber noted, however, that as soon as he turned his back, sounds of slurping and growling began. He smiled, and opened a tin of soup for himself.

After dinner, Silber poured a stiff drink and took it into the living room. He poked around in his bookshelf, and retrieved a dusty box of clippings from the *Fort Bastion Morning News*. Lately, there had been relatively few articles about EquaCare. But about 18 months ago, it had been on the front page nearly every other day. The reporter, Robert Carlisle, had been extremely thorough.

Keynes stuck his nose into the box, sniffed and sneezed. He began to wash his face furiously.

"Revolting, isn't it?" Silber said. "Go find yourself some juicy crickets for dessert."

But Keynes seemed uninterested in such strenuous activity. He jumped up on his favorite chair, sharpened his claws on the arm, then collapsed in a heap to take his accustomed post-prandial siesta. Silber noted that the cat was purring rustily, and smiled a little to himself, careful not to let Keynes know that he had noticed.

Then he settled down to read the yellowing papers. "EquaCare Contract Awarded to TU; Regional Preventive Health Centers to be Funded." Hmmf, Silber thought. Same day "wellness checks" at $20 a head. Sickness appointments were booked up for six months, though. "Governor Attends National

234

Symposium on Health Care Cost Containment"—and Eisig was in that delegation to explain how EquaCare was working. "TURPH Center Commended by Peer Review Organization for Outstanding Quality of Care." Silber snorted. "EquaCare Saves State $70 Million in First Year." That one was really interesting. The state had actually spent $130 million more than the year before. But the legislature calculated that the increase would have been $200 million if EquaCare hadn't been enacted, and besides, most of the money came from the feds. "Legislature Votes Overwhelmingly to Extend EquaCare Experiment for Five Years."

There were some articles that hadn't made the front page, too. The legislature failed to appropriate funds for an audit, saying a $5 million discrepancy in the books "didn't justify the expense of an audit." A grand jury deliberated in secret on accusations against one of the EquaCare founders; no follow-up report was ever released. One EquaCare "provider," a group of private doctors, was filing for bankruptcy; they claimed that the state owed them $11 million.

Silber shook his head. What a morass! He poured himself another slug of bourbon, and lit a cigar. As far as the politicians were concerned, EquaCare was a rousing success. And the medical journals loved it too. Prepayment was the discovery of the century. Just gather up the money in the pool, and appoint "gatekeepers," giving them the prospect of a bonus as an incentive for cost containment.

All that money up front was an incentive all right. And chances that it would ever find its way to the doctors who actually did the work of caring for sick people were remote indeed.

And there was the "balanced" assessment of EquaCare in the *Northeastern Journal of Medicine* that had brought Fort Bastion and Dr. Eisig the acclaim of all progressive health economists. It even mentioned the "anecdotal" evidence that EquaCare had a few growing pains. Mr. Post and Dr. Altman were anecdotes too, no doubt.

Silber's viewpoint about EquaCare when it was still in its planning stage had been called biased and unbalanced. He didn't have anything favorable to say about it. And balance was all important. Especially the bank balance.

Silber snorted. He had no statistics, no t-test for statistical significance, and no evidence that would stand up in court. Eisig was holding all the trumps; he made Willie Sutton look like a rank amateur. The bastard was probably going to get away with everything. Well, maybe not. An idea began to form. He picked up the phone and dialed the office of the *Fort Bastion Morning News*.

"Let me speak to Robert Carlisle, please," he said.

"Sorry, sir. Mr. Carlisle is no longer with us."

"Oh," Silber said, surprised. He really hadn't counted on this. But it made sense. Recent articles about EquaCare had been fewer and more favorable. "Thanks," he told the young woman on the end of the phone and hung up.

He poured himself another drink. So much for public exposure, he thought ruefully. He wondered why Carlisle was no longer with the paper. Maybe a change in job hadn't been entirely his choice.

Still wearing his scrubs, Silber padded over to the computer. Might as well get a little business done, he thought. At least fetch the day's closing quotes on the companies he followed. He yawned and sat down.

Keynes emerged from behind the table, looking pleased with himself, and sat at Silber's feet expectantly. "Aargh!" Silber exclaimed, realizing at once what the cat had been up to in his absence. A quick look behind the computer told the tale. The power cord had been chewed completely through. "Why do you do it?" Silber roared at him. "You destructive beast! You seem determined to deny me the one thing that pleases me most."

Keynes gathered himself for flight, apparently eager to resume his favorite game. But something was wrong. He looked at his master, who had stopped in mid step, as if to ask: was there to be no chase? No screaming? No threats? He regarded Silber quizzically from the safety of the kitchen.

"My God!" Silber said, collapsing into a chair. "That's it!" He was so excited he couldn't sit still. He leaped to his feet. Pacing the room, he threw back his head and laughed aloud. "Ha! That's the way to do it. You bastard, we'll get you yet!" He looked toward the kitchen where Keynes sat, puzzled. "And you, you great lump of masticating destruction, you've just redeemed yourself."

"Mfff," Keynes replied in disappointment.

• • •

Next morning, the idea still seemed a good one. An early phone call to Fitzhugh brought him and Stevens to Silber's house—Fitzhugh looking apprehensive, Stevens eager.

"You'll probably get us both fired," Fitzhugh muttered gloomily. But he drew a chair up to sit beside Stevens at Silber's computer.

"Probably," Stevens agreed, rolling up his sleeves and rubbing his hands in glee. "Maybe even arrested. But it will sure be fun. I haven't done any hacking in ages. Oh, don't worry," he told Silber. "It's like riding a bicycle. It all comes back." He took the bourbon-laced coffee that that Silber offered. Entering a few more numbers into the computer, he sat back and waited. The automatic dial feature of Silber's modem took over, and in a moment the proper connection had been made. "Bingo! We're in!" Stevens informed him.

Silber, standing behind him, clapped him heartily on his shoulder. "Good man!"

"Now what?" Stevens wanted to know, holding out his mug for more coffee.

Silber smiled, looking at his watch. It was well before noon. Lots of time to get the deed done and make a few phone calls. "We're going to play Robin Hood," he told them.

• • •

Feeling pleased with himself, Silber hummed a few bars from "Sheep May Safely Graze" as he turned into the Flying V's laneway. Even the horses seemed benevolent today. The smell of steak grilling outdoors met him at the end of the driveway. Hmff, he said. How very convenient. He had managed to arrive just at suppertime.

237

Maggie answered the door. Still pale, but evidently much better rested. Kate had apparently found her something to wear—an attractive green sweater and a skirt. Very becoming.

"Dr. Silber! It's good to see you," Maggie said, leading him through the house. "We're all out back. You've just missed Ryan, I'm afraid, but I'll tell Kate she has another guest for dinner."

So it was "Ryan," was it? Obviously young Fitzhugh had wasted no time introducing himself. Hmmf. Well, why not? They were both engaging young people. They could do far worse than each other.

"I know who it is. He doesn't like ranches," Kate's contralto voice carried well from the backyard. "I wonder if he's willing to eat steak, though."

"Certainly," Silber said, feeling insulted. "I like steak as well as anyone. But I don't recall having been invited. And I really can't stay," he lied. "I just want to check up on the patient."

Maggie showed him a neat flow sheet with her hematocrits recorded. They were quite stable. "I've been ravenously hungry," she reported. "Besides napping, I've done nothing except eat."

"Good," he said.

Kate, with the help of a young Mexican girl, spread out a plain but savory meal. Thick sirloin steaks, baked potatoes, bread, cornbread, and an assortment of vegetables.

"Come on, Milt," Kate teased him. "You don't have to be a horse lover to stay for dinner. And consider yourself invited." She smiled at him and he forgave her immediately. Well, perhaps he could stay for a few minutes.

Silber allowed her to press a beer on him, glad that he had put on a clean pair of khaki slacks and his new blue golf shirt. Bought with Kate in mind, he frankly admitted to himself. In fact, he had a hard time tearing his eyes off her. She looked particularly attractive this evening, he thought. Her white slacks and fuchsia shirt looked very good on her. And she had left her boots elsewhere, thank goodness. Hmmf. Better concentrate on what you came here for, he told himself. He noted approvingly that Maggie declined the offer of a beer. She was sticking to milk.

"I don't think an old fashioned Sippy diet would agree with you," Silber observed.

"Oh, no," Maggie declared, her eyes on the steaks. "I know I need to build up my strength. But I have certainly sworn off alcohol, coffee, and aspirin. That's probably what did me in."

"Not to mention worry," Silber added. "What you need most now is rest. For at least a week. Then you can think about what to do next."

"There's not much to think about," Maggie said.

"Sure there is," Silber said encouragingly. "There are lots of possibilities."

"Just one," Maggie said, spearing herself a thick piece of meat and carving it up neatly.

Silber had a sinking feeling. Surely the girl wasn't determined to go back to work.

She was. "They're extremely shorthanded at TU," she told him around bites of her steak. "I talked to Fred this afternoon. For one thing, they've transferred Charlie off the service. I don't know whether they fired him, or what. But I need to get back as soon as I can."

"Woodlands will survive," Silber said. "It's you we're concerned about."

"I'm not so sure TU will survive," Maggie replied. "We know something is going on there. Something that will destroy the place. Unless we do something about it." She looked quite determined. Well, he'd better talk turkey to her.

"Something will be done about it," Silber said, hating himself for sounding so cryptic. "In fact, something has been done," he told her. "The best that can be done, under the circumstances." She looked at him doubtfully. "I can't tell you all the details. Not yet. But soon. Maybe even tomorrow."

Kate raised an eyebrow. Silber wondered if her stepson had confided in her about yesterday's activities. Silber, Stevens and Fitzhugh—computer hackers. Probably not. Fitzhugh was pretty close mouthed.

Maggie didn't look convinced. "Eisig can't be allowed to get away with this," she asserted.

"He won't," Silber promised. "At least not entirely. But there's a limit to what we can do. We can't overthrow the whole system. It's far too entrenched."

"It's rotten," she said.

"I know," he had to agree. "But wait until you hear what I have managed to do. I'm sorry I can't tell you now, but there are a few loose ends to tie up."

"Is Ryan involved in this?" Kate inquired.

"Why don't you ask him?" Silber suggested.

"Yes, in other words." She shook her head in disgust. "I might have known." She served some vanilla ice cream, and Maggie took a huge helping.

Silber pondered what to say to Maggie. She was clearly too inquisitive, and too courageous, for her own good. He didn't like resorting to scare tactics, but he really had to warn her.

"I hope you haven't forgotten that only three days ago your life was in danger."

Maggie pointedly ignored him. "This is the time to take action," she told him. "Now. Before it's too late."

"You'll just have to be patient," Silber told her. "Eisig won't get away scot free. Not entirely, anyway." Damn. He should have waited until everything had fallen into place. Then he could have presented her with a fait accompli. Now, all he could offer were vague reassurances. Blast it! But the most important part of his scheme was yet to come—tomorrow morning would tell the tale. Well, she would just have to trust him. Hmmf. Would she? Perhaps more scare tactics would help. "And even if you're safe from Eisig himself, there are other problems." He looked at her thoughtfully. "That episode in the parking lot Saturday night might not have been just another random mugging."

Maggie flinched. He hated himself for reminding her about it. "Fred told me about it Sunday morning. When he came to check on you."

She turned down a second serving of ice cream, having evidently lost her appetite. Why did he suddenly get the feeling that she was hatching some plot of her own? She had clearly stopped listening to him. "Promise me you won't do anything rash," he said in his best professorial voice.

"All right," Maggie said meekly. Far too meekly for his liking. "Nothing rash."

Chapter 46

Silber peered nervously out the living room curtains, waiting for the arrival of dawn and the paperboy. Where was the little urchin? He was usually prompt. Most mornings he heaved the paper at Silber's window at 6:15 sharp. Of course today, when Silber was fairly dancing with impatience, he was late. Lazy little thug. Blast it! Silber wondered if he should get in his car and drive to the local 7-11. Maybe so. Ah—there he was now. Hmmf. About time, too. The morning edition of the *Fort Bastion Morning News* hit Silber's window with a thud.

He couldn't wait. On the front porch, in the light of the 40 watt bulb, he turned to Page 1 of Section B. So where was it? There were stories about the local transient shelter being removed from the Jackson Park area, the Viet Nam vets who were running a drug rehabilitation center, the Eurasian girl from Fort Bastion who had won the state spelling bee, but . . . Yes! There it was! He chortled in glee. The story, which ran across four columns and occupied the bottom six inches of Page 1 bore the headline "Local Firm Gives $1.3 Million to Crippled Children." He laughed aloud and began to read. "Whoever said corporate America has no heart?" the article began. "Harvey Consulting Corporation, a local firm, has proved that old saw false. Its extremely generous donation of $1.3 million to the Neighborhood Crippled Children's Center was surely a gift straight from the heart."

Silber dashed up the front steps and into the house, hooting like a madman. Keynes opened one eye, growled a little in irritation, and resumed his nap in the desk tray labelled "Urgent."

In the bedroom, Silber tossed clothes out of the closet until he found something suitable. Well, all right. His grey pin-striped suit. It was a little tight, but still very presentable. And, fortuitously, there was a clean white shirt still on its hanger from the laundry. And perhaps his maroon tie. Yes. That would do nicely. He certainly wanted to look his best this morning. For this was a day he felt sure he would remember forever.

• • •

"I'm sorry, sir—"

"—Doctor," he said, interrupting the gorgon who was trying to deny him entry. "Dr. Silber."

"I'm sorry, Doctor, but you can't see him right now. Why, you don't even have an appointment!" She riffled through the pages of her desk calendar. "The earliest appointment I could give you would be two weeks from Friday, and even then I'd have to squeeze you in." She smirked at him. "Dr. Eisig is a very busy man."

Silber leaned across the desk and lowered his voice. "I don't want to be squeezed. Miss McGee, if you don't buzz him and tell him that Dr. Silber is here and wants to talk to him about Harvey Consulting Corporation, I'm simply going to walk in."

"Oh! You'll do no such thing!" she told him. "I'm calling Security."

Silber grinned at her, walked past the desk and opened the door marked "Philip Eisig, Chief of Medicine".

Eisig sat at his desk, his back to the door, typing something into his computer terminal. He did not look up. "I thought I told you I didn't want to be disturbed, Miss McGee," he said testily.

"I'm afraid you're going to be very disturbed," Silber told him.

Eisig swivelled around and stared at Silber, regarding his former colleague with watery, reddened eyes. "You!" he exclaimed. "I have nothing to say to you. And how dare you come barging in? I'm going to call Security if you're not out of here in five seconds."

"Oh, I wouldn't bother," Silber said. "The efficient Miss McGee has already summoned them. But you'll want to send them away when they arrive."

Eisig gaped at him. "Send them away? Not bloody likely."

Silber tossed the morning edition of the paper onto Eisig's desk. "Page 1, Section B," he told him.

Eisig frowned, but opened the paper and skimmed the page Silber had mentioned. Almost at once he emitted a strangled sound of disbelief.

Behind him, Silber heard the heavy tread of the security guards, and the nervous twittering of Miss McGee. "Philip," she said softly. "The guards."

"What? Oh, yes." He looked past Silber to the trio who stood in his doorway. "It's all right, Ms. McGee. I'm fine. Dr. Silber and I have to . . . talk."

"But . . . but . . ." she sputtered.

"Ms. McGee, just close the door," he told her sharply. She did so with a bang.

Unbidden, Silber sat down.

Eisig stared at him from across the desk. "I think you've made a mistake," he said, confusion evident in his voice. So, that's the way you want to play it, Silber thought. The "it's-all-been-a-terrible-mistake" game. Hmmf. All right. I can play it for awhile.

Silber snorted.

"No, really," Eisig continued. "Evidently you're suffering from some kind of delusion."

Silber laughed out loud.

Eisig, seeming the soul of patience, looked at him kindly. "You really should seek help, you know. Shall I recommend someone?"

"This repartee is all very amusing," Silber told him, "but I'm eager to get to the best part. Aren't you?"

Eisig shook his head in despair. "Milt, look—"

"—no, you look. Do you think I'm joking, you larcenous bastard? I know all about Ararat and Harvey."

Eisig turned pale.

"And in case you think the article in the paper has no truth to it, I suggest you call your—pardon me, Harvey's—bank. I believe you'll find that an electronic transfer of funds was made yesterday from Harvey's account to that of the Neighborhood Crippled Children's Center." Silber smiled. "A move straight from the heart."

Eisig blinked several times. "That's theft," he said quietly. "I want that money back."

Silber hooted. "Theft! You should talk about theft. No, my greedy friend, I'm afraid the deed is done. And besides," he looked reproachfully at Eisig, "think about the bad press it would mean. And my associate at the paper might then want to do an investigative piece on Harvey."

Eisig swallowed several times and glared malevolently at Silber. He seemed unable to speak.

"So," Silber said in evident satisfaction. "That seems to be that." He really was enjoying himself, he noted. "Oh, well, there is one final thing."

"What?"

"I hope you understand that I have photocopies of all the documents pertaining to the Ararat/Harvey scam. Including a printout from the Woodlands computer detailing how, and how much, money was paid to Harvey. I think it would prove very interesting to the Attorney General's office. Oh, and one more thing."

"Which is?"

This time, Silber did not smile. "Dr. Altman. I believe you tried to kill her."

Eisig blinked quickly several times.

"I have a certain amount of proof for that, too. Most careless of someone to have left that tube of unclotted blood lying around."

Eisig sighed, then looked at Silber curiously, his eyes inscrutable behind his thick glasses. "Silber, what do you want? A title and a nice salary with no responsibility? A lump sum? How about $250,000?"

Silber was astounded. Does Eisig really think I can be bought off? Bribed? The bastard! What's medicine coming to when men like Eisig are appointed chief? Medicine is supposed to be a trust. But Eisig thinks it's a holding company.

Silber let the man squirm for a moment longer. "What do I want? Your assurance that Dr. Altman will be safe. And that no untimely accident should befall me. I have, of course, left all this information with a close friend. He'll make it public if I were to meet with misadventure." Silber smiled at Eisig. The bluff seemed to be working. "So, you see, it's a matter of interdependent utility functions after all. God, how I hated to hear you use that phrase." He shuddered. "In plain English—you're safe as long as we are." He slapped his forehead theatrically. "I almost forgot! How foolish of me! There is one other thing you can do for me, Philip."

Eisig bowed his head. Gutless bastard, Silber thought contemptuously. Chief of Medicine indeed. Why, you haven't the courage to even look at me.

"What?" Eisig asked weakly.

"Resign," Silber told him.

Chapter
47

Hearing tires crunch on gravel, Maggie opened the blinds on the living room window. Fred's truck was coming up the driveway. "He's here!" Maggie announced. Kate followed her into the foyer. "Thanks for everything, Kate," Maggie said warmly. "You've just been wonderful. But I don't want to impose on you any longer, and I really do need to get back to work."

"You're welcome to stay as long as you like," Kate told her. "And Dr. Silber will be really distressed to find out that you have left so soon. I know he wanted to talk to you tonight."

"I wanted to talk to him too. But we've both tried calling him, and he just doesn't answer. So it will have to wait until later." Maggie opened the front door before Fred could even knock.

"Please keep in touch," Kate said anxiously. "And be careful. We'll be worried about you."

"I intend to keep an eye on her," Fred promised. He extended his hand to Kate. "Fred Jenkins, Maggie's neighbor and fellow intern."

"Kate Fitzhugh," Kate responded, looking him over appraisingly. Fred did not look his best, Maggie noted. He had probably come directly from the hospital, which explained his bloodstained white pants. And it looked as though he had forgotten to shave that morning.

"Pleased to meet you, ma'am," Fred said pleasantly. "And this is quite a spread you have here. Really fine horses. Makes me long for home."

"So you keep horses?" Kate asked.

"My dad has a few. I could ride a horse long before I could ride a bicycle."

"Do you still ride?" Kate asked.

"Only in a Ford, ma'am. No time for it these days."

"Too bad," Kate said sympathetically. "Well, I'm glad to

have met you. Even though I'm not so sure I approve of your taking Maggie back so soon."

"She can change her mind," Fred replied. "Although she was very insistent." He looked at Maggie inquiringly. "I'm perfectly willing to come back another time. You've earned a rest. I can't say we don't miss you though."

"I want to go now," Maggie said firmly. "It's bad enough when everybody's there. With two people out, the patients are sure to suffer."

Kate gave her a hug, and looked after them with an anxious frown.

· · ·

"How have you been managing?" Maggie asked as they walked to the truck.

"The residents, even Blaine, have been playing intern. They're not happy, but the interns don't feel too sorry for them, I must say."

"Have you heard what happened to Charlie?" Whatever it was, he probably deserved it, Maggie thought to herself. But it had happened for the wrong reason. Eisig had needed a scape-goat, and Charlie was the obvious choice. That did eliminate one person from her list of suspects though, didn't it?

"Nobody seems to know," Fred told her. He helped her into the truck, and they set off for the highway. "Nobody cares very much either. Except that they don't like the extra work. Poor Charlie—he excelled at making himself obnoxious, didn't he?"

"I guess he did. I never understood him," Maggie said ruefully.

"Of course, I don't see how he could have made such a gross mistake either." Fred shook his head. "How could anyone do such a thing?"

Maggie looked at him curiously. Apparently, Fred assumed that Charlie had given her the heparin. By mistake. That must be what Dr. Eisig wanted everyone to think. Dr. Silber must not have told Fred about Eisig. Well, why should he? Maybe she should keep quiet about it too. But it was very tempting to confide in Fred.

Traffic was heavy on the highway, and Fred seemed pre-occupied with his driving. Maggie appreciated the silence. She had a lot of thinking still to do.

Maggie didn't have much doubt now that Eisig was the mastermind of the scheme to manipulate EquaCare for profit. Dr. Silber's evidence against him was damning. But he just couldn't have done it all alone. That had become increasingly clear to her. Collecting information and altering the records had the potential for increasing profits. But to "manage the case mix"—to see to it that the hospital admitted as many "winners" and as few "losers" as possible—required someone who could write orders. The chief of medicine couldn't do that. He had to have an accomplice.

She shivered as she thought of Mr. Post once again. Disposing of him had required more than an order. Would Eisig really have done that job himself? Or gotten someone else to do it? Fischbein had been on that night. Would he have given Mr. Post a fatal injection—something like potassium chloride? There had been an intravenous needle in place, she recalled. She had assumed that the radiologist had used it to administer contrast for the CT scan. No, she couldn't rule out Fischbein. Not even if he had been fired. Eisig might be willing—anxious even—to get rid of his accomplice.

Of course, Fischbein was just an intern. Somebody who had been at TU longer would be a much more likely candidate. And he really would need to be positioned at the entry to the system, rather than on the ward as Charlie was. Maggie nearly shouted aloud as a thought struck her suddenly. Why hadn't that occurred to her before? Blindness, sheer blindness. Denial, repression, a host of psychological defense mechanisms. Lately, she hadn't wanted to think of him at all. And for a time before that, she had been looking through a romantic haze.

But who was in a better position than Brent Stemmons, the gatekeeper, the Pit Boss ever since July? Maggie trembled at how she had told him about her suspicions. Of course, her ulcer was hardly his doing, and he had not been near her during her stay at TU, as far as she could remember.

Maggie was disgusted with herself. She had completely overlooked Eisig, and had instead suspected Dr. Silber. On grounds that looked pretty flimsy in retrospect. And she had nearly revealed everything to Brent Stemmons, who was now a prime candidate for Eisig's accessory.

She just hadn't been much of a detective. But now was not the time to give up. She needed to collect evidence, hard evidence. She did not share Dr. Silber's cynicism. She wanted this whole scheme to be exposed, and its perpetrators punished. She wondered again what Dr. Silber had planned to tell her today. Perhaps she should have tried to reach him one more time.

Fred looked at her with concern. "You're mighty quiet," he observed. "I can tell there's something on your mind."

"Yes," Maggie admitted. "I've been trying to piece together the evidence about what's going on at TU."

"I'm not so sure that's a good idea." Fred knit his brows. "It could be dangerous. And probably not worth it. Whatever is happening, a lowly intern isn't going to be able to do anything about it."

"But, Fred," Maggie protested, "what about the patients?"

"Well, you have to do the best you can for them," Fred replied. "You know, one person can't save the world or change the system. Soon we'll both be finished with the program, and we can forget all about it. I'm just anxious to get out into practice. Aren't you?"

Maggie sighed. Fred was probably right about the futility of it all. But surely he could see that something was wrong besides an organizational defect. "But what if you could prove that somebody was deliberately manipulating the system to make profits?" she persisted.

Fred frowned. "Who do you think it could be?"

"Maybe Stephen Blaine, with his piles of print-outs. He may be trying to 'make the system work' for all it's worth. Or Brent Stemmons. He certainly has been gatekeeper for the longest time."

Fred grimaced at the mention of Stemmons. "Good idea. Although I would have thought he was too busy chasing women."

Maggie blushed. She hoped Fred didn't know she had been dating Brent.

"Or Jim Thomas," Fred suggested. "He's in the Pit every day, and if you've noticed, everyone is extremely dependent on him. Or Charlie Fischbein. He really seems to hate the patients. And he was on the scene the other night. Or Jeannette Larkin. Who would ever suspect her? And she spends fewer hours in the hospital than any intern I know of, because she has the fewest and the easiest patients. And why not Fred Jenkins, while we're at it?" Maggie shook her head. She didn't think Fred was taking her seriously.

"Why just one person?" Fred went on. "The problem is, Maggie, that everybody has an incentive to manipulate the system. It's deliberately set up that way. The system profits from having more profitable patients in the hospital. And the doctors get more rest."

Fred had a point, Maggie conceded. Eisig may have been counting on people thinking just that way. If a problem were discovered, then he could easily respond by "policing our own ranks" and weeding out a bad doctor or two. Like Charlie. Or like Provider Number PGY1-14.

"What do you think of Dr. Eisig?" Maggie asked.

Fred thought for a moment. "The former Dr. Eisig. He used to be a doctor, but he's not anymore. He's a functionary. A faceless bureaucrat. I just don't pay any attention to him."

"Would you believe he is the sole officer of a shell corporation that has skimmed off over a million dollars from TU in the past year?"

Fred whistled softly. "I'll be damned," he said. "How did you find that out? Did your friend Dr. Silber tell you?"

"Well, there's no proof," Maggie said hastily. She had a sudden instinct that she shouldn't have divulged this information. Not even to Fred.

"You'd better not say a word about it then," Fred admonished her. "Not to anyone."

"I won't," Maggie promised. She rode most of the rest of the way in silence. She was very worried that she had taken on more than she could handle. But she was committed.

• • •

Maggie hadn't realized how weak she still was. It was only 4 p.m., and she was exhausted. She almost regretted her decision to come back so soon. Fortunately, she wasn't on call tonight.

"Dr. Altman, Dr. Margaret Altman, call 2824." So why was the ER paging her?

It was a bounceback. One of her patients who had been discharged during her absence. She sighed, and went down to pick him up.

She found the Pit to be in turmoil. Most of the staff was in crash room 1, trying to keep a patient on the stretcher. The man was thrashing about wildly, apparently having a grand mal seizure. Two handcuffed, Hispanic men were being escorted through the double doors, under heavy police guard. Brent Stemmons, sitting behind the bridge, was on the telephone. He looked tense, worried, Maggie thought. He replaced the telephone, and disappeared into the crash room.

Maggie felt relieved that she would have nothing more complicated than a relapsed lunger to deal with. The interns on call would have to face the disasters that were pending here. Her patient was not in his room. The blackboard said that he was in X ray, and Maggie went to look for him.

"Dr. Miltown, Dr. Everett Miltown, call 2262." Maggie drew in her breath sharply. That page again. Who was Dr. Miltown? And wasn't it always to the same extension? Well, if she were going to be a detective, she would have to try to find out. She picked up the house wall phone in X ray and dialled the number.

"Hello," said a soft male voice.

"Dr. Miltown," she said, feeling her heart thump.

"You don't sound like Dr. Miltown," the voice responded.

"I'm . . . um . . . covering for him. He's tied up right now." There was a pause. "Well, are you coming down?"

"Yes. Right away."

The phone clicked, and Maggie felt panic. She clenched her fists, and took a few slow, deep breaths. What she had to do was obvious. First, find out where extension 2262 was located. She hurried to the X ray reception desk, and obtained a hospital telephone directory. She skimmed it rapidly. There! She might have guessed. It was Pathology! Could "Dr. Miltown" be involved with Dr. Metzenbaum's "body snatching"? Well, they certainly wouldn't have to page Metzenbaum. He seemed to live in Pathology. They just had to knock on his door.

She ran down to the morgue, quickly, before she could change her mind. There, in the room with the lockers, was a man dressed in the uniform of an ambulance driver.

"'Bout gave you up, Doc," he said.

"Sorry," Maggie said breathlessly. "I got interrupted." The man looked her over calmly for a minute. Maggie wondered what his intentions were. Should she run?

"Dr. Altman, Dr. Margaret Altman, outside call," said the page operator. Maggie ignored it.

The man appeared to be waiting for something. "The money, Doc?" he said finally.

Maggie looked at him blankly.

"Surely Dr. Miltown told you about the money."

"Oh," Maggie thought quickly. "He wonders whether you can extend him credit, just for this time?"

The man sneered at her. "That deadbeat! This is a C.O.D. service, lady. We've been through this before. Tell Dr. Miltown that the stiff will be at the ME's office." He left, and Maggie looked after him in confusion. Why would Dr. Miltown be paying an ambulance driver for a dead body? Could this be part of the scheme she had overheard Silber and Metzenbaum discussing? But Dr. Metzenbaum had just had to sign a form. Most peculiar.

She turned to go upstairs, and nearly ran into Caroline. The nurse looked startled, even frightened.

"I'm covering for Dr. Miltown," Maggie said calmly, the first words that popped into her mind.

Caroline looked still more astonished. "You?" she said in disbelief. "Brent didn't say anything about a substitute."

Immediately, Caroline seemed to realize what she had just said. Brent Stemmons, Dr. Miltown? Maggie could hardly think straight.

"He told me he would tell you," Maggie said. "He must have gotten interrupted. He's really tied up in the ER at the moment. The police are there."

Caroline seemed to pale at the mention of police. Or it could be her imagination, Maggie thought. "All right," the nurse said, with obvious discomfiture. "Just give me the name and number, and I'll get the bed set up."

Maggie thought rapidly. The name and number of the corpse? Well, why not just make one up? She pulled her packet of index cards from her pocket and pretended to read from them. "Morton Smith, EquaCare number 4987165."

Caroline scrawled down the information, turned on her heel, and left.

Maggie wrote down the name and number herself, so that she wouldn't forget. She shook her head. What could be going on? She would have to think about it later. First, she wanted to get back to the real world, where people behaved normally. In climbing the stairs, she noticed that her knees felt quite weak.

• • •

Back in the X ray department, Maggie remembered her page and dialled the operator. But the outside caller had hung up, without leaving a message.

She had to stop to think for a minute to remember why she was in X ray. Oh yes, her patient, Jedediah Small. She would have to make a better effort to concentrate on her work.

Mr. Small's films were supposed to be hanging on the ER board, on panel 27, but Maggie had to wait until the radiology resident finished dictating a report on the abdominal film on panel 29.

"More than 30 well-defined, circular densities are scattered throughout the colon," the resident said to his dictaphone. "There is no evidence of obstruction. The nature of the densities is similar to that described for Type 1 cocaine packages in so-called 'body packers'."

Maggie looked at the film in amazement. It looked as though the patient had swallowed a bunch of ping-pong balls.

"I've never seen anything like it!" she exclaimed.

"I've only seen it in the journals," replied the radiologist—Dr. Mark Balford, according to his nametag. "It's quite dangerous. The cocaine is wrapped up in condoms or toy balloons or the fingers of latex gloves. The packages tend to rupture. That can be fatal." He flipped back to panel 28. "You can see the packages hung up at the ileocecal valve in this one." Obviously, the patient had an obstruction; the small intestine was hugely dilated with gas. He would soon be on his way to surgery, Maggie thought. Balford scribbled a brief report on the envelope. "I'd better call the Pit Boss. But first, I'll look at your patient's film."

Mr. Small didn't have anything remarkable on his X ray. Just the same blebs of emphysema. Maggie hoped it wouldn't take long to get him settled for the night.

• • •

At the last minute, a man stuck his arm between the elevator doors, and they opened again. Some people groaned and one shouted, "Wait for the next one." But two men elbowed their way into the crowd. Maggie stifled a scream. She recognized them.

Ignoring elevator etiquette, the men stood facing the back of the elevator, staring at all the people. Maggie couldn't move; she was wedged between Mr. Small's stretcher and the back wall. Just before the first stop, one of them looked right at her. She was sure he recognized her, too. Then they got off, on the second floor, surgery.

The scene blurred, like a static-filled television screen. No, Maggie said to herself sternly. You can't faint now. She tensed the muscles in her legs, hoping to increase blood flow. It seemed to help a little.

• • •

"Maggie, are you all right?"

Fred's voice penetrated her foggy consciousness. Maybe she really had passed out for a second. She tried to raise her head, then stuck it back down into her lap.

"I'm fine," she said.

"Sorry for the stupid question," Fred apologized. "Can I help you lie down?"

"Not necessary," Maggie replied. This time, she was able to keep her head up. Fred pulled down her lower eyelid.

"A little pale," he judged. "I am really angry with myself. I should have talked you out of coming back so soon. Have you noticed more bleeding?"

"No," Maggie said. "I don't think it's that. I was fine until I saw those men in the elevator."

"What men?"

"I think they're the ones I met in the parking lot the other night."

"Should we call the police?" Fred asked, reaching for the phone.

"No, I don't think so," Maggie decided. "What would they do? Besides ask me why I didn't report the crime in the first place."

"You have a point," he agreed. He stared at the walls thoughtfully for a while, then appeared to reach a decision. "I want you to come home with me tonight," he declared. "I'll sleep on the sofa with my .45. It's going to take me about an hour to get out of here. Why don't you lie down in the call room until then? With the door locked."

"I have some work to finish myself," Maggie said. "I'll meet you here in an hour."

She swallowed her Tagamet, and fortified herself with a glass of milk from the ward refrigerator. It only took about 15 minutes to get Mr. Small's orders written. She had enough time. Did she dare go to 6 West and face Caroline?

She would think about it for a minute or so. In the meantime, she dialled Dr. Silber's number. The phone rang and rang, but there was no answer. Next, she tried Kate Fitzhugh. No answer there either. Kate was probably out with her horses. But where was Dr. Silber?

Chapter 48

"Gone? What do you mean, gone? Gone where?" Silber demanded of Kate. He supported his aching head with both hands and tucked the phone between shoulder and ear. His hangover was enormous. Why in God's name had he decided to celebrate his victory over Eisig with a bout of solitary drinking?

"Home and back to work. In that order," Kate answered reprovingly.

In the kitchen, Fitzhugh emptied an ice cube tray into a metal bowl, and Silber whimpered in distress. To his fragile constitution, it sounded like a nuclear explosion. "So when did she leave?" he finally managed.

"Last night. I tried to call you," Kate said coldly, "but no one answered the phone. Maggie's friend Fred came for her. I tried to dissuade her, but she's a very determined young lady. Also, I gather she was waiting for a call or a visit from you. Something you were going to tell her. So, when she didn't hear from you, she tried to phone. Then, she just left. I'm surprised at you, Milton," she said accusingly. "You could have been more considerate. Maggie was counting on you." There was silence on the line for a moment. "And just who is this Fred character anyhow?" Kate wanted to know. "Rough looking lad. Even if he does like horses. Really, Milton, what do you know about him? Oh, did Ryan reach you? He was worried, too."

It was all too much for Silber. Question, questions. He groaned. "I know almost nothing about Fred. Maggie will have to take her chances with him. Damned stubborn female! Why can't she show a little common sense? And as for your son, he's detonating ice cube trays in my kitchen."

Kate sniffed in disapproval. "Common sense—is that a prescription? If so, I know someone who might do well to follow his own advice. Goodbye, Milton," she concluded frostily, and hung up.

"Hmmf," Silber said to the phone receiver. "Women."

"That was Kate, I suppose," Fitzhugh called from the kitchen.

Silber closed his eyes. No response seemed necessary.

"After we eat something, why don't you go back to bed?" Fitzhugh asked him.

Eat? Silber's stomach heaved at the very thought. "Coffee will suffice," he said. "If you're done blasting in the kitchen, you might bring me that bowl of ice. And a plastic bag."

"I've got them right here," Fitzhugh told him. "You really look terrible, you know. I hope the drinking bout was worth it."

Silber filled the bag with ice and held it against his eyes. "It never is," he told Fitzhugh. "I'm old enough to know better. But somehow, yesterday, it just seemed the thing to do. Coming home to this place was such an anticlimax after having bested Eisig. So I poured a drink to help myself feel better. Then a few more. Pretty soon I had forgotten that I was on my way out to the ranch." He winced. "I forgot all about Maggie. I drank and cried and sang and cursed. I know I offended Keynes. He went out around dinnertime and hasn't returned. Then I must have passed out. I didn't hear any of the phone calls I apparently received." Feeling suddenly self-conscious, he raised his bag of ice and glowered at Fitzhugh. "Is that coffee ready? And why aren't you at work?"

Fitzhugh brought the coffee. "Oh, I've given them my notice," he said. "One month. They don't want me to get involved in any major trades, so there's very little for me to do. Just routine stuff. No one really cares if I'm there or not. I can take care of my day's work in an hour and a half."

"Your notice?" Silber asked, interested. "So you're finally quitting."

Fitzhugh shrugged. "Apparently."

"Kate and the horses won, then."

"No. Not exactly. I thought maybe I'd take a few months and think things over. Maybe take a trip. I'd really rather not raise horses," he confessed, "but perhaps I'll have no choice."

"Bah!" Silber told him. "We always have choices. Something will come up."

Fitzhugh shrugged again and finished his coffee.

"I think I will take that nap now," Silber said. "I wonder if you'd do me a favor before you go home."

"Sure. What can I do?"

Silber looked at his friend sheepishly. "Find Keynes. He needs his dinner. And his breakfast. I called him unforgiveable names last night. Insulted his pedigree. He's probably at the Mexican restaurant down the street. He goes there to brood when his feelings are hurt."

Fitzhugh smiled, seeing Silber's distress. "I'll find him. Now just go to bed."

"Thanks," Silber said, stumbling wearily toward the bedroom.

. . .

Silber woke from an uneasy sleep to find himself being throttled by a sheet. He tore himself loose from its embrace and struggled to sit up. His head still thumped, but not as badly. He scratched busily at his beard, finally deciding that a shower might improve both physical and mental states. Yes, a shower definitely had its appeal. He stood up tentatively, took a step, and decided he could navigate to the bathroom. Hmmf. You're too old for adolescent drinking bouts, he chided himself. Consider your liver, if nothing else.

Showered and dressed, his thoughts turned to Keynes. Had Fitzhugh managed to locate the cat, he wondered? And had Keynes deigned to accompany him home? Carrying the beast was out of the question. The last time he had tricked Keynes into going to the vet, he had weighed in at 21 pounds, none of it fat. No, a bad-tempered feline heavyweight couldn't be carried far. Or in Keynes' case, at all. He discouraged such intimacies forcefully. No, Fitzhugh, who was somewhat acquainted with Keynes' foibles, would have had to use something other than brute force. Silber himself had found that an opened tin of shrimp usually brought success. The peace offering had to be preceded, however, by the requisite apologies and self-recriminations.

"You've met her I guess," a voice from the kitchen said.

"What do you think? Me, I just don't know. What would a woman find attractive in me? I'm not good looking. I'm socially inept—never did know the right things to say. No one wants to chat about yen and lire at cocktail parties. And I sure don't know anything about women—all I know is how to make money. Pretty dull, eh?"

Silber poked his head around the door. There sat Fitzhugh at the kitchen table, Keynes on his lap. He was feeding the cat shrimp one at a time from a tin, and talking earnestly to him. Keynes seemed most attentive.

"Mmmm?" Keynes said interrogatively.

"Oh, do you think there's hope?" Fitzhugh fed Keynes another shrimp.

"Nrrf."

"That's what I was afraid of. I'm a dull dog, pardon the expression. But I could try. You know, ask her out. She might even say yes." He looked off into space, frowning.

Hmmf, Silber thought. The 'her' of Fitzhugh's romantic musings was probably Maggie. Well, well. He smiled. Yes, the two of them might make a good couple.

Keynes bit Fitzhugh gently on the index finger.

"What—more? Sorry. Why not? After all, it's dinner and breakfast, too. A fellow needs to keep up his strength."

"So," Silber said, feeling absurdly like an intruder. "You found the prodigal Lord Keynes."

"Oh yes," Fitzhugh said, looking embarrassed. "He came with me right away. No trouble at all."

"Hmmf," Silber said, amused.

Keynes favored Silber with an aggrieved look, and butted Fitzhugh's hand.

"He's still hungry," Fitzhugh explained. "I'd better carry on."

"Oh, by all means," Silber said, rummaging in the cupboard. "I think I'll make myself some soup."

"Why don't you come on out to the ranch for dinner?" Fitzhugh asked him. "Consuela will have cooked something. There'll be plenty."

"Well . . ." Silber hesitated.

"Oh come on, Milt. Kate will be glad to see you."

Silber gave the young man a doubtful look. "All right. Just let me make a phone call. Maggie doesn't know yet about our friend Dr. Eisig and his generous gift to the NCCC." He sighed. "I meant to call her yesterday. She was most eager to see some form of justice done. Of course, it's not good enough, but it's something."

"I don't think she'll approve of your Robin Hood tactics," Fitzhugh remarked. "But it was a fitting punishment."

"Blast it!" Silber said, slamming the phone down with a bang, and collapsing into a chair. "She doesn't answer her page!"

Fitzhugh looked up suddenly from feeding Keynes. "Milt, something just occurred to me. Do you think Eisig is the only one in the hospital involved in the scam?"

Silber blinked quickly several times, a sinking feeling in his stomach. "God, what an ass I've been—imagining that Eisig was running this operation himself. Of course there has to be someone else. Someone inside the hospital to make it work. Someone to see that the right patients get admitted."

"I was afraid of that," Fitzhugh said. He was so pale his freckles stood out like tiny copper coins. "But it's only logical. We're a terrific pair of sleuths, aren't we?" he added bitterly.

"No time for self recrimination," Silber said, heaving himself to his feet. "I'd bet money that finding the 'inside man' is one of the reasons Maggie went back to work."

"Damn!" Fitzhugh swore, depositing Keynes and his tin of shrimp on the kitchen counter. "Where do we start looking? It could be anyone!"

"No, not anyone," Silber disagreed.

"Almost. It could even be that guy who picked her up at the ranch. Fred what's-his-name." Fitzhugh clenched his fists. "Milt, you may have gotten Eisig's promise not to harm Maggie, but what about him—whoever he is. And she may be at TU with him right now!" He started for the front door. Fear in his heart, Silber hurried after him.

261

Chapter *49*

"Raúl, I'm telling you it's impossible!" he hissed into the phone. "I couldn't do it! The police are turning everyone away. I've already tried to bluff my way in. They're going to take the coke back to the station with them as soon as it's all recovered. There's not a damned thing I can do about it."

"Listen, my friend," Raúl told him. "You assured me that you would be able to intercept it. That it would be no trouble at all. What happened? Did you change your mind when you saw the size of the shipment?"

"What do you mean?"

"Please, don't play games with me. A man could go into business for himself with such a large amount of merchandise. Especially merchandise that he didn't have to pay for. Don't you agree?"

He began to sweat. "No, I wouldn't do anything like that. I didn't. I swear I didn't."

Silence.

"You've got to believe me!"

"What I believe is this, Doctor: that you will be a very sorry young man if you persist in this madness. Benny and Carlos are on their way now to attempt to reason with you. As you know, they can be most persuasive. You will get my merchandise and give it to them. And they will allow you to live. That is the end of this discussion." Raúl hung up.

"No!" he yelled into the phone. "Damn you, I don't have it!"

He stood in the hallway, shaking, the noises of the hospital around him. Move, he told his numb legs. Run! You've got to get away. He remembered his previous meeting with Benny and Carlos and thought he might vomit. Somehow, he persuaded his legs to move. Down the hall, past the ER, and out into the parking lot, heedless of anyone who spoke to him. He had room for only one thought in his terrified mind—escape.

. . .

Think! he told himself. Calm down. Be sure to take everything you can pawn. He tossed the contents of his wall safe onto the floor, rummaged through the mess and pocketed his gold Piaget wristwatch, the platinum and diamond ring his mother had given him for his birthday, and four numismatic gold coins. How much cash was there? He counted out almost $1200. Not enough. He might have to be gone for months. No time to sell his cars. He looked at the phone. Should he call her? Why not. She'd always been good for it before. Why should she refuse him now?

The phone rang 11 times before she answered it.

"Mother!" he said, feeling faint with relief. "I have to borrow a couple of thousand dollars. Tonight. I'll be right over."

"No. Not this time," his mother said wearily.

"What?"

"No, I said. Don't you recall what I told you last time? Really, darling, you have to learn to manage your own life. These recurring financial emergencies are so tedious."

"But . . . but. . ."

"No buts. My mind is made up."

"You don't understand! They'll kill me!" he wailed.

"Hardly, dear," his mother answered unfeelingly. "It only seems that bad. After all, it's merely money. You'll straighten it out. And please don't call again about so bourgeois a subject." She hung up.

"No!" he screamed. "You can't do this to me!"

"Hiya, Doc," a voice said from behind him.

He spun around, his heart hammering. Benny and Carlos stood just inside his apartment door. Benny leaned against the door, arms crossed; Carlos approached him slowly, flicking his knife open and closed. No! Not again! He remembered his pain and terror in the parking lot, touched his barely healed earlobe and panicked. Throwing himself headlong at Carlos, he took the other man by surprise. The knife spun away, and Carlos was on the floor before he knew what was happening. Sobbing with terror, he scrambled awkwardly to one side, and charged at Benny. The smaller man moved to intercept him, and stumbled, falling toward Carlos. He shoved Benny violently, and the two enforcers struggled in a tangle of arms and legs, gaining him precious seconds. Then he pulled open the door and fled.

He was winded by the time he got to the bottom of the stairwell. Sounds of pursuit drifted down to him—Benny and Carlos were only three or four floors above him. But the door to the parking garage was just ahead. He was going to make it! He staggered to his Ferrari, unlocked it, started the motor and put it violently into reverse. Then he floored the accelerator. He sped by the stairwell door just in time to see Benny and Carlos stumble into the garage. Whimpering in fear, he raced up the ramp and onto the street.

He shot out of the garage like a rocket. Barely under control, the Ferrari skidded out onto the wrong side of Broadway Boulevard. A green VW van came hurtling toward him, and he screamed. He swerved violently to avoid a collision, and the Ferrari jumped the curb and careened down the median strip. He struggled with the wheel and, too late, saw in the car's headlights the scaly bark of a palm tree. Time seemed to slow. The Ferrari floated, light as a feather, directly toward the palm's trunk, and collided with a distressingly noiseless crash. What was happening to him? Was this a dream? His last thought, as he was crushed against the steering column, was a curious one: now that the Ferrari had been in an accident, he'd probably get a lousy price for it. He heard a crash, the tinkle of breaking glass, and felt something warm running in his eyes. God, he thought, I'm going to need that plastic surgeon again. But why don't I feel anything? Maybe it's worse than I think. Maybe I'm dead.

• • •

A horrible wailing noise woke him. He opened his eyes and became aware at once that he was inside a vehicle, which was hurtling somewhere at great speed. The noise went on and on, rising and falling. Oh, my God! He was in an ambulance.

264

"Don't worry, Doc," a familiar voice said. He finally recognized it—Daniel's voice. "We're just five minutes from TU. You'll make it."

He closed his eyes, hoping this was all a nightmare. He took a couple of deep breaths, alarmed that he couldn't remember how he had come to be here. Well, nightmares were like that, weren't they? But when he opened his eyes, everything was just as before. Unable to move, unable to feel, he felt as if he were suffocating. Fear gripped him. He seemed to be rushing headlong toward something unspeakably horrible. What nameless thing waited for him at the end of this ride? What was going to happen to him? He felt enormously sorry for himself. Tears began to course down his cheeks, and when he thought of the ambulance speeding toward TU, bearing his broken and disfigured body inside it, he began to weep. Soon he was sobbing uncontrollably. Life was so damned unfair!

Chapter 50

As soon as Maggie stepped into the 6 West nursing station, she knew that she had made a mistake. Caroline glared at her icily, and without saying a word to Maggie, picked up the telephone, and dialled an extension.

"Dr. Stemmons, please," she said.

A long pause ensued. Maggie tried to think about what to say, but her mind was blank. She noticed that she was holding her breath.

"Damn!" Caroline said, banging down the receiver. Apparently, Dr. Stemmons was unavailable.

"Is there some problem?" Maggie asked, as calmly as she could.

"Of course there's a problem," Caroline said. "There's no such name in the computer, and that number is unassigned!"

How could she have been so dumb, Maggie thought. The computer had to verify eligibility! Since doctors weren't entrusted to perform this step, she had forgotten about it.

"Well, why didn't you call me?" Maggie asked, surprising herself with her brazen tone.

"You!" Caroline sneered. "You can't even get the name and number right! Didn't you get his papers?"

"No," Maggie said. "I guess there weren't any. I'll just see if I can check on the name." She fled from the ward. She had no idea what she was going to do now. She apparently had learned just enough to get herself into trouble, and not enough to be of any use. It was sheer luck that Caroline hadn't been able to reach Stemmons yet. He was probably still busy with the police. Or with the patients. Perhaps more bags of cocaine had burst in the body packers' intestines. But no interns had been paged recently to take admissions, she had noticed.

Maggie sat in the 6 East doctors' station, waiting for Fred and wondering what to do. If someone had had reason to kill her before, there was even more reason now. She needed to talk to somebody. She tried dialing Silber's number again. No answer. Could he have gone to the ranch? There was no answer there either.

Then a terrifying thought occurred to her. What if something had happened to Dr. Silber? He had been planning to take some kind of action. She had no idea what he intended to do. Suppose that Dr. Eisig had learned of Silber's investigations. If he was willing to kill her, surely he wouldn't have scruples about harming Silber.

And there was another nagging question. Just what did Dr. Miltown have to do with Dr. Metzenbaum, and his body snatching? And wasn't he a friend of Silber's? Silber had called the scheme "a little irregular." Maybe there was more to it than he realized.

Surely, she couldn't have things backwards again. Dr. Silber had saved her life, hadn't he? Of course, she didn't have any hard evidence for anything. Not even for the attempt on her life. The heparin could have been added to the tube of blood, rather than to her intravenous.

She was just too tired to think, that was part of the problem. It may really have been a mistake to come back before she was more fully recovered.

Fred would be here soon. Maybe a fresh point of view would be helpful.

Before her friend arrived, there was time for one more thing. Seeing Caroline had reminded her of it. She fished through the index cards in her pocket. There had been a patient missing from 6 West, in X ray, according to Caroline. Some time ago. She had kept the card, meaning to check on it again. Matthew Portman. His chart was not available on line. But the computer did inform her that Matthew Portman had died. The question was, had he died before or after becoming a "patient" on 6 West?

• • •

There was some excitement at the emergency entrance, as an ambulance was pulling up Code 3, with sirens blaring. It

267

was evidently expected, as a team from surgery was coming out to meet it.

"Must be an elevator case," Fred commented. "Let's stay away from the confusion. And let's look where we're going." They surveyed the people milling around the triage desk or smoking outside the entrance. Maggie did not see the two men who had been on the elevator.

"I'll walk you to your car, and watch you lock yourself in. Then I'll follow you home. Stay in the car until I'm right beside it," Fred instructed her.

Maggie didn't like having to be protected like this. But she was too tired to argue, and she was frightened, she had to admit.

They arrived at Colonial Manors without seeing a single suspicious person. Fred insisted on going into Maggie's apartment first, to be sure everything was all right. She collected some towels, her nightgown, her toothbrush, and other essentials for the night. She set a timer to turn off the lights in about two hours, and double locked the door.

"You have to promise not to comment on my house-keeping." Fred's apartment unmistakeably belonged to a bachelor. The furnishings were purely utilitarian, and covered with dust. There was a painting of a desert scene on the wall, a bookshelf containing a collection of country western records, and piles of medical journals on the floor.

"You know what they say about glass houses," Maggie replied.

Fred put two frozen macaroni and cheese dinners in the oven, and excused himself to clean up the bedroom. He emerged carrying a pistol and a box of ammunition. After checking to be sure a round was in the chamber and the clip was full, he placed the pistol carefully on the floor near the sofa.

Maggie watched him with a sense of unreality. She had fired a gun once or twice, but had never expected to use one. Could this be happening to her?

Maggie took her Tagamet, and mechanically ate the food that her friend offered. She no longer felt inclined to discuss the events of the day. They seemed to have happened to someone else. She had no idea how she would manage to get through being on call tomorrow. But somehow she would have to do it.

"You're exhausted," Fred observed. "Are you sure that you don't want to go back to the ranch tomorrow?"

"No," Maggie said. "There's too much going on here." Besides, she thought, there were questions in her mind about that too. Why hadn't she heard from Silber?

She didn't have the energy to protest when Fred steered her into his bedroom. He closed the door quietly. She heard him moving around in the kitchen, but only for a few minutes, before she was soundly asleep.

Chapter 51

"Pull into the ER entrance," Silber said to Fitzhugh. The car squealed to a stop and Silber heaved himself out. "Park it anywhere!" he called, hustling toward the entrance. But an ambulance, siren shrieking, lights flashing, beat him to it.

He was elbowed out of the way as the surgery team burst through the doors, retrieved the body from the ambulance and hurried back inside. There seemed to be quite a lot of blood, Silber noted anxiously. And try as he might, he was unable to get a good look at the body for the attendants milling about. He shuddered, and followed them into the ER.

"Did you see that?" one of the patients in the triage area asked another. "What a mess! One of their own doctors, too, I heard."

Silber thought his heart might stop. A Woodlands doctor? Had that bastard Eisig broken his word? Was that body on the stretcher Maggie's?

"Who?" he demanded of the patient who had supplied the information.

The man stared at him blankly. "What?"

"Who did they just bring in? Which doctor was it?"

A shrug. "Dunno."

"Was it a man, or a woman?"

"Beats me."

Silber ground his teeth in frustration.

"Milt, what's the matter?" Fitzhugh asked, hurrying to join him.

"The ambulance. They just brought in one of the Woodlands doctors," he told him.

"Oh, no," Fitzhugh said weakly and sat down in the triage area.

"Well, we don't know for sure that it's her," Silber told him. "I'll check around." But Maggie didn't answer her page, and her home phone went unanswered. Damn! He stormed back to the ER and accosted the clerk.

"Who was it in the ambulance?" he demanded.

The clerk bristled. "Sir, we don't give out that kind of information."

"Damn it to hell!" he cursed. The clerk took two steps backward. "Then tell me if Dr. Altman was brought into the ER this evening!"

"I told you—we can't give out that kind of information," the clerk repeated. "We only release it to family members."

"Aargh!" Silber exclaimed. "Page Dr. Jenkins for me! At once!"

"Sir . . ." the clerk demurred.

"No, not 'sir'. Doctor. Doctor Milton Silber. Internal medicine." He drew himself up to his full height and glowered at the clerk. She capitulated.

"Doctor Jenkins, Doctor Fred Jenkins." But there was no response.

"Page Jim Thomas for me. Get him here at once!" he ordered brusquely. Why hadn't he thought of that before? It took Thomas only a few minutes to respond. Silber could have kissed him when he saw him coming down the hall.

"Dr. Silber!" Jim exclaimed. "What's wrong?"

"Jim. Thank God there's someone here who has a brain in his head." He looked meaningfully at the clerk who sniffed and turned away. "Who was in the ambulance?"

"The one that just pulled up?"

"Yes." Fitzhugh had come over to join them, and Silber could hear him swallow nervously.

Thomas shook his head sadly. "One of our own." Silber fought the feeling of light-headedness that threatened to overwhelm him.

Silber clutched the front of Thomas' shirt, and the man put an arm around him to hold him up.

"Help me get him sitting down. Over here," he heard Thomas say to Fitzhugh.

"No!" Silber said in frustration, fighting giddiness. "Tell me! Who?" He collapsed heavily in a chair in the triage area.

"Dr. Stemmons," Thomas told him. "Brent Stemmons. Car accident. A real shame."

• • •

"Want another glass of water?" Jim asked him.

Silber shook his head, and tried to rise. There were far too many things to be done. His old body couldn't give out on him now. If Maggie wasn't here at TU, then where was she?

"Fitzhugh," he said weakly. "Bring me the phone book." Ryan hurried away for it, and Silber turned to Jim. "Thanks again, old friend. I'm all right. You'd better get back to work."

Jim left, casting a worried glance over his shoulder. Silber sighed.

"Here it is," Fitzhugh told him, sitting down, phone book open on his knees. "Now what?"

"Some elementary sleuthing," Silber said. "If she's not here, she's somewhere else."

"Terrific," Fitzhugh said in disgust. "Where, Milt?"

Silber riffled through the phone book. "4860 East Hudson Drive."

"Hudson? isn't that the street you live on?"

"Yes, it is. She told me that she lived only a few blocks west of me on Hudson. And this is the only M.E. Altman in the book who lives on Hudson."

"Look up that Jenkins character, will you?" Fitzhugh asked. "I've got a bad feeling about him."

Silber raised an eyebrow, but did as his friend requested. "Hmmf," he said in a moment. "The prescient Irish. It seems our friend Fred Jenkins also lives at 4860 East Hudson." He slammed the book closed.

"Come on," Fitzhugh said, fire in his eyes. "I want to get my hands on Dr. Jenkins."

• • •

"Look," Fitzhugh said, standing beside the fountain in the apartment building's courtyard, counting windows. "That's

223—Maggie's apartment. There's a light on! But why doesn't she answer her phone?"

"Hmmf," Silber said. "Time for some drastic action."

The apartment's manager was most dilatory in answering her door. Silber briefly thought of kicking it in, but rejected the idea. Fitzhugh fidgeted impatiently behind him.

"Yeah?" she said finally, opening the door six inches.

"I'm concerned about Maggie Altman, one of your tenants," Silber began.

"So?" the manager demanded, not bothering to remove her cigarillo, and blowing smoke in his face.

"Madam," Silber announced, standing tall, "I am her doctor. She has been under my care. I have reason to believe she may be grievously ill. Perhaps terminal. Bring your key at once and accompany me to her apartment!"

"Terminal?" the landlady said in alarm. "Don't want no one croaking on my property." She edged out through the partly opened door, slammed it behind her, and scuttled off down the hall. Silber and Fitzhugh hurried after her.

"Here it is—223," the landlady announced, knocking loudly. There was no reply, and she reluctantly unlocked the apartment. Silber hurried to the bedroom, Fitzhugh took a quick look in the closets.

"Nothing," Silber told Fitzhugh.

"All right," Fitzhugh said. "We know what to do now." Silber ushered the landlady to the door. "Thank you for your patience, madam," he told her graciously. "But Dr. Altman must have sought assistance elsewhere."

The landlady locked Maggie's apartment, and stood in the hallway, looking at them suspiciously.

"We'll just pay a visit to a friend of ours. Lives on this floor," Silber told her.

She shrugged and hurried away from them. " . . . crazy," Silber heard her mutter as the stairwell door closed.

"Come on," Fitzhugh said, setting off down the hall in the opposite direction. "I want to see Jenkins."

• • •

Silber hung back, expecting the worst. Fitzhugh raised his fist to pound on the door for the third time. It was fairly dark in the hallway, but Silber had the impression that Fitzhugh's face would soon be as red as his hair.

Suddenly the door to 237 flew open, and a young man dressed in a pajama top and jeans grabbed Fitzhugh's upraised hand and yanked him into the apartment. Off balance, Fitzhugh staggered forward until his momentum was broken by a coffee table. There was a terrific crash, and Silber saw him shake his head, then lie there where he was, amid the ruined furniture.

"Hmmf," Silber said.

Fred Jenkins pointed a very large gun at Silber.

"Inside," he said. "You can join your friend on the floor." Then he looked more closely. "Dr. Silber?" he said in amazement.

Silber stepped inside and closed the door. He calculated his chances of grabbing the gun from Fred, and abandoned the idea for the moment.

Fred looked briefly behind himself at Fitzhugh, who was struggling to sit upright, holding his head and groaning. "Who's that?"

"A friend." Silber told him. Damn! He should have gone for the gun when Fred turned away.

"Where is she?" Fitzhugh demanded. "What did you do to her? You little bastard, if you've hurt her, I'll—"

"—now just hold on a minute," Fred told Fitzhugh, moving to a new position from which he could cover both men. "By 'her' I reckon you mean Maggie. So you tell me what you want with her. And how you knew she was here."

Silber sighed. Tact was evidently called for here. There would be time for the gun later. And Maggie? He shuddered. If she were dead, they couldn't help her. And if she were alive? He squared his shoulders. There were two of them to Fred's one. They wouldn't leave this apartment until they found out where Maggie was. He decided on a plan of action and was just about to open his mouth when a voice called from behind him.

"Dr. Silber! Ryan!" Clad in a long flannel nightgown and

> 2

5ms!

"Go on back in there," Fred told her. "I'm about to find out what these two fellas want."

"They're my friends," Maggie told Fred firmly, after only a moment's hesitation. "I'm sure of that. You can put away the gun."

• • •

"Brent Stemmons!" Maggie exclaimed. "But what was he doing out of the Pit? He was on duty."

"He was being taken to surgery when we left," Silber told her. He groomed his beard, feeling foolish. "We thought at first it was you."

"Oh," Maggie said.

"But Jim Thomas told us otherwise. And when you didn't answer your page, or your phone, we assumed the worst," Fitzhugh told her.

Maggie nodded. "You thought Fred was Eisig's inside man. And that he had carried me off."

Fred glared at Fitzhugh, and the taller man glared back. Silber sighed. Those two would never be friends.

"Thanks for the vote of confidence," Fred told Fitzhugh, clearly insulted.

Fitzhugh glowered, but said nothing. Maggie looked from one to the other, a worried frown on her face.

"Well," Silber said placatingly, "as it turned out, we were wrong, and you're perfectly all right."

"For the time being," Fred said. "But we still don't know who the inside man is, or what instructions he's being given by Eisig. Maggie may still be in danger."

"I don't think so," Maggie said at last. "I think I know who he is."

"Oh?" Fred said.

Maggie nodded. "Brent Stemmons. He's the most logical choice. His position as Pit Boss gave him a wonderful opportunity to 'manage the case mix'." She shivered. "He—or Dr. Eisig— had a pretty elaborate scheme worked out." She told them about her experience answering the Dr. Miltown page, and about Caroline's role. "I guess they must prepare a fake chart and collect the full amount that EquaCare pays for the diagnosis."

"While the body spends the entire hospital stay in the freezer." Silber snorted. "So that's why you suspected Dr. Metzenbaum. Jake's 'body-snatching scam' was really very innocent. He claimed the bodies of John Does from the city. They pay $500 apiece for indigent funerals." Silber shrugged. "Jake knows a mortician who will bury them for $250. So he claimed the bodies, paid out $250, and kept the remaining $250 for Pathology's budget. A little ghoulish, but perfectly innocent."

Maggie smiled ruefully. "I think I've got it all straightened out now. But there are still a few things I'd like to know."

"What are those?" Silber inquired.

"What was Brent doing out in his car when he was supposed to be in the Pit?"

No one had any suggestions. What indeed, Silber wondered. If he were Eisig's minion, his place was at the hospital. Wouldn't Eisig have called him off? It was most perplexing. Silber slapped his forehead.

"It completely slipped my mind!" He turned to Maggie. "Eisig. I told you I'd find a way to see that justice was done."

"Milt! You mean you haven't told her yet!" Fitzhugh demanded.

Silber bristled. "I've hardly had a chance, have I? We've been chasing all over town, pounding down apartment doors and breaking up furniture."

Fitzhugh looked acutely embarrassed.

"It's a rather long story," Silber equivocated, feeling awkward. He suddenly decided that friend or not, Fred had no need to know the details of Eisig's electronic comeuppance. It was, after all, illegal. The fewer people who knew about it, the better. "And it's late. Perhaps it would be better saved for another day."

"All right," Maggie said. Silber saw understanding in her eyes. She really was a most perceptive young lady, Silber thought approvingly.

"Come on, Fitzhugh," Silber told the young man.

Fitzhugh stood up reluctantly. "Aren't you coming back to the ranch?" he asked Maggie.

Fred stood up, too, and Silber groaned. Were these two going to have at it again? "She's safe enough here," Fred told Fitzhugh. He looked at Maggie, then at Fitzhugh and scowled disapprovingly. "Unless you want to go back, that is."

"It's too late to go anywhere," Maggie said firmly. She smiled at Ryan Fitzhugh. "I'll be all right here. Fred's sleeping on the couch with his gun. Although I think it's pretty likely that those men from the parking lot were hired by Eisig. And if he's been . . . "

". . . neutralized," Silber suggested, liking the sound of the word.

"Yes, neutralized, then I should be safe. So I'll stay here. Besides, I have to go to work tomorrow."

Fitzhugh glowered. "You'd be safer at the ranch," he muttered.

Silber sighed, and took his arm. "It's late," he said. "Let's go." Fitzhugh allowed himself to be led away. At the door, Silber turned to Maggie. "Tomorrow," he said. "I'll find you at the hospital. We have to talk."

Maggie smiled. "See you then."

Chapter 52

Stemmons tried to focus his thoughts, but the pain was too great. Damn those nurses! They refused to give him morphine until exactly four hours had passed, and then it took them half an hour to draw it up. And that wretched surgery intern hadn't ordered nearly enough.

He squinted at the wall clock, which had acquired a bizarre halo. Another 20 minutes to go.

He wasn't sure which pain was the worst. His right hip had been driven back into its socket and shattered. A posterior dislocation, someone had told him. He didn't remember much about orthopedics. But it sounded like he'd never walk normally again, and would have chronic pain. His leg was attached to the traction device by a pin driven through his right thigh. He felt like screaming every time the nurses moved him. But that only happened once in a while; he had to breathe about 12 times a minute. With every breath, he could imagine the jagged edges of ribs scraping the delicate nerves of his pleural cavity. There were two chest tubes on the right side, and one on the left. Whenever he thought he might drowse a little, he would be awakened by the bubbling—the air being sucked out of his chest into the bottles on the floor at the side of his bed.

They were afraid of depressing his respirations, they said. That was the excuse for not giving him enough morphine. Really, they were just sadists. And if he did quit breathing, what the hell difference did it make? It was a lousy world.

Just when he had thought things were going pretty well. The marketing prospects had looked great. But he should have known better than to be so trusting. Just because those fools brought the stuff in all the time, he had assumed that they knew how to do it properly. They should have known about Type 3 packaging, which didn't show up on X rays. That was their specialty, wasn't it? It was hardly his fault that their careless packaging had caused them to get caught, but he was getting the blame for it anyway. Raúl had asked for his help in purging the patients and treating some "mild" symptoms, and he had agreed. But Raúl hadn't said anything about the police guard! Lying to the police was out of the question when the X rays were so obvious. They hadn't allowed anyone else near the patients when the purgatives were working.

And it was partly his mother's fault. She hadn't believed him when he had told her the money was a matter of life and death. Now she was out in the waiting room, probably sniveling. It was disgusting. He hoped she would have an accident on the way home. So she would learn what it felt like. He wouldn't have believed such pain was possible.

He buzzed for the nurse again. "Call the doctor right now," he demanded. "I've got to have more morphine!"

"I spoke to him already," she said sweetly. "It's too dangerous. But you can have a couple of Tylenol now."

Stemmons glared at her, imagining how much he would enjoy cutting her with a sharp knife. She probably hadn't called the doctor at all. But she would. He would see to that.

• • •

He learned how to get enough medicine. He just yelled and carried on until they gave it to him. The pain was dulled, and his mind was scrambled. He wasn't sure where he was, or what year it was. And he decided that was a fine state to be in. The sense of being disconnected was exhilarating. Picasso had the world pictured just right, he thought with a roar of laughter. He laughed again, just because he knew it was so inappropriate, and he liked the sound.

About 7:00 in the evening, a uniformed delivery man came into his room with an elaborate floral arrangement. All white flowers, like the ones on the altar at a wedding. Or a funeral. They had a halo around them too, just like the clock. The man tipped his hat and looked Stemmons full in the face.

"How's your ear, Doc?" the man asked, smiling. "Why, it's hardly noticeable." Then he walked away.

It was Carlos! Stemmons was sure of it. He felt a cold sweat break out and he heard a roaring in his ears. His throat was so tight that when he tried to scream, nothing came out.

Chapter 53

Maggie allowed Silber to buy her a glass of milk and a container of strawberry yogurt. He guided her to a quiet table in the corner of the cafeteria, and sat down rather self- consciously. His uneasiness communicated itself to Maggie, and for one terrible moment, she was afraid that the standoff with Dr. Eisig was no longer in effect. But then Silber smiled, and she relaxed.

"I didn't think that Dr. Jenkins' apartment was quite the place to make these disclosures," he told her. I'm glad you agreed. Quite frankly, the fewer people who know about this, the better. I feel quite awkward about it," he said, frowning fiercely. "It's not quite . . . proper, and I have the impression that you are a very proper young lady."

Maggie said nothing. She'd been told that before, usually by those who were critical of her ethics. It was a criticism that always made her see red, as the context usually was that she was hopelessly old-fashioned. Even Victorian. However, she had the sense that Silber did not intend criticism, so she listened intently.

"Sometimes," Silber sighed, "we can't get what we want." He laughed bitterly. "Listen to me! You're not a child, you know that. And I know that you know it. Hmmf. Let's start over." He combed his beard. "How do we mete out punishment to wrongdoers? We leave them to institutions. Or to God. But our institutions regularly fail us. And we're not sure about God." He looked up at her intently. "Consequently, we're often frustrated. We see wrongdoers escape justice every day. And we seethe, because we know it's not right." He sighed. "But if we take justice into our own hands, how are we different from those we seek to punish?"

Maggie's heart sank. What had Dr. Silber done? It sounded terrible. Come to think of it, she hadn't seen Dr. Eisig around for days. Dr. Silber couldn't have . . . could he? No! She wouldn't believe that!

Silber leaned across the table. "I gave the matter of Eisig's punishment a lot of thought," he told her. "And finally, when an idea struck, quite out of the blue, I knew it was right." He looked up at her guiltily. "Well, not right, maybe, but fitting. There seemed no way to get at the man. He had made himself untouchable. Except in one respect."

This was horribly fascinating. Maggie found she couldn't tear her eyes off Silber.

"His money," Silber continued. "It was hidden, but not inaccessible. And thanks to the wonders of modern electronic technology, it was all too accessible." He put an issue of the *Fort Bastion Morning News* on the table in front of her. "I don't expect you've had time to read the paper. And even if you had, this particular story might not have caught your eye."

She looked at it curiously. "Local Firm Gives $1.3 Million to Crippled Children", the headline read. Her heart beating faster, she skimmed the article. She looked at the date of the paper—Tuesday, three days ago—and laughed aloud. It was suddenly all perfectly clear to her. She reached over and took Silber's hand. "You did it!" she exclaimed. "You figured out a way to make him pay. Literally pay. You're a genius!" She squeezed his hand. "Robin Hood was always one of my heroes. People think that he stole from the rich and gave to the poor, in order to redistribute wealth. But he didn't, of course. He just administered simple justice. He gave back to the Saxon peasants the money that had been stolen from them by the real thieves—the greedy Norman barons and clergy. It's perfect!" she exclaimed.

"Hmmf," Silber muttered, his eyes a little moist. "Not perfect. Not even good enough for someone who tried to murder one of my friends. But the best I could do." He wiped his eyes surreptitiously, and Maggie pretended to be busy with her yogurt. She really felt a little overwhelmed. "I didn't do it alone," Silber said, smiling mysteriously. "I had a little help."

"Oh?"

"Yes. A certain Forex trader." Silber looked at her coyly from under his eyebrows. "He was most eager to help strike a blow on your behalf."

"Forex trader . . . oh! You don't mean Ryan, surely?"

Silber winked. "Indeed I do."

"Oh," Maggie said again. Well. It appeared she had more friends than she knew. But she'd think about that later. Now, she had another question for Dr. Silber.

"And how did you 'neutralize' Eisig? You used that word last night."

Silber laughed. "I bluffed! Persuaded him that I had enough evidence to send to the District Attorney's office. He was guilty, and he knew it, and didn't want to take any chances. So he agreed to leave you alone. And me, too."

"What about those men in the parking lot?" she asked him. "I suppose they might have been originally hired by Eisig. And if they were, I suppose now they'll leave me alone."

"I've been thinking about that," Silber told her. "It seems that they may well have been hired by someone to frighten you off, but that the someone may not necessarily have been Eisig." He looked at her steadily.

Comprehension dawned. "Not Brent Stemmons! He wouldn't have . . . "

"Why not?" Silber asked her. "He was involved in Eisig's scheme up to his neck. Maybe Eisig gave him an ultimatum." Silber snorted. "When I knew Brent Stemmons, he was a plagiarist and a liar. A coward, too. It would be just like him to get someone else to do his dirty work. Hmmf. Well, there's an easy way to find out, you know."

"Oh? What?"

Silber looked a little apologetic. "See if he'll tell you. You'll be tactful, I'm sure. It wouldn't do to let him know that you suspect him. Not just yet. But a short visit to a suffering colleague might not seem odd. He's upstairs, isn't he?"

Maggie blinked. Why not? She deserved to know the truth. Anger welled up in her, and something else, too. Disgust. Yes, she had a few questions for Brent. But would he answer them?

Chapter 54

Maggie thought over exactly what she would say to Brent Stemmons. How did you ask someone whether he had arranged to have you attacked? Or killed? Or about his involvement in a scheme to defraud a hospital that cared for the poor? Why would he tell her the truth? Still, she intended to see him. In spite of his injuries, which she had heard were quite serious.

The surgical intensive care unit was located in the most dilapidated wing of the hospital. The floor was dark with the waxed-on grime of years, the walls were covered with light gray ceramic tile, and the window coverings were old-fashioned venetian blinds with many broken slats. The unit was an open ward. The beds could be curtained off with ugly orange and brown striped curtains of some shiny fabric. What a horribly depressing place to be, Maggie thought.

She was appalled to see how bad Brent looked. His face was bruised and swollen. Apparently he had a laceration across his forehead, because a bulky dressing covered it. Automatically, she noticed that the toes on his fractured leg looked pink, that air was bubbling from the chest tubes, that he was receiving a unit of packed cells and a broad-spectrum antibiotic. And that there was no obvious irreparable damage.

He seemed to be awake, so she went up to the bedside and stood there awkwardly. "I was sorry to hear about your accident," she said.

It seemed to take him a minute to realize that someone was there. Then he looked at her, and his lip curled. What did the expression in his eyes mean? Contempt, anger, hatred? Maggie stepped back, feeling as though he had slapped her. She had the answer to her question, she realized. This man despised her, and was fully capable of carrying out everything she suspected him of.

"Well, if isn't Dr. Altman," he said. "The famous busy-

284

body. Always sticking her pointed, meddlesome nose into things. Thinks that she's smarter than everybody else."

Maggie would never have guessed at the hostility that this man had evidently felt for her from the beginning. What a consummate actor he was. And what a fool she had been!

"Bitch," he hissed at her.

Maggie looked at him in dismay. Certainly, there was no reason to stay here another minute. She would just walk away. Preferably, without letting him see that he could still hurt her.

· · ·

Good riddance to that bitch, Stemmons thought to himself. He should have known from the beginning that the direct method was the only way to deal with women like her. If he hadn't been so squeamish, he would be on top of the world, instead of in this hospital bed with his plans in ruins. He should never have left it up to Eisig. He had assumed that Eisig would use something reliable, like potassium. The man had proved himself capable of it with Mr. Post. But no, Eisig had to be too clever, and the bitch had survived.

No, he never should have gotten involved with Maggie. He should have stuck with women like Caroline. Ones that could be relied upon. The kind with normal, understandable motives. And subnormal intelligence.

But even Caroline wasn't quite as stupid as the ones they were hiring to work in the ICU. Stemmons cursed and pressed his call button again. The cretin working this shift hadn't brought his pain medicine yet. And he needed to turn a little.

She finally came and helped adjust his position in the bed. But she didn't have the medication.

"I asked for it 20 minutes ago," he said accusingly.

"Sorry," she said. "We're short-staffed. I'm trying to fill in, but I don't know the system very well. It takes me a little longer sometimes."

"You've always got an excuse," Stemmons said. "I'm about to report you to the supervisor."

"I'll get it for you right away, sir." She pulled up the

siderail of his bed and scurried away. Now that was the kind of response he liked to see.

He hadn't seen quick service very often in here. The help was pretty lethargic most of the time. You had to be assertive. Reporting one or two of them to the supervisor might set a good example. He resolved to do it at the next provocation.

The thought made him feel slightly better. Being helpless in the bed here was not agreeable at all. No, he was born to be in control. Well, maybe his absence would make Eisig appreciate him more. Once Eisig saw what things were like without a skilled gatekeeper in the Pit, he might even offer a raise. Of course, Stemmons wasn't at all sure that he would agree to continue, after Eisig had been so insulting in his last few calls.

Not even if he could solve his other problem. He looked at the flowers and shivered. Maybe he would have to go to the police. That might gain him at least enough protection to catch a flight out of town. And his mother might be prevailed upon to lend him the money now. Raúl's enforcers wouldn't dare do anything to him while he was here in the ICU, would they? A police guard. That was what he needed. And deserved. It might even turn him into a hero.

The nurse brought the IV morphine. It was nothing like cocaine, but still all right. The increase in dose had been effective. Stemmons began to feel confident again. He would turn this accident to his advantage. "TU Resident Thwarts Drug Dealers" would be a nice headline. As to his personal requirements, he would have to turn to medical sources. That would have been safer in the first place. He needed to be more careful about his choice of business partners. Be more sure that they really did have a common interest.

A nagging sense of being short of breath was intruding into his pleasant haze. It seemed to be worsening by the minute. At the same time, a tremendous pressure was building up in his chest, as if a balloon were being blown up, pushing his heart and lungs aside.

He struggled to breathe, but there was no room in his chest. He pressed the call button desperately. The world was beginning to dim.

He realized belatedly what was happening, but couldn't believe it. Not now—not just when his prospects were once again looking hopeful. A black abyss opened under him. Silently, he shrieked a curse at the universe. As he entered free fall, he could hear the page operator, more and more distantly, calling "Code Blue, SICU, Code Blue, SICU, Code Blue, SICU." After that, he heard nothing at all.

Chapter 55

Somewhat to Maggie's surprise, Stephen Blaine greeted her cordially. She had to turn down the proferred cup of coffee, of course. "How forgetful of me," he apologized. "Would you like some juice instead?"

"No, thank you," Maggie replied.

Blaine closed the door to his office, and sat down at his desk. "I want to talk some things over with you," he said, looking at her thoughtfully. "Some things I have just become aware of. Actually, I'm going to have to eat some crow." He fortified himself with a gulp of his own coffee.

"While you were ill," he continued, "I took over your service for a couple of days. Thank God it wasn't for very long. I'd forgotten what it was like to be an intern," he smiled a little. "I noticed a couple of things. One was that you had been doing a good job. And second, that you certainly had a lot of extremely sick patients."

Maggie felt a glow of satisfaction. It felt good to hear a few words of appreciation.

"That could have been just the luck of the draw," Blaine continued, pulling down a computer printout. "But I went over some stats. It was very consistent. All the unprofitable DRGs, and just plain complicated cases, were being admitted to you or to Fred Jenkins, whenever Dr. Stemmons was Pit Boss. I couldn't prove it, of course. But it sure looks like favoritism. Or a even a deliberate attempt to persuade you to leave the program."

Maggie didn't know what to say. It had seemed that she was a "Dr. Black Cloud," as Charlie had put it.

"I can't ask him about it now, of course." Blaine looked very serious. The death of one of their own number had affected all of them. "But our DRG profile has looked noticeably worse since our most experienced gatekeeper is no longer at the gate." Blaine shook his head. "I am really not happy with my own performance. When things were going so well in general, I wasn't paying as much attention as I should have been. And to tell the truth, I was relying on Stemmons for some of the statistics. He made himself extremely helpful to me."

Maggie wasn't surprised. She thought about it for a minute, then decided to tell Blaine about Dr. Miltown. He listened to the story attentively, and sipped coffee reflectively for several minutes after she finished.

"Caroline, and 6 West?" he asked finally.

Maggie nodded.

"Figures. Do you remember any of the names?"

Maggie pulled out her cards, and Blaine jotted down the information.

"I'll review the charts," he promised. "I'll bet they are just exemplary. Everything documented perfectly, so that they were all passed over very quickly at the death review. I'll probably have to talk to some interns. They might not have minded having their names used, in return for credit for a good admission—a dead one."

"Did Brent ever ask you about some software problems?" Maggie wanted to know.

"No," Blaine said. "I asked him, as a matter of fact, and he assured me that everything seemed to work perfectly."

Maggie shook her head. How could she have been so gullible?

"There are a lot of questions I'd like to ask the good Dr. Stemmons," Blaine continued. "And so would the police."

"Oh?" Maggie asked.

"Starting with why he happened to be in a one-car accident while on duty in the Pit. Particularly, right after a large shipment of cocaine had been delivered to TU in its unusual containers," Blaine watched her reaction carefully. "Were you aware of any connections Stemmons might have had with the drug trade?"

Maggie felt a chill, remembering the men in the parking lot. Colombians, perhaps?

"Well, looking back on it, there were times when he did behave a little strangely. He looked very tired one minute, then bursting with energy the next."

"The police are investigating TU now," Blaine said.

"For drug trafficking?" Maggie asked. Blaine nodded. That was one problem Maggie hadn't been aware of.

"Perhaps they should be investigating some other problems too," Blaine said, "but as yet I have no definite evidence. And we can't ask the person who knew the most about it. If only I had gotten to the code a few minutes sooner!"

"The code in the SICU?" Maggie asked.

"Yes. The surgery resident called me when they weren't having any success."

Maggie closed her eyes. "You know, I must have seen him just a few minutes before the code. He just didn't look as though he was about to die."

"He shouldn't have died," Blaine said bluntly. "In fact, it is a terrible embarrassment to TU. If I had to name the cause of death, I would have to say it was the hospital's skimping on the most important, most basic aspect of patient care: the nursing staff."

Maggie looked at him inquiringly. She hadn't heard why Stemmons had died. Probably, the hospital was trying to keep it quiet.

"They had the idea that he had received too much morphine. He had gotten a dose shortly before the code. The nurse from the agency—we've been relying heavily on temporary staff—was very concerned about that. She had asked the doctor for an order to increase the dose, and was afraid it had caused the patient to stop breathing. The resident was afraid of that too. He apparently didn't realize what a healthy tolerance Stemmons had built up. So they gave him about six amps of Narcan, trying to reverse the effects of the morphine. It didn't work, because that wasn't the problem."

Blaine paused. "The problem was that his chest tube had been pinched off by the siderail on his bed, and he still had a big air leak. He died of a tension pneumothorax, right in our surgical ICU! I stuck a needle into his chest and air rushed out. But by then it was too late."

"But he must have been gasping for breath! It wouldn't

have looked like respiratory depression!" Maggie exclaimed.

"If there had been anybody looking!" Blaine said. "Apparently, there wasn't. They were short staffed, and the nurses were in the back putting codes on those nursing flow sheets that nobody can read. The alarm on his monitor didn't go off either. It may have been sloppy maintenance, or somebody may have turned it off."

Maggie looked at him in disbelief. "By the way," Blaine told her grimly. "All this is strictly off the record."

"Is his mother going to sue TU?" Maggie asked.

"She certainly could," Blaine replied. "But fortunately for us, she refused an autopsy. The cause of death is being given as a morphine overdose. His family may not want his drug history to be investigated too closely."

Maggie felt numb. If she had stayed to talk to him for a while longer, Brent Stemmons might still be alive. But he had driven her away himself. She had heard the page to the SICU, but it hadn't registered at the time. It hadn't occurred to her to respond to it, or that it could have been for a man who had seemed to be so very much alive.

Blaine finally broke the long silence. "There may be a lot of things I will want to ask you. But the main reason I called you here today was to apologize for the way I have treated you. I was under a lot of pressure from Dr. Eisig about the DRG profiles. But I'll be giving you an excellent recommendation, and since he'll no longer be with us, you needn't worry about a letter from him."

"He's leaving?" Maggie asked, hardly daring to believe it, even though Dr. Silber had promised.

"Read this morning's paper," Blaine advised. "Of course, if you want to go into research, my offer to help you find a job is still open. Frankly, I can hardly wait to get out of clinical medicine. Even as an administrator, which is what I really am now."

Blaine rose and opened the door for Maggie. "I really thought this EquaCare system was a good idea, and that I could make it work. I was wrong."

Maggie shook his hand thoughtfully. "Thanks for coming in," he said. "I'll be talking to you later."

Blaine wasn't a bad person after all, she decided. And maybe he would be able to trace down some of the irregularities that had happened. But she doubted that the full story would ever come to light. A lot of it, she suspected, had been forever obliterated from electronic memory.

Maggie borrowed a newspaper from one of her patients, and found the article she was looking for on the front page of the metropolitan section.

TU EQUACARE DIRECTOR RESIGNS

Dr. Philip Eisig, EquaCare Director and Chief of Internal Medicine at Texas University Regional Preventive Health Center, announced his resignation today. He will accept an offer to start a new program modeled on EquaCare at Great Northeastern University.

Eisig said that he felt the program at TURPH Center has been remarkably successful, and now has the momentum to progress on its own.

"No one person is indispensable," he said.

Eisig acknowledged that the decision had been a difficult one, because he enjoyed his work at TURPH Center so much.

"But personal considerations must be secondary," he explained. "I am needed more at Great Northeastern, and I look forward to the challenge, even as I bid a fond adieu to my friends and associates in Fort Bastion."

Members of the EquaCare board of directors in the state capital accepted Dr. Eisig's resignation, expressing their regret.

"His dedication, foresight, and management skills have been extremely important to our success in containing health care costs," Chairman Bruce Maelstrom said. "We will miss him. In fact, we were hoping that he would seek greater challenges right here in our own state. We were ready to support him in a campaign for governor."

Eisig was asked to comment on Maelstrom's allusion to running for political office, in view of past rumors that Eisig might indeed be interested.

"Oh, I'm just a doctor," he said. My only ambition is to

continue providing high quality health care to the poor and high quality education to the doctors of the future."

• • •

Maggie sensed that someone was behind her, and started a little. "Sorry," Fred said. "I couldn't help reading over your shoulder."

"It's hard to believe, isn't it?" she said.

"Quite a snow job," Fred commented. "Great Northeastern, home of the *Northeastern Journal of Medicine*. They deserve Dr. Eisig, in my opinion."

"But, Fred, think of the patients!" Maggie protested.

"I do, I do," Fred pointed out. "See, I even cured something this morning." He displayed a large plug of wax. "I made the deaf to hear."

Maggie couldn't help smiling. Fred always did seem to enjoy his work.

"I've been looking for you," she said. "Kate Fitzhugh is giving a party for Hallowe'en, out at the ranch. Would you like to come?"

"Yes, I'd like to, but . . . " he blushed a little. "An old friend of mine will be in town that day. From my home town. She's going to be interviewing for graduate school at the University of Fort Bastion. I promised to show her around." He grinned a little foolishly.

Hmm, Maggie thought. Maybe more than just an old friend. "How nice!" she said sincerely. "Well, would she like to come too? She might enjoy seeing the ranch, and I'm sure Kate wouldn't mind."

"Thanks," Fred said. "I'll ask her."

Chapter 56

"I'm glad you could come," Ryan said, hurrying to Maggie's car to greet her. "The turkeys need some more basting—you're just in time to help." He smiled tentatively, and Maggie wondered if his pride was still smarting from having been bested by Fred. Maggie made a point of smiling warmly at him, and he seemed to take heart. Really! Men's egos were so fragile, she thought in amusement. As they walked into the house, she was impressed again by how red his hair was. And she'd never known any grown man with so many freckles. They made him look somehow boyish and engaging. But tonight he looked very much the gentleman rancher in jeans and a crisp blue cotton shirt with a string tie. She glanced down at her own jeans hoped she looked all right. They had been bought new for the occasion—Kate had insisted that everyone wear jeans, and Maggie had been dismayed to find that her one pair was totally unsuitable for wearing to anyplace other than the carwash. Certainly not to a Hallowe'en party at the Flying V. But she needn't have worried. "You look terrific!" Ryan said in evident appreciation.

Maggie smiled. "Thanks. New jeans," she said ruefully. "Kate was most insistent."

"Yeah, Kate's like that," Ryan said. "She wanted everyone to dress casually and feel at home." He gestured to the lighted pumpkins that adorned the front porch, each sporting a hideous grin. "Kate likes to observe all the special occasions properly," he explained. "But she likes to be comfortable, too. We're in here," he told her, directing her toward the kitchen. "Milton came early—ostensibly to make his famous barbecue sauce," he whispered. "But I think he came early to see Kate."

"Really?" said Maggie. "And what about Kate?"

Ryan grinned. "Well, it took her an hour to get ready. And she changed clothes twice. So I guess she wasn't unhappy to see him."

In the kitchen Dr. Silber, looking silly in one of Consuela's aprons, was busy basting two large turkeys that turned on a spit over mesquite coals. The smell made Maggie's mouth water. He was humming, she noted, and seemed to be enjoying himself hugely. She was rather amused to see that he had had yet another haircut, and that most of his wild looking beard had been shorn. He also seemed to have lost weight. What she could see of his plaid shirt and jeans looked very dapper. When he saw her, he positively beamed.

"Ah, the fashionably late Dr. Altman!" he called. "Just in time to tend these plump birds." He winked at her. "I have business elsewhere. Here, you may have my apron. I'm certain it will look more becoming on you than me." Still humming, he wandered off.

"I'll do that," Ryan offered, taking the apron and tying it around his waist. "I guess everyone's gone for walks," he said. "To look at the sunset, in Kate and Milt's case. Or the horses, in Fred and Joanne's." He slathered some sauce on the turkeys. "Dinner won't be for an hour or so. You could walk around if you like. Watching the turkeys won't be too exciting."

Maggie smiled. "I think I'd rather stay here with you, if you don't mind."

Ryan blinked a few times, and blushed furiously. "Oh," he said, evidently surprised. "Well . . . good! Oh damn. I'm such a lousy host. I was supposed to offer you a drink. Or something." He put down his basting brush.

"No, don't stop," Maggie told him. "I know my way around. I'll just get some milk out of the refrigerator. What about you?"

"A beer, please. There's some Mexican stuff there that I like. Don't bother with a glass." He grinned. "We ranchers drink ours straight from the bottle. No class at all."

Maggie brought him his beer and he took an enormous swallow. She sipped her milk, thinking how happy she felt.

"Now," Ryan said, pausing in his chore to wipe his hands and drink some more beer. "While everyone's outside, there's something I think you should hear."

Maggie raised an eyebrow. "What? Sounds mysterious."

"Well, I think it's something that shouldn't get around. It's about Brent Stemmons."

Maggie frowned, her heart sinking. Surely Ryan couldn't have found out what a fool she had made of herself over Brent? Still, she'd better hear what he had to say. "All right. Tell me."

Ryan took a deep breath. "A friend of mine, Alan Stevens, led a very colorful youth. Many of his activities took place on the other side of the law. Of course, he's gone straight now." He looked at her somewhat anxiously, as if eager that she understand. She nodded to encourage him. "But he has some contacts who haven't. And he still sees them from time to time. Well, in the course of, um, a social evening, he learned that Raúl Grijalva—a very big drug dealer here in Fort Bastion—would be taking a little vacation. It seems as though his mules were intercepted by the police when one of them had an accident and had to be taken to TU. Grijalva lost his whole shipment."

Maggie gasped. "The body packers!"

"Right. And guess who Grijalva's contact at the hospital was?"

"Not Brent Stemmons?"

Ryan nodded. "It seems he and Grijalva were about to go into business at TU. Stemmons was a user, too."

Maggie didn't want to believe it. But Blaine had brought it up, and when she gave it a little thought, it made sense. Brent's erratic behavior, his strange manic energy. It all fit. But cocaine dealing, too? Wasn't his one illegal activity sufficient? She shook her head. What could have been his motive? Money? But his family was wealthy. It was simply impossible to understand. And, she decided, she didn't want to try.

"One more thing," Ryan told her. "Grijalva is taking his cousins with him for a little vacation to Guadalajara. Benny and Carlos. They're his enforcers, but he's been known to hire them out. Stevens thinks you may have met them."

"Met them? Where?" Of course! "You mean those men in the parking lot? Why does Stevens think so?" she asked Ryan.

"Well, they're in disgrace. The story that's getting around is that some woman took them both on and won. A doctor. They'll never live it down. It's such a good story that's it's getting a little embellished in the telling." He looked up at her in admiration. "I guess the woman was you. And it must have been Stemmons who hired them to attack you. They're certainly not very loyal employees, because just a few weeks later, they were after Stemmons. Grijalva sent them after him to get his cocaine back. They were chasing Stemmons when he had his accident. Too bad. But at least now you know you won't have to look over your shoulder for the rest of your stay in Fort Bastion, wondering if they're going to spring out at you. They're gone."

Maggie wished she could have a beer. Or something stronger. "Thanks," she told Ryan inadequately.

He returned to basting the turkeys. Laughter floated in through the open kitchen window, laughter she recognized as Fred's.

"I'm glad Fred could come," she said. "He deserves some fun."

Ryan glowered. He really doesn't like Fred, Maggie realized. Was it the fact that Fred had embarrassed him by shoving him into the coffee table the night Ryan and Silber had come to rescue her? Or was it something else?

"He's been a good friend," she told Ryan. "And I'm glad Joanne was in town. He seems quite serious about her. He's planning to go back to his home town and be a country doctor. She's his high school sweetheart, apparently. They make a nice couple, don't you think?"

Ryan looked over at her in surprise. "Fred and Joanne? But I thought you and Fred were . . ."

"Friends," she told him firmly. "Just friends."

"Oh," he said feebly.

"So!" a voice called from behind them. "Slacking off on the job, are you? Hmmf. I see we'll have to take over."

Kate came quickly to embrace Maggie, and Silber took the apron and basting brush from Ryan.

"Go somewhere, you two," Silber told them. "Shoo."

"Dinner won't be for a while," Kate said. She took the brush from Silber, who seemed affronted. "We can manage the turkeys."

"Aargh! Not that spot, woman," Silber told Kate. "I have

my eye on that for Keynes. He likes his turkey plain."

"Really!" Kate said. "Oh, all right. And I saved the giblets. They're cooked and in a plastic bag in the fridge."

"Excellent!" Silber said. "The useless old rodent-catcher doesn't deserve such bounty, but it is a special occasion." He winked at Maggie. "And he does deserve some appreciation for his part in Eisig's comeuppance. Turkey is much tastier than power cords."

"Come on," Ryan said. "After all that hard work let's go collapse in the living room. I think Consuela's already started the fire. Are you warm enough? I think the night will be quite chilly."

"I'm fine," Maggie said, as they sat on the couch in front of the fire. "Have you given up the foreign exchange business for horse breeding, then?"

"I'm not going to breed horses, "Ryan said, "but I have quit Banque France." He sighed. "I'm too old for it. It got to the point where I worried too much."

"And now? What what will you do?"

Ryan smiled enigmatically. "Well, a couple of other financial institutions approached me, but I turned them down. You see, someone had already made me an offer I couldn't refuse."

"Oh? Who?"

"That famous financier, Milton Silber, who wants more time to indulge in a hobby."

"Dr. Silber? Oh, of course. *The Silber Report*. Well, congratulations are in order then, aren't they?" Maggie wondered whether Dr. Silber's "hobby" was really medicine.

Ryan shrugged, looking bemused. "I suppose so." He cleared his throat. "Maggie," he said tentatively, "I know you're busy, and are still recovering from your ordeal, but sometime, um, when you have some time off . . ." He seemed to lose the thread of his thought and began to look a little desperate. Maggie tried not to smile. "Perhaps you'd like to go out. Somewhere. With me, that is."

She finally let herself smile. "I'd like to go out. Somewhere. With you," she said, teasing him just a little.

He beamed. "Great," he said. "I mean, good. I'll call

you."

"Well," Silber said, bustling into the room with a silver tray bearing three glasses of effervescent liquid, "have you two young people got all the world's problems solved?"

"Hardly," Maggie told him. "But you seem to be in good spirits tonight. What are the glasses for? A celebration?"

"Exactly," he said. "Might as well laugh as weep, right? We fought the good fight. We should be able to sleep better at night knowing we did what we could. And not without risk to ourselves." He set the tray down on a table and handed Maggie and Ryan each a glass. "Medicine." He frowned fiercely. "I told you a long time ago that it was going straight to hell. You were innocent then. You didn't want to believe me. Well, it almost took you with it." He groomed his beard with his fingertips. "The new 'health care delivery system' is being designed by thieves for thieves. And there's very little we can do about it." He shrugged. "But we won a little skirmish, if not the war. So there is something to celebrate, right?"

"Right," Maggie said, smiling. She thought back to the beginning of her internship, that harrowing day in July when she had arrived at TU, and all the events that had occurred since then. Maybe there was even more to celebrate than Dr. Silber would admit just yet. Maybe he would even find a way to contribute once again to clinical medicine and teaching, despite the impediments in the system.

Silber looked at her closely and held up a hand as if to stop her from saying more. "No philosophizing," he said firmly. "And no speculating. How about a toast?"

"A splendid idea." Maggie stood up an held out her glass. Silber and Ryan clicked theirs with hers.

"To justice," Silber said, "which was served. After a fashion."